Gateway to Ithria

THE CHRONICLES OF ITHRIA
Gateway to Ithria

J.J. THOMAS

COVER DESIGNER: DEREMYRE JOHN

authorHOUSE®

AuthorHouse™
1663 Liberty Drive
Bloomington, IN 47403
www.authorhouse.com
Phone: 1-800-839-8640

Published by AuthorHouse   10/16/2012

ISBN: 978-1-4772-3142-5 (sc)
ISBN: 978-1-4772-3143-2 (e)

Dedication

For all those people who said;

"Oh cool, you're writing a book.
That's awesome!
Can I read it?"

Your words encouraged me more than you think.

Acknowledgments

I would like to thank . . .

My family for their endless support during my many long hours of writing; sometimes into the early hours of the morning and for providing me with the encouragement I needed to succeed.

My friends for giving me an escape when the world of Ithria became just that little bit too intense.

Nathan, who despite having an ever busy schedule, worked tirelessly to help make printing possible.

And a special thanks to Mel, for giving up her spare time after long hectic work days to edit my book. Without her help, my writing would never have evolved from the poorly punctuated, juvenile scribblings that they were, into the story you have before you now.

About the Author

Jonathan Thomas better known as 'Joff' by his close friends and family (A name given to him by his brother at a young age) lives just outside a small village in South Wales.

He was inspired by his love of the outdoors and has brought a sense of home into his novel.

Through the use of local areas and buildings, he has added an air of authenticity to his writing and hopes you are able to immerse yourself into the magical world he has created.

Map of Ithria

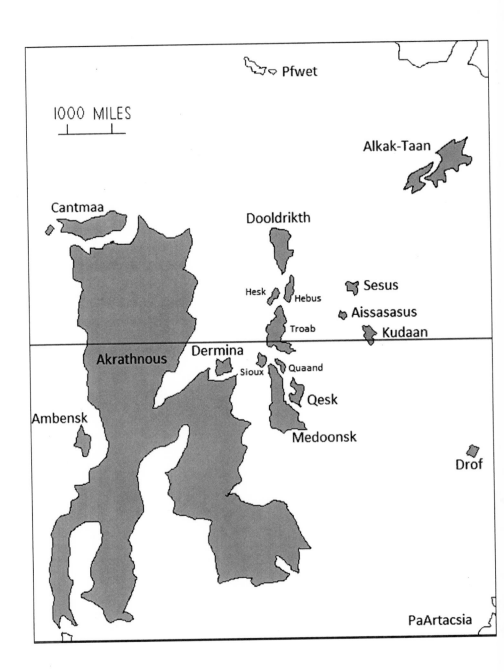

Map of Ithria

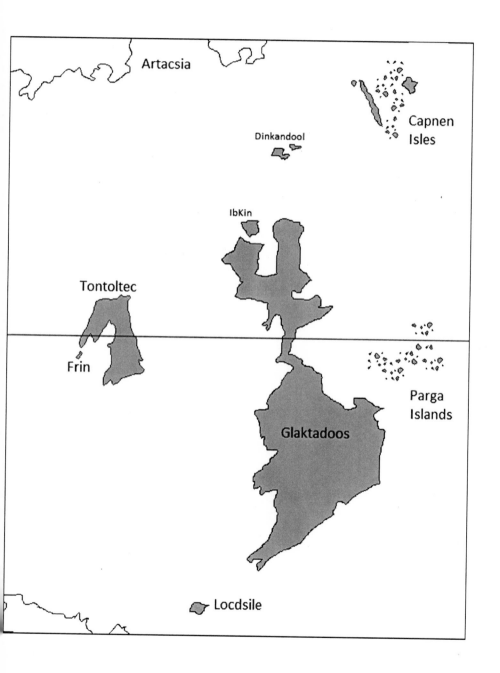

Artacsia

Capnen Isles

Dinkandool

IbKin

Tontoltec

Frin

Glaktadoos

Parga Islands

Locdsile

Map of Tontoltec

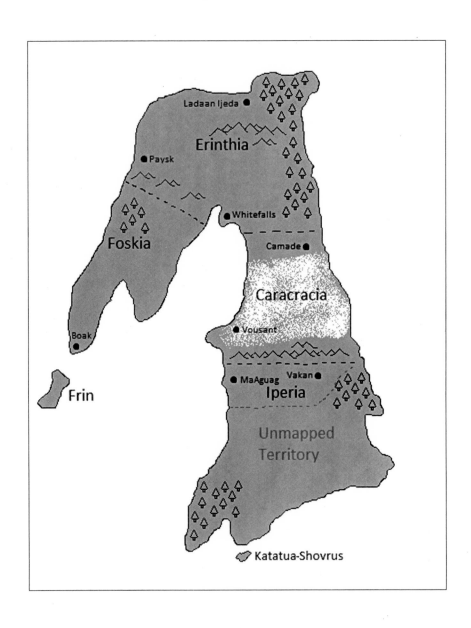

Prologue

Orak JaVrei's surroundings slowly slid into focus. He could feel the cold hard ground beneath him; like stone, but bizarrely smooth, flat and perfectly level. He blinked a few times and strained his eyes to try and focus on what looked like a giant rectangular rock, but it couldn't be, as it was reflecting like a fifty foot high mirror.

Once his eyes had settled, he was shocked to see how alien this world really was. He had seen it through the window, but nothing could have prepared him for the mayhem he now saw. The giant mirror was a multi storey building, but every inch of its walls were made of glass, and its edges were straighter than rulers.

Orak looked either side of him and saw dozens more buildings in every direction, all as spectacular as each other. Glancing down at the peculiar stone ground, he saw that it was pitch black and formed a path that stretched out as far as he could see.

There was a constant roaring on either side, and beyond some partial barrier he could see flashes of light streaking past, faster than any animal he knew could run. Something rumbled past him, and Orak shot to his feet when he saw how close it had come. His eyes followed the creature and his jaw dropped when he saw it in detail. It wasn't a creature at all, but a bright red machine, zooming along the flat like a cart losing control down a hill. A horn sounded, but like no call to war or warning he had ever heard before, he spun around to see another of these peculiar machines hurtling towards him.

Frozen to the spot with fear, he mustered the strength to move. He leapt away to one side with a mighty bound but was a fraction of a second too late.

Chapter 1

"You alright love?"

"Eh?" said a rather sleepy male nurse. He looked up from his reclined position on the staff room sofa to see a rather plump woman standing over him, holding a large mug of steaming black coffee. He smiled and accepted the cup. "I love you Gloria, my surrogate mum," he joked, "What would I do without you?"

"Join the dole queue," she replied bluntly, gesturing towards the clock, "Your break ended fifteen minutes ago John. Out again last night were you? This is really starting to affect your work. You mixed up Mr Albert's and Mr Alpert's medication this morning."

John said nothing and just sighed. This was the third mistake in two days. The worst part was that he hadn't been anywhere last night; he'd stayed in and gone to bed early. Something else had kept him up.

"I can't keep covering for you John," Gloria said more softly, "I'll have to tell Doctor Griffin, and maybe he'll be more lenient because it's you."

"Lenient? Are we talking about the same man?" exclaimed John. "When have you ever seen him go easy on anyone, especially his own children? Do you actually think he did anything to help me get a job in his department?"

"I'm sorry John," said Gloria, with an air of finality. She handed him a clipboard and left.

Hauling himself off of the sofa, John went to the sink and splashed water over his face to wake himself up. Once he had dried off, he looked at the notes he'd been given. He was to check on a patient who had been brought in after being involved in a road traffic accident a few days ago.

Everyone knew of this patient by now, even though nobody had spoken to him or even knew his name. He had been unconscious for three days, but apart from a relatively minor head injury and some heavy bruising, there was nothing wrong with him.

The reason every member of staff knew of him was because of his abnormal appearance. Standing at six foot, nine inches, he weighed significantly more than your average two grown men. They had needed to make adjustments to the bed to hold him. His thick mane of dreadlocked hair almost reached the floor in his reclined position, and his face was covered in hundreds of tiny scratch marks. This gave him a striking appearance, but what most people found strange about him were his clothes, which appeared to be made from thick furred animal hide and reptile skin. His boots were crudely made of what looked like leather, and he wore a necklace made of an assortment of polished animal teeth; all razor sharp and almost 5 inches in length.

If this wasn't enough for people to take notice, eye witness accounts claimed that he had materialised from nowhere, seconds before he was hit by a heavy goods lorry that had been hurtling down the dual carriageway.

John moved the curtain aside and looked in on the sleeping giant. The patient's huge arm had dropped and was dangling down beside the bed. He was surprised to see that the man's arm was as thick as John's leg, and that his hands were like dustbin lids. He stared into the face of this wild man in amazement; how could anyone survive that?

"Defies belief doesn't it?" came a young woman's voice from the next cubicle.

John turned to see Doctor Maria Bishop standing behind him.

"What?" said John, "That he lived or that the driver didn't see him?"

She smiled back, "You should have seen how long it took us to take a blood sample, his skin is as tough as leather."

John looked back at the patient and stepped back in shock; his eyes had opened. "Jesus Christ, he's awake!"

Maria seemed equally startled. The huge man, although still completely motionless was staring at her intensely. A moment later his mouth lolled open, and then quickly closed.

"How . . . How are you feeling?" John stammered, unsure of what else to say.

"Where am I?" the giant said in a gruff voice, sitting up on the bed. Even sat down he dwarfed both John and Maria. His accent was like nothing either of them had heard before.

"You're in the hospital," Maria said, "You were in an accident? Do you remember what happened?"

The patient rolled back his eyes and placed his hand across his forehead. "I was struck by . . . . no I don't," he grumbled.

"You were hit by a lorry," John explained, "You're lucky to be alive."

"I've had worse," the giant replied.

John and Maria just looked at each other. "Do you remember your name?" Maria asked.

"Orak . . . Orak JaVrei."

Maria confirmed the spelling with him then scribbled the name down on the notes. She followed up by asking the usual questions, most of which he could not recall or had no answer for. Five minutes later, she left with nothing but a bizarre name and a place she had never heard of.

John took Orak's blood pressure and tested him for signs of concussion. When it came to checking his heart rate, he didn't need to use a stethoscope. He could virtually hear it from where he was stood; it sounded healthy.

"I need more rest. Can I go back to resting, just for a little while?" Orak asked, lying back down on the creaking bed. Before John could say anything, the giant was fast asleep.

*

"Where do you think he's from?" Maria asked as she dragged her backpack out of her locker at the end of her shift.

"I don't know, but I don't think Tontoltec is a real place," said John. "I Googled it and found nothing."

"When did you have a chance to go on the internet?" asked Maria.

"On my break," replied John.

"You went on break before you saw Orlak, or Orak, didn't you?" Maria questioned.

"I may have taken another one," John said, shying his head away.

Maria tutted and shook her head. "Late for work two days running, mixing up patients prescriptions and taking liberties with breaks," she exclaimed. "Wish I was the boss' son, well, daughter."

"I'm doing my best here," John said. "I've told you about the nightmares. I can't be on top form after less than two hours of sleep a night. Do you want to meet up for a drink later? I finish in an hour."

"Not tonight sorry," said Maria. "I need to be up early tomorrow, and unlike you, I need at least six or seven hours before I can even think about getting out of bed. I'm off Saturday though, so tomorrow night definitely."

"Sure," said John, deliberately trying to sound casual. He had plans, but nothing which couldn't be cancelled.

John left the locker room with a spring in his step. He had more energy now than he'd had all week. He'd been infatuated with Maria since she had moved here only a week ago, but only now was he sure that she liked him too. The hour flew by, and before he knew it, he was working overtime.

After hurriedly changing, he walked briskly towards the exit, eager to get home and to his kitchen. Despite having more than his share of lunch and tea breaks, he'd not had a chance to eat anything all day and he was famished. On his way through the ward however, John noticed Orak's cubicle was empty. Strange, he thought, *they wouldn't have discharged him yet.*

Ignoring the rumbling in his stomach, he decided to check the toilets to make sure the big guy was alright. Before he even got to them, he saw the unmistakable silhouette of his patient heading towards the main door. John jogged to catch up with him, amazed at the pace needed to keep up with his vast strides.

"Has anyone told you that you're well enough to leave?" John gasped, virtually running alongside him.

"I feel fine," Orak replied, "I am rested enough."

"You were hit by a lorry doing seventy," John exclaimed, feeling as though his words lacked impact when this strange man's expression remained the same. "You've been in a coma for 3 days."

Orak stopped dead and turned to face the hospital worker.

"Thank you for looking after me during my sleep. Could you tell me who I need to talk to so I can get a message out to everyone? Or at the very least to your leaders."

"What?" asked John, dumbfounded by the question.

"A warning: a great danger is coming. I need to warn your people," said Orak.

"My People? I don't understand . . . What are you talking about?" asked John.

"What is your name?" asked Orak.

"Err . . . John Griffin."

"Can you take me to somewhere that serves food John Griffin? I am very hungry and I don't know this place at all? I also have a lot to explain to you," said Orak.

Chapter 2

Gloria Jones left the hospital shortly after John, having officially finished her shift an hour earlier. She drove a short distance to her house and parked her car in the double garage.

Her husband's sports coupé was already parked in the other bay and for a moment she thought he had come home early. The fact that the house door was locked reminded her that Mr Jones car-pooled on Thursdays.

Crashing down on the sofa, she switched on the TV. After a twelve hour shift, she didn't have the energy to do anything else. Today hadn't been an especially busy shift, with no major accidents and relatively few minor ones.

Gloria caught her reflection in the screen. She realised that she was starting to look her age and this saddened her. She would be sixty five within a few weeks and this had been on her mind much of late.

It wasn't as if she'd wasted her life, not by any means. She'd helped a lot of people throughout her forty seven year career, but she'd never had children, and although she cared deeply for her husband Mark, it was a loveless relationship. In her mind, she referred to their marriage as an arrangement of mutual contentedness.

Maybe this was why she treated John like a son. She had been close friends with Dr Griffin for many years, and it was her who got Griffin Junior his job in the hospital.

Gloria snapped herself out of her spiralling train of thought and focused on the TV. The news was on and the reader was reporting on what at first looked like a terrorist attack. She turned up the volume and leaned in closer.

"Earlier this afternoon, six were injured during the initial fire and one woman was reportedly killed when the air-borne creature was witnessed to return, although only partial remains were found . . ."

Gloria was sure she'd misheard the newsreader. It had been a long day. Squinting her eyes, she focused on the scene in front of her. It showed a glazed shop front that had been shattered. The products on display were all smouldering and blood was spattered across the pavement. A nearby lamp post had been bent in half, another actually torn in two with tangled cables scattered everywhere.

Gloria shook her head in disbelief, but carried on listening. The report cut to a member of the public who had witnessed the event.

"It flew overhead, clipped them with his wing," the shaken man gasped, gesturing towards the broken lamp posts. "It just clipped them! It coughed out a ball of fire straight at us. I was lucky; the others were taken to hospital."

The witness held up his reddened arm, where the flames had licked. "We thought it had gone," he continued, "But it came swooping back down, and it snatched her right off the street in its jaws, then shook her until she stopped moving, then it just flew away."

Gloria just stared for a few minutes, barely able to think. Once the report was finished she reached for the phone and began to call everyone she knew.

*

John took Orak to a café not far from the hospital, en-route to his house. He wasn't entirely happy about having to pay for this stranger's food, especially after seeing how much he ordered. His anger was reversed immediately when the self-discharged patient brought out a chocolate bar sized block of solid gold and said, "Am I right in thinking that this is quite valuable here?"

"You're kidding right?" John replied. His uncle, Robert Griffin was a jeweller, so John knew the current value of gold better than most.

"But I understand that I can't use it to pay here? So can I get the value to pay you back from this?"

John stared at him again and simply asked, "Who are you?"

"I'm not from around here," replied Orak.

"I guessed that," John laughed, looking again at Orak's clothes.

"Where are the teeth from . . . the ones on your necklace"? John asked.

"Prey," Orak simply answered before asking, "Do you have more money for food?"

John opened his wallet and handed him some money. "I think I know somewhere you can get cash for that gold," John added, eyeing the block of precious metal just sitting there on the table. If it was pure 24 carat gold, this little block could be worth thousands. "Where did you get it from?"

"From home, it's more common there . . . I have more." He took out two more bars, and noticed John's eyes light up. "If you help me out I will split the currency with you, half and half."

John stuttered, "I . . . Err . . . What do you need me to do?" He was well aware that many people would kill for less. Suddenly the insanity of the situation had advanced another step. One moment he was checking if a patient was ok, the next he was in a café, being given thousands of pounds worth of gold by a man with seemingly no understanding of the value of money. What could he possibly want?

"Right, firstly I should explain. I'm not from around here," said Orak.

"We've covered that."

"Secondly, and I have a feeling you're less likely to believe this, but I'm not the same species as you."

John snorted a laugh, "Is this a wind up?"

Orak didn't smile back. "I'm human, but not exactly the same type as you," he said.

"Ok, this is ridiculous. What's this got to do with me anyway?" John asked.

"Nothing," replied Orak, "But you've offered to help. I don't know anyone else here, and I need to find a way to put a message across."

"What message?" John asked.

Orak sighed. He had no idea how to explain everything in just a few short sentences like this medic was expecting him to. What made it harder was that he wouldn't believe a single word of it. Nevertheless, he decided to try.

"I come from a . . ." Orak was cut short by a sudden burst of music. He spun around looking to see where it was coming from, but there were no musicians and nobody else in the café looked remotely surprised. The song was immediately silenced when John pressed something on a small handheld device, and then began talking into it.

"Gloria, you'll never guess who I'm sat here talking to? What? What channel?" John asked. "Ok, I'll try. See you on Monday then, bye."

John left the phone on the table and went to ask if the manager could put the TV on to the 24 hour news channel. When he sat back down, he saw that Orak was fascinated by his mobile phone. He had picked it up and was looking at it from every angle. When the screen lit up, he dropped it in shock, sending it clattering onto the table.

The channel switched from a reality TV show onto the news. The same report had been circulating for the past half an hour, and what everyone in the café saw made them forget what they were doing and stand up to get a better view.

"Sweet Jesus, what in God's name?" an American tourist cried out.

Just when John was sure his day couldn't get any stranger, he found himself staring at footage of a giant winged reptile lying dead on the streets of Manchester. Florescent green police jackets were visible everywhere, as officers tried to stop the hundreds of curious shoppers getting near. The beast looked to be over forty feet in length, and was coiled like a snake. There was no other word for it; this beast looked uncannily like the ones in dozens of fantasy books and artworks. The dragon's great horned head bore a jaw full of razor sharp teeth, and it didn't take long for John to make the connection. He looked back at the giant of a man eating his fifth course of dinner, and saw the necklace.

John sat back down a minute later and said "Ok, I'm listening."

Chapter 3

Maria Bishop had received a similar phone call from Gloria and had watched in awe at every news report that the internet had to offer on the events of the afternoon. There were hundreds of theories about this mysterious creature, varying from the idea that it was a dinosaur that had survived hundreds of millions of years underground, to paranoid conspiracy theories about government genetic engineering. All but one was wrong.

Deciding that she was unlikely to make sense of any of this online, she switched off her computer and started cooking herself a simple meal. After a ten hour shift, she didn't have the energy to cook anything more extravagant than battered cod, rice and peas.

She had been thinking a lot about John since she had got back from work. Before he had asked, it hadn't occurred to her that he might be interested too. A nagging doubt told her that it was just a drink and nothing more. Maybe he just wanted to get to know her as a friend. Maria had never been lucky in love for exactly this reason, doubt.

Trying not to think about it, she carried on stirring the rice. Her thoughts strayed back to her day at work, specifically the patient she and John had seen together, and she wondered how he was recovering. She remembered seeing the x-rays, and not noticing a single broken bone. The reports of how he was injured must have been wrong, she was sure of it.

Glancing down at the saucepan, she saw that the water was starting to pour over the sides. She had put too much in, and now it was all over the hob. Quickly turning off the flame, she carried the pan to the sink to pour some out, scalding herself in the process. The metal saucepan fell to the ground with an almighty crash, soaking her feet in starchy boiling water.

Maria screamed, throwing off her slippers and running to the bathroom. After dousing her feet under cold water for a few minutes, she carefully treaded back downstairs into the kitchen.

When she got back, she noticed the pan was back on the worktop. Surely she wouldn't have picked it up before running off in pain? She was sure she'd left it where it fell.

"Don't be alarmed," said a quiet voice from behind her.

Doing the exact opposite, Maria nearly had a heart attack. Stumbling backwards on her swollen red feet, she fumbled for a knife from the draw and promptly dropped it. Snatching a potato peeler, she pointed it in the direction of the voice, but the room was empty. She was sure she had seen a figure there a second ago.

"I'm not going to hurt you," the voice said again.

This time Maria knew she wasn't imagining it. "Where are you? What do you want?" she asked, trying to sound brave and confident, but failing.

"I'm at your front door," said the voice.

Confused, Maria walked out into the hallway and looked through the peep hole to see a bald man wearing a long dark cloak, standing on her porch. "What do you want?" she repeated.

"I'm sorry I made you hurt yourself, I was only trying to make you think about when you saw Orak. I need to know where he is," demanded the man.

"What?" she shouted, backing away from the door. "How did you know I had hurt myself?"

Maria gasped when she saw the door unbolting itself from the inside. She leapt forwards to try and close it, but was a second too late. The door swung open and she fell straight through the opening.

Her eyes had shut tight reflexively, bracing herself for impact with the floor, but she felt nothing. Opening them, she saw herself floating several inches above the ground. Thrashing her whole body violently, she felt herself drop to the floor. She ran back inside the house and re-bolted the door. Sliding down the back of it, she broke down into floods of tears.

Maria found herself silenced when she caught sight of a piece of paper in front of her. It was folded into the shape of some kind of bird.

Her hands trembling, she unfolded it and read a note written in ornate calligraphic handwriting.

> *I'm not here to hurt you. Sorry I frightened you and I'm sorry about the incident in the kitchen. I have gone now and I will only return to collect your reply. If you know where Orak went after leaving the hospital, please write the location down on this piece of paper and leave it outside your door. Thank you.*

Maria read through the note a dozen times. She didn't even know Orak had been discharged. A few moments later, she scribbled the words '*I don't know*' on the paper, and then shoved it back through her letter box.

*

John decided that he needed something stronger than coffee before he heard Orak's story. The pair moved from the café to the local nightclub.

From outside, the building seemed out of place on the fairly modern street, as it was a converted stonework Catholic Church. Inside, the place looked more like a drinking establishment, despite some original features having been retained. There were several rows of pews on the second floor and the large stained glass windows were still intact.

They chose one of the quieter booths to sit in and John bought a large round of drinks, still thinking about the gold he'd been promised.

"You're not from around here. We've clarified that," John began, once he was halfway through his second pint. "So where are you from?"

Orak took a deep breath before continuing. "The country I'm from is called Tontoltec; a newly formed democratic nation which was formerly a collection of principalities. It is located in the northern hemisphere of a world called Ithria."

"So, you're an alien?" said John.

"I suppose so, yes," replied Orak. "There has been a link between your world and mine for thousands of years; a mutual point in orbit around sibling stars. I don't understand it either. This link causes rifts in space, allowing matter to cross over between worlds."

John said nothing, this may have been madness, but it was compelling madness. "Go on," he said.

"We thought the link had been severed during your thirteen hundreds," said Orak, "But four years ago, evidence arose that it was reforming. At first we were only able to observe your side so we learned a lot by watching your people."

"Like our language?" said John.

"Correct," replied Orak. "I learnt English, Mandarin, Russian, Spanish and French, because the journey is never the same. The destination is always geographically different, and we had no idea where we would end up."

"What do you mean by 'we'?" asked John.

Orak quickly consumed another pint of lager; even the cheap stuff here was far better than the alcohol they served in Tontoltec. "Three of us came through. The message that I need to get out will help them find me, so we can sever the link again."

"Why?" asked John.

"For your safety," replied Orak.

John thought for a moment. He didn't believe any of this, but if all this strange man wanted was to find his friends and was willing to pay as much as he said, there was no reason not to help. "I'll figure something out to help you. When you said you weren't the same type of human as me, what did you mean?" he asked.

"Ok, this might not be as easy to explain," Orak said, without even a trace of a slur.

John was amazed, not only by what he'd said but by the number of empty pint glasses sat on the table. He was very glad that it was a Thursday night when the drinks were not expensive.

"It would be easier to show you, but I'll try and explain," Orak said.

"Most of the people on Ithria are humans just like here, but there's a minority, less than half a percent, who are different. There's a state of energy called Anuma which can be manipulated and stored by those in the minority. There are three of these races, each determined by the recessive genes that they possess."

Orak was interrupted by a pretty young woman selling shots of different coloured drinks in plastic test tubes. From the look on Orak's face, John knew he was tempted. He sighed and got out his wallet once again. *This guy had better pay out*, John thought. "We'll have one of each," he said to the woman.

After downing eight flavoured vodka shots, Orak continued. "The three races re-named themselves for your tongue. Firstly there are those who've utilized this energy in enhancing their physical bodies, like me. We're known as Titans. We're bigger, tougher, stronger and faster . . . not meaning to brag," he laughed. "We can also heal quicker than any other human, even to the extent of growing back limbs given enough time."

"So if I cut off your hand . . . ?" John said.

"It might take a fortnight or two, but yes," replied Orak. "The next race we've called Telepaths. These people utilise the energy within their minds, giving them projective mental abilities. They can put things into your head, like words, ideas, pictures, as well as having telekinetic abilities."

"They can read minds?" John asked.

"No, they can only give, not take thoughts. The third race we've called Spellcasters. They have the ability to manipulate the energy into the form of fire, air, water, and electrical currents, sort of like the four elements . . ."

"Where are you staying?" John interrupted, not having fully paid attention.

"I don't know yet," replied Orak.

John thought, waiting for a moment of clarity. His next step could be a huge gamble. All his life he had tended to go with his gut instinct and it had usually turned out to be for the best. This time however, even though his gut told him to trust this stranger, his brain screamed 'bad idea'. Doing as he always did, he decided to take the risk head on.

"Well, as you don't have any money yet, you'll have to crash on my floor tonight. I'll take you to the gold exchange place on my way to work tomorrow morning, is that ok?"

"Thank you John," said Orak.

The two of them left just as the bar started to get busy. Everyone stared as this peculiar clad giant moved through the crowds, and nobody dared stand in his way.

*

The cloaked man returned half an hour later and read the torn scrap of paper. Dissatisfied with the answer, he left in search of the next lead.

Maria had calmed down and after cleaning up the mess in the kitchen, she put a ready meal in the microwave. She had planned on having an early night, but there was no way she'd be able to get to sleep now.

After some deliberation, she tried phoning John to see if he was free for a drink. She needed someone to talk to, and didn't know many other people around here. She tried a few times, but it always went to his answer phone. After giving up, she decided to phone the only other person she knew had been treating Orak JaVrei.

Gloria answered almost straight away, catching Maria off guard. Flustered, Maria tried to explain what had just happened. Missing out some of the less believable parts, she enquired as to whether she knew where their patient was now.

Having also been unaware of their patient's discharge, Gloria said, "Have you tried asking John?"

"I can't get through. Do you know if he has a landline?" Maria asked.

"He does, but it doesn't work," Gloria replied.

"I could visit him. Do you know where he lives?" asked Maria.

Gloria gave her the address and repeated it so that Maria had chance to write it down. Maria checked the time, it was already nine thirty, and so all hope of an early night was out of the window if she was going to go all the way to the other side of town.

"He said he might be going out for a drink, is there anywhere he usually . . ."

"The Phoenix," Gloria interrupted, "On Wyndham Street. But why don't you just leave it until tomorrow? By the time you get there it'll be a bit late for visitors."

Maria sighed, "You're right," she said. "It can wait."

Despite having such a burden on her mind, Maria eventually did manage to get to sleep. She knew that tomorrow would be a big day, but she had no idea just how significant it would be.

Unwillingly she would begin a journey which would change the course of her life forever.

Chapter 4

While Maria lay dreamlessly asleep, nine miles away John slept less peacefully. Instead of comfortably lying in bed, he was standing on an open plain, surrounded by jagged rocks. The warm sun had died, leaving only blackness. The icy wind howled like wolves. It cut through his clothes and chilled him to the bone, sending him to his knees.

The howling soon turned to screaming, and in the dim glow from the fallen star he saw winged silhouettes, like thousands of bats moving skywards. The swarm grew larger and began hurtling towards him, screeching ever louder. John began running, cutting his feet on the rocks with every step. The ground grew hotter and began to hiss as he trod over it.

The swarm was almost upon him, but as he looked back they scattered, vanishing into thin air. They had been replaced by a single dark shadow which flowed like black smoke. It engulfed his body and lungs as he was hurled back into his bedroom.

Gasping for air, John felt as though he had just surfaced from deep water. His body was trembling and drenched in sweat. *They're getting worse*, he thought to himself.

He stumbled out of bed and clambered into the shower. It was still only 4:30 in the morning, but he dreaded the idea of going back to sleep and returning to whatever hell he had just escaped from.

For the next two hours, he tried to keep his mind occupied by playing on computer games. After that, he woke up Orak and got ready for work. John walked with Orak to the gold merchants and arranged to meet him back at the house at the end of his shift.

Reluctantly, he handed his house key to the man who was almost a complete stranger and told him to stay there. Orak could keep himself entertained by watching TV or using the computer, but in order to stop him from using the internet, John had hidden the cable.

When John arrived at the hospital, although it was exactly the same, the place felt different somehow. It had been little more than twelve hours since he had last been here, but it felt like it had been days. In other ways, he felt as though he had never left. Yesterday had been without a doubt, the strangest day of his life.

One thing was different; Gloria wasn't there to greet him. This was her first weekday off in a long time, and John found it somewhat lonely knowing she wasn't there.

It was midday before he finally caught up with Maria. There had been a spate of casualties admitted, keeping them both busy and on different sides of the ward. Maria came into the staff room, blood covering her white coat. She tossed the dirty garment into her locker, and began changing into a clean set of clothes.

Maria nearly jumped out of her skin when she saw John lying on the sofa, and realising she was only wearing her underwear, tried to cover herself up.

"I won't look," John said, wishing he wasn't so gentlemanly.

"It's fine, you just startled me that's all," she replied, noticing the smile on his face as he forced himself to look in the opposite direction. "I've been meaning to talk to you all day," Maria added.

"Really?" said John.

"The strangest thing happened last night. You'll probably think I'm mad," said Maria.

"What happened?" John asked, waiting for the chance to tell her about his own bizarre meeting.

Maria explained every single detail. She told him about the disembodied voice, the cloaked figure outside her door and how he could move things without touching them, even her. All along, John was hearing Orak's voice, remembering what he had told him:

"These people utilise the energy within their minds, giving them projective mental abilities. They can put things into your head, like words, ideas, pictures, as well as having telekinetic abilities."

"He was telling the truth!" John said, interrupting her, "He was telling the truth."

"Who was?" asked Maria.

"Orak, the huge patient from yesterday, wait, that means . . ."

"You know where he is?" Maria asked.

John nodded, his head was spinning. Yesterday he was sure everything this superhuman had told him was all lies or delusions but with the dragon on the news, and now this, his mind was in turmoil. "I need a drink," he said.

"Phoenix? 8 o'clock?" he asked Maria.

"Maybe if I've finished what I need to do by then," she replied.

John went on to explain everything Orak had told him, or at least everything he remembered. As he went on, he felt less tense, and less like he needed a drink. Both lost track of time and without realising it, they were still talking half an hour after their breaks should have finished. "There could be a lot of money for me if I help him out," John finished, "I'll split it fifty fifty if you help me re-unite these strange people."

Maria smiled, she'd wanted to take a holiday for a while, but her funds were all tied up. "Count me in," she said.

*

During her day off, Gloria decided to treat herself to a spa treatment. She had gotten up early and headed to the health club a few miles down the road. By two o'clock she had managed to fit in an hour of swimming, a sauna, a full body massage and a facial. A friend had given her vouchers, so the whole thing barely cost a penny. By early afternoon, she was ready to go back home, feeling and looking fifteen years younger.

When she got home, the first thing she did was put the kettle on. She had bought half a dozen different types of herbal and fruit teas at the spa shop to try.

Relaxing on the sofa with her mug of camomile tea, she switched on the TV. The news was on again, but nothing quite as unusual as yesterday's big story seemed to be making the headlines today.

She found herself getting a little too relaxed, and a few times she felt herself beginning to drift off and so decided to just let it happen. As she was reaching for the remote to switch off the TV, the screen went blank of its own accord. At the same time, the lights flickered and every digital clock in the house reset to midnight.

Unhappy, Gloria got up to go and check the fuses. This was the fourth or fifth time this had happened in a just a few days. She found the switches had tripped. Resetting them all, she returned to the lounge, no longer feeling like taking a nap.

From the opposite side of the building, Gloria could hear a loud hissing. "What on Earth?" she said to herself. Fearing it was a gas leak, she went to explore. After listening to the exposed pipes in the utility room, she realised the sound was coming from the garage. Slipping on a pair of trainers, she went out to investigate.

*

For John, the next three hours seemed like the longest of his life. Not only were his views of the world and the universe around him changing fundamentally, but he was getting closer to the woman he felt sure he wanted to be with. On top of that, he had the potential to earn enough money to not need to work for a few years. He couldn't wait to leave this place and get on with what he needed to do. Things were running smoothly, despite the huge amount on his mind. That was until he was called into Dr Griffin's office.

Despite working in the same building, John had not seen his father and boss for several days. He lived away from his parents in a rented house, and they were usually on different wards in the hospital. He expected this meeting to be as awkward as their meetings usually were. Ever since John's mother died, his father had barely said a word to him, even though sixteen years had passed since then. He said his son reminded him of her, but John knew the real reason. His father was incapable of caring about anyone other than himself.

When he knocked on the door, an austere sounding voice called for him to enter. Mr Griffin looked a lot like his son, but older and greyer. He didn't look up when John entered, neither did he stop writing. Upon his nose were perched a pair of thin framed reading glasses and his chair was raised high, as if to show dominance. This reminded John of when he was called to see his father as a child when he'd misbehaved.

"I hear you've not been coping well here," Dr Griffin began, still not looking up. This was his attempt at being compassionate to soften the blow. John knew exactly what was going to happen.

"I've made a few mistakes, I admit," said John.

Their eyes met for the first time in weeks, "You and I both know it's been more than a few. I took a risk allowing you to work here, and I feel you've let me down," said his father. "I know you didn't intentionally do anything to harm any patient here, and I hate to say this, but you're becoming a liability. If we were in any other career, your performance of late might not be as much of an issue," he went on to say.

"Are you asking me to hand in my notice, or are you firing me?" John cut in; fighting back whatever urge was building up. He didn't know whether to cry or lash out.

"I think it would be better for you to resign before I have to step in," said his father, adding, "I hate to be harsh, but if you're letter of resignation isn't on my desk by the end of the day, I'll be informing the board of your indiscretions. If you resign on personal matters, you might still have a chance of finding work in another hospital."

"Thank you," John said, breaking eye contact. He stood up and left without saying another word.

He waited until he was halfway down the corridor before shouting and kicking the wall, but he was sure his father had still heard. Deep down, he knew his old man was right, but it didn't make it any less painful to hear he was a failure.

*

The hissing grew louder when Gloria opened the door to the garage, confirming that the source was in there somewhere. Stepping towards her car, she noticed the plastic sheeting covering her husband's power tools was flapping, like it was caught in a breeze.

She moved into the empty bay beside her car, and felt the airflow for herself. It was warm and powerful, but also strangely localised. It felt exactly like someone was pointing a hairdryer at her. Moving closer to the door, the breeze stopped immediately, but the hissing continued.

Baffled, Gloria waved her hands through the air, trying to find the air flow again. She stopped dead when she felt it blowing through her fingers once more. Her jaw dropped, this was impossible. The wind was coming from the direction of her other hand, which felt nothing. Hands trembling, she moved them closer together, but still only one hand felt anything. The air was coming from nowhere.

When her hands met in the source of this mysterious breeze, she felt a jolt of electricity through her arms and she leapt back. Backing up against the wall, she tried to catch her breath, her lungs gasping for air and all of her muscles aching.

The hissing continued for a minute longer, gradually quietening down until it was completely silent. Gloria took herself back inside and decided to try and put this to the back of her mind until her husband came home from work. Maybe he'd be able to shine some light on it.

Chapter 5

As soon as Maria heard about John's resignation, she ran to find him. She asked him to wait for her at his house, and said that she would come straight over once her shift had finished. The money seemed less important to her now, but she felt compelled to help him because she knew he would soon need it to live on.

During a fifteen minute break, she called the local hospitals, morgues and police stations, giving them each a description of the man who had terrorised her at her home; the man Orak was looking for. Losing track of time again, she had to hang up mid-sentence and go back to work. She'd had no success with these lines of enquiry, and just hoped John was having better luck.

*

When John got home, he was greeted by a kitchen table covered in bundles of £20 notes. He nearly yelled with excitement but managed to compose himself. This had taken the edge off the anger he felt over his forced resignation.

"Orak?" he called, searching the other rooms.

"In here," Orak's voice rumbled.

John found him in the study, sitting at the computer. He had no idea how, but Orak was using the internet. The screen was covered in messages about viruses and at first he felt like breaking the keyboard over Orak's head. He quickly came to realise that he could now easily afford another computer and his data was all backed up anyway.

"I found the cable in your bedside table drawer; that seems a place to keep it to me," said Orak.

"Yeah, I guess," John replied, "How much money did the gold fet...? he asked.

"More than I was expecting, but I don't fully understand your currency," Orak said "I also found my backpack, it landed in the park. It made quite a crater but it was in the shrubs so nobody found it. I sold the gold in there too."

"So . . . how much?" John asked.

Orak pulled a slip of paper out of his pocket and read the figure, "Two hundred and sixteen thousand," he said calmly.

"Two Hundred and . . ." John yelled, steadying himself against the door frame.

"Is that a lot?" Orak asked.

"So how much do I get for helping you?" asked John.

"I said half, so that's one hundred and eight thousand. Is that ok?" asked Orak.

"Well, I suppose it's enough," John said casually. He remembered his promise to Maria, which would make his cut only fifty four thousand, but that was still more than he would make in a year.

"I didn't have any luck searching on here," Orak said, switching off the computer.

"What's the name of the guy you're looking for?" John asked.

"WaMaktaJrei Kroez," Orak told him.

"Do you think he'd mind if we shortened it to Mac?" John joked.

"I don't imagine so. I put out a few adverts on the internet with WaMaktaJrei's and Shoadrina's description," said Orak.

"Shoadrina? She's the Spellcaster right?" asked John.

"Yes, we call her Shoa. I put your phone number on the adverts, so they can contact me," said Orak.

John sighed; he knew that he would probably need to change his number after this ordeal. The expenses seemed to be mounting, and he wondered whether Orak would be offering to pay them from his share.

"I asked a friend to help out. She should be coming around later," said John.

"I can't afford to pay her too," Orak said abruptly. "I need this money for . . ." He stopped mid-sentence.

"I said I'd split mine with her," John said.

"You mean half and half?" Orak asked, "She must be quite a special friend."

"She is," John said instantly, "Or at least I hope she will be."

As if on cue, the doorbell rang. John knew that Maria had said that she would be coming over about this time, but if it was someone else, he would need to hide the money. Quickly shoving the bundles of notes into the cupboards under the sink, John stuck a padlock on the doors and locked it. He put the key in his pocket, before rushing to the front door.

As he suspected, Maria was there. A wide smile appeared on his face, and she looked equally happy.

"I found her," Maria said, stepping inside without waiting for an invitation, "Well, she found me."

"How?" John asked.

"Oh, hello," she said, surprised when she saw the mountain of a man sitting down in John's study, "I didn't know you'd still be here."

"You were there at the hospital?" Orak asked, standing up to greet her. She shook his hand; hers looked like a child's in comparison to his shovel-like paw. "Thank you for looking after me."

"Just doing my job," she said instinctively, as if it were a reflex.

"You found Shoadrina?" said Orak.

"She phoned in to the radio station when I was listening to it on my way here. She said she'd bought a mobile phone. I was driving so I didn't get the whole number."

"How much of it did you get?" John asked, finding her excitement infectious.

"Nine numbers, well, eight for sure. I think the ninth is either a five or nine."

"That gives us about two hundred possibilities." John had known from the start that this wasn't going to be the easiest job in the world, but they each had access to a phone, how long could it possibly take?

Maria started work on writing down all of the possible combinations, while John fetched the spare mobile from his bedroom for Orak to use. It took nearly fifteen minutes to explain how to use the phone, and after losing his temper several times, it became apparent that the Titan probably had a mild form of dyslexia. Each time Orak had to dial a number, not only did he have to cross out each digit at a time, but his fingers were so big, he couldn't press the buttons properly.

Nearly two hours later, they were only halfway through the list and decided to take a break. Maria was starting to lose her voice after having an argument with several people, who she'd accidentally called two or three times, and John's phone had run out of battery.

Maria had written a side list of the numbers they had dialled where nobody had answered, making the list of total numbers tried at one hundred and forty. She was starting to wonder if she had gotten any of the other numbers wrong, but kept that thought to herself. She also wondered whether anyone else she knew had heard the phone in, but she was certain that nobody would have felt the need to write down the number. This was unfortunately the only way.

While John's phone was charging, he popped down the road to get a few takeaway pizzas for everyone to share. Using the money from the gold sale, he tipped generously and even paid a taxi to take him back just over a quarter of a mile home.

"Any luck?" he asked, dropping the sizeable order on the kitchen table.

"No," Maria said, already helping herself to a slice of pepperoni and ham, "But we're down to ninety numbers. Knowing my luck it'll be the first call I made where nobody answered," she said.

They all stopped for a short break while they stuffed their faces with food. All three of them were determined enough to stay up all night to find the right number if they had to.

Maria stared avidly at Orak while he finished off his third large pizza. She had never seen anything eat so much, and she had grown up on a farm.

"You never did tell me," John said after a long silence, "What danger are we all in if you don't close this rift thing?"

Orak stopped eating for a moment to explain. "Well, you know how I said we've been able to view your world from ours for the past four years? Well, it's not only our university who figured out how to create these gateways. A nation overseas from Tontoltec also developed a method. Alkak-Taan used to be one of the greatest empires on Ithria before the revolution about fifty years ago. Their rulers are a council made up of the three minority races, who still believe that they should have control over humanity. Over the past four years, they've been looking at your world's science; genetics in particular, and have been combining it with their advanced knowledge of Anuma energy. We knew about this work for quite some time, but we were naïve and ignorant, and thought it would never come to much."

Orak stopped to make a start on his fourth pizza. He got halfway through before finally declaring that he was full. Maria and John shared what was left between them.

"Anyway," Orak continued, "Their science and yours allowed them to produce a new race; a combination between humans, goblins and dragons. They called this creature a Drathmork and found it grew to full maturity in less than six months. These creatures walk and talk like us, but are winged and even more violent than the dragons they used to engineer them from. Although not as strong as us Titans, they are a lot tougher than you. At the rate they breed and grow, they would pick apart your world within months. They are the soldiers which will assure Alkak-Taan victory in the war that they will have started by now."

"Hell," John said casually, "I'm really sorry man."

Orak shook his head, "I'm not going back there," his voice filled with a world of regret. "WaMaktaJrei and Shoadrina aren't either. We need to be on this side to sever the link, and that was why we volunteered. You might think we're deserting our people, but believe me, there's nothing we can do now. Ithria is lost."

"So, that's why you need your entire share of the money," John said before asking. "What about Mac and Shoa?"

"We'll all have to find jobs. We'll share the money and buy a house together if it's enough. It'll take time, but we'll settle in," said Orak.

Orak excused himself and went to the toilet. John wondered whether the porcelain throne would even support the man's weight, but said nothing. He turned to Maria once he was sure his guest could not hear.

"Are you buying all of this?" he asked her.

"I think he believes it," replied Maria. "If you asked me this a few days ago, I would have said no, not for a second. Do you trust him?" she asked.

"I trust him about the money," said John "He's already brought the cash into my house, and let me lock it in my cupboard."

Maria frowned; she didn't know how to feel about any of this. If Orak was just telling them some elaborate fantasy, then what was his real reason for being here? Impossibly, only his crazy story really made any sense.

Before either of them could continue working through the list, John's charging phone buzzed. He snatched it up quickly. "Hello," he answered.

The woman spoke with an almost Hispanic sounding accent, but with unusual undertones. "Hello, is Orak JaVrei or WaMaktaJrei Kroez with you?" the woman said, sounding nervous but hopeful.

"Yes," John said a moment later, "If I give you my address, can you get here?" he asked.

Chapter 6

Gloria's hand had stopped hurting, but whatever she had touched had burnt her skin, forming a small scar between her fingers and thumb. She returned to the garage several times, wearing rubber gloves and protective goggles, but saw no more of this mysterious anomaly.

It definitely wasn't her imagination; she had the scar to prove it. Gloria had moved every box and sifted through every cupboard in search of anything that could explain what had happened, but nothing was out of the ordinary. She was starting to wonder whether she was going mad and had just managed to stick her hand in a power socket, or something equally careless.

Accidentally slamming her finger in a door, she yelped and banged into the shelving behind. Her husband's shotgun came crashing down onto the floor, firing a shot and blasting one of the work benches' legs apart. Wood splinters flew everywhere and the power-tools slid down onto the concrete floor. The stack of clay pigeons under the unit had also been knocked over, scattering orange shards amongst the wood and stray pellets.

Gloria noticed the side of her car had been scratched badly by a dozen or so stray shots. Screaming with rage, she emptied the weapon of its cartridges and threw it back onto the shelf. She had told him dozens of times never to store the damn thing loaded. *When he gets home I'm going to throttle him,* she thought. Gloria's heart rate took a while to return to normal; she could have been killed.

Her husband Mark had phoned her earlier to say he wouldn't be home tonight. His meeting had run late and as it was such a long commute, he needed to stay the night at a hotel. She had tried to explain to him what had happened in the garage, but he just said that he didn't understand her, and that they'd talk about it when he got back.

Mark had been away a lot lately, and when he was here, it seemed like he wanted to be elsewhere. The romance between them had died a long time ago, but she still cared enough to stay. The trouble was, she was starting to think he didn't. Like a lot of things lately, she put it to the back of her mind.

Gloria couldn't face tidying up the garage. She would leave it for Mark when he finally made an appearance.

*

WaMaktaJrei had booked into a hotel four days ago. He had traded a gold bar for a fraction of its value to a complete stranger, who looked as though he could afford it. It had given him enough money to book a fully catered room for a week, with enough left to buy a pay-as-you-go mobile phone and a laptop with a wireless internet card.

He had spent the time contacting hospitals, police stations, prisons and hotels, as well as researching the internet. Several hours earlier, he had heard Shoadrina's voice on the radio and managed to get in contact with her. She had recently called back and told him where she would be meeting Orak, but he told her to wait for him. There was something he needed to do first.

Sprawled across the desk in front of him was a map of the United Kingdom, as well as several smaller regional maps. He had circled the areas where the three of them had arrived on this world, as well as a large circle highlighting the possible areas the dragon could have come from. It was unfortunate that this beast had hitched a ride through with them, but something potentially worse had also gate crashed.

The map showed him a distinctive scatter pattern, from which he could fill in the missing pieces. It was a large area of possibility, but if it had moved, he would have heard about it by now.

WaMaktaJrei took a bus to the disused industrial site he had pinpointed on the map. After paying for the bus, he had less than £5 left in total. It was critical that he got to Orak after he had dealt with the loose end.

Upon the dusty ground he found an impact crater, from which led a strange set of footprints. They were edged softly like large paw prints, but were deep; clearly showing there was much weight behind them. These long thin impressions moved outwards, almost perpendicular to the direction to which they were going. They led to a building bigger than any he'd ever seen before. The huge brickwork structure bore several huge concrete chimneys and the entire row of high up windows had been boarded up.

As WaMaktaJrei got closer, he saw that the large main doors, which had initially been padlocked shut, had been smashed open. One door was hanging loose on its hinges; the other was a dozen or so feet inside the building.

Inside, the prints were no longer visible, as the ground had turned to smooth concrete. Just inside the entrance, WaMaktaJrei found a large flat headed shovel. His eyes surveyed the dark open space, lit only by a few gaps in the boarded windows. The place appeared completely empty, but it was too dark to tell. Venturing forwards, he listened out for the quietest of sounds.

In the darkness, WaMaktaJrei saw a flicker of light and a sudden movement of something shiny. He frantically searched for where the creature had gone, gripping the handle of the shovel tighter. He had a feeling he would need a bigger shovel.

The only other weapon he carried was a sheathed hunting blade at his waist. Although sharp, the weapon was less than a foot long, and curved, making it useless for stabbing.

WaMaktaJrei wished he had brought a torch with him and as he ventured further, the factory grew darker.

Out of nowhere, a deafening roar filled the air. A pair of shimmering black eyes appeared ahead, followed by a second pair just below.

The beast stepped into the thin ray of light from the high window, and WaMaktaJrei caught a glimpse of what he would face. Standing at ten or eleven feet high, the monster looked roughly human from the waist up. Below this muscular torso however, was the huge skeletal abdomen of a spider.

Roaring like a wounded lion, this huge beast sprinted towards him at an immeasurable rate. WaMaktaJrei reacted by sending the shovel flying towards it, twice as fast. Striking the creatures segmented lower body, the shovel merely bounced off, leaving no more than a scuff.

WaMaktaJrei levitated up from the ground, sending himself flying backwards away from the charging arachnoid centaur, and into the light.

Gliding back out through the main door, he was followed by the beast, smashing its shoulder through the timber frame effortlessly.

In the daylight, he could see this massive creature fully. He realised that it had a second set of humanoid arms below the first, giving it a total of twelve limbs. Its head contained not two, but three sets of beetle black eyes as well as a vertically closing set of jaws that bore a pair of razor sharp teeth.

Squinting its six eyes, it became clear that this beast couldn't focus in the sunlight, even though it was nearly nightfall. WaMaktaJrei took this opportunity to send his hunting blade spinning towards it, striking it deeply across its chest.

The monster barely reacted to the blow which would surely have killed any man. Storming towards him again, the beast appeared to have adjusted to the new light level. WaMaktaJrei caught his foot on a rock as he glided away and came crashing down to the ground.

He forced himself to roll away, seconds before the beast's legs thudded down where he had lay. Elevating the blade once again, WaMaktaJrei sent it hurtling towards his attacker. Catching the side of the predator's neck, the blade rebounded, leaving no more than another deep gash.

Seeing the flying knife, the beast lost interest in his prey and followed the shiny piece of metal. Amazed at his luck, WaMaktaJrei searched the dusty flat lands for a better weapon. He caught sight of a disused crane and mustered all of his strength to focus upon it.

Suddenly the heavy steel hook dropped, falling fifty feet, striking the beast square on the top of its head, shattering its skull and killing it instantly.

Clambering to his feet, WaMaktaJrei nursed a headache. His vision was blurred and dizziness set in, causing him to fall back down. He had overexerted himself and needed a moment to recover.

A few minutes later, he dusted himself off, picked up his blade and concealing it back under his cloak; caught the bus back into town.

Chapter 7

When Shoadrina arrived on this world, she had entered through a rift in Glasgow. She had not ventured outside the city until after she had spoken to John on the phone. Unsure about flying in a plane, she decided to take the journey by rail. It would be the following day before she reached John's house in South Wales, as it was a seven hour trip.

Maria had stayed the night at John's, sleeping in his bed while he slept on the sofa. None of them had gotten any sleep until about 4 am, and were woken just three hours later by a hammering on the door.

Orak was the first to get up, and was so excited when he opened the door that he forgot to turn the handle. John heard the noise from the living room and rushed out to the hallway.

When he got there, he saw two cloaked figures standing in the doorway. Maria arrived a moment later, wearing John's dressing gown, looking like she'd just crawled out of a grave. "What's going on?" she mumbled, rubbing her eyes.

"They're here," John said, sounding equally drowsy.

Orak embraced both of his friends in a hug, lifting them both off the ground. He invited them in, forgetting this wasn't his house, and then tried closing the door. "I'll buy you a new one," he said, flushing with embarrassment. He wedged a splinter of wood at the bottom of the door to hold it closed for the moment.

John looked at the two strangers who had been let into his home. The first, presumably WaMaktaJrei, was a man of average height, pale skin and completely bald, with bizarrely bright purple eyes. He wore a full length black cloak and was carrying an old battered canvas backpack. Dropping it on the sofa, he took out a laptop and a mountain of papers. "I hope you don't mind me being here," he said, "As soon as I figure out the time and position of the rift, we'll be on our way."

"Orak, I found a bed and breakfast just outside the town. We can all stay there whilst we look for a house," said WaMaktaJrei.

Maria eyed WaMaktaJrei with distrust. He had tried to break into her home, and now he had effectively broken into John's. She turned to see the silent stranger who had accompanied him.

Shoadrina was the most normal in appearance of the three foreigners. Despite wearing an unusual green cloak, she was not freakishly tall, and her eyes were a very ordinary brown colour. She had long auburn hair, tanned skin and a very pretty, young looking face. Maria would have guessed she was about sixteen, and she guessed right. She realised that Shoa had a fairly fresh cut above her right eye, and her cheek below was bruised. Blood stains were also visible down the leg of her robe.

"My God! What happened to you?" asked Maria.

"After I left the hotel, some men followed me," she said calmly in her sweet eerily soothing tone, "They tried to take my bag."

"They hurt you?" asked Maria.

"I hurt them back!" She said, anger rising in her no longer innocent voice. "I sucked the stinking breath out of their lungs until they dropped dead!"

Maria looked shocked. This girl was suddenly more frightening than the giant or the pale cloaked intruder. Nevertheless, she was a victim of a violent crime.

"I'm a doctor Shoa. Can I call you Shoa? Do you want me to stitch up that cut?" Maria asked.

Shoa nodded, looking away, ashamed of her violent outburst. Maria took the battered teenager upstairs to treat her wounds, eyeing John as she left. She wondered what kind of mess he was really getting her into, and doubts about whether this would really be worth the payout crept into her mind.

John was thinking the same thing. He had been ok with letting this strange man use his house for a few days, but now he was harbouring a murderer in his home.

WaMaktaJrei sensed his hesitation, "I'll make sure none of this causes problems for you when we've gone," he assured him, "I'll say you knew nothing about what she's done. I'll say she cleaned herself up before she got here, and there was no way you could have known."

"Thank you," John replied, feeling only slightly better.

"Wait, what happened to you?" Orak cut in, noticing that WaMaktaJrei's robe was ripped and covered in mud.

"Was I the only one to notice something else followed us through, other than the dragon?" asked WaMaktaJrei.

From the confused look on Orak's face, the answer was no.

WaMaktaJrei took out the mobile phone he had bought and showed them the picture that he had taken of the creature he had slain yesterday.

"What the hell is it?" Orak asked, looking genuinely worried.

"Something new," replied WaMaktaJrei, "And I have a feeling that it was just an infant. Its body may have been fully grown, but its mind wasn't. The Alkak-Taan's are engineering soldiers, not mindless beasts."

"Isn't this another reason you should hurry up and close that rift thing?" John added, unable to take his eyes off of this horrifying monster. He wanted to hurry things along as much as possible. The sooner he got rid of these people, the sooner he could get on with his life. "Also, your name is impossible to pronounce."

"Call me Mac," WaMaktaJrei interrupted.

"Ok, I will," John replied, taken aback.

Mac spread several papers over the table, and then set up his laptop next them. He had quickly figured out how to use the computer, and had already found most of what he needed from the internet. Orak looked down at a sheet displaying a map of the town, with dozens of lines converging in three different points.

Mac scribbled some numbers above one of the convergences. "This is the time that this rift will open," he explained, pointing at the position on the map. Using the calculator, he entered some kind of equation the other two couldn't begin to understand.

"Mac is our universities head of science and maths; he's the country's foremost expert on the Anuma Link. That's why he was chosen to come through," Orak explained.

"Why did you and Shoa come through?" asked John.

"We were randomly selected from about 100 applicants; at least that's what they told the others," replied Orak. "We were actually handpicked because we were the most competent of the few applicants who were of the three races."

"How will you close the rift thingy?" John asked.

"High powered electrical energy released at precisely the moment before the opening becomes fully active. Shoa is going to do it," replied Orak. "That will sever it temporarily, maybe for a few decades. When the link forms again, we'll have to do the same thing. After that, we'll probably have died of old age, and it will no longer be our problem."

"So where do you need to go to sever it?" asked John.

Orak looked to Mac for an answer. He was still working on it. The three convergences on the map were where the rifts would be opening within the next forty eight hours. He had worked out the exact time for each of them, but apart from rough grid co-ordinates, he had no idea whether two of these places were even possible to get to.

"We'll have to visit them in turn," Mac explained, "This first one will open in just under two hours. It's a few miles away, and I know it's inside a building so we should head off as soon as Shoa is ready."

"So where is this place?" John asked.

"17 Oakfells Road" replied Mac.

For some reason the name rang a bell. "Definitely number 17?" John asked, trying to remember why he knew the address so well.

"The anomaly is close to number 15, but definitely within the walls of 17," replied Mac. "I've got a floor plan of the property."

Mac brought out an A3 plan of the three storey semi-detached house. To the west side of the respectable sized building was a two bay garage with additional workshop space towards the back. A large hand-drawn circled asterisk was located at the convergence of dozens of lines, in the western parking bay of the garage. When John saw the layout it dawned on him why he knew the address.

"That's Gloria's house!" he exclaimed.

"You know this place? You can get us in?" Mac said, sounding hopeful.

"I can't just let you break into Gloria's house!" said John.

"So make her invite us in?" Orak cut in.

"I . . . I . . ." John stammered. He didn't have an answer. Confronted by these two vastly more powerful beings, he had no other reason to stop them other than it being rude and disrespectful. "Ok, but please, let me go in to explain first?" said John.

"As long as we get there in time that's fine by me," Mac finalised.

"Right," John said, he had no idea how he would explain any of this to Gloria. He wondered whether a share of the money would make her let them in, but he doubted it. Her husband Mark was a bank manager and earned £90,000 a year.

Maria came down a moment later and told the three men that Shoa was sleeping upstairs.

"I'm not surprised she's tired. It's the cities," Mac explained, "There's so much electromagnetic radiation in the air; radio waves and microwaves and such. We take much of our energy from the environment. This busy air messes with the natural balance of our minds and bodies. It affects Shoa more because she is so young."

"How old are you?" John asked.

"Forty one," replied Mac.

"Your people don't live like hundreds of years do they?" asked John.

"No, that's ridiculous. Why would we? Mac asked. "In half an hour we set off . . . Are you coming too?" he said, looking at Maria.

"Where?" she asked, having not been present during the recent conversation.

John led her into the kitchen so the others couldn't hear. He pushed the door closed so they were completely alone. "They think the rift opening thing is going to be in Gloria's house in a few hours. They want to go there to close it."

"What?" she blurted out, "Should we phone and warn her they're going to break in? Or phone the police and . . . ."

John interrupted, shaking his head, "I don't know what to believe, but if they go and do their thing, then they'll be out of our hair. They'll be out of all of our lives and we'll have our money."

"If they honour their word," Maria said.

"If they don't, then we call the police," said John.

"Ok, I'll go with you. It might take both of us to convince her to let them in," Maria smiled. "Tomorrow we'll be more than fifty grand richer and I'm going to take you out to dinner to celebrate."

"Only if you let me pay," he replied, taking hold of her hands.

"Deal," she laughed. Maria drew him closer to kiss his cheek, but he moved his head to face her and they kissed passionately. They both knew that regardless of whatever else happened, today was the start of something special.

Chapter 8

Before everyone left, John nailed several boards across his broken front door and then left through the back. On the way there, he struggled to think of what to tell Gloria. He knew he was a terrible liar and she wouldn't believe any story he gave, but how could he expect her to believe them? If he led these strangers into her home, how would she ever forgive him? She had been like a mother to him for years and he wasn't prepared to ruin their relationship over this. He doubted she would be happy to hear that his reasoning behind it was for his own financial gain.

Having Maria with him lifted much of the burden on his mind, but it would still be hard. When he looked at her, he knew she was thinking the exact same thing. Another worrying thought dawned on him. *What if Mark was home?* He would never let these crazy strangers inside. The idea of a confrontation terrified him. What if Mark tried to defend his doorway? He would be torn apart.

John had to tell himself again and again that in just under twenty minutes it would all be over. When he reached the front door, his hand began to tremble as he rang the doorbell. This was ridiculous; she was one of his oldest friends.

Gloria came to the door and her face lit up, "John, what a surprise . . . Oh, and hello Maria. To what do I owe this pleasure?"

"This is going to sound strange," John said, "Can we come in for a minute?"

"I don't see why not. I'm starting to get used to strange today."

Gloria noticed three figures standing on the pavement at the bottom of the front lawn. She immediately recognised the tall one to be her patient from the other day. She looked into John's eyes. "What's going on?"

"They think there's something in your garage . . . . A kind of anomaly . . ."

"Well they'd be right," she said, eyeing the strangely dressed figures, "How in God's name do they know about it?"

"They think it's a portal to another world," Maria cut in when she saw John was lost for words, "Their world."

"And you want me to let them in? Why are they here with you?" Gloria's temper was rising; fuelled by confusion.

"I don't think they'll leave us alone if we don't let them do whatever it is they've come to do."

Gloria shook her head, "I won't let strangers in my house, especially ones mad enough to think they're from a different planet. You two better come in and tell me everything, from the start."

Maria and John went inside and Gloria bolted the door shut behind them. She put on a pot of tea and led them into the living room. John started by explaining how Orak had asked for his help to reunite him with his friends and although it was stupid, he allowed him to stay over. Gloria remained silent while he explained, biting her lip not to comment on how reckless and greedy he had been.

When he came to tell her about losing his job, she couldn't hold her tongue any longer. "I'm so sorry, I told your father that you were struggling, I didn't think he would fire you, I'm so sorry."

John tried to assure her it was fine and that it was probably for the best. This side tracked them, and Maria had to cut in to remind John that they had a time limit.

Outside, Mac was starting to get agitated. He had spent hours finding this place and time, and they weren't allowed in because these humans were discussing private property access. He looked at the watch he had bought himself on the way down, and realised that they only had three minutes. There was no sign of anyone at the door to let them in, and if they didn't act soon, the opportunity would be missed.

He saw the garage doors just to the side of them, and realised how thin the sheet metal doors were. Orak had clearly had the same idea.

"We have to," Mac said, "If we miss this one, there's more chance of something coming through before the next opening."

"Oh for God's sake just do it," Shoa snapped, storming towards the doors. Orak followed, quickly overtaking with his vast strides.

Inside the house, they heard a loud rumble, followed by a squeak. Gloria ran through and burst into the garage "What the hell do you think you're doing?" she screamed at the top of her voice.

Even Orak looked scared. John and Maria ran through after her and noticing the broken work bench, they both assumed it was Orak's fault.

"Everybody step back!" Mac shouted, but nobody did. "I don't want anybody to get hurt."

"I want you all out now," Gloria yelled, brandishing a heavy stainless steel spanner.

"We'll leave just as soon as we've . . ." Mac glanced at his watch before shouting, "Shoa, ready."

Gloria was about to open her mouth when she felt the same warm gust of wind she had felt the day before. This time she saw where the wind was coming from. Like a bolt of lightning, frozen solid and hovering in the air, they could all see the rift. It fizzed loudly, and then began to crackle. A second bolt of motionless lightning appeared, mixing in with the first to form a geometric shape. The shape began to darken and the wind blew stronger, sending every loose piece of paper or plastic sheet spiralling into a horizontal tornado.

Shoa could barely see through her long hair as it was blown into her face, but she managed to brush it aside just as Mac yelled, "Now!"

Huge cracking arcs of electricity shot from her fingertips, striking at the heart of the forming portal. The eye shrank into a single glowing point. More bolts of lightning lanced out from the white orb of light, scorching the walls and ceiling. The orb grew larger, so quick that nobody noticed until they were inside it.

It felt warm, but they could no longer feel their limbs or their surroundings. Instantly the blinding whiteness turned to complete blackness, and the crackling became silence.

Chapter 9

John was back amongst the jagged rocks, the wind howling all around him. The air felt colder than ever. He moved himself behind one of the huge protruding masses, but the wind merely changed direction to face him again.

It wasn't long before the screaming started and a vast cloud of winged beasts blocked out the sun. John started to run, quickly breaking into a sprint. The creatures caught up with him, but he forced himself not to look back.

Catching his foot on a rock, he began to fall, only to stop in mid-air. He felt himself being lifted by hundreds of tiny sets of wings, as they began to bite hard, they tore his skin apart. As John struggled, the creatures let go one by one, and after enough had fled, he plummeted to the ground.

The landing was strangely soft, and the ground felt like sand in his hands. Suddenly the sun burst into life; burning his eyes. Warmth spread over his whole body and it took him a moment to realise he was awake.

Once his eyes had settled, John surveyed his surroundings. The sky was the bluest he had ever seen it, and even though it appeared to be mid-day, he could faintly see the moon. John did a double take; this wasn't the moon he'd known all his life. It appeared to be about three times the size, and distinctively red.

The biggest shock came when he saw a second, slightly smaller moon in the opposite corner of the sky. He had fallen asleep and woken up on a completely different world. He was on Ithria. Everything Orak had told him was true.

Sand was all around him, as far as his eyes could see in every direction. He grabbed a handful and let it flow through his fingers just to make sure he wasn't dreaming again. It felt coarse but fine, and drained the moisture from his hands.

John ran up a hill to get a better view. He fell several times, unable to grip the flowing ground with his trainers, but eventually he reached the top. The sandy dunes continued for miles, with nothing to give him a frame of reference, except for a tiny black dot about half a mile ahead. John decided to find out what the lone object was and began trudging towards it. Thirst quickly set in, and all he could hope for was that it was a fridge full of chilled soft drinks.

*

Eighteen miles west, Maria found herself lying on damp, muddy ground, with thorny creeping plants wrapped around her legs. Carefully pulling them off, she dragged herself to her feet.

Almost walking into a thin vertical trunk, she just about stopped herself with her hands. Gripping the tree with her fingers, she tried to find a better balance. Stepping off a protruding root, she walked into a flat area.

Maria brushed off most of the crispy bits of dry leaf that had clung to her clothes. She quickly came back to her senses, and realised she was in the heart of a dense forest.

How did I get here? She mused. A moment later, it all came flooding back; John, Orak, the gold, the garage and the blinding white light. The rift was real, and she'd gone through it.

"John," she called, "Is anyone out there?"

No reply came. A feeling of dread crept over her when she remembered that Orak and Mac had arrived on Earth in a different country from Shoa. They could be anywhere.

She knew she had to find them before she found anyone else. Even if she was lucky enough not to come across any of the dragon people that Orak had described, she was on an alien world, with no way to communicate with its people. She seriously doubted that very many of them could speak English.

Even when she had been on Earth, she had found it hard to cope without her phone. Here though, there were no mobile phones, no phone boxes and no fibre optic cables connecting everyone together. She was completely alone; more alone than she had ever been in her life.

Maria felt as though she should have been angry at John and the three strangers who had forced themselves into her life, but more than anything else, she just wanted to see them again; any of them.

For hours she walked through the forest with no sign of an end. Everywhere she turned, everything appeared to look exactly the same. She was well and truly lost.

The little light that broke through the gaps in the vast canopy above her started to diminish, and soon she had to guide her way by touch. The air grew cooler, but never reached a state she would call cold. As night fell, the forest filled with a multitude of noises; birds squawking, creatures screeching and insects clicking.

When her legs became too tired to carry her, she found a clearing and lay down. She knew one of the worst things to do now would be to go to sleep, but she felt her eyelids trying to close. Within two minutes of stopping to rest, she was out cold.

*

The object that John had seen, which had appeared to be only about half a mile away, was actually about three times that distance from him. As he finally got close to it, he was sure it was a mirage. Sticking out of the sand, six feet in the air was the tail end of Gloria's saloon.

Touching the shiny metal surface to check it was real, he recoiled in pain. The metal was scorching hot, but definitely real. Grabbing at the plastic handle, he found the door was open. Gloria had forgotten to lock it.

John wouldn't have thought it possible, but inside the car it was even hotter than outside. Clambering inside the vertical car, he stood upon the open door to search its contents. He opened the glove box and felt like his prayers had been answered.

Despite the fact that Gloria rarely drove late at night or on long journeys, she had three cans of energy drink stored in the compartment, as well as a bag of salt and vinegar crisps. The cans were not exactly cold, but were much cooler having been sealed in the glove box. Drinking one, he still felt incredibly thirsty, but with no idea how long he would be here, he left the others until later.

After a short rest in the shade of the car, he started digging away the sand from behind the front wheels using his hands. He knew that even if he could get the vehicle out, it was unlikely to start, and even if it did, it would not move very well over loose sand.

Nevertheless, he spent several hours digging, and ended up drinking the other two energy drinks. Fuelled by a huge dose of caffeine, he dug until his hands and arms ached so much he could barely lift them.

John lunged at the car from the other side, kicking at the bonnet. Even after shifting so much sand, it still wouldn't move. Hurling himself at it over and over again, it eventually gave way, thudding down onto its tyres.

Climbing back inside, he found the keys already in the ignition. "Thank you Gloria," he said out loud, "I've never been so glad of your terrible sense of security."

Turning the key halfway so as to switch on the electrics, he set the air-conditioning going. Still wide awake from the energy drinks, he began work on banking sand up against the side of the car facing the sun to block out the windows. Soon he had created a shelter, cool and dark enough for him to sleep in. The next day he would set out to find the others. He was sure at least one other person must have come through; they must have.

Chapter 10

Gloria's first sensation in this new world was the feeling of water splashing at her feet. She sat up; aching all over, but what she saw took her breath away.

Calmly swaying in the refreshing cool breeze, a pair of huge palm trees bordered a magnificent tropical landscape. Taking her feet out of the rock pool, Gloria stared out at the sapphire blue ocean and the towering rocky islands dotted all around it. This view would have put a smile on almost anyone's face, but the expression upon Gloria's was just pure confusion.

Grabbing a stick from the pool of water, she used it to haul herself onto her feet. The stick felt strangely cold and heavy. When she looked at it, it quickly became apparent that it wasn't a stick; it was her husband's crowbar.

Thinking back to when she was in her garage, she remembered the light swallowing everything around her. Could that be what brought her here? Had it moved everything to this place?

Gloria needed to find out where she was. It looked like somewhere in the Caribbean, but how could she have gotten here so quickly, had someone brought her here in her sleep?

Further along the beach, she saw a green cloak draped across the sand. Gloria hobbled over to explore, resting half her weight on the metal bar, having injured her knee. When she got closer, she realised it was a person.

Rushing over, she turned the body onto its back. She was looking down upon the face of the girl who had broken into her garage. Gloria shook the girl to try and wake her up, but she just rolled over and grumbled, confirming at least that she was still alive.

Leaving the girl to rest, Gloria searched the beach for the others. There were no signs of any other people on the thin strip of sand, which stretched for miles in either direction. Behind the beach were rows of trees, which seemed to stretch out just as far as the sand.

Gloria ventured into the trees to see how deep the woodland was, but seeing no end, she returned to the beach. Tapping Shoa with the cold metal bar, she shouted "Wake up!"

Shoadrina just moaned again, and a jolt of electricity shot through the crowbar. Gloria's hand twitched violently and the heavy piece of metal dropped down onto Shoa's stomach. Now definitely awake, Shoa gasped for breath. Tossing the bar aside, she sat up, wheezing for a moment.

"I'm so sorry," Gloria said, "It was an accident, you shocked me and . . ."

Shoa's response was to cast a gust of wind at the old woman; blowing her off her feet. "Masgra Krith Kiahaar!" she yelled in her native tongue, "You could have killed me you old crone."

"Well it's as much as you deserve," Gloria screamed back, shoving the mouthy girl. "You and your friends broke into my house and abducted me. What right do you have . . . ?"

"Abducted? How stupid are you? We were trying to save you and your people, you ungrateful KrithSprore!"

"What did you just call me?" Gloria came back at her, genuine with her question.

Shoa snarled, "We were trying to close the link so your people would be safe from this place. And now because of you interfering with things you clearly don't understand, we're back here. I hate you."

Gloria stood there, stunned. What was this girl talking about? What did she mean by your people? Shoa stormed off, and only turned around to point her finger up at the sky. Gloria's eyes followed, and she nearly fell over when she saw what was up there. She saw two moons within the same sky; one a lot like Earth's, the other several times bigger, but just as real.

Shoa quoted to this woman a line from the Earth literature she'd studied, "You're not in Kansas anymore."

*

Orak woke up the moment he hit the ground. Plummeting thirty feet through the air, he crashed through a thatched, timber gable roof and landed on a heavy oak dining table, breaking it in two.

When he moved, he felt a sharp pain in his forearm. Orak lifted his arm and felt queasy as he saw the bone had snapped in two. It was bent in half and dangling.

He heard a scream and looked to the end of the table. A small boy, about three or four years old was staring at him with eyes as wide as saucers. Beside him was a younger boy, wailing at the top of his lungs with tears flooding down his face. The two parents were sat on the opposite side, staring dumbstruck.

The man, who was a good two and a half feet shorter that Orak began yelling at him. "Droo Waka Degda," he screamed in a language he didn't recognize, "Kith greos maag Braham."

Orak scrambled to his feet, tears forming in his eyes from the pain as he ran out of the front door. If he had any gold, left he would have given it to them for the repairs, and if he spoke their dialect, he would have apologised. He didn't, so instead he just left without saying a word.

Down the dirt track road, he saw a house he recognised and realised where he was. Orak had arrived close to home. The house he had landed in was owned by a family of immigrants.

"Orak," a voice called from the doorway of the house he knew, "Was that you who fell from the sky a moment ago?" they said in the native Tontoltec dialect.

"I'm afraid so," he replied in the same tongue, nursing his broken arm.

"What are you doing here? I thought you weren't returning?" the elderly man asked, "Come inside, let me get you a splint set up for that. We don't want you healing with a bend in your arm."

The grey haired man held the door for Orak, who had to crouch to get through.

"Thank you Greaygo, it's good to see you again."

Greaygo led him into the main room and placed a blackened iron kettle on the grate above the fire in the corner. Orak had never been inside this house, although he knew it from its exterior. It seemed smaller than he had expected, only having two rooms downstairs and one on the floor above. The floor was entirely stone tiled, with several areas of loose carpet dotted about, and the walls were roughly lime plastered. Each of the rooms only had a single small glazed window, presumably due to the price of glass being so high.

Orak sat down on a heavy timber chair that creaked under his weight. He gritted his teeth while Greaygo slowly tried to bend his arm straight, more tears forming in his eyes. Tensing his arm suddenly as a reaction to the pain, the bone snapped back into place and Orak screamed. He wept as he held two straight sticks either side of the break while his old friend bound them tightly.

"It should take just a few days until it's as good as new. You were lucky."

Orak smiled, but only for a moment, "Thank you, but I shouldn't even be here. Something went wrong." He tried to hide the sorrow in his voice.

Greaygo didn't even have the chance to leave before things became too hard to cope with, not that it made a difference. Now they were both stuck here.

"Tell me, what has happened in the time since I left? Has the war reached our shores?"

Greaygo shook his head, "Not that I've heard, but I received a letter from my cousin in Frin this morning. He sent it the day after you left. He said Alkak-Taanan soldiers had come into his village and publically executed the wealthiest landowner as a message. My cousin and his family fled."

Frin was an island off the coast of the nation of Tontoltec, with only a few small trading towns and a dozen farming communities. The country was considered so small and insignificant that nobody had ever fought over it, but both Orak and Greaygo knew what the enemy wanted it for. The shores of Tontoltec could be seen from the beaches of Frin, making it the perfect staging area for an all-out assault.

"I hope your cousin made it out alright," Orak said, "I hope he made it to our shores and you will soon be re-united."

"I hope so too," said Greaygo. "He was always resilient. The house you landed on, the people who live there are from Drof. They sailed thousands of miles across the ocean to get here because of the war." Changing the subject he said, "Will you stay for lunch? My daughters will be returning shortly, and they are marvellous cooks."

"I'd love to, but I can't stay. When Shoa tried to break the link, it dragged us all back through. There were three people from Earth with us, I have to find them."

"I understand. I'll put word out so people can help with your search" said Greaygo.

"Thank you," said Orak, embracing the elderly man in a one armed hug, before setting off on his journey.

Chapter 11

WaMaktaJrei had twisted both his ankles on impact, slicing through the lake like a diving sea bird. Gasping in pain during his waking moment, water poured into his lungs. Sinking deeper, he fought to keep his airways closed, but there seemed to be no air left inside him. As he sank, the world around him grew darker, and the last thing he saw was a faint mesh forming before him. As it embraced him, he began convulsing and a stream of bubbles ascended from his mouth. A moment later he lay still, drifting into the abyss.

*

Maria had no idea how long she had been asleep, but it felt like it had been days. Crawling out of the indent she had formed, she felt her foot sink into the soft mud and realised she had lost a shoe.

Searching the immediate area, she saw nothing but wet leaves and puddles. Despite being soaked from head to toe, she still didn't feel cold.

Trudging through the mud, Maria tried to figure out which direction she had been going in. The forest seemed less dense than it had done yesterday, which must have meant she had been going the right way. However, today the trees looked almost identical in every direction. Ahead she saw a tree she could refer to as a landmark.

Unlike the others it was coniferous, about half the height of the others and stood out like a decorated Christmas tree. Maria approached cautiously, even though she doubted a tree could do her any harm. Around the tree, the soil looked cleaner than the rest of the forest, with only a few dozen pine needles on the ground beneath it. The earth looked as though it had been freshly dug and it became obvious that the tree had been planted there. Carved into the wood were several strange looking symbols running vertically down the trunk.

They were neatly cut, making Maria think that they were something more than just childish graffiti. Picking up a fir cone, she hurled it into the crown of a taller tree. The leaves rustled a little, but nothing fell down.

Maria was starving, but had no idea what was or wasn't edible, and was certain that she couldn't digest tree bark. Suddenly, she heard a steady whistling and a mound of leaves in the distance exploded into the air. A louder whistle caused her to spin around, just as an arrow thudded into the tree just a few feet away.

Maria desperately searched for the source, holding up her hands in submission. "Whatever I did I'm sorry," she said quickly.

Although she saw nobody, it suddenly dawned on her what the out of place engraved tree meant. It was a gravestone.

"D'o Gream MrKaal!" said a slow angry voice, seemingly from nowhere.

"I come in peace!" she blurted out, even though she knew he wouldn't understand.

"D'o Gream MrKaal!" the man repeated, as he stepped out from behind the trunk of a bare tree.

The man stood defensively, aiming his drawn longbow at the intruder. Maria realised why she hadn't seen him earlier; the man's clothes appeared to be entirely covered in a thick layer of mud and dead leaves. He stepped closer as Maria stepped back. She backed into a tree and could go no further.

"I don't know what you want!" she shouted. The razor sharp arrow head was so close to her skin, that she could nearly feel it. Her heart beat grew faster, and the stranger looked down at her chest which was breathing heavily.

Easing the strain on the bow, he took hold of the arrow in the same hand, and then reached for a knife in his belt. Maria took her chance to forcefully swing her shoed foot into his groin. The bowman doubled over in pain, screaming indecipherable curses at her as he slashed his blade wildly in her direction.

Maria started running. She had a good hundred metre head start before her attacker was back on his feet. She was not a natural sprinter, and it quickly became clear that this man was.

Changing direction spontaneously, she saw the bowman sliding to the ground before his body wrapped around a narrow trunk, snapping it in two. Maria continued to run, even though her attacker had given up. She bounded over roots and rocks, strafing and ducking under branches until she was sure that he could no longer see her.

Collapsing with exhaustion, she tried to figure out which way she had run. There was enough of a gap in the trees above her to see the sun; it was blinding. Maria found that she was almost completely dry, but her clothes were now abundant with dirt.

A little while later, she came across a fresh water spring. She shed her clothes and began to wash them the best that she could. She remembered how embarrassed she had been just a few days ago when John had caught her in a state of undress, but would have done anything for him to turn up now. It felt like she would be stuck in this forest forever.

*

John woke up to find the air-conditioning had cut out in the car several hours earlier. He was soaked in his own sweat, and the car stank so bad he had to clamber out. The sun had not yet risen, and the air was thankfully cooler outside.

He tried to siphon some of the water from the radiator using a straw from the glove box, until he remembered that antifreeze was poisonous. He remembered that Gloria's radiator leaked though, and because of this she kept a stash of water bottles in the spare tyre compartment. It tasted foul because it had been sitting there for weeks, but John drank it all. Even If he could get the engine working, without the emergency water supply and in such a hot climate it would overheat within minutes and would more than likely bury itself.

There was little more use he could get from the vehicle now. John decided to try and make as much distance as possible before the sun rose. Where this distance would take him he had no idea, but surely anywhere was better than here.

John had been stumbling through the sand for over an hour before he came across something other than sand; a rock. As the sun climbed higher he found more rocks, until finally the sand had almost stopped.

The grey layered rocks grew larger the further he travelled, giving him better footing and providing shade. Finding himself at the foot of a wide cliff face, he saw no way to move forward other than to ascend it.

He clambered up the rocks, feeling a sudden and unexpected burst of energy. He guessed it was his body giving him once last chance before he found safety. Eventually, he reached the top of the ladder like rock face.

John felt an enormous surge of gratification when he saw level ground, but the smile was wiped from his face very quickly. Just a few hundred feet from where he stood, the ground dropped back down even deeper. He had climbed onto the edge of a huge canyon, and the way around it was further than he was prepared to travel.

Walking further on the flat, John carefully made his way to the other side. The canyon looked as though it stretched for hundreds of miles, and there was no sign of anything even resembling a bridge across it.

As he looked down, he saw something he wasn't expecting; movement. This was the first movement he had seen since arriving in this place, besides the sands shifting in the wind. What had moved, he couldn't tell from this far away, but it was nothing to do with the wind.

A moment later, he saw something else unexpected; a step. Unlike the vaguely horizontal rocks he had walked up to get there, this step was smooth, and most definitely man made, as it had a rough timber post and handrail beside it. John cautiously looked over the cliff and saw more steps spiralling around a rock column. This structure was enclosed by timber rails, and wound all the way down to the bottom of the canyon.

This was the first sign he had seen that he wasn't alone in the desert, and gave him a sense of reserved hope. He was yet to discover whether they would be hostile or hospitable.

Chapter 12

The column of the spiral staircase offered little shade. John grew more exhausted with every step, and the distance to the bottom seemed not to change. About halfway down, he felt as though he could barely move and stopped dead. He was drained of all energy and his head was pounding from the effects of dehydration.

One thought kept him going; Maria. She was out there somewhere looking for him and he prayed that she had found herself in better circumstances. Just thinking about her gave him the focus to continue, but just fifty feet from the base of the canyon, his sheer will alone was no match for physical debilitation. Collapsing, he fell down several steps before catching onto a railing post. He lay there as voices shouting in the distance faded into nothing.

*

John didn't know how long he had been unconscious, but by now he had no way of telling whether it had been a day, two days, or even a week since he had arrived in the desert. All sense of time had been burnt away and all sense of purpose had been sucked dry by the hot yellow sand.

The first thing he noticed when he regained consciousness was a drop of water flowing down his cheek. Brushing it with his hands, he rubbed the cool liquid into his fingers to confirm it really was water. He'd almost forgotten what it felt like.

Trying to sit up, John found himself bound where he lay. Around each wrist was a leather clad iron strap, chained to the wooden bedposts behind him. His arms were suspended by the chains in such a way that his hands were level with his head, and his elbows pointed to the ceiling. Despite his arms and legs being fixed in place, this bed felt quite comfortable. The mattress appeared to be filled with the same fine soft sand as the desert, and had moulded to the shape of his body.

John looked around the room. It seemed dark but with several thin shafts of light coming down from the ceiling. He saw two figures standing in the doorway, completely motionless, and holding long wooden poles taller than themselves.

"Hello," he called to these figures. They remained still and silent. John guessed they must have been guarding him but couldn't understand why they would think he posed a threat.

"Can I speak to whoever's in charge?" he asked, still receiving no answer.

John could see that the wide opening where the guards were standing was blocked off by iron bars, stretching from the ground to the rocky ceiling. Two of the bars appeared to be segmented, held in place by a padlock around a metal lock. At the base of them, was a hole in which they could drop down to form an opening.

When he looked back to the side, he realised that one of the guards had disappeared. This wouldn't have made his escape any easier, he was still completely immobile. With people like Orak on this world, the bonds were probably designed to withstand a lot more than ones on Earth were.

The guard returned a moment later with a shorter man at his side. The shorter man unlocked the padlock above his head, and the two iron bars slid down into the floor. He stepped through the door with the guard still at his side, who then pulled the bars back up and relocked them.

The man who appeared to be in charge stepped closer and said something John didn't understand a word of.

"Do you speak English?" John replied.

The man continued to speak in the foreign dialect, seemingly changing language after each sentence. After a few minutes of getting nowhere, he walked to the bars and said something to the guard outside. He waited a minute before a thin flat piece of slate was passed through with a small piece of roughly shaped chalk.

After handing John the writing implements, he waited. John tried his best to explain his situation pictorially. He drew a picture of Earth, and a few dots to represent stars, and a picture of what he imagined Ithria to look like. He drew six stick figures and arrows depicting them travelling to and from worlds.

Once his captor had looked over his drawings, he took it to the bars and gave some kind of order to the guard outside, who took it elsewhere. A few minutes later, a fourth figure came to the bars and looked across to the prisoner. He pointed to himself, then to John and said three words, "Send speak, tomorrow."

John lay back, repositioning his arms in the least uncomfortable position. As the guard and his master were leaving, the man in charge turned around. He said something else in his language then took out a small key. Unlocking the arm restraints, but leaving the leg ones, he placed a metal goblet of water on the floor beside the prisoner and left.

As he walked out through the doorway, he waved his hands upward, and the bars shot back up by themselves behind him. The padlock flew into place and snapped shut, as the two guards stood back in place. John was in shock. He had actually witnessed telekinesis. This confirmed yet more of Orak's crazy story, and he had a feeling there was a lot more to come.

*

Mac spluttered water from his aching lungs. His chest gurgled with each agonising breath. Coughing endlessly, he cleared his airways before collapsing exhausted onto his back. He could barely move, but at least he could breathe.

He would not feel well for quite some time, but he was on his feet about fifteen minutes after being dragged from the water. He had landed in the net of a fishing vessel, snapping it from its chain. A crew member who had witnessed this, dived in, towing a hooked chain and reconnected the net.

Mac had been in the water for just under two minutes, several more seconds and he probably would have died. His slight physiological differences made him survive longer than a normal person may have done. His brain housed a small ATP store for extra boosts of energy. This allowed his brain to be fuelled for longer in a more relaxed state.

The ship that had rescued him was called 'Poleas Jijaf' meaning 'White Swan'. It was a large timber vessel, thickly painted white and held a crew of twenty men.

The crew agreed to take him ashore for a fee. As Mac had traded in all of his money and most of his worldly possessions for the gold to make his new life on Earth, he only had one thing to trade. The curved hunting blade had been a coming of age present, and he hated having to part with it.

Once he handed over the weapon, he felt lost. All he had now were the clothes on his back. He had succeeded in severing the link, but at the cost of trapping himself and five innocent bystanders on a condemned world.

While he was alone in the galley, Mac stole several steak knives and the largest chopping knife that he could fit under his robes. The crew allowed him a small amount of food and water, and gave him a small broken rowing boat for the last half a mile to shore.

The boat, despite having half a dozen leaks, took him almost the whole way. With his ankles still in pain, he was unable to swim, and had to use all of his strength to hoist himself to shore. Even though it had been a day since he had nearly drowned, his lungs still burned, and his breath was heavy and rapid.

From here, he would head for the former principality of Erinthia, where he knew Orak and Shoa would also go. Once they returned to the university, they could focus their efforts on finding the three Earth people.

Chapter 13

The interpreter didn't turn up until noon the following day. John had been fed meals of chicken, potatoes and green beans, and given as much water as he needed. He had been unchained, and was allowed to use the cell's toilet freely. The air inside felt fresh and much cooler than outside. His only real problem was extreme boredom.

As John was not wearing his watch and his phone battery was completely flat, he only had the light patterns outside the cell to judge the time.

The shadows changed suddenly as two figures walked down the hallway outside. They stopped and began to speak to each other. The first voice sounded like the Telepath who had visited him the other day. The second sounded like that of a middle aged to elderly woman. John couldn't understand a word of their conversation as it was in an alien language, but he could tell they were debating fiercely.

A minute later, one of the figures moved. The guard outside unlocked the padlock and let the bars slide down. A short woman wearing a lightweight hooded cloak stepped inside. Both guards outside stood on full alert, aiming their spears into the cell. John noticed that they each had a long curved blade very similar to Mac's knife, and wondered why they thought he would be mad enough to escape; it was like Death Valley outside.

The cloaked woman lowered her hood, and her long silvery hair dropped down over her shoulders. Her deeply tanned skin looked leathery and wrinkled with age. She walked with a slight limp and was aided by a polished hickory walking stick and greeted him in a language he didn't understand. Seeing John's disappointment, she switched to a language he did recognise.

"I don't speak French," he replied.

"Ah, English," she said in her hoarse weathered voice. "So you say you're from Earth?" she asked.

"I came through the thing, err . . . rift," John replied, still wary of the two on-edge guards pointing weapons at him. Despite being terrified, he felt immensely relieved to find someone who could speak his language.

"Where?" she asked. "Sorry, I'm being rude. My name is Udrok." She offered her hand, and John shook it. He gave his name, and started to explain how he got here.

Udrok interrupted him, "You must understand that you aren't a guest here."

John eyed the armed guards again, "I figured that part out by myself. Can I ask why?"

"You could be a spy," she said bluntly.

John involuntarily laughed. He tried to comment on the ludicrousness of their accusation, but had to admit they had a point. If he was a spy, this might be a good cover story.

"I clearly wouldn't make a very good spy," he said, gesturing to the guards again.

"You're inside our facility," she pointed out. "If you managed to gain our trust, you'd know where this place is."

"Not if you led me out into the desert blindfolded," he replied, starting to think this woman wasn't a trained interrogator. "Where did you learn English?" he asked.

"That would be information our enemy would want," she replied.

"Was it at a university, and were you taught by Orak JaVrei?" he again pressed.

Udrok didn't reply. John took this as a yes. He took the opportunity to press her further; turning the tables. "Was there a science professor called WaMatta . . . WaMakka . . . Mac, a bald Telepath? He's apparently the foremost expert on the link rift thingy . . . There was a girl as well, a Spellcaster, a student I think. Her name was Shoa."

Udrok glared at him, "How do you know about them?" she asked.

"I met them," John replied. They tried to close the rift and I got dragged through."

Walking back to the door, Udrok called out to someone. A moment later, the Telepath returned. They had another intense discussion in their language, before Udrok turned to John.

"You may leave any time you wish," she told him. John felt less relieved than he thought he would. He had been free until he arrived here, and he nearly burnt to death in the desert.

"Can I stay?" he asked, struggling to believe he was actually saying this. "I'll pay my way and I'll work for my food and keep."

Udrok had another discussion with the Telepath. The guards left as she spoke, and once the Telepath had finished speaking, he too left.

"If you're looking for Orak JaVrei, he was my language tutor, I know where he lives," Udrok explained to John. "If he's back on Ithria, he'll have headed for a city in Erinthia called 'Poleas Luffpa,' which means 'White Falls'. You've arrived in Caracracia. The border of Erinthia is about a hundred miles north, Whitefalls is a further fifty miles from the border."

"I appreciate you telling me, but I don't think I can make it a hundred miles through the desert," replied John.

"The people here will trade a means of transport for anything of value you have," said Udrok.

John shook his head, "I don't think I have any . . .". He stopped and thought for a moment. He had no idea what these people knew of Earth, or what they would think of what he had brought from it. He knew this woman could speak his language, but she had been taught by Orak and may never have viewed his world. "Actually I think I have something" he added.

Taking out his wallet, he presented her with a brand new twenty pound note. Laying it down on his palm, her eyes widened at the sight of the shiny metallic strip running through it.

"I've never seen parchment like this," she said, amazed at the detail.

John guessed that they didn't even have printing presses, and took the opportunity to exaggerate. "This is worth a lot of money where I come from. Painstakingly crafted by our finest cotton weavers and illustrated using the rarest of inks."

Udrok looked into his eyes, "What purpose does it serve?"

"It's art," John lied. "I was given it as a gift from the Royal Bank of England. See the name, Andrew Bailey, that's the artist's name; it's his signature."

"And you'll be willing to trade it for safe passage to Erinthia?" asked Udrok.

"I have nothing else to trade. Please, look after it," said John.

Udrok took the note to the Telepath who was now waiting outside the cell. Once again they spoke in their language for a whole five minutes. John had crossed his fingers and was silently praying they would buy his story. This Telepath, who was clearly in charge must have had less knowledge of Earth than the translator, and looked just as impressed by the small piece of parchment.

Once they were done, Udrok returned to the cell. "We're accepting the artwork as payment," she told him, "We should be able to exchange it for many useful things when the next trading party comes in a few days. We've agreed to give you two camels and some supplies. We'll fit one with a large water bladder and a pack containing a few weeks' worth of food. We will also give you some new clothes; the ones you have on are disgusting."

John sniffed his shirt and agreed. Udrok gave him a map and drew the quickest route out of the desert, as well as labelling the nearest towns he could stop at for shelter. She also gave him coins and a few pages of phrases that he might need when he got there. John stayed one more night in the cell, and then set off the next morning before sunrise.

*

Shoa had stormed off in a fit of rage, cursing the world around her. Gloria had no choice but to follow, the girl clearly knew something she didn't.

After explaining several times that they weren't on Earth anymore, and that they needed to find Mac so they could get back, Shoa lost her temper again, hurling a ball of fire in Gloria's general direction. Missing by a few feet, the fireball struck a tree and singed the bark, before dissipating into smoke. Gloria was silenced. If there was a God, she wondered why he would give superpowers to such a hormonal teenager.

Despite the threat of being electrocuted, or set on fire, Gloria felt safer with Shoa than alone in this alien world.

"Do you think the others came through as well?" she asked a little while later.

"I think the whole room came through," Shoa replied, as she bent down to pick something up. She looked in fascination at the red plastic casing of the shotgun round. There were more dotted about the sand, and Gloria began picking them all up.

"Do you have big pockets in that dressing gown of yours?" she asked.

"It's a robe!" she retaliated, throwing the spent round at Gloria, "What are these things?" she asked.

"It's ammunition. It goes inside a gun, which would be great if we could find it."

The pair of them scoured the beach, picking up about a dozen shots, but finding no gun. After eventually giving up, they headed into the trees.

Shoa seemed to know exactly where she was going, even though the entire forest looked the same in every direction. Gloria hated the feeling that someone so much younger than her knew so much more about something. She had always been the one with the answers; this feeling was new to her. When she saw Shoa looking up through the gaps between the crowns of the trees, she realised how the girl was doing it.

"You're using the sun to tell you which way is south?" Gloria asked, "What's south of here?"

"If we are where I think we are . . . Erinthia," replied Shoa. "That's where Mac and Orak will be; in a city we've renamed Whitefalls. It's where the university is, and where we could view your world from. We translated it to English because it reflects the fact that we can see Britain through it . . . Why do you call it Great Britain? It looks like a dump to me."

"I guess it is compared to this tropical paradise. How far is it to Whitefalls?"

Shoa shook her head, "I've got no idea, maybe two days walking, without stops."

"Without stops!" Gloria exclaimed. "I don't know if you've noticed, but I'm not as young and energetic as I once was. Do you think you could walk two days without stopping?"

Shoa stopped. She crouched down to pick something else up. Stuck in a soft patch of mud, was a flat, black women's shoe.

"It's Maria's," Gloria said instantly. She had seen this same shoe falling off Maria's foot in her house in what she thought was just yesterday. Calling out Maria's name, they searched the forest.

A little while later, they came across a small coniferous tree amongst the tall deciduous ones, and an arrow protruding from a tree trunk.

"She's in danger!" Gloria blurted out. Searching frantically for more clues, she saw a second arrow lying on the ground. Creeping plants had wrapped themselves around the wooden shaft, and moss had started to form on the flight.

"This has been here for a few days," Shoa realised, "This was here before her."

"Or we were asleep longer than we thought. She could be anywhere by now."

"So what do you want to do?" Gloria asked. "Keep searching?"

"We won't find her, this forest is too dense," replied Shoa.

Gloria knew she was right, but they couldn't just give up. "Can you use your powers to find her?" she asked, stabbing in the dark.

Shoa just shook her head, "We keep going south and hope she's had the same idea. Once we get to the forest edge, there should be a town close by. I'll ask if they've seen her."

Reluctantly, Gloria followed Shoa south. Whether she liked it or not, Shoa was her only hope of getting home. She was completely and utterly at her mercy.

Chapter 14

Maria started to get the feeling that she had walked in a big circle. She was once again looking at a small coniferous tree, engraved with strange symbols, but there were no arrows in any of the trees. There were no footprints in the mud either, making her realise that this wasn't the same tree.

Looking around for anything to suggest which way she should go now; she saw nothing out of place or anything of interest. She was glad that she didn't have a mirror on her because she knew she looked in a terrible state. She hadn't showered properly or changed clothes in days, and in some ways she felt glad that she was all alone.

She began tying rough knots in loose twigs so she could tell where she had been, and after a few minutes of doing this, she came across a knotted twig. "Damn it!" she shouted, enraged at how quickly she had managed to turn back on herself. Inspecting the twig however, she quickly realised that it was a different type of knot; somebody else had had the same idea.

"Hello! Is anybody out there?" she called, unsure of whether she really wanted an answer.

There was no response. She stood perfectly still, listening intently for a reply. The only sounds she heard were the birds and the leaves in the wind.

Maria continued knotting twigs every few metres, creating a trail. She wondered whether this was a good idea or not. She had already experienced one unsavoury character in this forest, how would she know if the next person she encountered would be any different.

On her journey, she came across a strange item. Glinting in the sunshine, resting on the branch of a tree was a 100 watt light bulb. Banging into the tree, the bulb dropped into Maria's hand. She inspected it, and it took her a minute to realise where it had come from; Gloria's garage.

She doubted she would find a bayonet fitting connected to a mains supply anywhere in the trees but she kept the item nevertheless. Carrying the bulb with her would serve as a reminder of where she had come from.

A little while later, she came across more items they had accidentally brought through with them: a half empty can of petrol, a length of string and some old cleaning rags were lying on the ground. Using the rags to construct a basic bag held together with the string, she placed the bulb inside and looped the string around the handle of the petrol can. She saw no use for these now, but she was sure sooner or later they would come in handy.

When night fell, she found a suitable spot to lie down and held onto her new possessions tightly. As sad as it seemed, these were all she had in this world.

*

Maria awoke on the forest floor for the third time. Her sleep had been deep once again, and she only had a rough idea of how many days she had been here.

It had not rained this time, and the ground was almost completely dry. She had been woken by crippling hunger pains. Maria had eaten only a few dozen red berries since she had arrived in the forest, and she wasn't even sure that they weren't toxic.

Maria knew she wouldn't be able to survive long like this. She had no idea how to catch or prepare animals, not that she'd even seen any besides birds and insects. Whilst searching the ground for seeds or nuts, she looked up and saw something she was sure would help her to get some kind of bearing.

Through a gap in the leaves above her, she caught sight of stone. Stepping back, she saw the peak of a rocky hill ahead of her.

Maria took off her remaining shoe and ran through the forest towards it. The bottoms of her feet had hardened through all the walking she had done, but the loose twigs and stone still dug in painfully. Clambering up a slope, she felt the soil sliding from under her feet and hauled herself up using every branch within reach.

Eventually, she found herself upon level ground and saw the rocks just ahead. Unlike they had appeared from below, these rocks were not of a natural formation, but were carved into pillars. Upon these pillars stood a large plateau which overhung where she stood. Maria circled the them, and found a staircase spiralling inside. This structure was the last thing she had been expecting, but it was a godsend.

Running up the stairs, she came out onto a flat stone floor. The tableland held nothing but a small mound of ash in the middle, circled by small stones. Walking to the edge, Maria looked down upon the forest. She was far above the canopy, and could see for miles around.

Her heart sank. Even from this vantage point, she could see no end to the forest. She strained her eyes staring at every horizon, but saw nothing but trees. Maria collapsed onto the stone floor. Hope had been all that had kept her going, but now that was gone. Tears formed in the corners of her eyes and the floodgates opened. Screaming at the top of her lungs, she broke down and wept.

Beating the ground with her fist, she did not hear the hurried tapping of footsteps below her. She had no warning before a figure appeared before her eyes at the top of the steps. Maria screamed and backed away.

He had found her. The same man who had tried to kill her yesterday stood before her, aiming his bow at her forehead. His eyes were filled with rage, and his hand trembled as he pulled back the string.

Maria didn't have the strength or the means to escape, she could barely move. Squeezing her eyes shut, she whispered "Just do it, please."

She heard the twang of the bow and the thud of the arrow, but felt no pain. Her eyes opened slowly. The bowman lay dead on the floor, an arrow protruding from his temple. Blood poured into his open eyes, and his tongue dropped from his gaping mouth onto the stone floor.

Then Maria heard footfalls approaching; someone was coming.

Chapter 15

Orak travelled on foot from the village, and crossed the border to Erinthia earlier than he was expecting. The journey through the Anuma link had exhausted him just as it had with everyone else, and he desperately needed sleep. He stopped at the next village to have a short nap, but ended up waking up twelve hours later.

The day was already wasted, so he travelled just three more miles to the next village and stayed at a bed and breakfast. He used all of the coins; Greaygo had given him for his journey on a bed for the night and two meals. The following morning he headed to Whitefalls.

In less than a day, his bone had healed enough for him to remove the splint. The arm still hurt; it would for at least another day, but it was now fully working. While it still felt sore, he kept it in a fabric sling.

On his journey, Orak spread the word about his missing friends, giving descriptions and instructions. Anyone who saw any of the other five would tell them where to find him.

It became obvious that the war had not yet reached Tontoltec, which gave him confidence that the others were relatively safe. He knew the enemy would not invade this great nation until its numbers were vast, but he was sure that at that very moment, the smaller islands all across the ocean were being attacked. When the enemy felt confident enough to strike, they would do so hard and fast.

Orak knew he was getting closer to home when he saw the dry dusty ground turning to luscious green grass. Taking a short cut, he walked through a vast plane of bright yellow wild flowers, unbroken by fence or hedge. Birdsong reached his ears, and for the first time in days, he was glad to be back.

He stopped for a break and sat down on the sawn off stump of a tree in the middle of a field. Shortly, he knew he would be seeing his friends and family again, and as happy as he should have been, it felt strange. He had said his final goodbyes; he'd opened up to people and gotten closure on this chapter of his life. Now he was back, after all that, his word surely meant nothing.

One of the worst things that he would have to face would be Shoadrina's parents. They had been heartbroken when she left, and would be overwhelmed if they ever saw her again. The trouble was, she wasn't here with him, and he had no way of knowing whether she was one mile or a thousand miles away, or even if she still alive.

Taking several deep breaths, he stood back up and continued walking. He found himself yawning, and somehow still craving sleep. The journey through the rift seemed even more tiring this time. He was sure that if it worked like this every time, a few more trips back and forth too close together would put him in a coma.

As Orak reached the ridge of a hill, he saw a huge black horse galloping at full speed straight towards him. Hurling himself out of the way, he saw the rider tugging violently at the reins to steer the stallion away, nearly garrotting the animal. They missed by inches.

Leaping from the saddle, a tall woman ran towards him. "I'm so sorry," she shouted in Tontoltec. "I didn't see . . . Orak?"

Orak looked up at the face of the woman. Dazed from the fall, and still tired, it took him a moment to recognise her. Standing at just over six foot, and with flowing blonde hair down to her waist, she was unmistakable in these parts. "Kyra?" he asked.

"Yes, it's me. What are you doing here?" she asked, single handily dragging him back onto his feet.

"It's a long story," he replied groggily. "But to cut a long story short, something went wrong. We're all back here and we brought three people from Earth with us. I have to find them."

"Did it work though?" she pressed him. "Did the link sever?"

"I think so, I won't know for sure until I find Mac."

Kyra stroked her animal under its chin, "I would offer to give you a ride, but I don't think she'd be able to support both of us."

The jet black horse looked about the size of a large shire, but ran like a racing stallion. It was bred specifically for Titans to ride, but even a beast this size could not carry the combined weight of the two.

"You take her," Kyra decided. "You look shattered. I'll walk beside you . . . It's good to see you again, even if the circumstances aren't the best."

She embraced her old friend in a hug, and then helped him up onto her horse. The animal seemed glad of a rest from running, while she slowly trotted alongside her master.

"Has there been any news of the war?" Orak asked.

"We received a message by pigeon," she explained, "More ships are arriving in Frin every day. There was no fighting, they just took over. They're building fortresses and they're setting up camps and training facilities. The Alkak-Taanan soldiers seem to be planning to strike Erinthia within a matter of weeks."

"Does our government have a plan?"

"They're sending every able soldier we have to the coast. They think that if our enemy gets a foothold on our soil, we'll have lost our advantage."

"And what do you think?" Orak asked, sensing she disagreed with the authorities.

"I don't think we have an advantage even while they need to cross the sea. They've brought Drathmorks to Frin; there are hundreds of them. They're long distance flyers, and they can strike like a swarm from above, gliding straight over our walls. Their skin is tough and rubbery like the skin under dragon's scales, so our Spellcasters can't harm them with fire or electricity . . . . They won't stop fighting until they are ordered to or until they lose their heads."

"You know every knight in Whitefalls will follow you whatever you ask them to do, you are their general. If you want them to stand ground and defend the city walls, they will."

"As good as my human soldiers are they're no match for the Drathmorks. I need Titans like us, but we're so few. A quarter of the city evacuated when the message arrived. They're heading south to Caracracia to hide out in the desert, or building ships on the east coast to sail to Groaska."

"I wish them luck," Orak said solemnly. On the east coast, living in camps and makeshift towns, their people would be sitting ducks if their enemy decided to take a less orthodox route. As for the desert, the

Drathmorks could walk on fire; the scorching hot sand wouldn't stop them.

"It's left us with only half an army, but as long as our people stay at Whitefalls, I'll defend it with my life."

Orak felt a pang of guilt. His mission to Earth had been important, but hearing her speak like this made it sound like he had been deserting everyone from home, and taking the coward's way out.

Kyra was the most skilled fighter he had ever seen. Although she was not nearly as strong as he was, she could halve his time on a mile sprint, and take on a small army by herself with one hand tied behind her back.

"You could just snarl at the enemy. I've seen you scare off dragons with your face first thing in the morning," he joked.

She went to punch him in the arm, but noticed the sling and stopped herself. "Rough time on Earth?" she asked.

"No, this was here."

Orak thought about the state he had seen Mac in on Earth, and the beast he had photographed. He decided not to share this information with Kyra; she had enough to think about.

"Is anywhere safe?" he asked a moment later. "When I find the Earth people, I need to protect them. It's my fault they are here."

Kyra thought for a moment, "I'm planning on sending my family south, not to Caracracia, to the gulf. They can sail, and although it's a hell of a long way, the safest place in all of Ithria will probably be the Arctic Islands."

"The Earth people are used to the cold I suppose. If I could stay and help, I . . ."

"You've never been a fighter Orak," she said understandably. "You're a teacher. You'll be more useful helping the evacuees . . . I have a platoon of soldiers who aren't ready for battle. I want you to take them with you. They will help keep the children and the elderly safe."

Orak found himself struggling to stay awake, even while his ride walked across rough uneven ground. As they reached the city of Whitefalls, he once again drifted off.

Chapter 16

Mac had also been spreading word about the missing Earth residents. Without knowing where anyone else had come through, he had no way of even beginning to work out where the others could be. He knew they would all be somewhere in Tontoltec, but it was a huge country, roughly the size of Mexico.

Wherever Orak had arrived, he would be able to cope, as he spoke both main languages of the country, but Shoa, although from the south originally, only spoke fluently in the northern dialect. John, Maria and Gloria would struggle wherever they landed. He prayed that everyone had arrived somewhere better than he had.

Barely able to walk, and unable to levitate for long periods, Mac made slow progress. He had nothing to barter with to gain a horse in the small fishing town he arrived at, nor did he have time to work for any money. He managed to craft a small cart out of scrap wood, which he had to push along by its back wheels like a wheelchair. The construction was very heavy for its size, and although strongly built, it was not a comfortable ride.

It was impossible to climb hills, or anything sloping upwards, so he stuck to flat roads. This increased his journey time significantly. It took him over a day to finally reach Whitefalls, and he was exhausted. His lungs still gurgled quietly whenever he breathed deeply.

The loose grey gravel road turned into smooth white paving stones, as it bridged in an arch across a stream. Beyond the bridge, he saw hundreds of people walking through the streets. Canvas stalls had been set up alongside the paths, the shouts of tradesmen and the conversations

70

between customers filled the air. Beyond the stalls were towering stone shops, with flags and banners outside, displaying their wares.

Dappled sunlight shone through the neat rows of Cyprus trees that lined a boulevard to his right. At the end of the vast thoroughfare, he saw the iconic waterfalls that gave Whitefalls its name. Torrents of rapid white bubbling water roared, as it coursed through the middle of the district. Fountains naturally pressurised by the river watered the trees, as marble statues seemed to welcome everyone into the market square.

Mac rolled through the stalls, passing many people who took no notice. He tried several times to haul himself up a step, before someone finally took pity on him and helped lift the chair up onto the higher level. He explained where he was going, and they offered to take him there.

Once he was outside the market area, he crossed another bridge onto a large island which curved the mighty river around it. The path steadily climbed, but without any more steps on the rest of the way, he thanked the stranger and said he could cope. At the peak of the hill, he saw the high battlement walls of the university.

Five decades ago, this had been a royal castle, where the eldest Prince of Tontoltec had lived. During the revolution, many royal families were exiled or even executed, and their homes went to better use. The castle had never been under siege, but was built to be impenetrable. It was therefore chosen as the site for Whitefalls University because of its isolation from the rest of the city.

When he reached the heavy oak doors, he hammered on them and waited for a reply. Turning around, he looked down on the city. From here, he could see the edge of the cliff, where the main waterfall dropped down onto lower Whitefalls. The city was divided in two by the geography of the land, and connected only by a series of carved staircases and underground tunnels.

The surrounding lakes glimmered in the sunshine; the water gently lapping in the breeze. For a moment, Mac wondered why he ever left this place.

The doors slowly creaked open, and Mac had to roll backwards away from them. The university's administrator stood there looking down on him with puzzlement.

"WaMaktaJrei?" he asked, speaking in English out of habit, "I thought you would have left by now? It's been well over a week. What happened to you?"

"We came back Shrax," he replied, short of breath, "I don't know how, but it brought us back. I don't know where the others are, have they not come here?"

Administrator Shrax led him inside and through the courtyard and into one of the large buttressed buildings within the walls. Mac noticed that the man he knew and had worked with daily looked as though he had aged within a matter of days. He had always remembered him with jet black hair, but now his short well groomed hair had several distinctive grey streaks. It was odd to see that he had thick stubble growing on his chin. Shrax would always turn up clean shaven, and often have a razor blade with him to shave on his break.

Mac did not say anything as he hauled himself out of the chair and began to levitate up the stairs. The administrator helped him along the corridor, and noticed how laboured Mac's breathing was. He lowered him into a chair in his office, and then sat at the desk opposite.

"You can rest here," Shrax told him, "many of the dormitories are empty, so you can take your pick."

"Thank you," he replied. Mac was still exhausted, and needed time for his ankles to heal.

"Much has happened since you left WaMaktaJrei. Since we received word from Frin, more and more people have been leaving every day, more than half my staff, but only a few dozen students. I've been juggling with organising new rotas and teaching several more classes than I should, as well as having talks with the local Parliamentarians."

"Is the government stirring up trouble again?"

"They want the military to take over the university. They say it's the best place in Whitefalls to defend its people, and that the city should hide behind its walls ready for the enemy's attack. It may be the only fortress we have, but there are over fourteen thousand people in upper Whitefalls alone, we barely have space for three hundred students. It'll be standing room only inside the building and there'll be people sleeping out in the courtyards."

"Has anyone even been in to assess the place? Surely they'd see that it's impossible."

"General Kyra. She says it can be done. Maybe her and her soldiers can sleep on camp beds stacked together like logs, but what about the elderly and the disabled? And it'll disrupt the student's education to no end."

Mac felt like telling him that compromises needed to be made in such times, but Administrator Shrax wasn't the sort of man you wanted to get into an argument with, there would be no end to it.

"Maybe by then, enough people will have migrated for it to be feasible."

"I doubt it. And with all their weapons and horses cluttering up the place, there'll be even less space. We could potentially accommodate her six hundred odd soldiers, but not the rest of the city."

Moving himself across to the window, Mac noticed how good a vantage point they had from here. The high walls obscured much of the view, but what he could see over them was astonishing. He could see right to the edge of the city, and to the farming colonies beyond. On the horizon, he saw the grey mountains which carved Erinthia in two. He had never been beyond these mountains on land, the roads were too hazardous. Even though the journey around was many times longer, and required sailing across several lakes, he would take that route every time.

The grey mountains were where he, Orak and Shoa had gone to journey through the link to Earth, but they were deemed dragon territory. Only the foolish or ignorant ever went there without reason.

"Do you know of anyone who would be willing to help out in finding Orak and Shoa? . . . There's something I failed to mention earlier," Mac remembered. "Three people from Earth came through with us. I feel it's my responsibility to find them, but I can't do it alone, and I need time to recover."

Shrax too looked out of the window to the mountains; he was now thinking the same thing as Mac. "There are plenty of men mad enough to brave it out there, but I'm not the person to ask." He gestured to the path below the window, where General Kyra was walking; beside her was the downtrodden hulking figure of Orak JaVrei. "Your quest just became a little easier."

*

Orak and Kyra were let into the building by its caretaker, who led them up the stairs to Administrator Shrax's office. They were asked to wait outside while the caretaker found out if they were allowed to enter. They sat on small wooden chairs outside, which seemed too small even for normal sized people.

The caretaker returned ten minutes later and said that they were both allowed inside. Shrax welcomed Orak with open arms, but didn't say a word to Kyra. With all of his worldly knowledge and charm, he acted surprisingly like a child when things weren't going his way.

Orak embraced Mac in a vice like grip. "Thank God I've found at least one of you . . . the others?" he asked with a hint of optimism in his voice.

Mac shook his head, "I've only just got here myself. We were discussing sending out volunteers to look for them."

"I've ordered a regiment to start looking. Every soldier has with them a letter written in English to give to the Earth people if they find them." Kyra said adamantly.

"Thank you," Mac said; glad of some positive news, I've been spreading the word about them in the villages that I've passed through."

Orak nodded, "So have I."

"Can the General and I speak in private?" Shrax asked; more out of courtesy than actually requesting permission.

The other two left the room. Mac had a feeling he knew what was going to happen. Although the administrator sounded firm in his belief that the university should remain as it was; with limited access, Mac knew that Shrax had no way to evict Kyra. He would be reluctantly giving his permission for the military occupation.

Orak stood while Mac sat on one of the undersized chairs outside. "What happened? With the rift?" he asked, having been waiting to know for days.

"I don't know, I only knew about the theory behind it," Mac explained. "It was a very long time ago when anyone last had to do it, and the records aren't especially concise. What I do know is that it worked. We broke the link."

Orak's head dropped, "So John, Maria and Gloria . . . They're trapped here?"

Mac nodded, "It will probably be many years before it reforms, hundreds if it's anything like last time. Once we find them, I'm going to devote as much of my time as I can into trying to find out if they can be sent back, but I'm not hopeful."

Orak began pacing around the corridor, trying to keep his anger bottled in. No matter how he looked at it, it was his fault John and Maria were here. Losing it, he smashed his hand into a thin timberwork wall, and screamed with rage. He knew right then that he'd ruined their lives.

Chapter 17

Maria crept towards the edge of the rock plateau and looked down. The drop was over a hundred feet, but she saw no other way of escape. She tried to make herself jump and land in the canopy of trees, but she was frozen to the spot. As the footsteps grew louder, she ran forwards towards the dead body, scrambling for his blade. Hands trembling, she fumbled with the sheath, and dropped the knife, which slid across the rock and fell down over the edge.

She found herself standing right beside the stairs, as a second figure stepped out in front of her. Maria tried to run but he grabbed her and dragged her down onto the ground with his body.

"Musasus, Masasus," he said in a calm soothing voice as he held her tightly, "D'o esk cik ak aap, shh shh."

Slowly he let go and Maria found herself free of his grasp. She knelt on the ground, unsure of what to do. The stranger crouched in front of her and all she could do was stare at him.

Unlike the bowman, whose body lay feet away, this man wore clean, fine quality clothes and looked healthily tanned. His eyes were a vibrant blue, and for a moment she felt captivated by them. He laid his longbow down on the ground beside them and placed his hand half over his face. Maria didn't know what this gesture meant, but she copied it and said, "Thank you."

"Woja eem KiKilip?" he continued, before realising she couldn't understand him. He held his hand to his chest and uttered the word, "Jekka," then placed it upon her just below her collar bone.

"I don't . . ." she replied. "Jekka? Is that your name?" She placed her hand upon her own chest and said, "Maria."

Jekka stood up and stepped towards the dead body. Rolling it over with his foot, he pushed the carcass over the edge, sending it crashing through the trees. He returned to Maria and gently helped her to her feet, then escorted her down the stairs.

With nothing more than a name and a face, Maria had no reason to trust this man, but she had seen more kindness in his eyes than she'd seen in a long time.

At the bottom of the stairs, Jekka picked up the dead man's blade and handed it to her. He said a single word Maria couldn't begin to understand, and then taking her hand he led her through the trees. She had no idea where they were going but she followed without question.

*

Gloria and Shoa had stayed the night in a makeshift shelter constructed of broken branches and leaves. Gloria had complained a lot about having to sleep on the soil and about her back, once again reminding Shoa of her age.

She had accepted the compromise of sharing Shoa's robe as a sheet to lie on, while Shoa slept in her thin underclothes. They had nuts and berries for breakfast, which only took the edge off the hunger. They set off shortly after sunrise.

By noon, they had reached the forest's edge, and they were both somewhat relieved when Shoa recognised where they were. "Those mountains . . ." she pointed out, "Whitefalls is on the other side. It's maybe fifty miles or so."

"Fifty miles!" Gloria blurted out, "Are you being serious?"

"Look, its fifty miles. There's nothing I can do about it," she snapped, "If you don't like it then follow me and the distance will get less as we go."

Gloria was speechless. These were surprisingly wise words, and she felt slightly embarrassed that this teenager, who was a fraction of her age, was acting more mature than she was.

The mountains didn't seem to get any closer no matter how long they walked for. The hills rolled, and at each apex, more land revealed itself before them. Eventually the grass became thinner, and stonier, and they found themselves looking directly up at the first peak. Gloria was already exhausted, and convinced Shoa that they should take a break.

After resting for a quarter of an hour, Shoa led them along the gentlest sloping path she could find. Gloria noticed that the girl seemed to be on edge for some reason, but said nothing.

It wasn't long before they lost sight of the forest and they found themselves completely surrounded by a grey rocky landscape. As they descended further into the valley, more mountains arose around them.

Every hour they would stop for a break, and Shoa could tell that her companion wasn't coping well. Gloria had the stamina to work long hospital shifts, which were by no means easy, but this was an entirely different ball game.

Years of smoking had reduced her lung capacity, and although she had quit a long time ago, its effects had stayed with her. Shoa took pity on this poor old woman; she had been dragged from her home without warning.

"There's a cave system not far from here," Shoa said, "It'll be dark by the time we reach it. We can rest there for the night."

Gloria was unsure, she needed somewhere with something resembling a comfortable bed. Her back couldn't take much more torture.

"We can try and make a mattress out of moss and dry grass, there's plenty of both about. We'll collect it on the way."

Gloria was once again surprised at how considerate this girl could be. When she thought about it though, it was the least Shoa could do after what she had done.

"With all of your local knowledge, I don't suppose you know where to look for some food?"

"Yes, but we'll need to hunt for it."

Gloria's face contorted. She wasn't exactly squeamish, but she disliked the idea of killing for her food. Like most people on Earth, she left that to others.

The thought of having a comfortable bed for the night gave her the focus and stamina to push forward. They did not come across any life for quite a while, but hit the jackpot when they stumbled upon a heard of grazing gazelle.

Cracking her fingers, Shoa quietly approached. She was within metres of a calf when it saw her and bolted. As it bounded over a small stream, the water seemed to come alive and drag it down below the depths. Blinding white electricity came from the tips of Shoa's fingers and passed through the young gazelle's body. It thrashed violently for several seconds before it dropped dead.

Gloria stared open mouthed as the stream spat the animal back out. Shoa turned to her, "I've done my bit, so you can take it to our camp."

Begrudgingly, Gloria dragged the carcass along behind her as they descended further. The valley had become completely engulfed in shadow, and as the sun went down, it grew even darker.

Shoa set alight a small dry branch, and using it as a torch, led them into the wide open mouth of a cave.

They set a ring of stones and brought more wood in to fuel the fire. Gloria noticed that much of the wood was already charred, and wondered if many people came this way. They cooked the meat on the fire, and piled up the hay and dried moss, laying Shoa's cloak over it. The make shift bed was nowhere near as comfortable as either of them had envisioned, but it was still far better than the uneven rock floor.

Gloria was delighted that they were finally co-operating, but wondered how long their patience with each other would last. The next few days would be a test of many things.

Chapter 18

The desert was as hot as ever, and even with the feather light clothes that John wore that covered his whole body, he was sweating profusely. The camels however seemed immune to the heat, and walked for miles and miles even when John could barely stay awake. He had not realised that the night air was freezing cold, as the past two nights; he had slept in the car or had been locked in a cell. The sand held enough heat after dark though, so that in his tent there was a fairly constant, comfortable temperature.

The sun was so bright that he spent much of the time with his eyes shut, while the beasts of burden carried him and his equipment. He rationed his dry bread and fruit well, but the camel's food supply quickly ran out.

He stopped briefly when he saw something small and red, half buried in the sand. Climbing down from his animal, he found a single gun cartridge just lying in the desert. Had someone else from Earth been here? He searched the ground for more, but only found the one. Inspecting it closer, he realised that it was intact and hadn't been fired.

Putting it in his pocket, he clambered back onto the camel and continued his journey. He remembered his night in the tent and realised that he hadn't had the nightmare for the first time in weeks. Instead, he had dreamt of an eternity of sand and walking for miles only to come back to the same place he had started from. Awake, things didn't seem very different.

The only thing making him aware that he was going in roughly the same direction was his compass. The map had illustrated several landmarks which he had already come across; mainly large rocks, telling him he was going the right way. Within two days, he had consumed more than three quarters of his large water container and had struggled to refrain from glugging down the rest.

With nothing but his thoughts to occupy his time, he pictured what he would say and do once he found Maria, and what they would do when they returned home. He fought the urge to think about where she may have arrived on this world, and had to try and trick himself into believing that she was already safe. Orak had mentioned Whitefalls to her, so surely she was heading there too.

John was pulled up from the depths of his own mind when he heard a noise. He was sure he had heard a human voice. Looking for the source, he saw a dark shape emerging through the heat waves in the sand.

More dark shapes formed, and as they walked closer they became clear. Dressed in bright white cloaks, were four men, each carrying a curved two foot long blade.

John climbed down from the camel and fell over the moment his feet hit the floor. He'd been sapped of energy though he hadn't moved for hours. Clambering back up, he had to rest his weight upon the camel to stand.

"M'a heedrei monemut!" the closest man shouted, brandishing his sword.

John froze to the spot. He should have asked Udrok for some kind of weapon, but he hadn't anticipated even coming across another person in the desert. He held up his hands in submission.

The armed men stepped closer, each pointing their swords. The closest gestured with his hand that he wanted John to give him something.

"I have no money," he lied. Udrok had given him a few coins for when he reached Erinthia.

The aggressors didn't reply but continued to approach. John tossed the small bag of coins down in front of him. The nomadic desert dwellers took the money, but didn't back away, they wanted more.

As one of them leapt forward with his sword above his head, John found the strength to leap out of the way. The swordsman hacked into the side of his camel, before delivering several more blows, sending the animal to the ground. His friends started taking every possession that it had carried.

They had taken his food, water, maps, and all of his equipment, but they still pursued him further. They must have wanted the clothes off his back.

Running up a dune, John felt himself swaying and zigzagging. Although the thieves were only walking, they were still keeping up with him.

John's foot caught on a stick half buried in the sand, and he tumbled down the other side of the dune. He saw the stick fall down after him and stop halfway. Shedding the upper layer of his thin cloak, he found he could move more freely. This didn't make him faster, but he ran towards the stick nevertheless. This was the closest thing to a weapon he could find. When he got closer, he realised it wasn't a stick at all, and remembering what he had found earlier, his heart jumped.

Scooping up Gloria's shotgun, he saw not four, but six men arriving at the top of the hill, just metres from him. John threw himself painfully to the ground and forced himself to roll back down.

The nomads broke into a sprint, and as John lay there in the sand, he clumsily loaded the shot into the gun. He had never done this before, and it took him longer than he had anticipated. By the time he had cocked and aimed the weapon, the wild eyed nomad was standing at his feet, his scimitar raised and ready to strike.

John closed his eyes and he squeezed the trigger. The deafening bang stopped the other five dead in their tracks, as they saw their friend fly backwards onto the sand. His bright white robe was covered in vivid red blood, which seeped right through his thin garments. The nomads fled, realising that they were no match for this new magic.

John scrambled to his feet, feeling the dead man's warm blood across his. He couldn't believe his luck. He had been outnumbered and seconds away from death. Furthermore, he had arrived in the heart of the nomad's deserted camp.

Climbing into one of the large tents, he saw food and water. To his delight, he saw the red plastic casings of three more shotgun cartridges sitting on a table top. These thieving scavengers had turned out to be the answer he didn't even know he was looking for.

He stayed the night in one of the smaller tents, which was in the shade of the largest. Sleeping with the loaded shotgun in his arms, he would be ready if anyone came back, but nobody did.

In the past, he thought he would have been ok with taking a life if it was necessary to save his own, but the act still haunted him. Once again he dreamed, but this time of blood soaked sand and a nomadic funeral; where cries of grief could be heard throughout the desert.

*

Gloria was pleased to wake up in less pain than it had been. She also found that Shoa had rolled over in her sleep, and was lying in a shallow puddle towards the edge of the cave. Deciding not to wake her, Gloria lit a fire ready for them to cook breakfast. Enough heat was coming from the embers for it to reignite once she had put enough dry twigs and leaves on.

Her clothes now reeked of smoke, but it masked all other smells. She had been wearing the same clothes since they had arrived on this world, and she desperately needed to change. Cutting more meat off the gazelle with surgical precision using Shoa's almost blunt pocket knife, she skewered it with a carved stick and propped it up above the fire.

"I couldn't find any salad to go with it," Gloria said when she saw Shoa was awake. For the first time she saw Shoa smile, and was surprised at how pretty a smile it was.

"Dagastra MrKraal, I'm soaking," Shoa exclaimed. "Did you push me over?"

Gloria shook her head, "I'm not stupid. You'd set me on fire, or turn me into a frog if I did."

"Turn you into a frog?" she asked, utterly bewildered.

"Nevermind . . . this is nearly cooked. I found some more of those berries outside, and some seeds I think are edible and also these."

She held up a large bright red tomato. Gloria wished she had access to some saucepans. She would be able to make quite a simple but tasty sauce with these ingredients.

Once they had eaten, Shoa doused the fire, and kicked the smouldering ashes out of the cave. They set off, feeling full for the first time in days.

The cave system stretched for miles and Shoa pointed out which one she thought they had travelled to Earth from. She also pointed out that it could be a long time before the rift formed there again, and they might not even see it when it did.

They travelled for two and a half hours before Gloria said she needed to rest again. In reality, she felt as though she needed to stop a long time before then. The two of them sat on boulders in a wide open plain towards the end of a valley. From here, they could see more of the mountains than anywhere else they had been so far.

Out of the corner of her eye, Gloria saw something darting through the sky. At first she thought it was a bird, but at the speed it was travelling, she couldn't see how it was possible.

The bat like silhouette grew larger as it approached, and Gloria realised that it had the same snake like body as the creature she had seen on the news the other day. As it came into focus, she saw its colours emerge, the dark red of its scaly body, the yellow of its teeth, and the white of its eye.

The dragon covered the distance through the air so quickly that all Gloria had time to do was shove Shoa away, before diving to the ground herself.

Its razor sharp teeth snapped shut inches from Gloria's ankle, as its hot breath blasted clouds of dust, engulfing them. Coughing, she saw the dragon flying away from them.

The giant lizard looped high in the air, before it swooped back down again. Directly in line with its prey, the beast opened its powerful jaws and a stream of fire erupted from its mouth. Gloria braced for the worst, but the heat, although intense, did not burn her.

Shoa was stood in front of her, and the flames seemed to be wrapping themselves around an invisible barrier. The wall of yellow fire disappeared as the huge reptilian monster began to loop back around.

"Run," Shoa yelled, dragging Gloria back onto her feet.

Without needing any encouragement, Gloria moved as quickly as she could.

They passed behind a huge protruding rock as the beast struck for the third time. The rock protected them from the blast. The fire only singed Shoa's damp cloak, which hissed out a puff of white smoke.

"We can't keep this up for long," Shoa gasped, as she searched for a cave opening.

Gloria steered her away from the caves. The fire would only be channelled in a tunnel of rock, and they would be trapped. "Here," she croaked, dragging Shoa towards the edge of a large lake.

Glancing backwards, Shoa saw the dragon was about a quarter of a mile behind, but she knew it would reach them within seconds, long before they reached the water. Stopping, she prepared to repel the next blast.

As the creature was about to strike, she heard it screech in pain and suddenly change direction. Shoa ducked as its tail whipped around fast enough to cut her in two.

Blood spattered the ground around her, and as it fled she saw an arrow protruding from its eye. Before Gloria even reached the water, the dragon had vanished over the horizon. She stopped running when she was knee deep in the lake.

"What hap . . . ?" she started to say, but her question was answered for her. Standing on the summit of a small mountain, was a tall man beside his steed.

Trudging slowly out of the water, Gloria approached him. A second horseman appeared over the brow, holding an upside down spear with a large canvas flag attached to the top.

Shoa recognised the crest on the flag and jumped with excitement. "They're from Whitefalls!" she exclaimed.

Chapter 19

Jekka kept hold of Maria's hand every step of the way, so as not to lose her. They walked for only about four or five minutes through the forest before they came to a clearing.

The clearing was small and entirely invisible from above, as the tree canopies stretched far enough over to conceal it. In the centre, stood a small stone walled well. Maria noticed there was a very decrepit old roof above it, and a fraying rope hanging from a winch.

Winding the rope up, Jekka withdrew a bucket full of water and took a long gulp, before passing it to Maria. She barely had the strength to hold it, and noticing this Jekka helped her lift it to her lips. She glugged it down like a thirsty horse, and Jekka had to prise the water away from her to stop her from drowning herself. Maria gasped for air when she swallowed the water, and had to brace herself against the stone.

Her thirst had been quenched, but now her hunger seemed worse. Leaving the well, they continued through the forest.

Maria felt optimistic for the first time since she'd arrived in this strange world. Jekka was a complete stranger, but she knew from the start that he wasn't out to hurt her. If he was, then he'd had plenty of opportunities. She was beginning to doubt his motives for helping her. Not everyone would go to this much trouble for a damsel in distress.

It wasn't long before they came across another clearing. Maria was surprised that she hadn't seen this from the stone tower, as it was far bigger than the last. In the middle of the glade, stood a large log cabin built upon raised stone foundations. It was constructed of tree sections varying in thickness, lashed together by thick bundles of vine and sealed with dry clay. The roof was clad with patchy thatch work and thick pieces of slate could be seen underneath, where its builder had tried to seal leaks.

The doorway held a gate made from thin branches and sticks, and clearly served the purpose of keeping out animals rather than people. It had no lock, only a primitive bolt. Jekka opened the gate and gestured for Maria to follow him inside.

"You live here?" she asked, noticing that the inside was pitch black, except for the illuminated grid of a window on the other side.

Jekka used some pieces of flint to light a candle in the doorway, which he then used to light a dozen more candles dotted about the room. He showed Maria to a single bed in the corner of the large room and sat her down on it.

He continued to speak to her, even though they both knew that they couldn't understand each other. Maria found the sound of his voice calming, and gradually she felt more comfortable in her new surroundings. Jekka brought her a wooden board full of messily sliced bread, which she wolfed down faster than he had ever seen anybody eat. The bread was dry and very hard, but to Maria it was the most delicious thing she had ever eaten. Like with the water, Jekka had to take the food away from her so that she wouldn't overdo it and get severe indigestion.

"Thank you," she said tearfully, as she lay down on the lumpy bed. She wondered where he would be sleeping, as she didn't see any other bed in the room. This didn't worry her for long, because she fell asleep virtually the moment her head hit the pillow.

*

Maria woke to see dusty beams of light flowing through the gridded window ahead. She looked around for Jekka, but saw nobody.

In the daylight, the room looked very different from what she was expecting. The walls inside looked much like they did outside; just exposed log sections that looked cleaner, had been sanded down and seemed slightly paler. The ceiling above her was made from neatly woven straw around long sections of pole, and the floor was made from stone slabs pushed down into the soil, with many large visible gaps.

The candles had all been blown out, but the smell from them still lingered in the air. She could see that this large cluttered room had nearly every piece of furniture a person needed; chairs, a bed, a table for dining, a worktop for preparing food, a clothes horse, and a set of cupboards. Hanging from brackets on the walls, were pots and pans, spoons and forks, and a huge collection of knives for every purpose. Maria noticed a doorway to a second room and went to investigate.

In this room hung all of his clothes, as well as his longbow and a suit of armour. Upon a small table sat a selection of swords, as well as a shiny metal helmet. An immaculately kept oval shield rested against the table, displaying an engraved crest; depicting a horse and rider and a dragon facing each other in battle. The rider wore exactly the same square helmet that sat on the table, and carried the same long broadsword that sat beside it.

Maria returned to the main room just as Jekka arrived, carrying two large buckets of water. He placed them down beside the bed, and took out a sponge and a piece of soap from one of the cupboards. "Zian," he said, miming rubbing himself with the sponge, before handing them to her.

"Thank you," she replied. Jekka left the room, closing the door behind him.

Maria waited to make sure he was gone before undressing. She scrubbed hard at the several days' worth of muddy stains, until her skin was red raw but clean underneath. Once she herself was clean, she started to scrub her clothes. Using the large cloth he had given her as a towel to cover herself up, she hung her clothes on the clothes horse.

When Jekka returned, he helped her lift the drying rack out into the sunshine. Maria noticed a campfire outside the house, where her host must have done all of his cooking.

"Did you build this place?" she asked, hoping something would get through to him.

Jekka just looked at her, puzzled. Maria mimed stacking stones and hammering nails, but he looked just as confused.

They sat in silence while Jekka prepared some food. There were so many things he wanted to say to her, but had no means. His face showed frustration, and Maria didn't understand why.

After eating a breakfast of porridge and more dry hard bread, Maria offered to wash up. This involved walking half a mile to the spring, carrying the bowls and cutlery with her. It made her realise how easy housework was for her back home.

She had left chalk marks on the trees she passed so she could find her way back. This worked brilliantly, but she wished she'd had access to this chalk days ago.

When she got back, she found Jekka sitting on a tree stump beside the camp fire, whittling a figure out of a block of wood.

The level of detail in this tiny sculpture was impressive, but resembled nobody she knew. Jekka looked up at her, held up the figure and said "Maria."

Maria looked closely at the carved figure; it looked nothing like her, but it was a sweet gesture nevertheless. "I wish I could understand you," she said quietly.

For the next few hours, Jekka tried to teach her, firstly how to whittle wood, then how to speak his language. He gave her another piece of chalk and a spare roof slate, which she used to write down everything he said in an attempt to understand it.

As soon as she had figured out what a word he had said meant, she wrote down how it sounded along with a translation. She would read the word back to him, and he would correct her until she got it right, and then he did the same with the English. After some time, they understood several very basic words of each other's languages, such as yes and no, and hello and goodbye.

As night fell, they went inside and Jekka lit all of the candles again. Some of them had burnt almost completely down to the bottom, and she wondered where he would get more of them. There was so much curiosity surrounding this place, and she was sure there must have been a story behind each and every item on display.

Jekka had enjoyed teaching Maria, and wanted to teach her more. Picking up one of the knives, he swished it around and stabbed the air a few times. "Conabas," he said, repeating the action.

"Duelling?" she asked.

Jekka picked up a second knife and did the same again.

"Conabas means fighting?" she asked. Maria put her fists up in the air and started shadow boxing.

Jekka burst into laughter, nodding his head. Maria couldn't help but laugh too.

"Oi, it wasn't that bad!" she said, playfully jabbing him in the arm.

Jekka pretended to attack her back, and they stopped when he found himself gripping her by both arms, backing her against the wall. He stared into her pretty green eyes, and she stared back. They felt each other leaning in closer, but just as Jekka was about to kiss her, she moved her head away.

"I can't," she said. There was an air of sadness to her voice, and Jekka dropped his head and backed away.

Maria walked out of the house. She'd never felt this connected with anyone without words before, but it wasn't fair on John. How could she think about doing anything with this stranger? She knew it could never come to anything. They were from different worlds after all.

She needed to learn to speak to Jekka. She needed to explain about John, and ask him to help her find him and to find her way home.

Chapter 20

The two riders led Gloria and Shoa down the quickest path through the mountains. They had brought a spare horse with them which the two women would have to share

It had been about thirty years since Gloria had ridden a horse but she hadn't forgotten how. She and Shoa took turns steering the animal and it quickly became apparent that Shoa was a natural.

They moved quickly out of fear of encountering more danger. Several times, Gloria found herself panicking when she saw things in the sky, but each time they turned out to be birds.

"Ask them if there is anyone searching the forest," Gloria said suddenly.

"What?" Shoa replied, slowing down the steed.

"Maria might still be in the forest," said Gloria. "Ask them if anyone is searching for her, please."

Shoa approached one of the soldiers that were guiding them. She spoke rapidly in their native tongue, pointing over the hill in the direction they had come from. The soldier spoke just as quickly back to her, gesturing in the same direction, holding up four fingers. Turning to Gloria, she explained that they did have more people searching every inch of the forest and enquiring at all the villages on the border. If she was anywhere near the woods, they would find her.

As they reached more open ground, their pace quickened once again. The flying predators that lived in the mountains had eyesight better than any bird of prey, but their prey would be relatively safe amongst the rocks and trees. Shoa was frightened of the beasts returning, but she was

90

more afraid of Gloria seeing through her. It was true that people were out looking for Maria but there were things she had failed to mention. They had crossed the narrowest part of the forest; the trees engulfed an area of land the size of Scotland. The soldiers would spend a day or two looking, before heading home.

Gloria also had no idea how far apart they had arrived on her world. Shoa had said John wouldn't have been far from Orak or Mac. If she knew the truth of how random the entry points were, she'd have been so worried about her friend that she would never have made it this far. Shoa knew that distorting so many truths was never a good thing, but it was the only way she could get the old woman to stay with her, under her protection.

The rider Shoa had spoken to, held out his hand as they began to ascend a narrow ridge. The others slowed right down and peered down into the valley half a mile below them.

A huge red lizard was moving amongst the trees, sniffing at the ground. Its severely bloodshot injured eye was visible from where they stood; petrified. Although they could see it clearly, it could not see them, the arrow had half blinded it.

The three horses moved as slowly as they could be made to. The riders were tense and cautious of every stone shifting and every twig breaking beneath their hooves.

As the ridge swept around, so did the valley, and more dragons seemed to appear below, all searching the ground for traces of blood; they remained unaware of the flesh so close by. One dragon they could just about handle, but as even more creatures crept out of caves and hollows, they became vastly outnumbered.

"It's a hive," Shoa hissed, holding onto the reins so tightly that her knuckles went white.

More than a dozen dragons were clustered together near the cave entrances; some were over a hundred feet long. They would have no trouble snatching up a horse and rider in one bite, and torching them to death in their jaws.

Hunters all over Erinthia had searched for this hive for years, and nobody had ever found it. Technically some had, but those who had found it never returned to make the claim.

Once they were near the summit, the ridge narrowed, but the ground either side became less steep. There was only one way they could go. The horses were extremely reluctant, but were pressed into heading down the slope, out of view of the hive.

Galloping down the mountain side, the horses accelerated to beyond what the riders thought possible. A single wrong footed stride could easily have been the end for both horse and rider, but they didn't miss a beat.

Finally, the ground levelled out and the horses slowed down. The soldiers leapt down off their steeds immediately, as did Shoa. Gloria was so shaken from such a terrifying experience that she stayed seated on the animal for much longer.

They stopped to rest beside a lake, knowing that the water's edge was the safest place away from the dragons. Shoa was starting to wonder whether they should have come this way to begin with, but if they hadn't, it would have added a whole week to their journey. She didn't regret it; if they had gone around the long way they could have lost each other, and Gloria would never have survived by herself.

Floating in the water just at the shores edge, Gloria saw one of the sheets of plastic which had covered her husband's power tools. It suddenly dawned on her how little she had thought about Mark since she had been there, and it saddened her to think that they had really got to that stage.

She wondered what he was doing back on Earth. He would be at a loss as to what had happened to the contents of their garage, if he'd even returned home by now.

They set off again, trudging across sand and wading through streams. They put their horses through trials like they had never seen, and carried on even after the sun had gone down. Ithria's two moons were both full and gave them enough light to see more than just paths and trees. The soldiers seemed unstoppable as they pressed on, but Shoa and Gloria had to take it in turns to ride while the other slept sitting up.

As the moons descended and the sun peaked over the horizon, they were scrambling up the side of a frothing white waterfall. At the top, a long fast flowing river led them the rest of the way. Shoa immediately knew where they were, and she felt a huge sense of accomplishment. This was the furthest she had, or had ever planned to travel in her life.

The river led them straight to the very same lake where she had spent much of her life growing up. Built upon the end, was the floating district in the furthest reaches of Lower Whitefalls. She was finally home.

Chapter 21

John had very little sleep that night; constantly being awoken by his own thoughts. He kept wondering whether there had been another way to survive. He gained little reassurance, realising he had taken the only option. The man would have murdered him, but was this the correct way to measure if a life was less worthy than his own?

With one less camel to carry him and his equipment, John looked after his remaining animal better than himself. Even though he gave the creature as many stops as it wanted, he expected it to carry a lot more than it had done. John had used one of the nomad's smaller tents as a sack to carry the food, water and clothes that he had salvaged. He used a stolen length of rope, tied it at the end to seal it, and then let it trail behind them in the sand.

Just as before, he drank the water far quicker than planned, but this time there, was a lot more of it. The food lasted longer as he had very little appetite these days.

Conventional time was no longer a concept to him anymore, there were now only three times; sunrise, high noon and sunset. Even with these guides, he still had no idea how many days he had been out here. Sometimes he would search the skies for signs of rescue helicopters or planes, before remembering where he was.

Many hours after he had left the camp, the yellow sands turned grey and rocky again. A little while after, he saw something he didn't expect.

Sprouting from the dusty sand just in front of him was a small green plant. John fell down on his knees and started to stroke the plant with his dry calloused fingers, it was real. John picked off one of its few leaves and took it with him back to the camel. This was the most beautiful thing he could ever remember seeing.

His attention was fixed on this single thin leaf, until more tiny sprouting plants emerged over the hill. An inane smile crept across his face and stayed there for quite some time. He had no idea whether he was losing his mind, but just to find something else living and that was unlikely to kill him, was enough to make him happy for now.

John crossed from horizon to horizon once more, but the view which opened up before him this time was very different. Patches of grass began to spring up, becoming larger and larger. Before long, he was standing on the bank of a fast flowing river, staring down at a huge body of water that stretched many miles across. Floating on the water, he saw half a dozen wooden galleons trailing enormous nets between them in pairs.

Across the water, John saw tiny white houses and even smaller ant sized figures walking around. He made sure he had his list of words with him before approaching.

Before he reached the distant houses, he came across another small community previously hidden behind several large trees. He stroked the tree bark, still struggling to believe that it was real.

John struggled to read a sentence to the first person he met, who didn't understand a word, and walked away. He showed the symbols to the next person he met. They handed him a small bag of coins, before taking his camel away. With several of the coins, he bought a small backpack off of the stranger, so that he could carry some of his supplies.

When he reached the larger town, he booked into a hotel for the night and bought a meal of fresh fish and slightly burnt sliced potatoes. Nothing had ever tasted so good.

*

Gloria and Shoa arrived in Whitefalls looking like they had been dragged through hell. Everyone around them; as they travelled through the upmarket area looked clean and well groomed.

Gloria couldn't stop looking around at the magnificent ancient looking city, built upon the most beautiful countryside she had ever seen. There were thousands of people everywhere, but no polluted air; not even the scent of wood smoke.

The section they had entered through was constructed of timber buildings, built upon a huge pier like structure, hanging over the lake, but now the buildings were all rendered with brick and stone. All down the paved roads, travelled horse and carts and what looked like primitive four wheeled bicycles.

When they reached a huge cliff face, a deafening waterfall cascaded down. The soldiers led them through a tunnel cut through the rock, which led them up a wide twisting staircase, reaching all the way to the top of the cliff.

At the top was a second city, with just as many lakes and streams. They crossed more bridges than Gloria could count, and she caught sight of the mountains they had just come from ahead of them. "Why did we loop around?" she asked, confused.

"Upper Whitefalls can only be reached by crossing the water or by the lower city," Shoa explained. "And we didn't bring a boat."

By the time they crossed the bridge onto the island, where the university stood, the soldiers had left them to go back to their barracks. Shoa was shocked by the sheer number of people climbing the hill towards the same building. The tall doorway between the gate towers was wide open, and hundreds of civilians were traipsing through without being stopped.

"What the hell is going on?" she asked a stranger in their language.

"It's the safest place," replied a teenage girl several years younger than she was, "The war is coming."

"When?" asked Shoa.

The girl shook her head, "I don't know. My dad says they'll be in the city in less than a week, my mum thinks they'll be here the day after tomorrow."

Shoa rushed passed them, dragging Gloria along behind her. "This can't be happening," she yelled. "We shouldn't be here. We need to find Mac."

Soldiers wearing the same thin steel armour, as the ones who had found them, stood guard on the inside of the doors. Shoa knew how much Administrator Shrax hated the military, and found it hard to believe he'd have allowed this. On the other hand, she also knew how powerful the general of Whitefalls was.

She ran up the stairs of the largest building in the courtyard and hammered on the main office door. It opened slowly, and an older looking administrator than she remembered opened the door. He looked delighted to see her and welcomed his student with open arms. Shoa was delighted by his reaction; it must have meant the others were already back.

"This must be one of the unfortunate people from Earth you brought with you. I must apologise profusely for any inconvenience caused to you," the administrator said, addressing Gloria.

Gloria hadn't expected this man to speak English, and her response was flustered. "I . . . That's ok . . . I . . ."

Shrax turned back to Shoa, "Professors JaVrei and Kroez are in the hall downstairs waiting for you. I'm sure you've noticed that our great institution has been taken over by the good general and her men, I can only extend my apologies for yet more inconvenience."

"How do you all speak my language so well?" Gloria interrupted.

"Orak JaVrei and I learnt it by observing your world through a window in this university. Professor JaVrei then taught it to his students and Professor Kroez," he explained politely.

"Madame, you are the first Earth lady I've ever spoken to. How do you find my grasp on your native tongue?" he asked.

"If I didn't know better, I'd have sworn you were from London," Gloria told the man.

Shrax looked delighted at her reply, "Shoa will show you to a comfortable bed for you to stay in," he said.

On their way down to the hall, they stopped off at the girl's dormitory. The first thing Shoa did when she got to her own bunk was to change her clothes. She found some old but clean clothes at the bottom of her hamper for Gloria to try on. As they were both about the same height, the clothes fitted, even if they weren't what she would normally wear.

Gloria looked at herself in the mirror and frowned at the bright red and black vertical striped robes. She wasn't used to wearing such vibrant colours, but it was still better than wearing week old clothes.

Orak and Mac were sat alone in the large dining hall, and both stood the moment the doors crashed open. A smile formed on Orak's face when he saw them, but it disappeared when he saw the terrifying snarl across the elderly woman's. Shoa jumped up to hug Orak, the same time as Gloria slapped Mac so hard that he was knocked of his feet.

Staring back at her through blurry eyes, he rubbed his cheek. It stung badly. He looked back down at the floor, unable to make eye contact.

Once Gloria had calmed down slightly, she looked around the room. "Where's John and Maria?" she asked, turning to Shoa, "You said they would be here?"

Shoa turned to the two men. Orak just shook his head, "There are a lot of people looking for them," he replied. "But I've not had any word."

"Why aren't you looking for them?" Gloria snapped, and Orak's hand twitched ready to defend himself, "You brought them here."

"Don't you think I know that," he retaliated.

"They could be in god knows what trouble. We were nearly killed by a dragon. What else is out there?" she asked.

Orak turned to Shoa and directed his anger at her, "You took her through the mountains," he roared, "You stupid little girl."

Gloria also turned to Shoa, "You knew those monsters would be there," she screamed.

Orak had to physically restrain her, as she tried like a stroppy child to break free and strike Shoa. He was amazed at the strength that this small woman possessed, but he kept her in place until she seemed less aggressive.

The argument that followed lasted longer than anyone would have liked, but was finally resolved when Mac said he was doing everything he could to find a way to take them all back. He explained that there was nothing anybody else could do in the meantime. It was his mistake that had caused this, and he would be the one to fix it.

Chapter 22

—◆◆◆◆◆—

Maria spent the night on Jekka's single bed again, and she realised that he was sleeping outside under the stars. She had not said a word to him since their misunderstanding, not that it would have made a difference if she had. Jekka had not seemed angry or especially upset, but Maria wondered how long he would let her stay. She had proved to herself that she couldn't cope out there alone.

In the morning, he still made her breakfast, this time consisting of a large smoked fish shared between them, with a sprig of some kind of herb she didn't recognise. Maria wondered where he had gotten the fish from, as she had seen no rivers or large streams during her time in the forest.

She wondered how she would find the others once she'd gotten Jekka to show her the way out of the forest. She remembered the name of the country; Tontoltec, but had no way of pinpointing them further. Unless this country was the size of the Vatican City, she would need more to go on.

After breakfast, Jekka decided to try and teach Maria how to use a sword, in case any of the murderous woodland scavengers came back. She found his broadsword too heavy, so instead used the shorter curved blade that he had taken from the dead man.

Firstly, he showed her how to hold the weapon so it couldn't easily be knocked out of her hands, and then demonstrated how to withstand a strike with it. Maria had never held anything bigger than a kitchen knife before, and found wielding this scimitar daunting.

As they duelled at a very sedate pace, he tried to teach her new words, such as the names for the swords and movements. By the end of their session, she felt more confident holding the sword. This was a start, and Jekka was sure she would learn more next time.

Maria had not exerted herself, but was drowning in sweat and went down to the well to wash herself. When she returned, she and Jekka tried to learn more of each other's languages. It became obvious to him that she would be staying for quite some time, so he started work on building a second bed frame. He also began constructing a small lightweight structure on the side of the house for Maria to have some privacy.

*

John left the hotel at first light. He had no money left, and very little food or water with him. Although he had left the desert far behind, the air was still sweltering, and the ample lakes and rivers wouldn't be as clean as his spring water.

It felt surreal to him that he could walk through a busy street with a loaded firearm in plain view. What was even more surreal was that none of the hundreds of people around him had any idea what it was. None of them knew what he was capable of doing with this strange looking stick.

Following his map, John left the town and started walking through a huge field of cornflowers. The map showed very little detail in most areas, but specified this particular field, so he knew he was going the right way.

Before leaving the hotel, he had changed back into his clothes from home, after washing them thoroughly. He glanced down at his belt and realised that he had moved down two holes since he had last worn them, but his jeans still felt loose. *Walking through Ithria is better than any gym,* he thought.

John took out his map again when he reached the end of the field. It showed a wide river between him and where he needed to be and he wondered why he hadn't studied this map more carefully. The map showed no crossings anywhere nearby, and when he reached the bank of the river, he saw nothing even resembling a bridge.

Thirty or so large flat rocks protruded from the calm river, each one less than a metre apart. John didn't have the best sense of balance in the world, and this would be a true test of it. Not all of the rocks were that big, towards the middle, some of them were no bigger than the soles of his shoes.

Just as he was starting to cross, he heard a deafening scream from beyond the field. John lost his footing and crashed down into the shallow river. Scrambling back up onto the muddy bank, he didn't know whether he should investigate or not. The scream had come from a woman, and it sounded as though she was in trouble.

John began to run back through the field when a figure appeared in the distance. At first it looked human, but as a huge set of bat like wings spread out from its back, he knew it couldn't be.

Skidding to a halt, John's trainers dug into the soil, uprooting several plants. Poised like a sprinter, with his hand upon the ground, he shot off in the opposite direction. Out of the corner of his eye, he saw more winged figures leaping into the air, as if they were spring loaded.

He darted across the stepping stones, nearly losing his footing several times on the first few, but clumsily regaining his balance later. Halfway across, John stepped straight past a stone and once again crashed down into the water.

Most of the creatures glided past, except one who landed with grace upon the stone John had missed. He heard it screeching as he looked up through the water at its hideously distorted face. The monster did not seem to want to submerge itself, and as John lay there at the bottom of the shallow river, fighting to hold his breath, he saw the shotgun lying on a rock several feet away.

The beast hissed and snarled at the human under the water; its needle like teeth exposed, and its large dark eyes glaring. This beast matched the description that Orak had given him of the Drathmorks, the weapon the enemy would win the war with. Even unarmed, this monster could easily tear him limb from limb.

It wasn't unarmed. Sheathed to a leather strap across its chest and waist, was an entire arsenal of daggers, swords and throwing knives, as well as a circular wooden shield hanging behind its back below its wings.

John couldn't hold his breath much longer and forced his head out of the water before the instinct to inhale cut in. As soon as he surfaced, the hybrid soldier swung its sword at his skull, missing by millimetres and shaving several hairs off his scalp. John scrambled backwards, snatching up the shotgun. He pulled the trigger as soon as he had a grip upon the handle and blasted the tip of the creature's wing off.

The Drathmork screeched again, beating its wings down and spraying blood across the water. It glided over several stones and before landing right next to its enemy, swung with all of its strength at the projectile weapon. The blade struck the barrel of the gun and sank straight through the metal; wedging in place. The sword flew from its hands, but John held on tight to the gun as it swung down and struck the stone, firing on impact.

The blast sent the sword flying, and broke off a two inch section of the barrel. John wheeled the firearm around and discharged the last round directly into the creature's chest at near point blank range. The winged soldier was thrown back into the water, where it thrashed violently in pain. Redness spread right across the river, but the creature kept moving. Its heart had been torn to shreds by the metal pellets, but it was still very much alive. John ran across the stones while the monster tried to crawl through the water. It clambered onto the stones and within seconds was running just as fast.

Orak had failed to mention that these creatures clearly had a second cardiac organ. Without any more ammunition, John had no chance of defeating it.

Changing tactics, John dived into the river. The Drathmork stopped as it saw his adversary floating away with the current. As he drifted downriver, John saw the creature doubled over in pain and gasping for breath. Suddenly it stopped moving altogether and fell into the river. Its additional heart couldn't sustain the creature alone for long.

John's heart felt as though it was about to give up too. He knew he wasn't especially unhealthy, but he never thought he would have lasted this long with everything he had been through.

Clambering back onto land a quarter of a mile further along the river, John saw a huge stone bridge, consisting of two large ornately carved wide arched sections. Polished marble gate pillars stood either side of the bridge and upon them; an intricate mesh of wrought iron sealed the bridge off from both sides.

John jumped back into the water, tucked the shotgun into his belt, and then swam under the bridge. He surfaced just outside a fenced off garden, and saw more gardens all along the bank. Behind each garden was a house; far grander than any of the ones he had seen in the last town. He looked down at the river that he had just crawled from and saw water pouring into it from a rocky stream between the mansions.

The stones acted like very wet steps, and took him all the way up into an open courtyard. From here, he could see a towering rock face, and billions of gallons of water cascading down it into a large pool.

John pulled out the map, but the ink had run and he could no longer read it. He was sure he didn't need it though, this had to be Whitefalls. Where else could he be?

Chapter 23

John saw a large archway cutting through the vertical cliff face. He approached, and saw lights flickering inside. Reaching for his phrase sheet, he tried to find a way to ask where the university was, but like the map it was also too water damaged to read.

He searched for signs, before realising that this world wouldn't have the same symbols for letters as on Earth. With nowhere else to go, he headed through the tunnel.

It was lit by fire torches mounted on wall brackets every few paces, and illuminated the passage enough for him to see where he was going. It took him up a wide spiral staircase, almost as high as the one in the desert canyon.

He had noticed that nobody in this city was panicking, running or screaming, and therefore oblivious that the enemy was so close by. John had to warn them, but the only way to do that was to find the others. He sprinted up the stairs close to the centre, quickly getting dizzy. Stopping to get his head straight, he sat down on a step.

Suddenly a thought struck him. *What if they weren't there? Or if they'd been and left because he took too long to get here?* John had no way of knowing, but if they weren't at the university, how would he get the message out to these people? They needed to flee their homes, take up arms, anything but wait in ignorance to be slaughtered. At that moment, John found he had more responsibility over something highly important, than he'd ever had before.

Standing back up, he continued to run up the stairs. He was right up against the outer wall, using it to help guide his way. Eventually he reached the top.

The staircase opened out into a huge courtyard on which stood four cast iron statues, each portraying a very different looking person. The first statue was of a huge mountain of a man with a battle axe in one hand and a long broadsword in the other. The second depicted a smaller man with his arms spread out like an eagle, and with his feet elevated from the plinth by a partially visible metal bar. The third showed a man with fire coming from the palm of his hand and the fourth showed a less fantastical looking man with an open book in his grasp. John guessed that they were erected to show that there was meant to be a sense of equality in the city amongst the four races.

The statues weren't vandalised, which was a good sign. John walked passed them to a large fountain, which he used to cool himself down. He stopped every pedestrian that walked past and asked "Do you speak English?"

Most of them just ignored him but some replied, saying something in their language before walking off. After ten minutes and hundreds of strangers, he got a reply he was looking for.

"Yes . . . Are you in Professor JaVrei's class, I don't think I've met you before," said the young man.

"I'm not in his class, but I need to find him," John said so hurriedly that he had to slow down and repeat himself.

The student nodded his head and gestured for John to follow him. They crossed over dozens of bridges and clambered up a hill, before arriving at the gates of the castle he had seen from the city below.

"This is the university?" John asked, sounding surprised.

"Well, yes . . . I didn't know any other universities taught English," the student asked, showing off his fluency.

"You learn something new every day," he replied, before thanking the stranger and entering through the open gates.

It took him less time to find someone to give him directions to where Orak might be, and after paying the administrator a visit, he was led back downstairs to a dormitory common room.

Hundreds of people littered every corridor and every room he passed, as temporary beds filled every other inch of space. This was not like any university he had ever been in before. Armoured soldiers stood guard on every other doorway, motionless and staring into space.

The common room was lavishly decorated, with a grand fireplace and many comfortable looking sofas. Sitting at a large circular table, he saw them. Gloria, Orak, Mac and Shoa were there playing some kind of bizarre looking card game. Gloria did a double take when she saw him and leapt to her feet.

Before she could take a step, John had rushed up and hugged her, "I'm so glad you're ok," he said tearfully. "I'm so sorry, this is all my . . ."

"None of this is your fault," she corrected him, tears welling up in her eyes too. "Where have you been all this time?" she asked.

"It's a long story," he replied, looking around the room.

"Where is she? Is Maria here?" John asked.

Gloria's face sank. John looked around at the others, their faces looked equally grim.

Mac was the first to speak, "We hoped you two came through together. There are people looking, we think she . . ."

But John had already turned away. He buried his head in his hands, and began pacing. "It's been over a week," his troubled voice quietly said, "She's been all alone in this world for over a week."

John could barely breathe and his legs felt uneasy. He held onto a table for support and clenched his fist. Everything he had told himself to give him the strength to get here meant nothing now.

Gloria placed a hand on his shoulder, "We found her shoe in a forest. We couldn't find her, but there are people looking," she said, consoling John.

"People she doesn't know . . . who don't speak our language?" he replied.

"They'll find her, I'm sure," was all that she could say.

John spun around and pointed a finger at Orak. He wanted to attack the man, but he was more than twice his size. All he could do was speak with a tongue poisoned by hatred, "This is your fault, not mine. You should never have interfered with our lives."

Orak said nothing. The giant just sat there hunched in his chair, staring at the floor. Despite his size, he looked like a child who knew he had done wrong.

"If anything happens to her," John spat, "Nothing you do will ever make me forgive you."

John caught sight of the window and was suddenly reminded of the world outside this room and of matters unrelated to Maria. "They're here," he said. John's tone of voice had changed from rage to fear so quickly it was as though a different person was speaking. "Less than a mile outside the city, I saw one, I fought it. The Drathmorks are here."

"You fought it? Orak asked, finding it hard to believe this human could have done so and be standing here alive.

"I found Mark's shotgun," he explained to Gloria, before turning back to Orak, "I only saw a handful, I don't know how many more there were. They attacked a town east of here. Where are you going?" he asked.

Orak stormed out through the door before he could even answer. Mac left through a different door, but Shoa stayed.

She held up a deck of cards "Want to play? I'll explain the rules," she asked, with a faint smile on her face. Her attempt to lighten the mood didn't work.

*

Upstairs, Orak burst through the administrator's office door, only to find that it was empty. Sprinting back downstairs he frantically searched for the general.

He didn't want to cause a mass panic so he said nothing to the many confused civilians clustered in every corner of the building. The guards didn't try to stop him as he charged down the corridor towards the offices that the military had commandeered.

When he eventually found Kyra in what used to be the staff room, she was drawing up a formation plan on a map of the castle. She didn't seem surprised when he told her about the Drathmorks being a stone's throw from Whitefalls.

"I received word from a rider ten minutes ago," she told him, calmly scribbling several words inside the illustration of the gatehouse.

"Are we ready?" Orak asked, suspiciously. From what he had seen, the fort didn't appear to be on red alert.

"The creatures that attacked the town were just a scouting party. My soldiers have dealt with them," Kyra explained. "The ones we didn't capture and execute retreated. They've gone back to tell their commanders what to expect when they get here."

"So they have the advantage of knowing our landscape," Orak said.

Kyra shook her head, "We have the advantage. They don't know how prepared we are for them; we let those scouts escape. It will give them a false sense of confidence, and they might send less of a force if we're lucky."

"I think you're the one with the false confidence," he replied, scanning the battle plans she had been annotating.

"Don't confuse real confidence with outward confidence," she said with a smile, "I'm terrified Orak, but what good would it do letting my soldiers know that."

"They're too close for me to lead a party of evacuees. We'll be caught up right in the middle of the battle," he said.

Kyra nodded, "I wish we'd had more warning. What you can do for me, is help gather as many people from Upper Whitefalls as you can, and bring them back to the castle. I'll be closing the gates and dismantling the bridge tomorrow. I know the river won't stop the enemy, but it will help. Their human soldiers can't cross it very quickly and we have a few Spellcasters who might be able to contribute."

"Do you have any jobs for me? I may as well help if I'm here for the battle," Orak said, bravely.

Kyra thought for a moment. She noticed he was still wearing his necklace of teeth. "I think I have something, yes. Put your old dragon hunting skills to use if they aren't too rusty."

Orak left her to continue strategising. He felt less worried than when he had entered her office, but this calm was only temporary. It was just a matter of time before the serenity of Whitefalls would shatter like glass.

Chapter 24

Four whole days had passed before any more news of the enemy reached them. A messenger rode into the city with a broken arrow sticking out of his thigh. He was carried to the university on a stretcher to be seen by the professor of medicine, but when Shrax remembered about their new residents, he asked for the help of the Earth people.

For the first time since he had arrived, John felt useful. The instruments weren't as clean or precise as the ones he used in the hospital, and all he had for sterilising the wound and anaesthetising the patient was a strong drinking spirit. He successfully removed the deep arrow head without causing significant nerve damage, but left stitching the wound to Gloria who had much steadier hands.

The message was for General Kyra, telling her that the enemy army was seen marching across the border of Erinthia, just thirty miles away. The enemy war machine had well over a thousand cavalry and infantry units, as well as siege weapons and at least five hundred armoured Drathmorks.

The messenger also told her about several dozen creatures that he had never seen before; with the abdomens of giant spiders but the upper bodies of men. This news sent a chill down Kyra's spine. She felt as though her control over the situation was slipping. What else did the enemy possess that she didn't know about?

Through John's experience of the Drathmork scout, she had learned how resilient these creatures were, and she surmised that the only sure way to kill one quickly was decapitation. She had also learnt that they seemed to be petrified of submergence in water, but this information was currently of no use to her.

*

Another two days passed before anyone in Whitefalls received confirmation that the enemy had taken over a town five miles west of the city. Their army had demolished the bridge to the university and had sealed and reinforced every single one of the castles external doors, and soldiers had been posted ready for whenever the invaders struck.

John had not spoken to Orak or Mac since he had arrived in Whitefalls, but Shoa had tried to talk to him on their behalf. He had pushed her away too, even though he knew deep down that just like when she had broken into Gloria's garage and sent them here, she was just doing what they had asked her too.

Gloria had also been keeping her distance from Mac and Orak, but although she now understood that Shoa had knowingly taken her on such a dangerous path, she did not attempt to push her away.

Every day they would wait for news from the soldiers in search of Maria, and every day they were disappointed to hear none. Orak had even tried to convince Kyra to send more soldiers to search, but she was highly reluctant to do so, being so close to the eve of battle.

She had agreed to send a messenger to Ladaan Ijeda, a city close to the forest, asking whether they could send out people to search. She received a reply by pigeon, saying that they would send an entire legion on the condition that she warned them when the enemy approached in time to bring back their soldiers.

When Orak told John about what Kyra had done, the silence between them was broken. "It's a huge forest, but there's more than sixty men searching now," he explained. "They're bound to find her."

"How many people were looking for me?" John asked.

"Nobody knew where to look," Orak replied. "We know roughly where Maria arrived in the forest. She won't have travelled as far as the rest of us because she doesn't know where to go."

"But she's alone," John snapped, slamming his fist down on the common room table, "Don't you get it? I only survived because I was lucky."

"We'll just have to hope she's lucky too," said Orak. You need to be together over the next few days, there's going to be a lot more casualties. You and Gloria are the best field surgeons we've got."

"I'm not a field surgeon though," said John. "I work in a hospital or worked in a hospital . . . as a nurse, and not an especially good one."

"I beg to differ," said Orak.

John had not been thinking much about this war. He thought it would be like the wars in Afghanistan and Iraq, where the fighting was hundreds of miles away, while he sat at home perfectly safe. When Orak spoke about him being a field surgeon, it dawned on him that this conflict would be right up close. The armies wouldn't just pass them by. Whitefalls was a prime target for the enemy. He wouldn't be as safe behind these thick stone walls as he first thought. None of the thousands of people in the castle would be.

"What are our chances?" he asked.

Orak sighed, standing up to leave. "Kyra's a good general, and our soldiers are highly skilled. If you can kill a Drathmork without any training, then maybe it'll do good to let everyone fighting know that."

John decided to take a walk around the university. Maybe seeing how secure the place was would make him feel less troubled. However, walking around the courtyards seemed to have the opposite effect. The walls formed a good perimeter, but within them, the buildings had no means of protection. Most of them had large glazed windows and thatched or timber shingle roofs. Once the enemy breached the walls, they could access anywhere with ease.

John would be inside the building with Gloria and her shotgun. Shoa had collected twelve rounds from the beach, giving them a chance to take out up to twelve enemies. Some of the civilians hiding out would have swords, but very little skills. The odds definitely seemed stacked against them, but instead of fleeing they sat there waiting.

Despite how crowded it was inside, the grassy playing fields and patios between the buildings were deserted. Maybe people were frightened that a stray arrow would fly over the walls, even though the enemy was still far away from the city.

John was staring intently at a large oval drain that went through the wall, trying to assess whether it could be a weak point. It had two thick metal grids across it, but without them it would be big enough even for a person as big as Orak to crawl through.

He was so focused on this vent and working out whether it could pose a problem that he didn't see Shoa walking up behind him.

"It'll be bricked up," she said, causing him to jump.

"Still doesn't solve the problem that our enemy can fly," he replied. "Are you going to be fighting?"

"I'll do what I can," she said simply.

"What do you think our chances are?" he asked, as Orak hadn't given a straight answer.

"I try not to think about it. You look like you could do with a drink," she said.

John smiled for the first time in days, "Are you old enough to drink?" he asked.

"I'm seventeen," she replied, "And what do you mean?"

"Back in Britain, you need to be over eighteen but yes . . . a drink sounds good," he said.

Shoa took him to a small tavern just outside the castle walls, through the only door which hadn't been barricaded shut. It looked a lot like any other traditional pub back home, except that it was meant to be a very modern student bar. When they got there, they found it was almost completely empty.

Shoa bought them both drinks, as John had no money. Whatever it was they were drinking, it tasted like cheap lager mixed with a strong liqueur tasting of aniseed.

Unused to this drink, John drank his at the pace he usually drank at, while Shoa sipped hers slowly. "You'll kill yourself if you're not careful," she said.

"Hey, we're all going to die soon anyway," he slurred, spilling his drink, "Probably tomorrow."

"Maybe Mac will figure out a way to get you home soon," Shoa said, more in hope than expectation.

"And maybe pigs will fly. Do pigs fly on this world?" John asked.

Shoa shook her head, then glugged down her drink to catch up with John, "Like you said, we'll all be dead tomorrow anyway."

Her face contorted and she stuck out her tongue. It didn't taste anywhere near as nice when drank quickly.

"I'll get this one," John said, dropping his empty wallet on the floor.

Shoa picked it up and flicked through his cards, laughing at the ID pictures. She came across a small tattered photograph amongst the thick wad of receipts. "She's quite pretty," Shoa said.

"You can see where I get my good looks from," John replied, "That's my mother."

"Do you miss her?" Shoa asked.

"Every day," he said, "Do your parents live in Whitefalls?"

Shoa shook her head, "They left the day after I went to Earth. I don't know where they went, but it's somewhere safer than here. This stuff tastes nicer the more you have of it."

"Hey, show me some of those magical powers you've got," John said, changing the subject before they could talk more about their impending doom.

"It's not magic," she replied.

"Magic is just science you don't yet understand. Do you understand how it works?" asked John.

"Well . . . no, nobody does fully," replied Shoa, "But do you understand how a computer works?"

"No, not really," he replied.

"So surely, to you computers are magic too," she said with a smile.

"Ok, show me your powers then," said John.

"I can't. We're in a public house, it's illegal," she replied.

John suddenly imagined a poster campaign; *Think. Don't drink and throw fire from your hands.* He laughed out loud. "Where else is it illegal?"

"Sports with normal humans like yourself, parliamentary buildings, libraries and shops. It's not recommended indoors anywhere, but not always enforced everywhere."

"Is it the same for Telepaths?" John asked.

"Telepaths are considered far more dangerous," she replied. "A lot of bars don't even allow them in, but some cater exclusively for them."

"Why?" asked John inquisitively.

"If you have someone who can put thoughts into people's heads in a building full of drunken people, they can essentially completely control someone's mind. Often people need to declare their race before entering," replied Shoa.

"So much for equality," said John.

Shoa shrugged, "When you think the powerful minority posed as gods and ruled as tyrants for thousands of years, I think people are being quite lenient. It has been fifty years since the revolution though. Most of the people who were ruling then are long gone."

"This place that's invading . . . Alkak-Taan, how are the magical minorities still in power?" asked John.

"The revolution just didn't reach them" Shoa replied. "There are still quite a few countries like it where nothing has changed."

John took a small sip of his second drink. He had slowed down; after one drink he had already started to lose his balance. The strange tasting beer helped him forget about the coming siege to some extent. More than anything, it just made him care less.

Without him realising, Shoa had somehow drank more than him, and was giggling inanely at nothing in particular. She tried to stand up, but caught her sandal like shoe on her robes and fell onto John.

Catching her in his arms, John shuffled backwards, before sitting her down on a table. "We should go back," he suggested.

"No, I want to stay," she snapped, pushing him away, "I don't want to go back to the castle, packed full of strangers, with no room to breathe."

John got two glasses of water from the bar. Shoa glugged hers down, and then stuck her finger in the empty tankard. The water vapour in the air began to condense on the inside of the vessel and pour down to the bottom. By the time the glass was half full again, John asked, "Should you be doing that?"

"As long as I'm not brewing my own beer, they won't care," she replied.

By the time Shoa was ready to leave, they had both sobered up a bit. They reached the castle door just as it was about to be bolted shut. As they reached the dormitories, before going their separate ways, Shoa turned to John. "If we survive, we should do this again."

Standing on tip toes, she kissed his cheek. He looked at her and gave a weak smile before saying goodnight and closing the door behind her.

Shoa sighed. She knew she was wasting her time. Returning to her own dorm, she went straight to bed. She needed her rest; tomorrow would be a big day.

Chapter 25

Maria had been unable to leave the immediate area around Jekka's house, not because she wasn't free to do so, but out of fear of getting lost again. They had gotten into a routine over the past few days. They would get up at sunrise, hunt for or just cook breakfast then spend an hour or two trying to learn each other's language. After that Jekka would repair or build furniture for the house, then after lunch he would try and teach Maria more combat skills until tea time.

Today was different though. They had breakfast as usual, and left without washing up. Jekka took Maria on a different route through the forest, making sure she was close by. They walked for the best part of three quarters of an hour, before stopping for what Maria thought was to rest.

They had stopped right by a tree which had either been dyed or painted bright red. Jekka shouted something in the air then waited. A moment later, a heavily built man carrying a spear and a sheathed sword came through the trees to greet him. The two men exchanged a few short words, before the stranger tied a length of rope around Jekka's wrist and led him in the direction he had come from.

Maria had no idea what was going on, but followed in silence. She nearly gasped out loud when she eventually stepped out into an area not surrounded by trees. After blinking a few times, she stared out at the open fields. More trees could be seen about a mile in front of her, but to the west she saw nothing but dark grey mountains.

Running to catch up with Jekka and whoever seemed to be holding him captive, she saw a small town emerge beyond the towering crops as she fought through them.

People all around stared and backed away from the prisoner, as he was escorted to a large open market area. With his free hand, Jekka took out a few large heavy coins and handed them to Maria. "Help me," he said, pointing at one of the stalls.

She now understood where he got his candles and the flour for his bread from. Maria found a woven basket to carry all of the products that Jekka pointed out to her. Once they had finished, the basket was full, and Maria struggled to carry it. Jekka took it off her with ease.

The guard still had Jekka's other hand bound to his, so he gestured to the one remaining coin in Maria's hand. "You for," he said.

Maria looked around the market. She had no idea what this coin was worth, but she tried matching the price tags of the products with the symbols on the coin. The mystery of where he acquired most of his possessions had been answered, but two far more baffling questions had arisen. *Why was he bound by rope and under constant supervision, and where was he getting this money from?* She was starting to realise that she still knew nothing about him.

This was the perfect opportunity to break free from the forest, but where could she go from here? Despite having less of a sense of whether she could trust him than before, Jekka was her best chance of survival.

She stayed close to him while she searched the market. Her eye was caught by something she wasn't expecting to see. Sitting on the table beside some vases and unlabelled bottles, was a 350ml bottle of triple distilled vodka. The strangest thing was; the label was in English.

Maria laughed. This must have been in the garage when they were brought through. Buying the vodka, she just about managed to fit it into the already over flowing basket. This would be useful as an antiseptic if ever they needed it.

The guard escorted Jekka back to the forest, until they were at the painted tree. He sawed through the rope and left Jekka with a sore, reddened wrist. Maria stared at him, waiting for some kind of answer.

"Later," Jekka replied.

She knew that later meant another day. She was sure the explanation wasn't a simple one, and that it would take time to learn how to put his message across.

*

John woke up late, expecting the enemy to be at their gates, but they weren't. The entire castle seemed to be on heightened alert. The large open windows had almost all been blocked by upturned tables or doors torn from their hinges. Not a single soldier could be seen inside.

The army had been up all night, evicting people from their homes in Lower Whitefalls, and forcing the people of the upper city to share their homes. A platoon had been assigned to stay camped out at the top of the two spiral staircases near the edge of the cliff. They had been digging trenches for hours, and when John saw this, he was worried this would be a repeat of the First World War.

On top of the wide castle walls, barrels could be seen every few metres, packed tightly with thousands of arrows. The steel arrow heads were as sharp as anything he had ever used to shave with, and would cut through flesh like a hot knife through butter.

Kyra seemed frantic as she made sure everything was exactly right, and that everybody was ready. It was mid-morning when a deafening long drawn out horn blast sounded. A second later, an alarm sounded. A dozen large brass bells fixed to a rig, all connected, sounded at once. It could be heard from anywhere in the city and was harrowing.

The castle burst into life. Soldiers who had been strolling around the courtyards ran to their stations, while huge warehouse style doors opened and massive wooden contraptions were wheeled out.

Orak was hauling out what looked like a gigantic crossbow. The device was over three feet long and resembled a medieval Ballista. Once it was in place, he turned a hand crank until the siege weapon was pointed up towards the sky. He checked the device was secure before returning to bring out another of these weapons.

John was ordered to go back inside the building, to the hall which had been emptied out to use as a hospital ward.

Kyra stood on the wall amongst her best archers. She held a large brass telescope to her eye and looked down at the evacuated city below. Several people, who had previously refused to move, were running for their lives towards the tunnels. At the edge of the city, moving like a black flowing shroud, the enemy approached.

The rows of marching soldiers stretched out as wide as the district they entered, covering every square foot of open land. They bashed their swords against their shields in unison in an attempt to unnerve their opposition, nearly drowning out the sound of the alarm.

Kyra scanned the crowd; they were all human. She had been told that many Drathmorks were among the attacking party, and suspected that as these creatures could move so much quicker, they were holding back; waiting.

"This is what we've trained for!" she shouted, "Positions!"

Every available soldier congregated on the walls and guard towers. Shoa, who had also slept in, ran out into the courtyard to join the other Spellcasters that the general had recruited.

She looked up at the wall where over a hundred archers stood. From here, she couldn't see anything beyond them, but noticed that the large drain at the base of the wall had not been blocked off. A small party of bowmen were stood beside the hole, ready to fire through if necessary.

Through the gap, she saw the horizon beyond the furthest reaches of the lower city. One second it was completely clear, the next she saw nothing but fluttering dark shapes, as a vast cloud of winged soldiers dominated the skyline.

Chapter 26

Hundreds of soldiers in smoke blackened armour ran through the streets of the lower city. With their shields held above their heads, they defended themselves from the arrows raining down from above.

Reaching the tunnel at the base of the vertical rocky cliffs, they began to ascend the staircases. More arrows descended down the shaft, cutting down the unfortunate, while their brothers in arms stepped over their bodies. The tunnels filled with a mass of armed men, trying their best to move quickly in their heavy armour, while rocks hammered down on their raised shields.

Bursting out from the open doorway at the top, a lone soldier was dazzled by the blinding light reflected from the sun. He staggered backwards and the last thing he saw before a projectile pierced his skull was a set of large mirrors angled to face him.

As several others surfaced, blocking their eyes with their bucklers, they heard a Tontoltec solider yelling something, before hearing a metallic clang. Their feet began to feel wet, and they looked to see a huge wall of water crashing down upon them.

The emptying canals gushed down the tunnel, swirling at speed, dragging everything and everyone down. Those who didn't drown were impaled on their comrade's swords or grated against the walls.

At the bottom of the staircase, the water pouring out was tinted red from the bloodshed, dragging more soldiers down into the pool and under the raging waterfall.

"Seal the shafts," a commander at the top of the cliff yelled.

A dozen men hauled a heavy iron circle across, before dropping it down over the tunnel entrance. On the other side of the waterfall, the other staircase was sealed off.

As the foot soldiers retreated, the swarm of bloodthirsty Drathmorks streaked through the sky towards the castle.

"We've delayed them, three days at best," General Kyra said to one of her troops as she watched the enemy infantry fleeing through the telescope. As confident as the general sounded, the legionnaire couldn't keep his eyes off of the sky.

*

The winged beasts approached faster than any army she had ever seen. In the air, they began to form rows, each spaced enough apart for them to strike in waves. They were far more organised than she had hoped.

The cliff top guards fired into the sky as the swarm passed over, knowing this would be their last battle. A few arrows struck, and even fewer made kills.

The wounded Drathmorks swooped down, followed by the rest of their regiment. A second volley of fire struck down many more airborne enemies, but there was no time for a third.

The battle was now on the ground. The Drathmorks drew their swords and metal clashed with metal. Now the real battle had begun.

Screeching like enraged eagles, the creatures attacked with unrivalled violence, biting and clawing when they could no longer duel. With the ability to glide, the invaders could strike downwards on even the tallest of humans with great force, and the feud was short lived.

Sustaining heavy casualties, the humans fought until the point of death, taking as many enemies with them as they could. Once every man lay on the ground, unable to fight again, the handful of surviving creatures flew off to join their brothers.

*

Behind the university's palisade wall, the Spellcasters stood ready to act on the general's word.

"You know the plan?" an armoured man standing beside Shoa asked her, noticing that she had just arrived.

119

She nodded, red faced and out of breath. The other Spellcasters took several steps back on command, giving them a better view.

Kyra screamed a command at the top of her voice. A sudden powerful gust of wind blew against the enemy, catching in their wings and pushing them backwards. They flapped hard to push against the gale, and for several seconds while the forces marched, they were stationary in the air.

Every archer fired at once and the Drathmorks dropped like flies. The powerful wind stopped suddenly and unharmed creatures swooped down and began hacking apart the soldiers on the wall.

Kyra drew her sword and picked up the shield of a dead soldier. Every creature which landed near her was swiftly beheaded, and every slash in her direction was blocked or dodged. Men all around her were being cut down, but many prevailed.

Their armour, although thin, was good at defending slashes rather than stabs. This was a slight advantage because the enemy carried curved scimitars. In spite of this, the shear strength of these hybrids meant that they were slicing through chest plates like they were tin foil.

Shoa was ordered to go back inside. As she ran to the nearest building, a creature that had crossed over the wall dived for her with its talon like claws ready to strike.

Turning around, she hurled a bolt of lightning at its throat. The creature didn't even react. She fired a second crackling stream of electricity into the beast's eyes.

It screeched again, and unable to see, it collided with a large stone buttress as Shoa darted through an open door. The door was swung shut and bolted. Other creatures behind battered against it inefficiently, unable to break through.

*

In the great dining hall, which was temporarily being used as an infirmary, a sudden and large number of patients were brought in. Many died before John, Gloria or any of the student medics could even see them; the enemy was very thorough. Most of the survivors would be unable to return to their duties; many wouldn't see tomorrow.

Gloria had relocated a patient's arm for the first time in her life, but felt no satisfaction in doing so as he walked off ready to rejoin the battle. She turned to John, who was struggling to stop an arterial bleed. With no machines, few tools and no drugs other than medicinal herbs, their job was torturous. A moment later, he turned away as a student draped a cloth over the deceased's body.

"There's nothing we can do," he said, looking across at the vast sea of patients waiting for them. These were just the priority cases. There were dozens more outside with missing fingers and broken bones.

A man John had given an emergency tracheotomy to just minutes ago was walking amongst the beds, with a tube still sticking out of his throat, labelling the patients with red dye. Those who could be treated had a circle and those who couldn't; a cross.

"We need more space!" John shouted.

"What's this?" the student asked.

"Sprite venom, it's the fastest acting thing we've got to end their suffering," he replied.

John couldn't believe what he was doing, but even in a hospital back home, many of these patients would never survive. They would cling on for hours in unimaginable pain; it was the kindest thing he could do for them.

He wished he could pause to grieve for everyone that passed away under his knife, but there was no time.

In the corner of the room, was a bed of hot coals and an iron poker. These practices were far more basic than anything he'd encountered, but they were all he could do. His next patient was bleeding heavily from a shoulder wound, which he cauterised with the red hot piece of iron. With no forms of anaesthetic at John's disposal, the patient had to be restrained and passed out with the pain.

The room emptied quicker than he had anticipated, but it soon became obvious why. The students, who had been helping treat the patients, were stacking the bodies in the next room, many with tears streaming from their eyes.

Gloria began mopping the blood soaked floor, while every few minutes somebody would bring a bucket of fresh water. Where John had been working there was so much of it that he could barely walk without slipping. He wanted to crawl into bed and cry, but he knew there would be many more to come.

*

Orak swivelled the heavy ballista around, tilting it back on its turret. The taut cable held a small wooden rack where four short spears were slotted. Attached to these giant arrows was a chain mesh.

The creatures still soared over the wall. Orak aimed, and then yanked the trigger back. The spears shot from the bow like a bullet from a gun. Only one projectile struck flesh, but the large net hanging between them engulfed a swarm of Drathmorks. Closing around them, it forced their wings shut, causing them to plummet thirty feet onto the battlements.

Soldiers nearby rushed towards the trap full of creatures and stabbed repeatedly through the holes in the net. Orak began reloading the device, while another Titan fired the second weapon.

Another cluster of flying warriors was dragged down, colliding with the thatched roof of a dormitory building. The doors burst open and everyone who had been hiding inside ran out into the court yard. Most reached the stone tower safely, but several perished by the scimitars of the enemy.

The once empty courtyard was now the site of the battle. The clash of metal and the cries of pain were all that could be heard.

Orak looked up at the wall to see only a handful of soldiers left fighting. The number was cut by one, as he saw a man cut in half by two blades closing on him like scissors. His upper body fell back, crashing down onto a barrel of arrows which scattered across the gravel.

The Titan beside Orak reloaded in time to catch a group of creatures as they flew towards him. One attacker dodged the net, and swung its sword at the man, slitting his throat.

The Drathmork grabbed the handles of the siege weapon and tilted it to face the wall. Orak ran to stop it, but another creature swung for his head. He ducked, narrowly avoiding the blade.

As he fought off the creature, the siege weapon was fired at the wall. A spear cut through Kyra's thigh, as the wide net wrapped around a section of the wall guard. She screamed as the weight of the full net dragged her and many of her men over the wall.

The spear snapped as she struck the hard ground outside the castle, tearing through the muscle and nearly severing the limb entirely. She dragged herself along the ground by her fingers, while more creatures swooped down to snatch up the wounded men to finish them off. She managed to hide in a corner where a guard tower joined the wall, with only the broken head section of the spear to fend off any attackers.

Orak duelled with the beast until its weapon was knocked from its hand by a powerful blow from the Titan's broadsword. He took the opportunity to swing for the beasts head, severing it in one strike.

Sprinting up a set of steps leading up the castle wall, he jumped all the way down to the other side, rolling to disperse the force of impact. He ran to Kyra and scooped her up into his arms. Swinging her over his shoulder, he fought off another creature with his free hand.

He carried her to the back of the castle once the beast was slain. With his sword and his foot, he smashed through the small barricaded door. Dropping the general off with a few of her soldiers, Orak stood guard at the now open doorway.

"Get her to the hall," he shouted, glancing back at the barely conscious woman lying across the stone floor. He knew that even after such a horrific injury she would be walking again within days, but he still felt concern.

Very few Drathmorks remained, but the castle which had been packed full of soldiers was now the site of a massacre. Bodies of both species littered the ground, their blood staining the grass and soaking into the soil.

With few men to stop them, the enemies smashed through an unblocked window on the top floor of the main tower. A volley of arrows cut most of them down, but the survivors cut apart the armed civilians while they were reloading.

The four remaining Drathmorks ran through the corridors unchallenged. They reached a turning and began to go down it, before seeing that it was a dead end. They turned back to see that a wall was now blocking the way they had come.

Confused and panicked, the creatures looked at each other, but saw only humans. Screeching with rage, they attacked.

When only one creature stood bleeding heavily from his wounds, he looked down at his own kind lying around him. The doors either side of the corridor reappeared. As the beast died, the last thing he saw was a pair of cloaked humans standing in the doorway.

Chapter 27

The following day, a foul stench filled the air around the university. Dozens of wooden carts were piled high with bodies and a huge pyre had been erected in one of Upper Whitefalls' many large squares. The enemy soldiers were tossed onto the fire, while the soldiers and civilians who had lost their lives awaited burial.

Several patients still remained in intensive care, but without any monitoring equipment, they could slip away at any time. John had not had any sleep since the battle, and had only stopped for half an hour to have something to eat.

Gloria had left the hall to sleep for a few hours. When she returned, John went for a much needed rest. There was little more either of them could do to help, but they felt compelled to stay with their patients in case there was.

Kyra had left the hospital ward in an iron wheelchair that morning, and by midday she was using crutches to move around. Her leg was far from healed, but had been crudely stitched back together, and was well on its way to reattaching itself. Every bruise and scratch had vanished, but she still felt the broken ribs that she'd told nobody of, shifting under her skin. Another night and they would be back to normal.

She had told Administrator Shrax that they would be pulling out of the castle, but the enemy would be back at the gates within six or seven days. Without being able to use the passages through the cliffs, the Alkak-Taanan foot soldiers would go the long way around, which meant sailing across the lakes. Although the invading force would be more vulnerable in the water, they were still outnumbered twenty to one, and most of her soldiers would be in no fit state to fight by then.

She would be leaving the city, and suggested he do the same. The nearest fortified town was more than fifteen miles away, but if people left early enough, she was sure most of the city could get there safely.

Shrax didn't apologise for trying to stop the military takeover. He wouldn't have apologised if he had started the war, but Kyra knew that he was sorry.

*

Above the hall, a disused laboratory had been commandeered by Mac for experimental purposes. Upon an operating table lay a deceased Drathmork. Of all the bodies outside, this was the most intact.

Using a steel bladed scalpel, he had cut away sections of the creature's tough flesh. He had used a saw designed for cutting metal to cut through ribs, and prised open the chest cavity. He saw a large cardiac muscle in the usual place, but several inches lower and more in line with the spinal cord was a second slightly smaller heart. If the primary heart was lost, the second would keep them alive long enough to fight for a few more minutes. This creature had been specifically engineered to squeeze that little bit more life out of it on the battlefield.

There were very few major blood vessels in the creature's body, but vast numbers of capillaries to transport its blood. This meant it was less likely to bleed to death from deep cuts, with the exception of its jugular vein, which had been severed in this specimen. Another interesting feature that he discovered was that its spine was covered by a thick casing of dark coloured bone, far tougher than calcium phosphate, more like the density of tooth enamel. This explained why, when the soldiers hacked at the back of the creatures necks, they had been unsuccessful.

Mac had discovered first hand that the Drathmorks were not as intelligent as humans. They had been so easily influenced by mental suggestion that he had helped trick them into killing each other. He also knew that they were frightened of water, possibly as they would be too heavy to swim, even though their powerful wings would allow them to move easily through water.

Once he had finished writing up what he had discovered from the post mortem examination, he asked the soldiers overseeing him to take the body to the bonfire with the rest of them. Mac's head still throbbed from the exertion of creating such a powerful illusion, but it took his attention away from the pain that still lingered in his lungs.

On his way back to his dormitory, he met Orak in the hallway. He tried to explain about the research he had been conducting, but was interrupted by the irate looking Titan.

"Six days," Orak exclaimed.

"What's in six days?" Mac asked.

"That's how long before the enemy invades again, which means we have four before we have to leave," replied Orak.

"Go where though? Nowhere is safer than this castle," said Mac.

"Then we use distance to protect us," suggested Orak. "We go south like we discussed, sail through the gulf and keep going to the southernmost point of Tontoltec. The enemy won't reach us for months."

"And in a few months?" exclaimed Mac.

Orak shrugged his shoulders, "We think of a new plan. Do you have any better ideas?" he asked.

Mac didn't reply. He had been thinking the same thing himself, but it only delayed the inevitable. "We'll talk it over with the others first. Ask Shoa, John and Gloria to meet us tonight for dinner. Did you lose anyone . . . In the battle?"

"A few of the soldiers I knew, but not well. A student of mine died as well . . . Adra Kree?" explained Orak.

Mac nodded, "I taught her too. She should never have been involved." After saying this, they both went their separate ways.

Over the next few hours, the castle became quieter. Most of the refugees went back to their homes to pack their most treasured and important possessions. There would be a train of carts leaving the city in the morning, and if it was up to them alone, Mac and Orak would be on that train.

By nightfall, there were less than a hundred people left in the university. John had never seen it this quiet, as he had arrived during the chaos. For the first time, he could admire the craftsmanship that went into decorating each and every room. Compared to the places he had been in this world up until this point, the university was a palace.

He arrived in the small dining room at eight o'clock, before the others got there. He guessed this room was normally reserved for staff dining, as the large oak table only had eight chairs around it.

A chef stood waiting in the corner of the room, ready to take their order. A menu had been written on a piece of parchment lying on the table, but it had been written in Tontoltec. The chef was a student of catering and fine cuisine, and had agreed to do this for only the cost of the food ingredients in order to earn extra credit.

Orak turned up later, shortly followed by everyone else. He read out the menu in English, and once they had ordered, he started to explain why he had brought everyone here.

"I've come to think of the five of us as a team," he said, "Through unfortunate circumstances I know, but we're bound together through obligation and necessity, and I'd like to think eventually, trust and friendship."

"What's this about?" Gloria cut in.

He went straight to the point, "We need to leave the castle and I think we should all travel together. This would mean sailing together, and we would be in each other's company all day and every day for a long time."

John frowned. He had been deliberately keeping his distance from them since he had arrived in Whitefalls. "Go where?" he responded, "We need to wait here for Maria, she'll come here when she's found."

Orak and Mac exchanged glances, "It's been a long time," Mac explained, "I know you don't want to hear this, but the chances of her still being alive aren't high."

"I'm not going anywhere without her," snapped John.

"We can't just forget her," Gloria added, "If she's out there, the only way she will find us is if we stay."

Orak reached into his pocket and took out a folded piece of lambskin parchment. He unfolded it and scanned its contents. "This is a copy of a letter that the general is sending the Government of Tontoltec," he explained, "She's said that the army will be moving out in two days, and that as many civilians as possible should also leave. It requests sanctuary in other towns and cities, and assistance of food rations and temporary shelters. It also specifies that the enemy, after being attacked from the cliffs, have started to travel around them. It says they will be here in six days."

John felt his heart lurch. "There's going to be another battle?" he said.

"No, there's going to be a massacre," replied Orak. "We can't wait longer than four days, and even that is taking a risk. We're leaving four days from now, whether Maria has found us or not. I'm sorry; that's final."

"Oh, really?" Gloria snapped before John had the chance to, "And you just expect us to follow you?" The argument fell apart in her mouth. She had to go with them.

"The thing is, I think leaving it four days is cutting things too close," Mac added. "The human foot soldiers might take six days, but they've also got a small number of those creatures I saw when we were on Earth. Without an army, if those things arrive earlier than the rest of the Alkak-Taanan soldiers, we've got little chance of fighting them off, even if there's only half a dozen of them."

Shoa was about to open her mouth, when Mac prematurely answered her question. "I'd guess they'd be here in three days, so we need to leave the day after tomorrow."

"If there's only likely to be a few of them, we can fight them off," Shoa contributed. She had settled back down here, and didn't want to be uprooted again so soon. "You killed one before and we've got my powers, Orak's strength and John's got that shotgun."

"My shotgun," Gloria corrected her. "I know how to use it, it'd be better off in my hands."

Mac shook his head, "You don't know how tough these things are. It was a very one sided fight, I just got lucky. I'm not staying to fight them. Am I going to have to leave by myself?"

Orak placed his hand on the Telepath's shoulder, "If you believe they'll be here that soon, I'm with you."

"What about Maria?" John asked again.

This time, it was Gloria who told him that they couldn't wait around. "I know you don't want to fight anymore. It makes no sense in us dying waiting for her John."

Without saying anything more, John slowly nodded his head in agreement. He still held a glimmer of hope that two days would be enough for Maria to find them.

Chapter 28

The next morning, General Kyra had woken early and ordered every soldier to assemble. She had been able to walk to and mount her horse unaided, although her leg was still in a lot of pain. She addressed the small gathering of less than fifty men, which several days ago had been close to a thousand strong.

She instructed them to prepare to leave, and within half an hour they were ready to go. Before setting off, she paid a visit to Orak. Kyra pleaded with him to leave with them, but he was adamant they were staying for one more day. She offered to leave a few of her men with them, but he refused. Saying their tearful goodbyes, they parted.

Administrator Shrax had already left without telling anybody. With no presence of authority at the university, and with no lectures or assignments, the students were at a loss. Despite having nobody to enforce the rules, there was no anarchy. No one had the energy or the will to misbehave.

The whole city was shrouded with gloom, and as more and more people left, the sombreness turned to loneliness. Once again, the university became crowded; in a time of such despair, people needed each other's company.

True to her word, Shoa went back to the tavern with John. Unlike last time, the place was packed. They had to queue to get to the bar, but on the plus side, the drink prices had gone down.

In the middle of the bar, where you might expect a pool table, was a large square drawn on the ground, where two students were standing either side of a tall stool. John stared as they played a bizarre game involving pieces made of stone, which they circled around a map drawn on the stool.

"It's complicated to explain," Shoa said, "Even more so when you're drunk."

They took their drinks away from the busy main area to a partitioned off room, where there stood an actual pool table.

"So you learn more than just our languages looking through that mirror thing?" John asked, "Do you have to put 50p in to play?"

"No. They make enough profit here from the drinks. You know how to play then? Can you teach me?" she asked.

John knew he was good at pool; playing amongst his friends back home, he would almost always win. Setting up the balls, he noticed that they appeared to be carved out of wood and were well polished. Instead of being different colours, they had either a circle or a triangle painted onto them, and the black just used a dark wood stain. The baize on the table seemed to be made of short animal fibres, but had been dyed green to match the ones from Earth.

He demonstrated a few times, potting every ball he aimed for, and then passed her a cue. He knew this might take some time when the first question she asked was "It's this end you hold, right?"

Laughing, John gave her his cue and stood behind her, guiding her hands. He gave her detailed instructions, but she wasn't listening. Shoa struck the white ball and sent it flying off the table.

The ball rebounded off a nearby wall and smashed into a tankard, knocking it onto the floor. Shoa looked mortified then terrified, as a huge Titan well over eight feet tall got up. He threw his chair across the room and stood there with beer all down his previously clean shirt, fuming with alcohol fuelled rage.

Shoa stepped back, and John darted in front of her. The Titan grabbed the edge of the heavy pool table with one hand and tossed it to the side, like it was just a stool. Swinging his football sized fist through the air, he missed the human's head by a hairs width.

John grabbed Shoa's hand and ran, dragging her along behind.

Once they were outside the tavern, they both exploded into a fit of laughter. Barely able to stand up straight, Shoa said something in her native tongue before remembering and translating. "Did you see his face? Are all of your Earth games so dangerous?"

"If you're the one playing them, yes," he replied, nursing a stitch. "We probably shouldn't go back in for a while. What do you want to do?" he asked.

John found it strange that even though there were many English speaking students his own age around, he found a girl more than eight years younger than him better company. When he was around her, he found himself starting to forget about the worries elsewhere.

"We should go for a swim," she said excitedly, "I know a big lake with very few leeches and no sea serpents."

"I haven't got any trunks," said John, before asking, "Wait, did you say sea serpents?"

"Yeah, they're like dragons, but don't breathe fire or fly and live underwater, but there's none in the lake around here," replied Shoa. "Orak and his friends used to hunt them and they wiped out the local population years ago. You don't need trunks, nobody will see you, and it's outside the city."

"There are no sea serpents, but what else should I look out for? Man eating fish? Giant squid?" asked John.

"There's nothing dangerous, come on, it'll be fun," insisted Shoa.

"No, I'd rather stick to dry land," said John,

"Ok, I'll show you some of our sports," said Shoa. "There's a playing field not far from here."

Shoa took John to a huge field of cut grass. As skilful as he was at pool, John was incompetent at the games Shoa tried to teach him.

They played for hours, changing to a new sport every so often. While they enjoyed themselves, forgetting about the troubles around the world, a rowing boat was being moored in the harbour close by.

*

Administrator Shrax left his vessel unguarded and ran through the city towards the university.

He reached the castle to find the main doors wide open. This would never have been allowed under his watch. Strolling through the halls in a hurry, he saw students leaning against the walls looking bored. One stepped forwards to ask him if lessons were back on, but he just dodged past them without breaking pace.

As he entered the staff area, he hammered on each door, each time receiving no reply. When he reached Professor Kroez's office, he found Mac staring out of the window and bouncing a rubber ball against the wall without touching it.

When he saw Shrax he stood up and the ball flew out of the window. "You're back?" he exclaimed.

"Yes, I must apologise for leaving so abruptly, but we have bigger things to focus on right now," the administrator replied.

"What's this about?" asked Mac.

"I'll show you, follow me. I witnessed something in the wheat fields east of here. If it's what I think it is, we may have a problem."

Shrax led Mac up a flight of narrow wooden stairs behind a locked door. The staircase opened out onto an old, poorly maintained corridor. Moss and lichen grew on the exposed stone walls and the bare timber floor creaked with every step.

Most of the doors were wide open, despite all having heavily rusted iron locks. Mac knew these corridors well; they were used to store all of the learning institution's text books and spare lab equipment. Something else none of the students had ever seen was also kept here.

At the end of the corridor was a heavy solid oak door with a brand new steel lock. Shrax brought out a large key from a pocket inside his robes and slotted it into one of the two keyholes. Mac did the same with a second key, before they turned them simultaneously.

Through the door, was another narrow set of old wooden stairs. The passageway was dusty, and some of the steps were so rotten that they had fallen through. They walked up along the edge where a large timber ran underneath and was therefore more stable.

At the top of the stairs was a tall attic, spanning the whole roof of the building. A single small window in either gable wall dimly lit the space, aided by several well placed mirrors.

In the centre of the room, was a large raised stone circle, in which sat the biggest single piece of crystal in the country. The crystal was tinted blue and was cut and polished to be as flat as possible. The disc shaped stone gave off a faint glow, as if there was a light bulb beneath it.

"In the fields, I witnessed a man walk through the source of a warm breeze, and was knocked to the ground from an electric shock," Shrax explained, "When you severed the link, I knew it had worked because the glow from the window went out."

Mac looked down at the illuminated crystal, shaking his head. "This is impossible," he said incredulously.

"Yes, but quite obviously true. If it's like last time, it'll be . . ."

"Four years before we can go through," Mac cut in, "But this shouldn't have happened yet, not for many decades. What could be doing this?"

Administrator Shrax shrugged his shoulders, "You're the expert, Professor."

"I need to do some studies," said Mac. "Most of the students will have gone by now, I'll need a few volunteers to take soil and water samples."

"Do you think you'll have time? When are you leaving?" asked the administrator.

"Tomorrow," replied Mac.

"You're a braver man than I, WaMaktaJrei. I was reluctant to come back, but I felt you should know about this."

Shrax left in a hurry once again, stopping to say goodbye to nobody else but Mac. He did not disclose his destination out of fear of it being discovered by the enemy.

Once Shrax had gone, Mac looked down into the crystal window. No static electricity was present in the area like before, and he was unable to view anything through it, but there was definitely something there.

Chapter 29

John heard no word of Maria for the rest of the day, nor the following morning. As he packed a bag with the clothes and possessions he had accumulated, he felt lost. Once they were gone, all chance of ever finding her would be lost.

He had no idea whether she was even alive, but his gut instinct told him she was lost forever and it was his fault.

At noon, he met up with the others just inside the main castle gates. They crossed a newly built timber footbridge over the river, and arrived at the edge of the lake surrounding the upper city.

Shoa looked back at the white stone buildings amongst the glittering waterfalls. She was saying goodbye to her home forever, but this wasn't the first time. A confusing cocktail of emotions forced her to look away and push forward. As they all clambered into the large canoe like boat, she saw the same sadness in everybody's eyes. The city slowly disappeared into the distance, and Shoa brushed away a tear before anyone else noticed.

Gloria held her bag close, nervously looking at the water as the boat rocked from side to side. She could see all the way down to the bed of the shallow lake and felt queasy. She saw nothing but pebbles and sand. There wasn't a single shopping trolley or discarded drinks can in sight.

"How did the research go?" Orak asked, remembering Mac's revelation yesterday.

"I didn't get anywhere, there weren't enough people left to help," Mac replied. He turned to John and Gloria, "The link is starting to reopen."

Both their jaws dropped. "That means we can go home?" Gloria blurted out.

"I don't know how long it will take for the link to fully form, but it's happening quicker than last time. Something new is affecting it, but I can't understand how."

John said nothing and continued to stare out at the mountains beyond the lake. He wasn't especially excited about going home anymore. True he had lost his job, but he had enough money to tie him over. What would he do with Maria's money? This hadn't even occurred to him before now. He'd never allow himself to spend it, but he couldn't leave it in his cupboard, waiting for the rest of his life for her to come back for it.

He turned to Orak, "Will you all be coming back to Earth when the thingy opens properly?"

"I don't know," was his reply.

John turned to Mac, "You are though, right? You need to go back and close the thing again to stop this war getting to Earth? That's what all of this was about, right?"

Mac nodded, "Yes, when the link reforms fully, I'll take you back. Hopefully I'll find a way to reduce the spread of disconnected matter passing through as well."

After just over an hour of gentle rowing, they were across the lake. As it was a further twenty miles to the coast where a ship awaited them, they bought a horse and cart in the nearest town.

They all realised how well hidden the city of Whitefalls actually was as they rode south, now just two miles away. To John and Gloria, it had been more of a large town than a city. Regardless of its insignificance in the whole scheme of things, they all knew they would miss it.

The journey ahead was long, and nobody fully knew what to expect at the end of it. The south of Tontoltec had several cities similar in size to Whitefalls, but there were also vast areas of unmapped land. It was in these hundreds of square miles of uncharted territory that they would hide.

Orak, Mac and Shoa took turns at the front, steering the two horses while John and Gloria sat back not contributing. Neither of them had ridden a horse and cart before, let alone been in control of one. The road was very bumpy and the cart had nothing resembling suspension.

Suddenly a thought occurred to John, "Wait, are they called sea serpents because they live in the sea?"

"Well . . . . Yes," Mac said, baffled by this question.

"And we're going to be sailing on the sea?"

John looked to Gloria for support on this matter, but she was fast asleep.

"They aren't that common," Orak explained, "Like dragons, they were hunted a lot in the past."

"Yeah, but some of us have already encountered dragons . . . ," he said, gesturing to the sleeping passenger and to the driver at the front.

"Relax, we'll have a harpoon."

This did little to ease John's worries. Making his state of anxiety worse, Shoa jumped away from the reins into the back and screamed something in Tontoltec.

As Orak tied the canvas strap down, he looked at John and exclaimed, "Harpies!"

"What the f . . . ?!"

Before he could finish, the sound of thousands of beating wings surrounded them. Creatures bashed into and scraped across the sides of the carriage. One of them screamed like a frightened woman, before several others joined in melodically.

The screeching of the swarm drowned out the noise from the horses, and the speeding carriage slowly came to a halt. Within no time at all, there was silence.

Unfastening the flap, Shoa found her fear had been confirmed. John poked his head out to see neither of the animals who had been towing them. Spread across the floor, he saw several clumps of hair and spatters of blood. His stomach churned.

"What were those things?" he said, thanking whatever Gods may be out there that they were under cover.

"Harpies," Orak explained. "Piranha's of the sky, flesh eating swarm reptiles. They've been on your world before from what I've gathered, but I guess they all died out . . . . That swarm isn't likely to come back, they've had their feed."

"What did I miss?" Gloria asked sleepily.

"You don't want to know," Shoa told her.

John thought about the swarm and remembered his nightmare. It was hard to forget it.

"Mac?" he asked. "What do you know about the meaning of dreams?"

After explaining his recurring dreams down to every minute detail, including the ones he had in the desert, he saw the expression on the

Telepath's face. The expression was mirrored on Orak's, and his eyes darted between the two of them.

"What is it?" John asked, a slight quiver in his voice.

"Tell him Mac," Orak said, still looking at the two of them in turn.

"What you've just told me," Mac began, "Is an exact description of my own unconscious visions for the past few weeks."

"What? You're kidding right? That's impossible?"

"Impossible . . . but quite obviously true," Mac quoted.

"What does it mean?"

"I don't know, but I'm going to find out."

Leaving the cart, they all spent a long time searching the sky. Nothing else came, and they were glad when they found shelter.

They stopped for the night in an almost deserted town. As they were now on foot, it took them all of the next day to reach the harbour. They found the gallant sea vessel floating in the deep water, just a short row away from the pier.

It was nothing compared to the huge yachts or commercial ships John or Gloria had seen on Earth, but was large enough to carry fifty people in comfort.

The Black Diamond was a sturdy, well-made boat, with shining brass railings and a proud white sail, towering into the sky. It looked magnificent in the glistening water and far outshone every floating bathtub around it. This would be their home for more than a season, as they sailed to the unknown.

Chapter 30

Maria had stopped counting the days since she had been at Jekka's home. It had been nearly two months since he had first let her stay the night, and even now he gave no indication that he wanted her to go leave.

Every other week, they would go to the village, where Jekka would be escorted by guards to buy supplies. Every time they went, Maria received no word of explanation, but she knew he would tell her when he was ready.

Jekka regularly took her out hunting, and taught her the skills she needed to survive out in the wilderness. Twice he killed an animal she had never seen before, and took its carcass to another nearby town. He received similar treatment there too, but was paid large sums of money for the dead animal. He explained to her in very few words how the villagers would use every part of the animal for different things, and that they were very rare and hard to catch.

They still spent at least an hour a day sitting down, talking to each other. As their grasp on each other's languages improved, they spoke about the other's cultures, personal lives and views on anything and everything.

Maria's combat skills improved more and more with every session, as he taught her more and more weapon techniques and to strategise. It became apparent that Jekka had been a lot more than just a soldier, but that was long ago.

The building now had an extra two rooms built on to it; one for Maria to change and wash, and another for storing the clutter that accumulated in the main room. As time passed by, Maria thought less and less about the home she had left behind.

One day, when she had run to the well to collect a bucket full of water, she came across something she had failed to see every other time she had been there previously. Lying in the dry thatch of the well's roof, she saw something glinting in the sunlight. Hopping up onto the wall, she reached up and grabbed the object.

The reflection had come from the smooth shiny plastic screen of a mobile phone. She didn't recognise it as her own; it was far too old. She doubted it was John's either; she remembered he had a fairly new device. Maybe it was Gloria's.

Pressing the end call button down for several seconds, the screen lit up and she nearly dropped it out of surprise. The phone had a tiny amount of charge left, and a low battery warning flashed immediately. A second later, it died and she was unable to switch it back on.

Maria turned the mobile over and saw a label with the name Mark Jones written across it. She wondered why Gloria's husband would leave his phone in their garage.

As she went to put the phone in her pocket, it slipped from her hand and crashed down onto a rock. A wide crack appeared across the screen, and the battery fell out. Beside the sim card slot, was a silver sticker with a company logo and the words, 'Ithria Ltd' above it. Maria gasped in surprise, picked up the phone and re-read the name. There was no way this could be a coincidence; it made no sense.

She took the broken phone back with her, hiding it from Jekka, purely because it would take too long to explain what it was. He barely understood the reason she was here; this would just complicate things.

"You take longer this time," he said when she got back to the bungalow.

"How can you tell?" she asked.

Jekka shrugged his shoulders; he just knew. Maria didn't understand how or why, but he had a body clock almost as accurate as a real one, and could keep rhythm like a metronome. Maybe it was his lifestyle, or something in the water. Whatever it was, it wasn't rubbing off on her.

"Can take we walk?" Jekka asked, still not grasping the full complicated nature of English Grammar.

"I've only just got back from one," she replied, pointing at the full bucket of water.

"I show you something?"

Jekka disappeared outside to the storage room, then returned a moment later. He filled two hip flasks with water, then made sandwiches and wrapped them in large green leaves. Maria got the sense that this would not be a short walk.

She realised how right she was when after he rolled up a large wool blanket, he packed two sticks, some old rags and filled another bottle with some of the petrol that Maria had found. These were obviously to make torches; they would be going somewhere over night.

"Are we ready?" Jekka asked.

*

The Black Diamond had sailed through the gulf of Tontoltec without a hitch. With land always within forty or so miles, and with a vast peninsula shielding them from the powerful oceanic currents, they encountered nothing but gentle waves for over a month.

Now though, they had hit open sea. This had happened at the worst possible time, as a storm had formed around two hundred miles away and they were definitely feeling the effect.

The ship rocked violently, one way then the other. Water sloshed over the sides and poured into the cabins through cracks that had formed. For the first time in months, everyone inside felt cold.

Orak had hurried to drag the sails down, and had brought the specially designed mast level with the deck. As soon as the wind picked up, they safely sealed themselves inside, in fear of being blown overboard, and to shelter from the driving rain.

Shoa had tried hard to use her powers to reduce the effects of the elements, but the weather battled hard against her and she had been no match. Exhausted, she held on tight to the fixtures of the ship along with everyone else, waiting for the storm to pass.

Eventually, they decided it was too risky to continue on their current path; against the direction of the unyielding wind. They all assisted in using the vessel's emergency rows to change course and head back towards land. They would make berth over a hundred miles north of their intended destination and find somewhere safer to stay for the next few days.

The Black Diamond skimmed across a large jagged rock as it got closer to the shore, jolting the ship suddenly and changing their direction. The vessel twisted out of control and struck another rock, tearing a hole down the side of the wooden hull.

Mac leapt up as he saw water pouring through under the door. He burst through and saw it coming through the wall of the next room.

Turning a table over, he and John pushed it against the tear. The water trickled down underneath it, but the majority of the flow had stopped.

Orak regained control of the vessel, but nearly tore the rudder off. Once he had gotten the ship back on course, he ran to help out with the next problem. He hammered large iron nails into each corner of the table, fixing it tight enough against the hull to stop the flow completely.

As the coastline became visible through the thick fog and sheets of heavy precipitation, the waves became less extreme. The ship came shuddering to a halt when the stern of the ship encountered sand. It cut through the land and wedged itself in place, while the sea whipped and shoved against it. Orak hurled the small rowing boat overboard, while the others climbed down a ladder into it.

They arrived on the beach, soaked to the bone. Shoa formed a temporary shelter by stopping the water from reaching them as they ran to find cover, which they found in the form of a large tunnel.

They had arrived in what looked like an abandoned town. The tunnel was built of clay bricks and had slots where gates had been. It had once served as a passageway into the settlement. The buildings looked half demolished and were covered with ivy and moss.

"Do you see any that have roofs?" John asked, squinting to try and make out some detail through the downpour.

"How long do you think it will be like this for?" Shoa said in response.

Nobody could give an answer. It had been raining for so long, that they could barely remember what a clear sky looked like.

"Looks like quite a big place," Mac added, looking at the sheer number of buildings beyond the ones they could see clearly.

"Do you think anyone still lives here?"

"I doubt it," Orak said, taking out the telescope he had borrowed from the ship. He scanned the town from the shelter. All he could see were abandoned buildings and fields of mud, but he caught sight of one almost completely intact structure. "Follow me," he said, before squelching towards the undamaged house.

While the others trudged through no man's land, Mac glided just above the ground. Orak broke open the locked door and looked around the house. The wooden floor was as wet as outside and he nearly slipped as he stepped over the threshold. Mould had grown all over the walls, and gave off a smell that made Gloria retch.

"We've had enough vomiting this week already," John said to her, "We're on dry land now."

"Oi! Cheeky bugger! I don't travel well," said Gloria, punching him in the arm.

Mac began checking each room. All were void of furnishings, and had been completely flooded. He opened what he thought was a door, and found a staircase. At the top of the stairs, they found that the rooms were much drier.

"I guess we could stay here for the meantime," Mac suggested, noticing that there were several double beds upstairs. "I've found three, so some people will have to share."

Shoa looked towards John, but he looked away.

"Orak will need one to himself and the girls can go together, so I'll have to share with Mac; top to tail. I hope you don't snore."

*

Jekka led Maria down a path she had not walked before. She had started to get to know the forest well, but within a few minutes of leaving the house, she was somewhere unfamiliar.

The forest now looked just as it had when she'd first arrived, with every new section looking the same. At no point did she allow herself to drift further than a few metres from him, through fear of getting lost again.

The ground which had been more or less level the whole way, suddenly started to slope downwards. The trees became less crowded the lower they got, but as the ground flattened out they became just as close as before.

A little while later, a second drop appeared. Jekka steered them away, and Maria saw why. The drop was even higher than that of the watch tower.

The makeshift shoes that Jekka had made Maria were starting to rub, and she asked if they could stop for a few minutes. She had to remove the heavy stiff footwear and carefully walk barefoot.

Fortunately at this point, Jekka told her they didn't have much further to go. He even offered to carry her for the last half a mile, but she declined.

Jekka asked her to close her eyes. As he stood behind her, guiding her forwards, a smile appeared across her face. For the first time in a long while, she felt excited.

They stopped and Jekka took his hand away from her eyes. Maria almost fell over backwards when she saw what was ahead.

She had felt the ground change under her feet, but she had not guessed it was sand. They were standing on a beach of fine white sand, looking out at the crystal clear ocean.

Maria ran towards the sea and dipped her feet in the cool water. She laughed when she saw a dolphin leaping up and arcing through the air; so close that she felt the splashes as it broke the surface and crashed back down into the water.

"Where are we?" she asked, feeling as giddy as a school girl.

Jekka pointed to the sea and said "North."

The sun beat down hard on Maria's skin, and with no sun cream anywhere on this planet, she sought shade. Jekka led her to a cluster of palm trees, and laid down the woollen blanket in their shadow.

"We're here for a picnic?" she asked.

He looked at her blankly; she hadn't taught him that word yet. Maria had guessed right though. As he unpacked the sandwiches, he patted the blanket beside him for her to sit down.

Maria wondered why he hadn't brought her here before now. The place was completely secluded, and she guessed that she thought of it as his own. She felt honoured that he'd let her see this view.

Once they had finished their food, they lay back and stared at the white fluffy clouds floating across the vibrant blue sky. Maria wondered how anyone in a world so peaceful could hold enough hatred to start a war.

At this moment, looking down at the setting sun, she wondered how anywhere could be more beautiful. She turned to Jekka and saw the orange light reflecting in his eyes, and suddenly she was blind to all else.

"Thank you for bringing me here," she whispered softly.

The hesitation had gone. Her doubts and reservations were no more than concepts now. This time she instigated the kiss and Jekka didn't object. All thoughts of John and what they had together vanished from her mind.

With nothing but the trees as witnesses, they made love under the setting sun and fell asleep in each other's arms.

Chapter 31

John had not slept at all that night. He had been thinking far too much about what they had all been through and dreaded the idea of having more nightmares.

For the past month, he had been forcing himself to stay awake for days on end, and then sleep only when he was incapable of remaining conscious. He knew he could not maintain this routine; it would soon take its toll. For now though, it was the only way he could cope.

When he slept, he still dreamt; either of the harpies and the jagged rocks, or of the battle and an endless stream of mutilated soldiers being wheeled towards him.

He did everything he could to occupy his mind. So much had happened since he had arrived on Ithria that his life on Earth was now a distant memory.

He strolled around the house, searching for something to help him forget. He peered into the bedrooms and saw that everyone else was fast asleep. He knew that he could always talk to Gloria, and Shoa could help him take his mind off his worries, but only when they were awake.

The rain had nearly stopped, and the wind had died down a lot. John took this opportunity to go out and explore.

By the time he quietly crept down the creaking stairs and out of the front door, it wasn't even drizzling. It was warm enough to quickly dry his clothes, but the muddy ground still had the consistency of soup.

He looked inside the other crumbling houses but saw nothing of interest. In the clear daylight, he could see how big the town truly was, and quickly realised that it wasn't a town; it was a city. He walked further, and found himself leaving the residential area. Towers up to ten storeys high dwarfed the houses, but were just as dilapidated.

A huge sunken colosseum had become the home of hundreds of plants, but not a single human sat in any of its thousands of seats. The grass in the sports fields and children's playgrounds was over a foot high, and the swings and slides were just frameworks for vines and other creepers. John saw nobody; dead or alive.

An abandoned town he could understand, but this place was bigger than Whitefalls. No war or plague had struck this civilisation. The people had just left it to rot a long time ago.

By the time he got back, Orak and Mac were already awake. The first thing he said when he walked through the door was, "I've got a bad feeling about this place."

"We're not staying anyway," Mac replied, "As soon as everyone's awake and fed we're going back to the ship."

"What did you find?" Orak asked, noticing how unnerved John looked.

"Nothing," he replied, shaking his head, "That's what's worrying me. Something drove everybody out, and it wasn't this war."

"Did you find any food?"

John held out his empty hands, "We still have plenty of food on the Diamond."

"I think we're all getting fed up with dried or pickled stuff," Mac added, "Did you notice any fruit trees? Any fresh food?"

"I want to go back to the ship."

"Alright, you take the women back to the boat. We'll go and scavenge."

John did just that. He didn't like this place one bit. They took the rowing boat and left a flag on the beach for Mac and Orak to signal them when they needed collecting.

The two men left on land headed in the opposite direction, splitting up to cover more ground. After a little while, finding nothing but toxic or inedible plants, they crossed paths. Orak looked just as worried as John had been, but Mac seemed unfazed.

"What do you think happened here?" the Titan asked, emphasising the word 'you'.

"Well, this place looks like quite an affluent civilisation, and it's been abandoned for around fifty years. So I'd guess that during the revolution, these wealthy people were driven out by the peasants."

"If that was the case, why don't the peasants live here now?"

Mac opened his mouth, but no answer came out. He looked around, and then shrugged. "Whatever it was happened decades ago, I can't see it still being a problem today."

They walked together, coming across several trees, but only finding a few seeds worth eating. They had started to head back via an alternative route when Orak caught sight of the top of an apple tree. An orchard full of healthy looking berry trees and bushes was hidden behind a crumbling wall.

The barrier between them and the juicy ripe food looked too unstable to climb, and as Orak was preparing to break through it, Mac glided up towards the top of the tree. He picked an infestation free red apple and threw it down to Orak. As he reached for another, his hand stopped midway.

Staring down beyond the wall, he saw a huge hole dug into an open field. Thousands of flies buzzed around the area, and when they cleared Mac saw why they were there. "I think I know where the people went," he said as his skin turned pale.

*

Back on the Black Diamond, Shoa worked on bringing the mast back up. The hinged wooden pole weighed well over a tonne, and had always been raised and lowered by the ships only Titan. As he was not currently here, she had to improvise.

After John and Gloria unrolled the sails, Shoa sent a powerful gust of wind through them. They all hauled the timber the rest of the way by tugging at ropes tied halfway up, and eventually it locked into place.

The next problem would be to break free from the sandbank, which held the hull out of the water. They all tried rowing, but this did nothing. Shoa used her control over the water to move it back a few feet, but nearly collapsed from exhaustion. They had no choice but to wait for Mac and Orak to return before they could do any more.

The sea was so calm and the sky so clear, it was hard to believe they had recently been caught in such a catastrophic storm. Despite receiving such a heavy beating, the vessel remained almost completely intact.

Once the crew of three were sure there was nothing more they could do, they unpacked the sun beds from out of storage and relaxed out on deck. Both Gloria and John were now just as tanned as Shoa was. Ultra violet radiation was not considered a problem. Shoa had explained that Ithria had a thicker Ozone layer than Earth's.

"I don't know why they're bothering," Shoa said, as she watched the clouds, "We'll be arriving at the most southern point in a week or so, and we've got plenty of dried fruit still on board."

"Maybe they fancy a change," Gloria suggested, "I'm getting a little bored of what we've got."

"Me too," said John, "I'm got a craving for some proper food, like chicken kievs and potato wedges, with garlic bread . . . Curly fries, oh and steak. This world is nice and all but the food is . . ." He stopped mid-sentence and held out his hand for the others to be quiet. "Did you hear that?"

"Are they back?" Shoa asked, scanning the beach.

"No, whatever it was sounded closer, like . . . on the ship."

A second noise carried through the timber deck. This time all three of them heard it. Gloria rushed into the cabin and picked up her husband's shotgun and loaded it. Normally this would have been considered as overreacting, but they were all on edge after leaving the nearby city.

John picked up a relatively sharp kitchen knife and noting Gloria's firearm and Shoa's natural talents, felt like he had drawn the short straw.

The three of them slowly descended the stairs into the bowels of the ship. Passing the galley, they saw through the open door that pots and pans were scattered across the floor, and one of the wooden cupboard units was broken into several pieces. The storm had loosened many fittings, and this piece of furniture must have been gradually coming apart for a long time.

Gloria relaxed her grip on the trigger, but a second loud crash almost made her fire it. Shoa rolled up her sleeves as she crept out of the room to explore.

As more crashes and bangs came, they realised that they weren't coming from just one direction. When Shoa heard an eerie high pitched cackle from up ahead, she knew exactly what their problem was. She opened her mouth to speak, but as she did a glint of metal flashed before their eyes. A small knife streaked past John's head, millimetres too close, slicing through the flesh of his ear. Strafing out of the way, he felt the stinging wound and saw blood on his fingers.

"Goblins!" Shoa hissed with loathing, darting a glance through the doorway from which the projectile had flown. She had only seen one creature, but knew how easily they could hide. There could have easily been a lot more.

With their backs to the wall, John and Gloria had no idea what to do. Nobody had even told them there was really such a thing as a goblin. Their knowledge of children's fairy tales gave them little insight into what to expect.

Shoa darted across the doorway and in the split second she was in view of the opening, sent a cloud of yellow flames into the room. The goblins screamed and ran out through the door. As soon as Gloria saw one enter her field of view, she fired, blasting two creatures to the ground. Another two disappeared so quickly that they looked like blurs.

John looked down at the bodies of these small, thin grey skinned creatures. In stature they looked like people, but their protruding faces and large pointed ears made them look more like bats. The creatures looked to be between four and five feet tall, and were completely nude except for their loin cloths and leather chest belts, where they kept sets of throwing knives.

Leaving the bodies where they lay, Gloria followed Shoa up the stairs back out onto the deck. John ran up after them when he heard another eerie cackle nearby.

At the top of the stairs they saw a yellow light swish around the corner out onto the open deck. The creature had taken advantage of Shoa's attack to light a torch to further its plans.

Shoa tried to put out the flame with a blast of wind, but was too late. The creatures were too fast for her.

"Look out!" John yelled.

A stray rope whipped down from the sail, narrowly missing Gloria's head. The goblins had started to climb the mast, and were slashing wildly at every cable and patch of canvas within reach. One leapt down from the crow's nest, striking Shoa's chest with its foot. She fell over backwards; smashing her head into the metal rails, while the creature crumpled into a pile of broken limbs on the deck.

John ran to her, slashing another creature's throat as it leapt up at him. More goblins were appearing every time he looked around; they were being overrun. Gloria stumbled backwards, firing at the invaders as she tried to escape.

"We've got to go!" John yelled. He dropped his knife as he hauled Shoa onto his shoulder.

A quiet click replaced the loud bangs when Gloria pulled the trigger, forcing her to swing the butt of the shotgun into the chin of an attacker.

"I'm out! We've got no more rounds!" she said hysterically. She threw the weapon at another goblin, knocking it off the railings and into the shallow sea.

John laid the unconscious Shoa down in the boat, and with Gloria's help pushed it over the side. The boat crashed down into the water with a tremendous force, nearly tipping it over. Shoa rolled back into the middle, steadying the vessel.

John dived overboard, narrowly missing one of the oars. His feet hit the sand, but the water broke his fall and forced him back up to the surface. Gloria landed in a deeper patch of water and surfaced as John was clambering onto the boat.

As they pushed towards the shore, the smell of wood smoke followed them. John looked back to see the sails engulfed in flames.

Chapter 32

Mac and Orak approached the open mass grave. Through the tangle of mutilated limbs, they saw several layers of dead bodies. Half buried in the soil, were several old clean bones, elsewhere there were corpses just weeks old.

"You know what this means?" Orak asked rhetorically.

"Goblins," Mac replied, "We should go back."

"I've never seen an attack this big before. Their colonies must be pretty close."

"This is why we should go back."

"I've never actually seen a goblin colony before."

"That's a good thing."

Reluctantly, Orak followed Mac back towards the shore. When they saw black smoke above the rooftops of the abandoned buildings, they broke into a sprint.

They arrived just in time to see the charcoal black mast fall into the sea, breaking into two as it hit the water. The Black Diamond, their only means of transport was now no more than charcoal and driftwood.

The rowing boat had reached the shore, despite being followed by goblins also fleeing the ship. It became apparent that these creatures were useless swimmers, and suddenly the Drathmork's aversion to water made sense, owing a third of their genetics to the goblins.

Shoa had regained consciousness, but her head felt like it had been split open. When Gloria explained to her what had happened, she rushed towards John and kissed him, "You saved my life!"

"I . . . It wasn't all me . . ." he said, flustered. "Rambo helped out," he added, referring to Gloria and her gun skills.

Gloria glared at him, and then mimed shooting him in the face with her fingers.

"We've got to move," Mac cut in. He wore a grave expression on his face while he stared out at the smouldering shell of their ship.

Orak waded into the water, "We should gather up what we can." When the water reached his chest, he began to swim towards the wreck. He returned ten minutes later carrying two large bags full of soaking wet clothes and a few bottles and jars.

With nothing but a badly damaged rowing boat to take them the remaining hundred miles, they had no choice but to walk from here.

"Goblins don't live in big cities," Mac explained, "Their settlements are small and quite far apart, so for there to be so many of them, there must be a huge number of colonies, probably spanning tens of miles. This is their territory we're passing through, so be extra careful."

John noticed how out of breath the Telepath sounded, and was surprised because he didn't think he'd run far. Maybe it was due to the shock they'd all suffered.

Orak used the ship's telescope to scan ahead in search of the goblin's colonies to give them the best possible warning. He led the party, stopping them every hundred feet or so to do a more thorough sweep of the area.

They kept as far away from the open grave as they could, but the smell was harder to hide from. Eventually the air became fresher, and the signs of human civilisation faded away. Dirt tracks and goblin footprints remained, constantly reminding them that they were trespassers in these parts.

Catching sight of something, Orak hissed at everyone to duck. They all hid down behind a short stone wall. While the others slowly crawled along out of sight, Orak peaked over the capstones and looked across the field to the settlement.

Dotted across the muddy ground were over a dozen dome-like structures built of woven branches, clad with dry mud. These waddle and daub houses had normal sized doorways, but looked huge as the dwarfish creatures passed through them.

In the centre of this hamlet was a pile of timber, where atop sat what looked like their leader. A goblin wearing the clothes of a human child and a crown made of polished bones shouted garbled commands at the other creatures. He turned towards the wall when he heard a noise. Orak ducked, but even crouched low, his head still stood out above the capstones.

The goblin yelled something with its low guttural voice, and his followers leapt into action. Snarling and wielding whatever weapons they had in their hands, they charged towards the wall like a bloodthirsty army.

Orak got back up, revealing his full height. As he did, the other four stood and the stampeding rabble slowed right down and stopped. Shoa sent sparks between her fingers to demonstrate their intent, even though the others were unarmed. Very quickly the hoard realised they weren't a serious threat and sped back up.

"Run!" Shoa yelled, as the others were already fleeing.

Gloria began to lag behind, and the goblins were inching closer. Turning on the spot and running towards her, Orak hoisted Gloria onto his back, before booting an attacker in the chest. The goblin flew back, knocking over two creatures like bowling pins.

Eventually the creatures gave up the chase and John nearly collapsed from exhaustion. While everyone else caught their breath, Mac bent over in pain and started gasping.

"Did you get hit?" Orak asked.

Mac shook his head, unable to speak. Suddenly he began coughing violently, and fell onto his hands and knees. Gloria and John rushed to his aid as blood spattered from his mouth and nose.

A moment later he stopped coughing and lay down panting.

"I'm ok," he heaved. It was clear to everyone that he wasn't.

Gloria tried without a stethoscope or any equipment to check his heart rate. It seemed fast but sounded healthy enough. She placed a hand on his chest to try and ascertain what was wrong. "I'm out of my depths here," she said aloud, shaking her head. "There's no way I can find out what's going on in there without an x-ray. Your left lung seems weaker than your right. Have you been hit in the chest at any point?"

Mac shook his head again. He was in too much pain to speak. If he opened his mouth he would have just cried out. Shoa looked down at him and felt lost. While Orak was being useful watching out for the goblins through his telescope, she felt useless.

"What's wrong with him?" she asked, despite knowing full well that the trained medics had no idea.

Gradually his breathing returned to normal, but neither John nor Gloria would let him sit up. They discussed his symptoms, using several words that none of the other three had ever heard before.

Orak was satisfied that the goblins were not likely to return, and started work on building a stretcher using some of their spare clothes tied between poles from a bamboo-like plant. Shoa tested it to make sure it could support human weight, despite weighing about two and a half stone lighter than their patient.

As they carefully lifted Mac onto the makeshift carrier, John gave his diagnosis to Gloria. "I think it's an infection in his lungs. When he nearly drowned in the lake, dirty water was left in the alveoli of his left lung. Some kind of bacterial pathogen must have been present and the water in his lungs would be a perfect breeding ground for it."

"So we need antibiotics," she realised, "That might be difficult; I've not seen any pharmacies around here."

"We'll have to find some, because if we don't, he'll die."

Chapter 33

Maria and Jekka didn't leave the beach until noon the following day. They held hands walking through the forest, partly so as they would not be separated. Every so often she would look at him and smile, nearly walking into trees on several occasions.

Last night had been special. She felt like she had been waiting a long time for it to happen. The only thing stopping them had been Maria's over active mind, but as her lifestyle became simpler, so did her desires and feelings. In the forest each day was a new and unique experience, never planned or scheduled. They only had each other to worry about.

All the way back to the bungalow, Jekka had been thinking through what he needed to tell his new companion. Since he had been living away from society, he had not been close enough to anyone to have to explain his predicament and was unsure how to go about it, especially as he would be doing it in a new tongue.

He cooked a pheasant for her, which she made into sandwiches for them. Once they had eaten, he led Maria into the small room where their clothes and his armaments were kept. Jekka sat her down on one of the chairs they had built together.

"I tell you why I live here . . . Why we live here," he began, picking up the immaculately kept broad sword. Maria noticed that there were a few small chips across the blade, where it had struck armour and other weapons.

"You were once a great warrior," she guessed. He had taught her how to duel with sticks, and to hunt with a bow, as well as freehand combat. The skills he possessed were of no conscript or amateur.

Jekka shook his head, "I was no soldier. I was a Lieutenant General."

Maria looked shocked, "You were in charge of men?"

"I was second to the leader of fifty warriors. General of our legion died in a battle, and I took his place. We were at war with our own people, and the king had sent us to slaughter the rebellion . . ."

"You don't have to tell me this," Maria cut in, not liking where this was going. She wanted her life to be a fresh start, and she wanted the same for him; they had to forget their pasts.

"I have to tell you Maria. You need to know."

"Okay, but whatever you say . . . It won't change anything."

"I followed orders," he continued. "I did what king wanted. I followed the order to attack the rebels' homes. They were unarmed and I sent the cavalry to cut them down . . . . We burnt their houses and slaughtered their cattle, because I had been told to order them to . . ."

"But you had no choice," Maria cut in, "If you hadn't, another general would have."

Jekka shook his head, "Another general might have been courageous enough to say no . . . After we had thwarted the rebels, the prince of Erinthia came over from Whitefalls to congratulate the troops."

He placed the broadsword down on the table and picked up the shield. He pointed at the figure depicted on the shield opposing the dragon and at the knight on horseback. "This was the great Prince of Erinthia, but he never fought that dragon, I did. The Prince was an arrogant spoilt brat, who never even fought his own battles in the playground . . . He gloated about our victory in front of the rebels' children that I had let live. He laughed and joked about their mothers and fathers who died under my command and he taunted them. They were so frightened that they tried to run from him, and he instructed a young foot soldier to chase after them . . . I countered his order, telling the soldier to stay."

Maria could see that Jekka was shaking. She held him close and wiped away a tear as it formed in the corner of his eye. "They exiled you for speaking against him?" she asked.

"The young swordsman listened to me and not the royal, so the prince went after the children himself. As he chased them into a stone hut he drew his hunting knife, but I had drawn my sword first. I cut through his back and twisted the blade, and then I stabbed him again and again until I was sure he was dead . . . . Many men offered to confess to the murder, but I couldn't let anyone else take the blame . . . . When the king found out he tried to have me executed, but my soldiers were loyal and stood up to the royal guard. To stop any more bloodshed I chose to be banished, so my warriors would have no death to avenge. The king let me live on the condition that I live many miles from any town under his law, and only enter his district with permission and supervision. When the king died and the government took over, my sentence remained enforced."

"Anyone would have done the same thing," Maria told him, "You made the right choice."

"No," he said, shaking his head again. "I should have taken his head before he even set eyes on those children . . . I should never have followed his orders in the first place."

Maria knew he was right. Jekka like many men in his position had made the wrong choice and he would regret it for the rest of his life. He had spilt the blood of innocent civilians because they expressed their views; for holding the same beliefs that he now held.

"A band of men who had been under my command ambushed the funeral proceedings and desecrated the Prince's body. Because of their actions, the whole legion was lined up and executed . . . . The man who attacked you in the forest the day we met was a mercenary. He was sent by those still loyal to the late royal family to kill me."

"It'll take more than one badly dressed archer to take on the mighty Lieutenant General Jekka GraKratoa," Maria said as she kissed him.

Jekka leaned away, "I don't deserve to be happy. I deserve to suffer alone for the rest of my days. I destroyed the lives of those children, and condemned every one of my soldiers to death. I ruin everything I touch . . ."

Maria placed her finger over his lips to silence him, "Don't I deserve to be happy?" she asked. "I can't do that without you, I love you Jekka. Everyone has made mistakes in their past. It's what we do from now on that matters. Our lives begin today. Whatever happened before has happened to someone else."

"Don't ever leave Maria. You have etched yourself into my heart. If you ever went away you would tear it apart and I would die."

"I'll never leave you," she replied. Throwing the broken mobile phone she had found out of the open window, she turned back towards Jekka. The device and everything associated with it meant nothing anymore. Earth, her career, her distant family; that chapter of her life was now closed.

Chapter 34

Having to safely carry one of their party slowed everyone right down. They continued south, encountering no more goblin colonies. Cautiously crossing a shallow but wide valley, they felt confident that they had seen the last of the violent creatures.

Mac's condition showed little improvement and it became obvious that rest would not help him heal. They had stopped somewhere they felt was suitable and attempted a very primitive blood transfusion.

John sterilised a small sharp blade with the strong drinking spirit that they had salvaged from the wrecked ship. He made a small cut on Orak's wrist and another cut on Mac's. They drained a few millilitres of the Titan's blood into a sterilised bottle and slowly let it seep into the Telepath's wound. They hoped that Orak's superior antibodies would help reduce the rate of infection. Afterwards, they bound the wounds tightly with clean strips of cloth.

An hour later, Mac's symptoms seemed to have eased, but they all knew this wasn't a cure.

"We need to find penicillin mould," John explained to everyone else while the patient slept.

"I don't even know what it looks like," Gloria replied.

"I do and I think I have a good idea on how to process it . . . . It won't be the all clear though. We need to get him to Earth. We need to keep him conscious and on form so he can figure out how to get us home."

"Do you know where to look for this mould?" Orak asked him.

"Normal places where mould grows I guess . . . . Not sure how I can test for it though."

John realised just how long this problem had been growing. Mac had contracted this infection the day he arrived here. Orak's landings in Ithria and Earth had been just as dangerous. He was almost certain that Maria was no longer alive. Even if she had been lucky enough to survive arriving, she would surely not have survived months alone in this dangerous world.

He forced himself not to think about it. He had to focus on saving the only man who could get him and Gloria home. He fought to convince himself that he was not responsible for Maria's death.

"Is this it?" Shoa asked, breaking John from his downwards spiral of self destruction.

"No, that's lichen," he replied.

"How do you know so much about antibiotics?" she asked him, "I know you were a nurse, but you didn't do pharma . . ."

"Pharmaceutical?"

"Yeah, that stuff?"

"Don't tell Gloria, or the other two for that matter but all I'm going on here is what I learnt from a late night documentary on a medical channel."

Shoa frowned, "I don't think we'll find it looking at cave walls and rotten trees. We need to find a town that's likely to sell medicine."

Later that day, they set up a second transfusion. This time they let out more of Mac's blood first, and gave him close to half a pint of the Titan's. The process had the same effect as before and gave him the strength to travel unassisted. By now, he looked severely bruised and very pale, but it sustained him for now.

They decided that they should repeat this process every day or two, providing Orak was able to donate, until they could find a way to clear the infection properly. The longer they relied on Orak's blood using such low tech means, the bigger the risks became to both of them.

*

Unlike the crew of the Black Diamond, General Kyra led her troops north. They sailed through the lakes to avoid the mountains, and arrived at the city of Ladaan Ijeda long before the war reached that far. Her skilled soldiers would become a unit in the city's army, but had to set up camp just outside the city limits.

The settlement was smaller than Whitefalls and was entirely encompassed by castle walls. The land inside the walls rose up in a hill like Mont Saint Michelle, but instead of a cathedral at the very top, there was a domed palace resembling an Mosque.

The city had grown to fill the perimeter walls and as a result, there was barely enough flat space to pitch a two man tent. Kyra's surviving legion was allowed to use several of a wealthy farmer's fields close to Ladaan Ijeda in exchange for a small fee.

The platoon sent from the city in search of the Earth girl had returned unsuccessfully weeks earlier and now every single soldier was restless, waiting for the inevitable conflict.

After two weeks of living under canvas in the agricultural plot, Kyra was invited to live in the upper levels of the city. Their head general had succumbed to a long suffering illness that he had contracted from a dirty wound, and so his quarters and position within the barracks had become vacant. The governors had heard the story of the battle at Whitefalls and were impressed by Kyra's strategies and leadership skills.

Since her instatement as Ladaan Ijeda's military leader, she had run drills and training sessions with the newly formed army to keep them on form. More soldiers came from other cities regularly as the enemy claimed more land. She now commanded a unified force greater than any Tontoltec had seen in decades.

When they received word that a strange anomaly had occurred nearby, Kyra sent a small party of horsemen to investigate, leading the group personally. The enemy was over a hundred miles from the city and there had been no news of an attack on the northern coast, so she felt it was a good time to leave the city.

The anomaly had started out as just a gust of wind, but had quickly become a startling display of electrical lights. Before anyone knew what was happening, a small boy helping to plough the field was dragged from the ground and vanished. It had been witnessed by half a dozen other workers, so wasn't dismissed as rumour.

When Kyra arrived at the farm, she was told of more of these events occurring close to the same time. She knew from what Mac had taught her that this meant the rift was nearly fully formed. This was impossible though; she had been told that it had been closed.

After a few hours of being at the farm, a small girl came running to the house screaming. The hysterical child said she had seen something coming from a 'sparkling cloud'. Kyra and several of her riders went with her to see the alien object.

It had dropped straight down from a cloud high in the sky and cut deep into the ground, sending clumps of soil flying across the field. Half buried in the mud and surrounded by cart horses and men with pitchforks, the long metal box couldn't have looked more out of place.

"Get it out of the ground," Kyra instructed.

Her soldiers slung ropes around the strange object and after tying them tightly around it, began to pull. The heavy object didn't move more than an inch, and was even a struggle to shift when they tied the ropes to their horses. When Kyra chipped in, the box jolted free, but it still took them a long time to move it off the wheat field.

"Take five minutes break," she told them. "We're going to try and open it later."

"What do you think is inside?" asked one of the farm hands.

"I can't begin to guess," she replied truthfully, "But I'd bet every single person here is as curious as I am."

She closely inspected the construction of this box. It was over ten feet long and more than four feet wide and tall. It was built of polished steel and bolted together with large protruding rivets.

Kyra gripped the end of the bolt with her strong fingers and tried to pull it out, but it remained in place. She saw no way of getting it open without completely destroying it. Borrowing an axe from one of her soldiers, she struck the bolt head several times before it broke off. The crate appeared to have at least twenty of these identical bolts going through the lid, and was clearly designed to be opened only by whoever had the right tool. As building such a tool would take time, she began methodically hacking off each one in turn.

After destroying two axes and badly denting a third, the lid was finally free of obstructions. The heavy steel lid was tightly slotted into the crate, and it took Kyra all of her strength to try and prise it open. She stopped to wipe the sweat from her brow. "Can someone help?" she asked reluctantly.

Three soldiers and another two farm hands grabbed one of the sides of the lid and in one heave yanked it free. The lid weighed more than all of them put together, and they dropped it to one side, narrowly missing several sets of toes.

Inside, the box was completely filled with solid grey foam. Kyra prodded the dense polystyrene and felt around the edge. Dragging the shock absorbing material out, she revealed what was inside. Everyone who had helped had gathered around in anticipation, but none of them knew what they were looking at.

Four long white metal tubes sat within the box, spaced apart by two squares of thin poles. These tubes had fins protruding from them, and some kind of exhaust vent at one end. The other end was conical, giving them a streamlined look. Kyra had no idea what their exact purpose was, but she knew they were weapons and she knew they were from Earth.

"I need to contact WaMaktaJrei Kroez," she said to one of her soldiers. "Can you assemble a team and prepare to go out and search for him?"

The soldier nodded and set off back to Ladaan Ijeda. The combined weight of the thick steel crate and its contents probably weighed close to one and a half tonnes. They constructed a rig and recruited more help to lift it onto a cart that had been originally designed for mining. They used every horse available to tow it back to the city.

The war would soon be coming to this region. If Kyra could understand how to use these weapons, she was sure they would come in very useful.

Chapter 35

The cart towing the missiles was under so much strain that the rear axle bent shortly after leaving the field. Night had already fallen, and they decided it wouldn't be possible to move it further.

General Kyra did not want to leave this potentially valuable asset unattended, so instructed her men to make camp in the field. Their tents formed a perimeter around the broken cart and the alien object.

She made sure that there were at least two people awake at all times, so they slept in shifts. The general had just finished her shift when her patrol partner saw a flicker of light from behind the crown of a tree.

"Did you see that?" he asked, wondering whether he was seeing things. It had looked like a flash of lightening, but there had been no other signs to suggest such weather.

"Go and check it out," she ordered, "Wait!"

They both stopped dead and could clearly hear someone moving. A moment later they heard voices. Kyra had no idea what was being said, but she recognised the language, English.

"Get everyone up! Battle stations!" she hissed, drawing her sword.

The soldier went into each tent, shaking everybody awake. Most came out onto the field still in their night clothes, carrying their swords and frantically searching for the enemy.

They found their general standing perfectly still, staring intensely at some shrubs. "I've counted four," she said so quietly that it was barely audible, "I need a bow."

A soldier crept barefoot towards her with a longbow and a small cluster of arrows. She prepared to fire, but slackened the bow when she saw the figures moving away.

"Get ready," she instructed them, "I need two of you to stay with the crate, everyone else follow me."

*

It had been four days since Mac had been violently ill, and although the Titan's blood was sustaining him, he was not in the best of health. The infection was likely to mutate, and if Orak's antibodies couldn't cope with a new strain, then Mac would succumb to his illness.

Despite spending much of their time searching, nobody could find even the smallest patch of penicillin mould growing, and they hadn't come across any signs of civilisation. They were now in uncharted territory, and had no way of knowing whether the next town was a mile or a hundred miles away.

"Have you thought much about why we are having the same dreams?" John asked Mac, as they trekked across a bridge which looked twice as old as the abandoned city they had just left.

"I've thought about it . . . . But I've not come up with an explanation," he replied. Mac had been speaking in short or broken sentences for the past few days due to his severely reduced lung capacity. "It's happened many times in history, between two Telepaths . . . . But it seems unlikely that you'd be a Telepath and never have realised it."

"Is that a possibility?" John asked, "Is it possible to have these powers and not realise it?"

"I don't think so . . . Usually these things develop at the age of about five or six . . . . Telepathic children have little control, and . . . . cause lots of trouble until they can focus . . ."

Mac stopped to catch his breath. The others waited for him, deciding to sit down on the wall of the bridge. Gloria was also glad of the rest. Although her lungs were fine, her leg muscles were exhausted.

"I've had a thought," Gloria said to John, "I'm no geneticist, but what if you do have something in common with Mac? The Telepaths have two recessive genes which contribute towards them having these abilities . . ."

"Those with just one recessive gene don't show any traits," Mac cut in.

"But what if in this case they do?" she suggested, "If people have been crossing over between worlds, maybe someone in John's ancestry was from Ithria, possessing DNA that we don't normally have."

"But people with one gene don't have any traits . . . . Not even thought projection," Mac repeated.

"Then maybe you've been sending him your dreams? Maybe John is more receptive?" she suggested. Clearly she had been thinking this for quite some time, a thought that had only just occurred to her. "John, when did they start?"

There was a long silence when he thought about it, then he stared at Mac and said, "The night before Orak first turned up in the hospital."

"Why would I be projecting my subconscious thoughts?" Mac asked.

Gloria didn't have an answer for this. They had reached the limit of her theory. "You tell me?"

"This is all going way over my head," Shoa said quietly to Orak, who nodded in agreement.

Shortly after crossing the bridge, they found more abandoned buildings, and realised that the goblin problem had been a serious epidemic. If the war was resolved, these creatures would be no problem in Northern Tontoltec, as the desert of Caracracia divided the country in two. Here though, they had to keep their eyes open.

*

The squadron followed Kyra right across the huge farm at a slow irregular pace. They were stealthily tracking an enemy only she had seen, and had to closely follow her every command. Having the element of surprise was paramount.

In the long grass they were well hidden, but keeping quiet was a harder task. It also meant that only their eagle eyed leader could see beyond the crops.

None of the soldiers had seen the enemy when their general shouted, "NOW!"

Kyra fired off two arrows in quick succession. Several other arrows flew off in roughly the same direction but without planned targets.

A short metallic rattle sounded and the soldier to Kyra's left collapsed dead, dotted with small deep wounds. "Take cover!" she yelled, as a second cluster of invisible projectiles flew towards them.

The corn exploded around them as the barrage of bullets continued, and they were forced out into the open. Kyra fired another arrow, this time only guessing at her target.

Two more of her men were struck down, and the enemy came into full view. At first the soldiers thought they were some new horrific creatures like the Drathmork, but they quickly realised they were human like themselves. These people wore jet black clothes and had their entire faces covered by masks and goggles. They had pipes leading from their masks to canisters on their backs and they carried barrelled weapons in their gloved hands.

More of Tontoltec's fighters fell before they could even reach these bizarre people. A knife was thrown, cutting one of the gunman's throats. Another lay dead from Kyra's arrows.

The remaining Earth warriors backed away from the charging mob, firing off single rounds to conserve their ammunition. A click sounded the end of a gunman's magazine and as he tried to reload, he was beheaded with a single forceful blow. The last thing he saw was the snarling face of a woman as terrifying as the legendary Boadicea.

The remaining Earth warrior ran out of ammunition and threw down his assault rifle. He then threw his hands up in submission. The primitive soldiers circled around him. He had lost the fight.

The general approached and pulled off his mask. She yelled something in an alien tongue, before throwing him to the floor. Two of the soldiers sheathed their swords and hauled him up from the ground. They dragged him to a large stone barn, binding his hands and feet.

Chapter 36

Jekka had finally completed every carpentry project that he and Maria had planned in the bungalow. He had now drawn up plans to build a hut on the beach for them to stay in. They had gone to the sandy shore again but it had rained. The walk back had been dark and unpleasant. Because of this, they both agreed on the new project.

While Jekka gathered wood for the construction, Maria went out into the forest with her own longbow to hunt for their food. She caught a young boar and carried it to the beach, where Jekka had set up a campfire.

She inspected his progress, which at present was a pile of thick straight branches and a few stones. "Not very homely," she said.

When Jekka saw her, he helped carry the carcass to the fire. "Did you bring bread?" he asked. Since Maria had introduced the idea of sandwiches to him, Jekka put all of his food in between slices of bread. He frowned with disappointment when she told him she hadn't.

"I need to learn how to make nicer bread," Maria told him. "That stuff we've been having is breaking my teeth."

"We need money to buy bread," he replied. "I'm finding fewer animals to sell these days and I have to buy twice as much food."

"Are you saying you want me to get a job?" she laughed. Maria thought for a moment and realised that finding employment wouldn't be such a bad idea. Jekka was restricted to the forest, but she wasn't. "My Tontoltec is getting better," she added, "I could ask in the village market we go to?"

"There is work at the tavern. I saw a poster last week."

Maria frowned, going from a doctor to a barmaid didn't seem to be the best career move, but it seemed like her best choice at the moment.

She knew very little of the medical methods used in Ithria and was sure she wouldn't cope with such simplified practices.

"You are tough enough to handle the drunks," Jekka added. "You've become a good fighter."

"Still not as tough as you and I'm sure you've been going easy on me."

Jekka smiled but said nothing. He had. He began explaining how he was going to go about erecting the shelter. Just as he started talking about the roof, Maria felt a drop of rain and laughed. Gathering up the hunting tools, they rushed towards the trees for cover. Out of the corner of her eye, Maria saw a flash of white sail.

"Is that a boat?" she said out of surprise.

Jekka stepped out into the rain to get a closer look. Beyond a small rocky island, they saw the silhouette of what looked like an old Spanish Galleon entering the cove.

"Do ships come here often?" Maria asked.

Jekka shook his head, "Never."

As the ship came closer, the huge white sails came into focus. The square-rigged vessel bore three towering masts and painted across the bow was a large golden crest. The crest depicted an axe and a sword lying upon an open book, representing industry, war and culture. Jekka recognised the symbol immediately and his eyes became wide with fear.

"Alkak-Taan!"

"Are they coming here?" Maria said hysterically.

Jekka nodded and backed away out of the ships view. "We have to run, back to the house. We need to pack what we can and get as far away from here as possible."

They left everything behind on the beach and headed through the forest. Maria was still unsure of the way, so kept close to Jekka at all times. This would be the worst possible time to get lost again.

When they got to the hut many hours later, Maria was exhausted. She was far fitter than she had been on Earth, but still her level of stamina was nothing compared to Jekka's.

"The enemy won't be here for a long time yet," he explained. "They'll make camp on the beach, we have time to rest. At sunrise we go to the town."

*

Mac constructed a test to see whether Gloria's theory about John had any truth to it. The others watched with anticipation as the two of them sat upon boulders facing each other.

Firstly, Mac drew up several cards with letters on. He shuffled them and gave them to John, who took one card, looked at it, then put it face down. Mac would then try to see if the number came to him. If it did, then it meant John was projecting his thoughts.

The first number, he guessed correctly and Shoa gasped. After that though, every letter he said was wrong. It had just been a lucky guess.

After fifteen minutes of this exercise Mac concluded, "He's not transmitting, that's for sure. I have another test, but it requires me to be asleep. So it'll have to wait."

"No tests to see if I can pick up things with my mind?" John asked, only semi seriously.

"Hmm . . . Try and pick that up with your mind."

John focused on an object for a few seconds, raising his hand in a Jedi like manner. "No, nothing."

"Then you don't have telekinesis," he said, followed by a short laugh and a sharp cough. "A simple but effective test."

"See if you can do this?" Shoa cut in, clicking her fingers and producing a small flame from her thumb.

"Now you're just showing off," John laughed.

"We should probably make a move . . ." Orak reminded them, "If we want to find shelter by nightfall. I don't want to sleep under a cliff overhang during a rain storm again."

Mac looked up at the clear blue sky. It was unlikely to rain tonight, but they set off in search of shelter anyway. They split into two groups to cover more ground, agreeing on a call so they could find each other again. Orak and John went one way; Mac, Gloria and Shoa went another.

Both parties would occasionally call out and wait for a reply to make sure the other wasn't too far away. An hour into their search, the two groups found themselves on opposite sides of a huge deep river, with no bridge in sight.

"We'll swim to you!" Orak called across. He then looked down at John, "You can swim right? I just don't want Mac trying it, and Gloria . . ."

"Isn't the youthful Olympic swimmer she used to be?" John replied, mimicking her typical response. "If we wait until it gets narrower, I'll do it."

"I've found an abandoned hut!" Shoa called across to them. "We're going to stay here! If you find somewhere on that side to stay, come meet us here tomorrow!"

Orak showed his thumb as a sign of agreement, then waved goodbye. He turned to John, "I saw a small cave . . . well, more of an alcove, but it's big enough for both of us."

John sighed. He knew at this point that finding a five star hotel was too much to ask for. They slept on soil once again and had a view of the stars. As long as the rain came from any direction but west, they would keep dry in this location.

They both fell asleep quickly, despite the fact that this was one of the least comfortable holes they had crawled into. While John slept, the nightmare about the harpies amongst the jagged rocks returned.

The red sky was on fire and steam erupted from the ground. The black smoke was back, but the winged beasts were flying through it. For the first time he could see that this desolate area was the site of a volcano. He had never noticed the cratered black mountain in any of the other dreams, but now it was spewing out hot fast flowing lava. He couldn't overlook it.

The harpies moved quicker than the smoke and instinctively John ran. The sharp rocks cut the soles of his bare feet, leaving a trail of blood. The creatures bit and clawed at his back, screeching so loud that his eardrums burst. All he could hear now was a loud ringing.

During his futile attempt to escape the swarm, he ran across a puddle and caught sight of his reflection. What he saw shocked him awake and he sat bolt upright, his ears still ringing.

Chapter 37

The prisoner was stripped of all his weapons, tools, and shoes. He was then sealed within the timber barn, the doors bolted from the outside. He had been tied to a pillar and gagged, and was under constant supervision.

Kyra had yelled at him for over half an hour, causing him to sweat, plead and finally break down into tears. In all this time, he did not speak a single word of Tontoltec, and the general was now certain his language was of Earth origin. None of her soldiers or the citizens of Ladaan-Ijeda spoke any other worldly dialects, and she had no idea where Orak or any of his students were.

The crate of weapons had been moved back to the city, and was being held in one of the highest buildings in a maximum security bank vault. Inside, Northern Erinthia's best scientists were working on a way to understand and use these weapons, having little success.

Kyra and a few of her soldiers stayed another night camped out at the farm to guard the prisoner in shifts. He would not be moved to the city, as its prisons were already overcrowded, having up to seven convicts per cell. The enemy was approaching, but were still many miles away, so the general could afford to keep the army behind the walls running their own drills.

No other Earth warriors came through anywhere near the barn, but Kyra was sure they would try again. Their worst fears were becoming reality. The link was still active, and it would only be a matter of time before it became a serious problem.

At midnight, she called a meeting. She addressed the platoon under the darkened sky, hoping for progress to have been made by morning light.

"We need WaMaktaJrei," she told the group of soldiers. "We need him to speak to this prisoner and to find out what he can about the Anuma Link."

"Where do we start looking?" an armoured Spellcaster asked.

"You don't start looking; you'll never find him by looking. We spread the word. Tell everyone you meet to tell everyone they meet. He's in Southern Tontoltec, that's all anyone knows, but it would take decades for a hundred men to search the whole region. If thousands are keeping an eye out, he'll be spotted sooner or later."

"The message won't reach the south country unless we cross the desert."

"Then we use airmail. We use the emergency method."

The gathering of soldiers looked around at each other; half of them had no idea what 'the emergency method' was. Those who knew explained to the others.

Locked inside a converted cave, behind heavy steel bars was a captive dragon. Not many people are aware that dragons have homing instincts better than almost any other animal. The imprisoned dragon had been taken from its home in the south country and shipped to the most northern city in Tontoltec. Upon release, the dragon would be administered with a slow poison that would kill the creature within thirty hours, as well as having a secure message tied to its leg. The dragon would also be fitted with a chain of brightly coloured streamers so it could be seen and identified from miles away.

The people of the south would recognise this streamer, and follow the creature to where it would inevitably die. If the timing was right, then the beast would die shortly after getting to its destination, and the message could be recovered. This was the fastest way to get a message across to such a vague destination.

"There are no guarantees that it will work," Kyra explained, "But it's the best option we have right now."

"So where do we fit in?" the Spellcaster asked.

"I need volunteers to tend to and release the creature. I won't lie, it's extremely dangerous and unlikely to succeed, which is why I'm sending nobody against their will."

Every soldier stepped forwards and Kyra was shocked. They all believed they stood better chances with the dragon than with their enemy, and this was a chilling sign.

"You will definitely be of use," she said to the confident Spellcaster, "I'd like you to select a team of five and get on with it."

She left them to it, wondering whether such a wild stab in the dark would work. The enemy would be unable to stop this messenger, but dragons were not famed for their reliability. Their chance of tipping the balance of the war in their favour was reliant on a beast she had spent much of her youth hunting. Kyra had little confidence in this plan, but it was their only chance.

*

John had eventually managed to get back to sleep, and surprisingly didn't dream. His head had been spinning, trying to make sense of things. Why hadn't the volcano been present in the nightmare before? And why could he feel pain in a subconscious fantasy?

The most baffling thing was the reflection. He had expected to see himself, or if not himself, then Mac. Instead he saw a face, which at first was that of a complete stranger. He quickly realised where he knew the face from, and the shock had sent him hurtling back into the real world, if he could call Ithria the real world. The last few months had been like one long dream, but there was no way they could have been anything but reality.

He had never seen the man in the puddle as young as he was in his dream, but knew it was him. His hair had appeared a dark blonde, but was now all but white. How could a bank manager from South Wales be the man walking through a geological disaster on another world? How could Mark Jones, Gloria's rarely seen husband be involved in any of this?

After a short sleep, John was woken again by a nearby birdcall. It was still dark, but the two moons were full, and bathed the world in an ethereal red light. He rolled over to see a large vacant human shaped dent in the soil beside him. Sitting up straight, he looked around and saw no sign of the Titan that had been sleeping next to him.

"Orak?" he called, clambering to his feet and searching all around.

John lay back down; his companion had probably just gone to the toilet. After ten minutes with no sign of any huge figures returning, he began to get worried. He was sure Orak wouldn't leave him here alone.

Ditching the shelter, John set off back to the riverbank where they had seen the others. He counted the steps to gauge the distance, but when he got to the exact point, he looked across and saw no hut. Had he managed to get lost? "Hello?" he called across, "Where are you guys?"

"Over here!" he heard Shoa's voice calling.

John bore a look of utter perplexity; her voice had come from his side of the river. Had they found a bridge? He had searched the river and not even seen a stepping stone, and there was no way Mac could have swum across in his state of health.

"Where are you?" he called back

He waited for a reply but heard none. Running to the source, he saw nothing but the entrance to a dark cave. He edged closer and peered inside. If Shoa was inside, she'd light a flame for him to see, but there was nothing. Turning, he saw the back of her green cloak and ran towards her. John reached for her shoulder, but as his hand grabbed the cloth, the body within it vanished into nothingness. The robes fell to the floor, sinking into a puddle.

I'm still dreaming, he told himself, trying to shake himself back into consciousness. He tried to see his reflection in the puddle, but it was too dark. Feeling his face and his hair, he checked that he was really himself.

"Over here!" Shoa's voice hissed directly in his ear, and he span around so quickly that he lost balance and collapsed onto the ground. Suddenly the scene around him was different.

The moon had changed colour, and the world was now tinted blue. The cave had vanished, and in its place was a brickwork tunnel just like the one they had seen in the abandoned city. At the end of the tunnel he saw daylight, even though he saw stars in the sky above him. John closed his eyes tightly and recited, "This isn't real," over and over.

He opened his eyes again, but nothing had changed. Slowly he crept through the tunnel, but the further he got, the further away the end seemed. He broke into a sprint, and the archway began to spiral, causing him to collapse from dizziness. There seemed to be no escape, and he curled himself into a ball, trying to hide away from the madness.

John looked up when he heard footsteps coming from both directions. From the sunlit archway, he saw the silhouette of a hooded man approaching. "Who are you?" John demanded.

"My name is Mradraak," the figure replied in a snake like hiss, which echoed all around him. "Tell me where he is John! Where is Kedos?"

"Who the hell is Kedos?"

"Don't try to trick me with your lies!" the figure screeched, "You have been communicating with the traitor. He has been feeding you secrets. Tell me where he hides and I will spare you and your friends."

"I don't know what you're talking about!" John yelled back, standing up to the mysterious figure.

The stranger suddenly grew two foot taller, as did the tunnel. John backed away, and he began to tremble. He saw a black void where the man's face should have been. A long straight blade slid down from the creature's sleeve, "You will tell me!" it hissed again.

As John reached for the knife in his belt that wasn't there, a second figure walked straight through the wall of the tunnel and slashed wildly towards the cloaked creature. Orak drew a second blade from his sheath, and the cloaked man backed away. The dark tunnel faded away as the stranger ran from the Titan. The stars above reappeared in the sky.

"Are you alright?" Orak asked, knowing that John clearly wasn't.

"Are . . . Are you real?" he stammered, gripping a tree for support.

"You've just been under the spell of a very powerful Telepath. None of what you saw was real. It was all an illusion, but I assure you I am real."

John did not get back to sleep that night, but Orak stayed up with him. They lit a fire for warmth, but even the hottest of fires couldn't warm the chill John felt inside. His mind had been violated, and his very grasp on reality had been tampered with.

Chapter 38

Maria and Jekka slept through the darkness. Using a primitive alarm, consisting of a balanced sand timer and iron cookware, they rose as the sun did.

They each packed a small bag, taking only their most treasured or important possessions. Once they were ready, they said goodbye to Jekka's house, and set off into the forest without looking back.

"Five years," Jekka said solemnly. "This woodland has been my home for five years."

"We'll make a new home together," Maria replied, "It'll be a fresh start."

"Another fresh start!" he replied angrily. Maria had never before seen him lose his temper, and it was a terrifying sight. "What's so bad in your past that you want to leave behind? I've told you everything about my life, but you've given me nothing in return!"

"There's nothing to say!" she snapped back.

"There must be something, or you wouldn't have made such a point about starting again!"

"I left my whole world behind Jekka! I'm not from Ithria, I'm from Earth! Every time I think about what I left behind, I want to forget everything! I had family and friends, a career and more money than you could dream of!"

"You never talk to me about this," he said more calmly.

"You are the only good thing . . . The only thing I have on this whole planet Jekka. The house, the forest, the beach don't mean anything without you in them."

"You are all I have left too," he replied. "I don't want to fight and push you away."

Maria doubted anything he could say would push her away. Even if she wanted to leave him she couldn't. She depended on him more than he knew.

They eventually passed the red painted tree, and without attracting the attention of his escort, strolled straight into the village.

He reached the centre of the market before anyone noticed him and within moments, a pair of heavyset men appeared, carrying truncheons and lengths of rope. They both stopped when they saw the broadsword sheathed to his belt.

They spoke so quickly that Maria couldn't understand a single word. A heated argument kicked off between the exile and the law enforcers, each maintaining a safe distance between them. Maria kept quiet, her grasp of their language was very limited and she didn't want to say the wrong thing.

The argument was ended when Jekka slowly but forcefully explained, "The enemy has arrived on the northern coast. They will be here within hours! I will not stay and be slaughtered by them! If you want to try and stop me, go ahead and try!"

The large men looked at each other, nodded in mutual agreement and let him pass.

"I'll inform the mayor," one of them decided, "You should send a message to Ladaan-Ijeda . . . Jekka! This doesn't change things. Once this battle is over, you return to those trees and your banishment is back in place!"

Both men left in a hurry. Jekka also made sure that he and Maria were outside the town before the mass panic set in. Neither of them knew their destination, but made sure it was out of the likely path of the invaders.

Outside the town were several thousand hectares of farmland, and they cut across the grazing fields. Several large timber framed buildings overlooked the fields, and Maria wondered whether they would find somewhere as comfortable to stay when they did decide to stop for the night.

Jekka hoisted her over the bordering hedges, and then vaulted over them himself with ease. The fields ran parallel with the edge of the forest, and they both agreed to head away from the trees.

Just as they turned away from the woods, Jekka heard a loud rustling. He held out his hand for Maria to stop, and she almost tripped over her own feet. The rustling continued, and the couple searched the trees for the source. Jekka crouched down and peered through a large gap in the hedge.

Maria spotted them first, trudging between the trunks without even trying to be stealthy. In formation, the men in jet-black armour marched out onto the field. Jekka was shocked; there was no way that they could have gotten here this quickly! The only explanation was that a second landing party had arrived on a closer shore.

"Don't move," he whispered, pulling Maria down onto the ground beside him, "Wait for them to pass."

The soldiers remained unaware of the couple hiding just yards away. The Alkak-Taanan unit was twice the size of the one Jekka had once commanded, so even with this legion he wouldn't stand much of a chance. The enemy quickly passed them by, but he could see more men marching deeper in the forest.

"Quickly!" he hissed, grabbing Maria's arm and dragging her across the field to the next row of shrubs. Waiting for her slowed him down more than he had anticipated and a soldier, head and shoulders above the tops of the hedges, caught sight of them.

"You and you! After them!" the armoured Titan bellowed at a pair of his troops.

Two eager warriors hacked their way through the hedge and sprinted up the uneven sloping field. As Jekka and Maria reached the brow of the hill, they came face to face with a row of white horses. Their riders looked down on the pedestrians, then downhill towards the enemy.

Maria noticed that many of these horsemen wore armour and carried shields identical to the ones Jekka had left at the bungalow. At the head of this army, was a towering long-haired woman upon a huge black snarling steed, waving her heavy sword through the air with ease.

"Charge!" the general screamed.

*

For much of the morning, the five travellers in Southern Tontoltec walked alongside each other, but on opposite sides of the wide river. By early afternoon, the river was shallow enough for Orak to wade across. John sat on his shoulders while the Titan fought the current of the waist high water.

When they were reunited, John hugged Gloria and Shoa who both showed concern when they saw how pale and shaken he looked. John noticed that Mac looked in a far worse state than he did.

As soon as it was convenient, they set up another blood transfusion. It took longer to show any effects this time, and despite saying he felt better, Mac still looked very unwell. His heavy breathing was audible to everyone, and they all knew that Orak's blood was starting to lose its effect.

Mac was just about well enough to talk, and started by asking John about the events that had occurred during the night. After John had explained every detail of the illusion, Orak added, "I hadn't left the cave. I was still there when you went out searching for me. The Telepath, this Mradraak, put an image in your mind that I wasn't there. He did the same thing with the hut."

"I can try and teach you how to resist a Telepath's mind games if he ever returns," Mac told him. "Did he say anything about this Kedos you were supposed to know?"

John shook his head, "Only that he is a traitor, and that he's been telling us things. How can this guy be telling us things if we've never met or even heard of him?"

He looked at Gloria, as her last theory had seemed the most plausible, but she just shrugged her shoulders. Shoa was equally clueless of what to suggest.

"Did you have the dream about the volcano?" Mac asked.

"Yes . . ." he remembered suddenly, and tried not to look at Gloria. Mac would have no idea who it was they saw, so it was up to him to bring it up. John didn't know how to tell Gloria that Mark was somehow involved without anything more to go on.

"The volcano wasn't erupting in the other dreams. It looked very different, but it was definitely the same place as the others," Mac replied.

"Yes," John confirmed. "I'd not noticed the mountain before either."

"Because it wasn't there before, a previous eruption created it."

"I don't understand."

"These dreams are memories, but they are older than both of us. That mountain was formed seventy seven years ago."

"Wait, you know where it is?" Orak cut in.

"I didn't before, but I do now. The ash field in mine and John's dreams is on a volcanic island ten miles south east of Tontoltec."

*

Kyra stormed down the hill, followed by the combined armies of Whitefalls and Ladaan-Ijeda. In each hand, she wielded a broadsword, but carried no shield to hinder her.

The two Alkak-Taanan footmen who had been running up the hill quickly changed direction, but weren't quick enough. Simultaneously, they lost their heads as the general struck at them with both blades.

She saw the enemies running away, and thought they were retreating. Victory had come at the cost of only two enemy soldiers. Several horses jumped the hedge and continued pursuing the foot soldiers into the forest, but slowed right down when they saw that they weren't fleeing at all, but joining the ranks of a second assault party.

Kyra saw the enemy double in numbers, but it was too late to stop, she was hurling downhill at full speed towards them. All around her, she saw her cavalry cut down by arrows and spears, as she tried to control her wounded animal. A sword stroke had deeply cut the thigh of her horse, causing it to lose control of its limb and buck violently.

Leaping from her stead, she clambered onto the horse of one of her fallen soldiers. She saw her black stallion bolting into the forest, but couldn't watch where it went because she had to be in the moment of the battle. Piercing the heart of an enemy soldier through his solid iron chest plate, she swung his body from the end of her sword into another solider. Despite having a considerable height advantage over the grounded army, they were greatly outnumbered.

"Retreat!" she yelled, steering her commandeered animal back up the hill, hoping her men would follow.

At the brow of the hill, Jekka and Maria watched in terror as so many of their countrymen were brutally killed. Jekka stood in front, covering Maria from any stray arrows coming their way. His hand rested upon the hilt of his sword, ready. This was a battle he could not win, but he couldn't stand by and do nothing.

"Don't even think about it," Maria stopped him. "You said this is all behind you now. You aren't a military man anymore."

"I'll always be a fighter," he replied. "But this isn't my battle."

Before he was able to do anything about it, the enemy was flooding towards them. Kyra thundered past them, shouting for them to follow. Going against his word immediately, Jekka took the bow from his back and shot down an enemy soldier just as he was about to take a swing at a horseman. The horseman slowed down and offered his hand to Jekka.

"Take her!" Jekka yelled, thrusting Maria towards him. The knight hauled Maria onto his horse as she screamed and fought against him. She reached out for Jekka, as he stood alone in the battlefield. As they stampeded over the hill, Maria saw him standing before a goliath of a man, preparing to duel while a hundred bloodthirsty warriors watched in anticipation.

Chapter 39

The charging army had stopped to confront one man. Lieutenant General Jekka GraKratoa had challenged the Alkak-Taanan centurion to combat. The enemy leader had accepted the proposed conditions and thrown down his shield, helmet and chest plate to make the fight fair.

If the challenger won, he would be rewarded with his freedom; if the centurion won the challenger's army would stand down. Jekka had shown an old medal which declared him as a military leader, and had strung them a story about not being on duty that day to explain why he wore no uniform.

From the top of a man made mount, the former site of a wooden fort, General Kyra watched through a telescopic lens. Her soldiers waited behind the hill. If the challenger failed, the cavalry would be ready to intercept the attackers.

Jekka stared up into the slit-like eyes of the huge Titan, maintaining a confident stance. He stood about six feet away from his opponent, waiting. He had taught his fighters never to make the first move in a battle.

The Titan began walking sideways, forcing Jekka to shift opposite, forming a circle with their path. Changing direction suddenly, the centurion tried to catch his opponent out. Jekka was one step ahead of him and took the opportunity to lunge forward with his sword, cutting several inches into the Titan's abdominal muscles.

A heavy battle axe swung for Jekka's head in response, missing by millimetres. The wound had not deterred or slowed the huge warrior down at all; it had just made him angry.

Crouched down atop the mound, Kyra pulled back the string of her bow, ready to strike at the heart of the centurion if the challenger failed. If this mysterious fighter fell, the victor would be dead within seconds.

Jekka had backed further away from the Titan again. He maintained eye contact with the gigantic warrior, who now knew not to underestimate him.

"You got lucky!" the Titan snarled, touching his wound with his free hand. He then began tossing his sword between hands, tempting Jekka to strike again.

"Who's to say I won't be lucky again," Jekka replied calmly, while slowly pacing around. He also began switching the sword between his hands.

"You won't get a second chance!"

The centurion leapt forwards while Jekka's sword was in mid-air, and batted the blade away. He swung for the challenger's head, but missed once again. Jekka staggered to the side, diving to the floor. He then caught the handle of his sword and rolled back onto his feet in one smooth motion.

Kyra was forced to look away from the duel when she heard hurried footsteps coming up the hill behind her. A dark haired woman sprinted up the slope, and the general re-aimed her bow. "Stop right there!" she screamed.

Maria skidded to a halt, spraying mud across the horse and rider before her. The arrow shot through the air and sliced deep into the ground inches from Maria's toe. Both women looked horrified.

"I didn't mean to fire," Kyra blurted out.

Ignoring her, Maria took out her own bow and aimed it at the centurion on the battlefield below. "I can't get a clean shot!" she snapped, "I can't shoot at this distance! Please! Help him!"

"If you release that arrow we're all dead. Let this play out."

"I can't! He needs help!" she said hysterically. The longbow was shaking in her hands. She could never make the shot.

Jekka had regained his footing, and like before, kept his distance from the enemy. Living in the forest had taught him patience, and this gave him an edge, as he was sure the big headed Titan was desperate not to look bad in front of his soldiers.

Sooner than expected, the centurion bound forward, slashing so deeply that the only way Jekka could dodge was to jump. The blade cut through the sole of his boot and skinned the bottom of his foot. Landing on one foot, he felt his sword being knocked from his hand once again.

The Titan stood on the flat of the fallen blade and laughed, "You're a fool to challenge me! And now you'll pay the price for your foolishness!"

Faster than Jekka could even blink, the Titan had covered the distance and thrust his sword into him. Jekka felt it slice through his gut and punch out through his back. He curled around it, gasping with pain as his eyes blurred. Reaching for his boot, he fumbled around a sheath while the blade was still inside him.

"You attacked too soon!" Jekka wheezed.

As the Titan laughed, he felt the cold steel blade cut up underneath his chin. As it severed his spine he fell back, drawing the blade out from Jekka's abdomen.

Both armies looked on stunned as the two men lay on the ground. The challenger and the centurion had both fallen, but it was clear who the winner was. Jekka clambered back to his feet, tightly holding either side of the wound. Maria ran towards him but was overtaken by the woman on horseback.

Kyra grabbed the wounded victor and dragged him onto her steed. "I'm not leaving you to die after that performance," she explained, "We need people like you."

*

As the river curved round to the east, the five travellers continued south. They had left goblin territory behind, and found houses occupied by humans. Orak had asked a local lumberjack for directions to the nearest guesthouse, as only he could speak the dialect.

They were directed to a town a stone's throw away. After searching for what felt like hours through a maze of narrow streets, they found the small hotel.

None of them had any significant amount of money left, so they had no choice but to barter. They had been fortunate enough to have arrived at a time when travellers were few and far between. The owner was so desperate for business that he accepted what they had, which was a quarter of the price he usually charged.

They were all so exhausted from walking huge distances each day, that the straw filled mattresses were the most comfortable any of them could remember.

"Can we stay a few days?" John asked the rest of the group, "We all need a break."

Gloria in particular looked like she needed to lie down for a week. Compared to Mac though, she looked like she'd just got back from a fortnight at the health spa.

"We can't," Mac replied, "We've got no money . . ."

"We can make some money. We can ask around, and see if anyone needs workers . . . Or we could work for rent."

"What about food?" Orak cut in. "You might be able to survive on berries, nuts and the occasional rabbit, but I can't. Mac isn't going to get better on a malnourished diet, receiving my malnourished blood . . . My cuts are taking twice as long to heal."

"Ok, so food is our priority. Any better ideas how to get any?"

"We could sell Shoa," Mac suggested.

"Oi!" She went to punch his arm but stopped herself. They all knew how weak he was at the moment. "There's a city on the south coast. I went there as a child. I don't know how far away we are, but we'd have better hopes of finding work there. Maybe we'll even find some penicillin."

"We could go there in a few days, after we've rested and eaten," Orak added. "I still have a few things we can sell for a bit of cash."

"What have you got left to sell?" Gloria cut in. "We've got the clothes on our backs and one change of clothes."

"I've got my knife . . . Ok, maybe not . . . There's the telescope . . . John's compass . . . I know which way south is without it."

"There's this too," she remembered, taking off a gold bracelet. "And my wedding ring."

John saw how willing she was to part with the ring and remembered his dream. He was sure that whatever Mark was doing on Ithria, Gloria knew nothing about it.

Now wasn't the right time to say anything though. Instead, he suggested more things they could sell. "Would my watch fetch anything? I know the days here are half an hour longer, and the time measuring system is completely different . . ."

"It's shiny, if you're a good salesman you can get something for it," Orak replied.

Everyone handed their un-needed possessions to Orak, who went out with Shoa to try and sell them. The village had over two hundred residents to ask, and many of them appeared to be very wealthy judging by the size of their houses.

Gloria slept in the shared room, while Mac and John sat in the lounge downstairs. They both felt very drowsy, due to the dim lighting and scented candles relaxing them more than necessary.

"There's something I haven't told the others yet," John said, repressing the urge to yawn.

"Is it to do with Shoa?" Mac asked.

"What? No, why?"

"Well, I've just seen the way you look at her."

"We're just friends," John said a little too quickly. "I'm not interested in her."

"It's ok to move on. Maria's been gone for a long time."

"It's not that. Shoa's a nice girl, but . . . Why are we even talking about this? I was trying to tell you something."

"She's a pretty girl, and she's crazy about you."

John ignored him, "It's about the dreams. Do you remember the puddle?"

Mac looked at him blankly, "Puddle?"

"I . . . We ran across a puddle in the dream. Did you see a reflection in it?"

He thought for a minute, "Yes, but . . ."

"It wasn't either of us was it?"

"No, it must be whoever is sending the thought. Another Telepath I expect."

"It was Mark Jones, Gloria's husband."

Mac's jaw physically dropped. He didn't know if it was caused by the shock or his illness, but it gave him a headache. "How can that be? He's from Earth."

"I've been trying to make sense of it, but I can't exactly ask Gloria about it."

"Well, you have to. This could be important, and she needs to know."

"Okay, but not yet. I want to try and figure it out first."

Mac frowned. He couldn't exactly tell Gloria himself, as he'd never met Mark, so he had to wait until John was ready to. "Once we get to the city Shoa said about, we can find out what we can about the island in our nightmares."

"What do you know about it?"

Hobbling towards a cabinet at the back of the lounge, Mac began searching through the drawers. The landlord had told him he kept maps in there, and when Mac had expressed an interest in geography, he allowed him to look through them.

After finding nothing but old guest books and drawings from children who had stayed there, he searched the cupboard underneath. Buried underneath several more books was a string tied pile of canvas maps.

Mac sorted through them and brought out what he was looking for. The map unfolded to the size of a large tablecloth, and he spread it across the floor. "This here is the southernmost county of Tontoltec," he explained, pointing at the large landmass dominating the top half of the map. "We're up here somewhere, in either of these two towns. The city Shoa was talking about must be this one, which is about fifteen miles south west of here. The island is twenty five miles south east of here."

John looked over the huge map. He could see the area that they had been in was completely blank, as nobody really knew it well enough to document. "It's not very big," he said, trying to look for a scale on the map.

"It was when this map was made, but it's growing all the time. The volcanoes make new land every time the lava flows out into the sea, thousands of tons of it. On this map it's called 'Katatua-Shovrus', which means 'Cold Fire'. Not much lives there, except for a few plants, some grazing animals and obviously harpies."

"Do you think we should go there?"

Mac shook his head, "I think the dreams are a warning."

"About the harpies?"

"Maybe, or they could just be the manifestation of something else. Dreams aren't always literal."

They both heard the front doors closing from where they were, and knew that such a heavy slam could only be from Orak. They had guessed he was angry from the manner in which he stormed into the building, but the Titan's behaviour was not always that easy to judge. When they saw him in the foyer, both Mac and John were surprised to see him happy.

"We both got jobs," Orak said, lifting Shoa up in the air like she was a trophy.

"Turns out there aren't any Spellcasters or Titans anywhere near here, so our skills are useful," Shoa explained, laughing as she was dropped back down onto the floor. "They paid us in advance so we've brought food, lots of it!"

"Looks like we're staying for a few days after all."

Chapter 40

Jekka was taken to Ladaan Ijeda's only hospital while the enemy soldiers stood down. They made camp in the farmland, leaving a day before moving towards the city.

Maria didn't let any other medics near Jekka while she tended to his wound. She couldn't believe how lucky he had been. The blade had missed every organ, and although had caused a lot of bleeding, had done no lasting damage. General Kyra had even given a vial of her own blood to help him heal as a token of her gratitude.

The soldiers kept watch over the surrounding land day and night, but the Alkak-Taanan army remained static. The consensus was that they were awaiting further reinforcements.

Kyra however, had another theory. They had arrived not long after the weapons had come through from Earth. She didn't know how, but she was sure there was a connection. The moment she learnt who Maria was, she had sent the woman, whom many of her soldiers had been searching for, on an errand.

In the uppermost quarter of the city, deep inside the rock, she was led through torch lit catacombs. She passed hundreds of tombs built into the walls, many depicting the deceased body in stone carvings. At the end of the old dusty passageway, was a more modern looking section. Two very glum guards stood outside an iron cage built into a large recess.

"We brought him here so if anyone came for him they wouldn't know where to look," her guide explained. "We'll be right outside if you need us."

Maria was not as fluent in Tontoltec as Jekka had become in English, but she understood enough of what had been said. The gate slid across, and once she was inside, it was locked shut.

Lying on a thin mattress on the floor was a pale tired looking man wearing black synthetic fabric. Maria knew at first sight that this person wasn't from Ithria. She felt drawn to him as it had been so long since she had seen someone from her own world. She knew that she wouldn't have a meaningful conversation or friendly catch up. This man was a prisoner, a dangerous criminal, and she was there to interrogate him.

"Stand up," she told him.

The man didn't reply. She didn't know whether he was dead or just asleep, but he wasn't moving. Crouching down, she shook him by the arm. Slowly the prisoner groaned and rolled over to face her.

"Well hello there," he said when he saw her face.

"Get up!" she snapped, hoping this would knock back his advance.

"I thought I was cranky this morning," he replied.

Maria noticed that he had an American accent, and what may have once been a healthy and handsome face, was now gaunt pale and sweaty. She suspected that he hadn't been fed at all, and the cuts across his skin looked infected. This kind of treatment would never be allowed in the civilised world she came from, and she realised just how primitive this place really was.

"What's your name?" she asked, trying to maintain her tough demeanour.

"Maxwell . . . Maxwell Stanton. And yours?"

Maria ignored his question, "Why did you come here?"

"Why do you think? Why did you come here? You're from England right?"

"No, I'm not from England. I came here because I had no choice. Why are you here?"

Maxwell stood up slowly, revealing dozens of thin but deep razor blade cuts on his legs. He was built like a wrestler, but appeared to have almost no strength in his whole body.

"Stay there!" Maria shouted, taking up a defensive stance.

"I ain't gonna hurt you," he laughed, "I'm a true gent, just offering you my seat."

"No . . . But thank you. Why are you on Ithria, Mr Stanton?"

"You mean you don't know? Your bosses didn't tell you?"

"Tell me what?" she was beginning to get angry now.

"The warheads . . . . They came to the wrong place; we need them back."

"Warheads?" Alarm bells went off in her head. Suddenly things had gotten a lot worse. "You mean nuclear warheads?"

"Yeah, nuclear. Sixteen kiloton experimental warheads. Four of them."

"Oh shit! Why the fuck did you send nuclear bombs to this planet!" she screamed, punching him in the arm so forcefully that he fell back down to the ground.

"Whoa, relax lady. We can get you off this rock before they detonate. They weren't meant to come here anyway. We were delivering to our partners; they've already paid, so we kind of need them back."

"What partners? Who the hell are you working for? Is it the government?"

Maxwell laughed, "The government, hell no! Ithria Ltd is a private company."

Maria had to take up his offer to sit down as her head had just started spinning. "Do you work for Mark Jones?"

"No, Jonesy is only middle management. You've heard of us?"

"Only in passing. Who are your partners?"

"Well, the only nation who can afford our services, Alkak-Taan."

*

From a window high above, Kyra looked down on the entrance to the catacombs and wondered what progress her interrogator was making.

From here, she could see almost the whole north side of the city below, and beyond the walls she could see thousands of hectares of farmland. A faint green line on the horizon highlighted where the forest began, and with the aid of a telescope she could see the enemy encampment. There were now well over two hundred Alkak-Taanan soldiers, but not enough to storm the city. She was sure the flying units and arachnid infantry would soon arrive, and tip the scales considerably in the enemy's favour.

Until then though, they were safe. The general left the window and headed further into the building. In the very centre of the bank, was the largest most secure vault in the city. Dozens of skilled, educated men and women were working around the clock, trying to understand the most advanced technology they had ever seen.

The missiles had been removed from the crate, and the metal framework holding them together had been disassembled. The metal on the pipe sections was as light as the lightest metal they knew of, but stronger than the strongest. The projectile weapons themselves had a propulsion system that could only have come from another planet. They had successfully removed the explosive component from the rocket section, but still had no idea how to detonate it.

"We think the weapon is triggered by a certain frequency of electrical signal," the scientist's spokesman explained to the general. "But we have no way of successfully navigating the propulsion system to a target. If we can drop this section on our enemy and successfully set it off, then it will cause more destruction than you could imagine."

"Keep working on it," she instructed. "This could be our only way to win this war."

Across the room, a Spellcaster was using small electrical impulses on the separated rocket section. They stopped to talk to another technician, before continuing their experiment.

"Can you give me a timeframe for when they'll be ready?" Kyra asked the team's spokesman.

He shook his head, "We haven't even begun to understand what we're doing here."

As Kyra was about to reply, she saw a blinding flash of light. She leapt out of the way, just before a table was blasted across the room. A smooth stream of fire erupted from the exhaust of a rocket section, setting the furniture all around them on fire within seconds. The restraints holding it down burnt to a crisp, and the huge white projectile broke free, shooting it straight through the wall. It smashed through the rock, striking the next wall at an angle. The engine cut out, and the rocket crashed down onto the floor.

Kyra clambered back to her feet. "Lose the tail sections, they're too unpredictable. Focus on the explosives."

*

Maria couldn't believe what she was hearing. This man showed no remorse over the fact his company was contributing to a war for personal profit.

How could they justify their actions just by saying it wasn't their world they were destroying?

"How are they paying you?" she asked.

"A little exchanging of our tech for a chance to explore the Anuma state of energy, but mostly gold."

"Gold?"

"Alkak-Taan alone has more gold than our entire planet, its worthless over here, but back home it makes us one of the wealthiest international companies nobody has ever heard of. We own businesses in every continent, but they are just covers."

"And I suppose Mark Jones' bank is one of those fronts?"

"That's right. He was one of the founders of the company, he first discovered a rift in his own garage, can you believe it?"

Maria wanted to strangle this man, but she couldn't, not yet. She still needed to find out more. "What else have you sold to the Alkak-Taanan government?"

"The warheads were the first stolen weapons we could get our hands on. But we had labs . . . they asked us to engineer soldiers for them. They had blood samples and living specimens for us, which we used to engineer their hybrid warriors. Took us years, but I couldn't believe what our geneticists managed to do."

Maria did nothing to disguise her expression of disgust, but this didn't seem to deter Maxwell from telling her everything. Mac had told her that the link had re-formed four years before, but they had only been able to observe in that time. Obviously the enemy had been able to pass through long before he could.

"What did you make for them?" she asked, dreading the answer.

"We made dragon people called Drathmorks, which I've been told have been a resounding success. The other ones we made later we call Arachno-Sapiens. They are built from spiders and the Anuma enhanced people called Titans. Jonesy personally oversaw their development and deployment; how do you know him?"

"If you'd made these for Alkak-Taan, why send nuclear bombs through?"

Maxwell shrugged, "I guess they just got impatient, battlefield warfare is slow, even if your soldiers can fly. Maybe they thought it would be more humane."

Before she knew what she was doing, Maria had turned around and slammed the base of her hand into the mercenary's chest, winding him. She then grabbed the back of his neck and threw his head down into the path of her knee. "You son of a bitch!" she spat, kicking him in the gut while he lay on the floor. Jekka was lying in a hospital bed because of this man and his greedy company, and she wanted to see him suffer like he was suffering. Maria had to walk out of the cell to stop herself from doing any more damage to the prisoner.

She slammed the door closed and spoke through the bars.

"How did you and your team know you would arrive at the same place the bombs did?" she asked as calmly as she could.

"We planned it?"

"How?"

"I want to make a deal."

"What?"

Maxwell tapped against the bars to attract the attention of the men guarding his cell. "Tell them I want to make a deal. I want freedom and passage back home in exchange for the information."

"Nobody is going to make a deal with you"

One of the guards left to find the general. Maria also went off to find her. She didn't want anyone to have to torture the prisoner any more, but she knew they would if he refused to tell her more. Even though she wanted to see him suffer, she didn't want to be any part of what was bound to happen. Instead, she decided to make a deal on Kyra's behalf.

She returned a few minutes later to the cage. "Start talking and they will let you live," she said.

"That wasn't the deal I wanted," he replied. "If it's a choice between being imprisoned on this backwards world or death, I choose death."

Maria banged her hand against the bars, "You bastard! I'm trying to do you a favour!"

"Freedom and safe passage to where I can get to Earth, in exchange for any information you want," he repeated.

Maria explained the request to the guard who had returned unsuccessfully. She spoke in broken sentences, and asked whether anyone but the general could make him an offer.

"If he tells us everything we need, then you could offer to take him."

"No way, I'm not taking him anywhere . . . I've got a new deal." She turned back to the mercenary and switched back to speaking English. "We let you go free, but you make your own way from there?"

Reluctantly Maxwell accepted. He hauled himself back to his feet making it look like the hardest thing in the world to do. He wished he could have negotiated some food for his journey, but he knew that would be pushing his luck.

"Jonesy built a machine, moved it to Calais in France," Maxwell explained. "He worked out that the rift only formed in the UK and parts of Northern Europe. He found the epicentre, and put it there. He sent a team of engineers through with the components to build a duplicate machine at the corresponding point on Ithria. We use the machines to send us where and when we want on both worlds using the Anuma link."

"That's impossible," Maria replied, but the idea of the link itself still seemed impossible to her. "Where is the duplicate machine?"

"The rift only forms in Tontoltec on this side, unless you're already here, but that's a separate issue. The epicentre and the machine are on a volcanic island way south of here called Katatua-Shovrus."

Chapter 41

Orak and Shoa both left for their first day of work the following morning. The others stayed in the hotel to continue resting. John very quickly got bored of sitting around indoors playing board games he didn't understand, that he went to visit Orak and Shoa's new work places.

When he arrived at the address the Titan had given him, he realised why he had not disclosed the nature of his new employment. John found him at the back of the stables next to a mountainous pile of manure, holding an extra large makeshift shovel.

"A bit of a step down from Professor of Languages," John laughed.

"My abilities mean I can shovel twice as much shit as a normal person, so they can pay out less to get the job done."

"How many hours are you doing?"

"About three a day, over four different stable buildings. It's enough to pay the rent for all of us."

"Is Shoa working here too?"

She had told John how good she was at horse riding, and he wondered whether she was teaching it or not. He found the idea funny that an undergraduate student of Orak's could be teaching while he was clearing excrement.

"No, she's found a much better job than me. They've appointed her the town mayor."

John laughed. For a split second he believed him.

"She has found a better paid job though, as security at the tavern."

"Seriously? Is she allowed to use her powers?"

"Technically no, but the customers know she has them, it's enough of a deterrent. They offered it to me first, but I had to take up this one because they only offered this to me. It was the only way we could both get work."

"How long are we planning on staying here?"

"As little time as possible."

"Well I'd love to stay and chat, but I better pay Shoa a visit."

Orak gave him detailed directions to the tavern. Although the town was fairly small, it was incredibly easy to get lost in. If Mradraak returned, this place would be the ideal labyrinth to put in his mind.

On his way, he passed the hotel, but didn't go back in. Mac and Gloria needed all the rest they could get. He couldn't remember any phrases to ask for directions, so he had to make sure he didn't make any wrong turns.

Eventually, he found the tavern at the end of a street of terraced houses. It was four storeys in high, built of stone and had large stained glass sections on the top two floors of the gable end. It resembled a catholic church, and reminded him of the local bar back home.

Shoa was just finishing her shift when he got to the door, and she decided she had a bit of money to spare. It felt like it had been a very long time since either of them had had a drink.

Inside, the pub looked very much like the one in Whitefalls, but there wasn't a pool table or dartboard in sight. They sat towards the back where it was quieter, and just like before, Shoa bought the drinks. The only beverages on sale were strong liquor tasting of almonds, and even stronger liquor that had more in common with surgical spirit than alcohol.

They had bought the almond liquor, and mixed it with lots of fruit juice. Even the smallest measure was about the size of two double 25ml measures, and was about the proof of absinthe.

John winced when he first tried it, but after a few sips he found it quite agreeable. "How was your first shift?" he asked.

"It was a trial, that's why I finished so early. I passed, so I'll be here a few hours, finishing at midnight every day now."

"Any disruptive customers?"

"One, but he was too drunk to do anything but complain and shout. The barman helped me drag him outside."

Shoa looked around at the other customers. Most of them looked sullen, and must be here to try and take their mind off of the war that would inevitably come. She looked back at John, who appeared to be thinking the same.

"So what's next?" he asked.

"What do you mean?"

"When we reach this city, and if Mac is cured . . . If he can't get us back to Earth, what next?"

Shoa shrugged, "We wait until he can. We can't go back to Whitefalls. What other choice do we have?"

"Katatua-Shovrus?"

"The volcanic island where you and Mac keep getting eaten by harpies?"

John frowned. He had to admit that the dreams had a clear meaning, but there had to be a more important reason why they had been brought to their attention.

"Mradraak told me someone called Kedos was giving us information. What if the dreams are the information he's giving us?"

"So this Kedos is on our side?"

"Not necessarily. There are not always just two sides to a conflict."

"So why do you want to go there?"

He stopped halfway through taking a sip of his drink. He had absolutely no idea. Just as Shoa had been doing all night, John shrugged his shoulders.

They both felt slightly queasy halfway through their second drink, but Shoa felt compelled to buy another. The drinks were dangerously cheap, and Shoa had been paid in hand at the end of her shift.

"Do you think the others are wondering where we are?" John slurred a little while later.

"I think they could do with some quiet and peace."

John burst into a fit of laughter. "You said it wrong," he said like an amused child.

"You up shut!" she giggled. They had already forgotten their concerns of the other three.

It had gone dark long ago, and nearly all of the other punters had left. Most people in the town worked six if not seven days a week.

The bartender looked about ready to close up when he saw his new bouncer get up to spend the rest of her pay check. She couldn't walk straight, she could barely stand without John's help, but there was no law against serving someone who had clearly had too much.

She ordered the stronger liquor neat this time, and when she tasted it asked, "Is there any alcohol in this?"

The bartender gave her and John some free food, to make sure that Shoa was alive for work the next day. They devoured the food like starving animals, making more mess than the barman had seen in a long time. "Northerners," he tutted.

Without realising what he was doing, John fed Shoa food from his own plate. She pretended to bite his fingers, laughed and then kissed his hand.

"We should go," John said, trying to get out of his chair. It felt as though the floor was tipping, and for a moment he was back on the Black Diamond during the storm.

The pair of them supported each other when they left, nearly walking into the doorframe.

"Can you remember the way back?" John asked her.

"Can I remember the . . . No, no I can't. I'm cold."

"Have my . . . I don't have a coat," he laughed.

John wasn't remotely cold, but when Shoa hugged him for warmth he didn't push her away. Neither of them cared that they were lost. All they cared about was that at least for tonight they were free from the war, free from Mac's illness, free from the worry that followed them everywhere they went.

They stopped staggering when they reached a crossroads. In one direction was a road they both recognised, in the other, open parkland. Swaying left, they walked across the grassland.

They sat down in the middle of a playing field and lay down on the short cropped turf. Staring up at the moons, Shoa's eyes seemed to shimmer with happiness.

The next moment John was holding her, "You look so pretty," he told her sweetly, "You've always been pretty."

Shoa leaned in and kissed him, slipping off his shirt. "Are you sure you want to do this?" she asked.

Without a second of thought, he said, "Yes."

Passionately, they made love until both of them were too exhausted to continue. They stared into each other's eyes until they fell asleep, John first then Shoa a few minutes later.

Chapter 42

John woke, confused to be looking up at a cloudless starry sky. He felt warm bare skin next to his and looked down to see Shoa naked in his arms.

As he moved his head, a debilitating headache struck him like a hammer. A few hours ago he hadn't felt cold, but lying in the wet grass he definitely did now. Slowly and carefully, he moved away from Shoa and gathered up his clothes.

Once he was dressed, he found Shoa's robes and laid them down over her while she slept. It was still dark, but he couldn't guarantee nobody else would come here, so eventually he would have to wake her up.

For now though, he sat with his head in his hands, wondering how something that had felt so right a few hours earlier could feel so wrong now. He dreaded having to tell Gloria about this, as he could already imagine her voice yelling at him for being so irresponsible:

> "You had unprotected sex with a girl who's barely of age! On a planet with no safe emergency contraception! No STD tests! And with medieval medicine! What were you thinking? I never thought you could be so reckless!"

John also knew that Shoa wouldn't think of this as just a one night stand. He didn't even know if this kind of thing was even tolerated in her culture like it was in his. He also knew despite how much he liked her, they could never sustain a relationship, their age gap was too much, no matter how juvenile he was, and no matter how mature Shoa sometimes acted.

The worst part was that even though he had never got this far in his relationship with Maria, and he had not seen her in such a long time, he still felt guilty. He needed to move on, but without knowing whether she was dead or alive, he couldn't.

When he turned to look back at Shoa, he saw her eyes were open. She gave him a wide smile, and he wondered how she had such white teeth in a world with no toothpaste. That thought was brushed away and his heart sank when he realised she wasn't feeling any of the regret he was. She didn't even look hungover.

"Morning," she said elatedly, looking up at the stars, "Well, not quite."

"Morning," he replied awkwardly.

"You gave me a blanket, you're so sweet. Can you remember the constellations I taught you?"

"Some of them," John mumbled, unable to pick out any shapes amongst the celestial bodies, "You should get dressed."

"Why? Are you shy?" she laughed, dropping the loose sheet like robe, "Have you seen my underwear?"

John shook his head then stood up, "I'll meet you back at the hotel. The others will be wondering where we are."

Shoa's mood changed in an instant, "You said you wanted this last night!" she shouted, covering herself back up.

"It's still last night!" He shouted back, "And I'd have said anything!"

John traipsed back through the dewy grass, so consumed by his own thoughts that he didn't realise he was walking the wrong way. Turning back, he walked along the furthest edge of the field so as not to run into her again.

He made the same mistake several times once he re-entered the residential area, but eventually found himself back on track. The stars had faded into the dark blue sky, and grey clouds had begun to form. By the time he got back, the moons had vanished and it was nearly daylight.

Despite him not getting especially lost, Shoa had somehow got back first. She had not held back any details, and John was welcomed by Orak's fist to his gut. He had imagined what being hit by a Titan would feel like, but it was ten times worse.

Gloria didn't wait for him to recover before saying her piece, and her wrath was also much worse than he had envisioned. Mac just looked down on him, disappointed.

"I'm sorry, I acted stupidly," John croaked.

"Too right you did," Mac replied once the others had gone, "Was this what you thought I meant when I said it's okay to move on from Maria? Get Shoa so drunk she doesn't know what she's doing, sleep with her and then dump her like she means nothing?"

"If anything, she took advantage of me," John replied, "I . . ."

He stopped halfway through his sentence when he realised how pathetic he sounded. It wasn't as if he had no self control.

"How is she?" he asked.

"Upset, how do you think she is?" Mac replied, "She's not blameless though, Shoa spent all of her money, which means we barely have enough for food."

"I'm sorry," John said sullenly.

"I'm not the person you need to say sorry to. We've bought food for me, Orak and Gloria; it's you and Shoa who are going to have to go without."

John didn't like the sound of going more than a day without eating, but he didn't give a word of protest. He knew he deserved it, but Shoa didn't.

*

As soon as Kyra was told about the machine on Katatua-Shovrus, she ordered the assembly of an elite unit of soldiers and the acquisition of a long distance sea vessel. She also persuaded Maria to look at the Earth weapon, and asked if she could try to explain how they could get it to work.

Maria was led through a series of torch lit corridors, through more iron security grates than she could count, and into the vault.

For the first time since the artifacts had been brought into the city, the room holding them was completely empty. The scientists had been ordered to leave the Earth woman to study the objects in peace.

She entered the cell knowing what to expect, but when she saw the state of the weapons, a feeling of dread crept over her. One of the warheads itself had been partially dismantled, exposing the encased radioactive component. Although she was sure it was completely sealed within non-conductive material, she understood the dangers that nobody else here did.

Maria had tried to explain these dangers to the general, but she had ignored her. Kyra was determined to use these weapons to her advantage. Words had no effect, and Maria expected the only way Kyra would truly understand would be to see the results herself. This had to be stopped.

With no knowledge of nuclear weapons, she would be relying on guesswork. Maxwell had told her that these warheads were experimental, and designed to be dismantled easily for safe transit. This gave her some confidence, but not much.

She asked the guards outside to leave so she could concentrate better, and after talking it over, they moved further down the corridor, out of sight of the vault door.

"What have you gotten yourself into now?" she muttered to herself, staring at the nuclear devices.

One mistake could result in an explosion which would kill her, Jekka, the general and her army, as well as the rest of the city in an instant. Slowly she removed the outer casing of the partially dismantled bomb, and placed it underneath the table. Using the knife Jekka had given her as a present several weeks ago, she cut through the wires connecting the power source. Once it was separated, she concealed it within her backpack and continued. Without a battery, she was certain the device couldn't be triggered, but her hands still trembled uncontrollably.

Once she had done the same with the other two partially dismantled bombs, she moved on to the most hazardous component. Carefully, she disconnected and removed the encased plutonium cores and placed them in her backpack. Once all three were safely stowed away, she replaced the warhead casings.

The final weapon had been untouched, and she saw that it was held together by a large number of screws. Using her knife as a screwdriver, she began trying to remove them, just as Kyra entered the vault to ask if she had made any progress.

Maria's heart jolted and the knife fell from her hands.

"I didn't see you come in," she replied quickly, mashing her words.

"Do you know how we can use them?" Kyra asked.

"No . . . I err, I don't think they are complete."

Maria held her bag tightly, and then dropped it to try and avoid suspicion. She went to pick up her fallen knife, dropping it several more times before putting it back on the table.

"If its incentives you want, I can make it worth your while?" Kyra asked, "I already owe your partner for holding back the enemy forces, I can make sure the two of you get exactly what you need or want. Is there anything I can do for you?"

Maria knew exactly what she wanted the general to do, bury the remaining intact bomb and tell nobody where it was. "I'll let you know," she replied, forcing a smile.

Several men entered the vault. At first Maria thought it was the research team returning, but when she saw their chainmail vests, she realised that they were no scientists. They gathered around the tables and helped each other to lift and move them through the door.

"What's going on?" Maria demanded when she saw the unopened warhead being taken.

"We're loading them onto the ship," Kyra explained, "So once we know how, we can send them straight to the enemy using this machine our prisoner told you about."

"But I'm not done! I need to . . . I need to find out the . . ."

There was nothing more she could say, the general would never be swayed. The only answers Kyra was interested in were violent, and Maria feared violence would be the only thing to stop her.

*

John did not speak to any of the others for the rest of the day. He tried to think of a way to make it up to Shoa, but his mind was a blank. The following morning he set off to try and find a job himself.

With very little understanding of the local dialect and few useful skills here, he found no success. Failing to find employment, he went down to the market to see if he could sell something. As his only possessions were his clothes and his tatty trainers, he unsuccessfully tried to sell his worn hole-filled socks.

John was so hungry he would have eaten anything. He was tempted to steal from the fruit stall, but feared the repercussions. A taste of an apple wasn't worth him losing a hand over.

Instead, he walked all the way to the edge of the town, and picked as much fruit as he could from the trees and bushes. He tied his shirt into a bag and loaded it up with fruit for Shoa and the others.

This would not earn him forgiveness, but it was a start.

Chapter 43

Jekka rested in Ladaan-Ijeda's hospital for three days, even though after two days, there were only scars from his wounds. The general's blood had given him strength and vitality, and he felt more alive than he ever had before. Maria on the other hand felt and looked ill.

When she came with the general to visit Jekka, she had been mistaken for a patient. She could not express her concerns in front of Kyra, as it would involve admitting her guilt. Maria had taken the components from three of the bombs and hidden them within her temporary quarters, planning to throw them in the deepest body of water she could find.

The team of nurses, who had been assessing the patient's recovery, left the private room when the two women entered. Maria hugged Jekka tightly, neither of them wanting to let go. Jekka could sense her fear. They separated, allowing Kyra to talk to the hero she felt she was indebted to.

"Many people are alive today as a result of your bravery," she began, kneeling so they were nearly eye to eye.

Jekka leant across the bed and grasped her hand to thank and accept her praise. "I was just doing my duty to my countrymen," he replied.

"You showed skill greater than any fighter under my command, unrivalled by any mere human. I wish to offer you a reward for your courage. I know all about your banishment, and would like to start by requesting a full parliamentary pardon. I know the government will listen to me on such a matter."

Jekka and Maria's faces lit up.

"Thank you," Jekka replied. "Thank you so much."

"You don't know how much this means to us," Maria added, wanting to hug the general, but refrained from doing so.

"I'd also like to make you an offer, and feel free to discuss the terms. I owe both of you," Kyra continued, "I was impressed by your fighting, and as I said, you showed more ability than the soldiers currently in my command. I understand that before your discharge, you were acting centurion?"

Before she could even ask, Jekka shook his head. "I won't go back to the army," he said firmly, taking his hand away. "I won't fight or lead more men to their deaths."

Kyra stood up. "This world is at war and there are only two choices: fight or flee. Sooner or later all those who flee will run out of places to hide," she said sternly, "The offer still stands if you change your mind."

"I've made my decision," he replied, taking hold of Maria's hand.

"I have a hundred men preparing to set sail to Katatua-Shovrus. I need someone more than competent to lead them; this could be the most important move we make in the war . . . The ships leave port in twelve hours, in six, I will ask you again. I hope you will reconsider."

Kyra didn't leave in the best of moods. For several minutes afterwards, they could hear doors slamming throughout the building, but once it had ended Maria turned to Jekka. She offered to help him out of bed, but he clambered out by himself.

To demonstrate to her that he was no cripple, he hoisted her up into his arms and carried her out of the room, kicking the door closed behind with his foot.

"Maybe I should try some of that Titan blood," she laughed.

When they got back to the room Maria had been staying in, Jekka saw his sword lying across the floor and propped it up prominently against the wall. The sheath had gone missing during the battle, and he could see that the once well looked after weapon had huge dents and chips all down it.

Maria looked out of the window at the clock tower near the palace above them. She remembered how much time Kyra had given them and thought about how she could approach the subject.

"You do know I would follow you anywhere?" she asked him.

"And I would follow you to the edge of the world if there was one," Jekka replied, "But I don't want to go anywhere. If we find work, we can stay here for as long as we like."

"There's something I need to tell you, and something I will ask you to do, but you won't like it."

Jekka sat down on the bed, "I don't understand?"

Maria sat down beside him. She knew they had hours yet, but she wanted him to know as soon as possible. He would not understand as well as she did, but she had to try.

"The general asked me to look at some devices yesterday," she explained, "They were weapons, but they came from my world."

Jekka suddenly looked frightened. Had she found a way back to Earth? Was she asking him to leave his world to go to hers?

Standing back up, he walked across the room. "Erinthia is my home," he said, gazing out of the window towards the forest.

"Can you let me finish, please? This is hard for me."

He turned back to her, but remained standing.

"The weapons from Earth, Kyra doesn't understand what they can do," Maria continued, "Nobody on Ithria does. I can't let her use them. I managed to render three of the weapons useless, but I couldn't with the fourth. We have to stop the weapon from reaching that island. It could kill millions."

"What can I do though? If you can't get to this weapon again, what makes you think I can?"

"Because if you lead her soldiers to that island, the weapon will be on your ship."

"I won't leave you to go to war."

"You won't have to, I'll come too."

Jekka turned away again, he didn't want her putting her life on the line, but he couldn't bear to be away from her for so long. "The general offered me a job, but not you, what makes you think she will allow you on her ship?"

"I'll have to convince her that I'm worth having on board. This is really important Jekka. We have to get rid of that weapon any way we can."

Angrily, he slammed his fist into the door. He began pacing the room, muttering things in his native tongue, only partially understood by Maria. "Do you know how long it has been since I commanded soldiers?"

Maria knew exactly how long it had been, he had virtually yelled it at her the last time he had lost his temper. "I believe you can still do it. I bet you would be better than Kyra at running her army. Unless you suffer from sea sickness, I don't see how you would have any problems. I don't want to go out and fight, it's the last thing I want to do, but I know you can protect me."

"I don't want you in harm's way. I want us to flee, not fight."

"I'm going to ask Kyra for a place on those ships," Maria said with an air of finality. "If you want to come too, then you'll have to make your mind up soon."

Maria prayed that he would stick with her, now more than ever. She would never cope without him on this mission; she wouldn't survive.

*

After nearly a day of hunger, Shoa refused to spend any of her next few cash payments without discussing it with the rest of the group. They stayed in the hotel, but with combined incomes they could now afford a room each. Shoa and John had been located on different sides of the building by Orak, causing much protest. John was twenty-five, and he was being treated like a naughty teenager, but there was little he could do about it. Shoa on the other hand, was a naughty teenager.

News of the war had reached the town. Alkak-Taanan soldiers had been seen on the southern border of Caracracia. Although this was many hundreds of miles away, people had already started to pack. Mac guessed that over two hundred people would leave the town within the week and head across the oceans to lands safe from the war. Orak and Shoa's jobs would become unnecessary fairly soon.

They had decided to keep working until their jobs became redundant, or until they felt they had enough to comfortably travel to their next destination. It wasn't long before Orak's hours were halved, as several stables closed and were boarded up. Shoa's shifts stayed the same, but as dread crept over the streets, the customers became more and more unpleasant. They knew Alkak-Taan was run by those who wanted the Anuma-using minority races back in power, and this caused bitter feelings towards the residing Spellcaster.

She returned from her third shift so late, that it was starting to be early. She had seen starry skies throughout her shift, but as she walked home the sky was a lightening blue, and she saw several people leaving their homes to go to work. She was so exhausted that she could barely keep her eyes open as she climbed the hotel stairs to her room.

When she unlocked her door, she heard a noise from inside and stopped before she could open it. She wondered if one of the others had gotten the wrong room. This didn't seem possible as she had the only key. Preparing to cast out a bolt of lightning from her fingertips, she threw the door open and looked inside.

The small one bed room was completely empty. From the doorway she could see the desk, wardrobe, the bed and beneath it. Glancing at both sides of the door, she saw nothing but the shadows cast by the furniture. Checking the wardrobe, she saw nothing but a single robe hanging from a wooden hanger. It must have been coming from another room.

Shoa fell into bed without getting changed, and before she could finish yawning, she had fallen asleep. The dim flame of the gas lamp upon the mantle flickered away, plunging the room into darkness. Several hours later she woke up in blackness.

Slowly she felt her way across the room towards the door. Touching the wall, she ran her hands along in search of the frame. After moving several feet to the right, she stood where she was sure the door should be, but still felt only the smooth plastered walls. Panic stricken, she felt all the way around until she had passed all four corners of the room. She had not encountered any of the furniture along the way, and tried to find some bearings.

Sure that she was having a bad dream, she made her way back to the bed, but after walking back to the middle of the room, she found nothing. "Hello! Is anyone outside?" she called, laughing nervously, "I can't find the door."

Reply came in the form of a muffled distressed sounding voice, followed by loud hammering on the other side of the studwork wall. Shoa banged the wall, trying to signal that she was there, but as she did, she saw a thin slither of light forming in the wall. Three more lines appeared, forming the shape of the doorway.

Yanking the door open she found herself outdoors. The door promptly vanished behind her as she tried to turn back. She could feel the damp grass under her bare feet, and the cool breeze flowing through her hair but knew that none of this could be real. She couldn't have left the hotel. "Mradraak!" she hissed under her breath, trying to snap herself out of this illusion.

*

Maria left the room shortly after giving Jekka the ultimatum. She wandered through the corridors without aim or direction to give him time to think. They both knew that in a few days the enemy would attack the city, and that if they didn't leave before then, they would have to fight anyway.

She despised the idea of close quarter combat. She knew she wouldn't last long against men who had probably been training their entire lives. Maria knew she would last even less time if they encountered any of the enemy's hybrid soldiers, and was sure they would have better chances upon a moving ship with a hundred other swordsmen on board than they had here.

When she returned to their suite, she found Jekka sitting on the bed just as she had left him. "Do you still want to go on that ship?" he asked her.

"Yes," she replied, knowing that he could sense her hesitation.

"If the general thinks this mission can win us the war, and if you feel stopping this weapon is the right thing to do, then what choice do I have? I'll accept her offer."

Maria hugged him, not wanting to let go. Tearing herself away she told him to pack, before rushing out through the door. She sprinted up the steps outside the building, taking her to the higher parts of the city. Without knowing exactly where she was going, she asked everyone she saw for directions to the barracks. Once she had found the barracks, she was directed back down to the training fields in the lowest part of Ladaan-Ijeda.

By the time she found Kyra, she was exhausted. The general was stood in front of the team she had selected for the mission to Katatua-Shovrus. Maria stood close to them and listened to the briefing.

Kyra explained that there would be three ships, and that the crew would be split so that there were two teams of thirty three and one of thirty five, making a total crew of a hundred and one. They would sail from a port forty miles from the city, and it would take them approximately four weeks to reach the island. Once they reached the volcanic landmass, they would make camp on the eastern shores, then search every square mile until they found the machine. Kyra gave no detailed instructions as to what they were to do when they got to the machine, but several men standing close to her had already been told.

Fifteen minutes after arriving, Maria saw the men being dismissed. Kyra signalled for her to join the group of soldiers standing beside a large sandy dugout. All but the general and one young man were left to return to the barracks, and Kyra introduced Maria to her second in command.

"KloHadras will be standing in for Jekka as commander of the fleet," she explained, "How can I help you?"

"Jekka will only accept your offer if I come too." Maria replied confidently.

"Can I trust you?"

Maria felt her heart jolt. Standing before these two towering warriors, she felt two feet tall. *Had the general figured her out? Had she found the stolen batteries and plutonium cores?*

"I . . . I don't . . . Of course you can trust me?" Maria stammered.

Kyra stared at her, unsure what to make of the woman's response.

"What use will you serve on my ships?"

"I can fight, Jekka taught me."

The general started to walk away, but stopped beside a sword lying on the floor. She picked it up and threw it towards Maria.

"Prove it!" she said as the young soldier beside her drew his sword, "First to draw blood wins."

Chapter 44

Shoa wandered the field, searching for a reason as to why she was there. Looking up, she saw the sky was a pale green colour, reflecting the vegetation upon the ground. She wondered whether this was what the sky would look like in a world with no oceans.

"I know you're trying to get my attention or frighten me!" she called out, "I know this is all a trick."

This time nobody replied. Nothing changed, and she continued to walk along the endless meadow. She was reminded of the field where she and John had spent the night together, and wondered whether this was some kind of punishment for it.

Since it had happened, Gloria had treated her differently, whether it was her being protective of John or just worried for her, Shoa didn't know. One thing she did know was that John was the one being treated like the bad guy, despite the fact that she had seduced him. He had knocked back countless advances in the past few months, and only when he had been too drunk to stop did he succumb.

Shoa was not panicked or frightened by the imaginary world around her; it seemed far too serene to be scary. She was confused however, why would Mradraak take her here? Wherever here was supposed to be.

After a few minutes of being completely alone, a cloaked figure appeared from a ditch she had not previously seen. He approached fast but his feet remained still. Shoa tried to cast fire from her hands, but nothing happened, and before she could move, the figure was upon her.

"What do you want!" she screamed, striking the figure with the side of her open palm. Her hand sliced straight through as if the man was a ghost, and she tried backing away.

As she ran backwards, the ground below moved in the opposite direction, while the cloaked stranger hovered a foot above it. The hood fell, and she saw the face of a grey haired elderly man she didn't know, looking down on her.

"I will not let you go until you tell me where Kedos is!" he demanded in a deep booming voice, which sounded as though it was coming from all directions at once. As he spoke, the ground shook, and the sky turned a deep blood red. The clouds ignited, and fire streaked across in every direction.

"Okay, I'll tell you!" she screamed, "I'll tell you, just stop this!"

The quaking meadow calmed down, and the burning clouds vanished. "Where is Kedos?" Mradraak repeated.

"In the desert, Caracracia . . . That's all I know!" she lied. Shoa still had no idea who Kedos was, but she was sure now that he was on their side.

"Where?" the Telepath demanded, "Where in Caracracia?"

"I don't know! Just get out! Get out of my mind!"

"TELL ME!!!" he roared, and the ground began to shake again.

Shoa felt the soil shifting beneath her, as tentacle like roots wrapped themselves around her legs. "ReDrok Palace!" she yelled so loud that everyone in the hotel could hear. When she opened her eyes, she was lying on the shared bathroom floor, with the shower curtain wrapped around her feet.

Her desperate attempt had obviously worked, but as soon as this dangerous illusionist realised she was lying, he would try again. He would not stop trying until he found Kedos, but she had bought them all time.

*

Maria stared into the eyes of her opponent. He was human like her, but still looked far stronger than she was. The determination she saw in him, told her that he would not give up until he proved his worthiness to the general. He would not give up after just shedding her blood.

"Never make the first move," she heard Jekka saying in her mind.

The young swordsman facing her seemed to have the same idea. He began pacing sideways just as the Alkak-Taanan centurion had several days before. Maria felt herself rooted to the spot and had to force herself to move her feet around like a boxer.

The only way she could think of forcing him to start, was to lure him into a false sense of security. Glancing in Kyra's direction, she took her eyes off the energetic soldier. He kept his distance, forcing Maria to take her plan a step further.

Tossing her sword from hand to hand, she dropped it to the ground. The soldier's eyes lit up like an excited child when the opportunity arose and he ran full speed towards the unarmed woman.

Ducking backwards like a limbo dancer, Maria avoided the swinging blade. As the man's arm was outstretched, she pulled a knife free from his belt and stabbed it deep into his arm, a few inches below the pit. Screaming in pain the young warrior fell to his knees.

Falling backwards in horror, she looked at what she had done. "I'm so sorry," Maria wept, "I'm a doctor, I can help."

As she reached for him, the shamed fighter pushed her away. Kyra stepped in, having only been observing until now, and separated the two fighters.

"The rules were clear," she said sternly, "First to draw blood wins, so Maria, you've won. Tell Centurion Jekka that you will be sharing a bunk with him on the TMV Victory."

"Can I help him first, I was a trained medic back on Earth?" she pleaded.

"I can do more for him than you," the general replied, showing a scar across a vain in her arm. Kyra escorted the wounded man from the training grounds, after leaving instructions for Maria on where and when to meet the rest of Jekka's new unit.

Once she had gone, Maria picked up the fallen soldier's knife and cleaned the blood off in a patch of grass. This would be her lucky weapon, it had been there when she had needed it, and she expected it could be of such use again.

Maria rushed back towards the building they were staying in. Bounding up a dozen sets of steep steps, she felt a new energy in herself. Throughout her training with Jekka she never thought she would ever want to use what she had learnt, but realising how skilled she had become, she felt a great sense of victory.

By the time she was halfway there however, she was exhausted and had to stop for a break. She had stopped in a part of the city she couldn't remember seeing before, and realised she must have taken a different route from before.

The courtyard she found herself in belonged to a school and for the first time since she had been on this world, she saw children playing. For the first time, she knew exactly what Kyra, the young soldier she had hurt and Jekka would all be fighting for. There would be no room for children to play in a world run by winged monsters.

The boys playing something resembling football looked to be about five or six years old, and didn't have a single care or worry in the world. Maria thought back to when she had been so at peace in the forest, and was saddened by how things had changed so much.

She left the courtyard in less of a hurry. Now she knew what was at stake, she felt bad for placing so much responsibility on Jekka's shoulders. When she got back to their suite, it was over two hours later than when she had left, and she found Jekka asleep on the bed.

They both still had plenty of time before they needed to leave, so Maria lay down next to him. When they awoke, they would set off towards another new beginning, but one Maria was far less inclined towards.

Chapter 45

Maria and Jekka were each given a set of lightweight armour plates, as well as new swords, bows, knives and large oval shields. Jekka's armour and shield, unlike every other soldier under his command, was plated with gold to show his status as leader. He was also awarded a medal of honour for his courage and ingenuity during the farmland battle.

They both packed a small backpack and left the suite as the sun was setting. Their new quarters on the Tontoltec Military Vessel Victory would not be as comfortable, but they both felt they now had purpose, something Jekka had not felt in a long time.

As they approached the ship, they saw a large cube about the size of a transit van being wheeled towards the ship. The cube was completely covered with a large piece of canvas sail, except for a small section at the bottom, where iron bars were visible. Among those transporting the heavy object was the general herself.

"I no longer have any use for him," Kyra explained, "But you might, he's likely to know more about this machine on the island than anyone else . . . If he's of no use, feel free to throw him overboard. I thought you could also make use of the hand held weapons his people brought."

Maria peeked under the canvas. Maxwell Stanton was sitting upon a mattress in the middle of the dark cage. She only caught a glimpse of him, but it looked as though he had lost a stone since she had last seen him. If they kept starving him, he would never survive the trip.

"He'll be of use," she said. Out of the corner of her eye, she saw several large wooden crates being carried towards the furthest of the three ships. "Which vessel will we be in?"

"The captain's quarters have been set up in this one closest to us," Kyra told her, "Have you got everything ready?"

Maria nodded. Disposing of the weapons would be harder than she first thought, but once they set sail, things would hopefully become much easier. She hadn't thought much about when they actually reached the island, she hadn't had much time to, everything had happened so quickly.

"There's nothing left but to say goodbye then," Kyra said a moment later. She embraced Jekka by the hand and said something Maria didn't understand, then turned and did the same with Maria.

"Bring my ships back in one piece," she added.

With military promptness, Kyra left to go back to the city. The battle was just days away and she had little time to waste.

Maria waited until she was far enough away before she spoke again. "Jekka, we can't throw the prisoner overboard."

"I won't," he replied, staring up at the bow of the huge timber galleon. He had never been on anything bigger than a fishing boat before, he had been a land based commander.

"And we can't let him starve to death either, it's just too cruel."

"I know, but we can't let him roam free, he'll remain incarcerated until we reach the island."

"I know, it's for the best."

"Have you ever sailed before?"

Maria shook her head, "I've been on a ferry though."

Jekka looked at her with a puzzled look. There was so much of her world she was yet to tell Jekka, but it would take their whole lives to tell him everything. Maria wondered whether he would ever want to go to Earth with her, but she would never ask. She didn't know if she even wanted to go back herself anymore.

At that point, Maria realised that after speaking to Kyra, she hadn't switched back to English to talk to Jekka. She had truly integrated herself into this world, more than she ever thought she would.

*

When Orak learnt of the mental assault on Shoa, he asked that when they were not working, everybody stayed together as much as possible. They all believed that Mradraak would return again, but he would not confront anyone unless they were alone.

Shoa was shaken by the experience, but not as much as John had been. It hadn't been the first time a Telepath had tried to trick her, which was why she knew what was happening straight away. She was sure that Gloria would be the next target, as Mac and Orak had training against such attacks.

As more people left the town, Shoa's hours at the bar were reduced. To make sure they all had enough money to get by, she had to take on shifts doing the job of security and barmaid for the same pay. Orak's job was eventually replaced by several children, who could be paid a fraction of what he had been given.

"We can't stay here much longer," Gloria told the group. There was very little she could do but look after Mac, and the days seemed like weeks. They both grew more tired as time passed, having nothing to occupy their minds. "I never thought I'd say this, but I miss working in the hospital. It's time we went home . . . all of us."

"If it was that easy, we would already be back on Earth," Orak replied, "We'll have better chances in the city, but we have to make sure we have enough money before we go there. I was talking to a local down the tavern yesterday who told me that you have to pay to enter Jopaka-Rafree, the city south of here."

"How much?" John asked.

"Not a lot, but we're spending everything we have on food and to stay here. We can't go without sustenance or beds anymore."

"So what can we do?"

"There's not a lot of choice, we go to Katatua-Shovrus." Mac interjected.

"We've been through this, it's too dangerous, and we don't even know what we're meant to find there," Orak replied.

"Whatever it is, Mradraak doesn't want us to find it, and Kedos does. I'm pretty sure Kedos is on our side," Gloria added.

"We don't even know who Kedos is."

"I know it's dangerous and we don't really know anything about it," John explained, "But I think we should go, I think it's what we've been looking for, and I think everyone else believes it too . . . . We've already got a majority vote on it haven't we?"

"We'll ask Shoa what she thinks when she gets back . . . If she says yes as well, then I guess we're going to Katatua-Shovrus."

Despite Orak's suggestion that they all stayed together, John left the hotel a few minutes later. He would not visit Shoa at work this time, as he was sure he wouldn't receive the same welcome as before. Instead, he told the others he was going to explore the areas of the town he hadn't seen.

Mac had given him instructions of how to fight against telepathic illusions, and although he had not practiced these with him, John felt confident he would not be lured into a trap so easily again. He was not as confident however, in the belief that Mradraak was gone. Someone as determined to find something as he was, wouldn't trust his enemy's word so willingly.

John was sure that if he saw the Telepath again, he would find answers. Mradraak would not hurt him before learning what he came here for. Alone, John was a target, and he could set up a trap of his own.

Waiting in one of the playing fields, he sat cross-legged and closed his eyes. Like before, the whole area was deserted, but now it was daylight, he could see everything.

After half an hour of waiting, John knew that Mradraak would not come. Whether the Telepath knew John was expecting him, or whether he really had left the town, John was certain that he wasn't coming.

Just over a quarter of a mile away, Mradraak stepped onto the market square. Like most of the town, the square was deserted. Reaching into the deep pocket inside his cloak, he produced a small metallic box. Opening the box, he saw the LCD screen light up, and he punched in a series of numbers into the keypad.

Placing the long range radio to his head, he spoke. "Take me home," he said, "Then I need you to send people to Caracracia, to ReDrok Palace. Kill everyone you find. If Kedos is there, you find him!"

Closing the device he placed it back into his pocket. Staring straight ahead, he waited.

Seconds later, a sudden wind blew through the air, kicking up dust from the ground and billowed through the flapping canvas market stalls. A bolt of lightning shot across the timber frames, cutting down the structure. A second stream of electricity crossed the first, and in an instant, the air became still and Mradraak was gone.

Chapter 46

No date was set for Shoa to quit her job and for everyone to leave the town, but they had all agreed on the plan. The following day she went to the tavern as scheduled, and was welcomed by the usual small crowd of daytime drunks. She now knew the full names of each of the regulars, and despite having little respect for most of them, enjoyed their exaggerated stories and jokes. The last thing she wanted was to feel settled here though, as they may need to leave at any time.

"In the revolution I was on the front line. I was just a young boy then, probably younger than you are now," an old man said to her while he inadvisably bought another drink. "There were a lot of us fighting, which was how we killed magics in big numbers you see . . . No offense to you and your kind."

"None taken," Shoa lied. She'd heard this man talking to his other racist friends, and knew his politeness to her was just a front. If she wasn't the one fuelling his habit, he wouldn't even have given her the time of day. If she cut him off, he would quickly change his behaviour, and she wasn't prepared to deal with any abuse.

Turning to the manager, Shoa asked whether she could have a break to use the toilets. Reluctantly he let her go, but turned a sand timer over before she left.

As she walked away, she heard the elderly man at the bar muttering, "The freaks shouldn't even be allowed in here, let alone serve us normal people."

Clenching her fists, Shoa pretended she hadn't heard and tried not to slam the door too hard behind her. The toilet was a wooden cabin outside the building, and in a fit of rage, she kicked the door open. Not satisfied, she sent out a blast of air so powerful it blew out a timber panel. Picking up the panel, she smashed it against the stone tavern wall and screamed. If she hadn't been working, she would have knocked the old man's teeth out.

When she returned, she was glad to see that the opinionated old fascist had left. "Has he gone?" she asked her boss.

The manager nodded his head, "He'll be back tomorrow though, you'll just have to ignore him."

Sighing, she started polishing the mahogany bar. "Somebody's vandalised the toilets outside."

"Again? I'm going to need to hire security for back there if this continues."

"I know someone who would be good for that."

"No, I can't afford any more staff; I can barely afford to keep you here."

Shoa remembered that she had seen one of the taverns best customers leaving town with his family that morning, but felt it best not to say anything. "Things will pick up," she lied again.

As she started putting the empty bottles into the bin, she saw several other customers getting up to leave. Walking the width of the building, she collected all the used glasses before starting to clean the sticky liquor stains from the tables. She didn't dare appear idle while her boss was looking, so soon after him mentioning his financial situation.

"Are you closing early?" she asked, hoping her hours would not be reduced.

"Doesn't look like it" he replied, smiling for the first time that day. The front doors had opened, and a crowd of heavily built field sport fans staggered in.

Shoa didn't know there was another drinking establishment in the town, but these men had obviously found one. Her heart sank when she saw the old man she had been serving minutes earlier in the crowd.

"Hey, there she is, the freak!" he shouted, pointing roughly in her direction.

"Your sort shouldn't be allowed in here!" a loud man, with a neck thicker than his head exclaimed.

"No, this place is only for cavemen like you, is it?" she replied, but regretted it the instant she opened her mouth.

An empty glass she had missed flew towards her head, luckily missing by miles. Not giving up, the troll like drunk picked up a chair and swung it wildly in her direction.

Shoa felt the leg of the chair strike her ribs, but before a second blow could be made, a cloud of red hot flames engulfed the chair. The thug dropped the piece of furniture and frantically brushed down his burning sleeves.

This hadn't served as much of a deterrent, and two of his friends moved in on Shoa, trying to box her into the corner of the room. Closing her eyes, she crouched down under a table, as she forced the air to evacuate from both sets of lungs. The attackers fell to the ground and kicked violently as they clutched at their throats in a futile attempt to breathe.

"Stop it!" she screamed, "I don't want to hurt you! Go away!"

The table above her was dragged out of the way, and the cockeyed old man dragged her to her feet. "We don't want your sort here. I'm going to make an example of you!" he snarled.

She felt his hand reaching into her robe and grope at her breasts.

"Get off!" she screamed. She tried to push him away, but despite his age, he was far stronger than her. Closing her eyes again, she sent a wave of electrical energy through him, and after a few seconds his whole body went stiff.

His muscles had gone as hard as rock and his cold dead eyes were wider and more frightened than Shoa's. Shoving him away, she saw him tumble to the floor like falling timber. She had stopped his heart.

"You killed my best customer!" the manager shrieked, "You're fired!"

In a moment of panic, Shoa darted behind the bar and snatched up the locked metal cash box from the lower shelf.

"You put that back!" he squealed, his pitch rising so high that most people in the tavern winced.

Shoa sprinted towards the back door, but when she yanked at the handle found that it was locked. Smashing the heavy box down on the handle, she saw the old rusty lock crumbling apart, and she kicked the unlatched door open.

The troll man who had thrown the glass at her, kicked the swinging door back open after it swung closed behind her. "You killed my uncle!" he roared.

For someone so big, he moved quicker than Shoa thought possible. Before she had left the porch, he had grabbed her by the collar and thrown her into the wall.

Shoa couldn't breathe. He was punishing her in the way she had tried to punish his teammates. With his free hand, he threw a punch straight at her chest, and Shoa was crippled with pain. She hadn't even felt the blade slicing across her forearm, and only realised when she saw blood droplets on the grey stone floor.

When she looked up, all she could see was a blurred figure nearly as wide as he was tall, and the shadow of another approaching quickly. The next second, she dropped to the ground and saw blood spots everywhere. The hulking drunk had fallen next to her, and she saw splinters of wood upon his bleeding face.

John had appeared, and in his hands he held the broken legs of a barstool. Shoa just about had time to grab the moneybox before he hoisted her up onto his shoulder. Before blacking out, she just about had the strength to ignite the broken timber in the doorway and send the flames soaring above the height of the door. Even the drunkest of men wouldn't try to pass through.

She felt the cash box dropping from her hand, and reached out hopelessly. The ground shook beneath her, but all was darkness, and she was spiralling out of control.

Her eyes opened and she saw that she was back in the hotel, lying in bed and looking at the moneybox on the bedside table.

"I couldn't leave it back there," she heard John's voice say, and turned around to see him sitting on the bed next to her.

"You saved my life again," she replied groggily.

"Well, I didn't want to miss a chance to knock out one of those pumped up bastards. I didn't know you had steroids on this world."

"We don't. They buy Titan blood. Doesn't make them that much stronger though, just bigger . . . . John, I killed a man in there."

"I think I did too," he replied gravely, "I didn't see him get up . . . I don't regret it though; I couldn't let him hurt you."

"I didn't think you cared," she replied, turning away.

John took hold of her hand. "You know I do. The way I reacted the other night, after we spent it together, well, I was wrong to treat you like that. I was stupid, really stupid. I hope you can find it in your heart to forgive me."

Shoa kissed him, "We'll see. Where are the others?"

"Downstairs, keeping an eye out. Does anyone in the tavern know where you're staying?"

"No."

"Good. That gives us time to let you rest, but we have to leave first thing in the morning."

John opened the metal safe box Orak had snapped open earlier, and showed her contents. There were several dozen large bronze coins inside. It was enough for them to leave and to hire a boat once they reached the docks. "You did well," he told her.

Chapter 47

The fire Shoa had started in the doorway had burnt down the timber porch, but had not spread into the building itself. It had died down enough for people to walk through within an hour, and was used by many of the town's residents when a meeting was called later that day. The man John had broken a stool over was now conscious, but severely concussed, and wouldn't stop ranting about the freaks and their sympathisers.

The stable owners told the ever increasing crowd about the Titan he had hired, and told stories about how he never put much effort into his work. The market workers told of how they had seen a frail looking Telepath lurking around the town, always with a group of followers he had tricked into worshiping him.

A funeral pyre stood in the centre of a square visible through the tavern's windows. A verdict was quickly reached; these strangers from up north had to leave.

*

Orak used some of the money to hire a caravan and a pair of horses, of which he did not intend to return. He was saddened by the fact that they had been driven to break the laws of this land, but he had no sympathy for the people of the town. He understood their prejudices, but could never condone their behaviour.

As he peered through a window to the back of the hotel's lounge, he saw that the streets were busier than they had been in days. Alarm bells in his head rung out when he saw that many of them were carrying weapons, from pitchforks to scimitars.

"I think we've stayed here long enough," he told Mac.

"They don't know we're here yet," Mac replied, "But it won't be long before they do. I don't think we should wait until morning, we should go under the cover of darkness."

"And if they come before then?"

"I hide us," he said, tapping his head, "If Mradraak can mess with our minds, I can mess with theirs."

"Not in your condition you can't, and not to that many people. I'll fend them off if they come."

Orak helped Mac upstairs. The Telepath no longer had the strength to use his telekinesis, and would need as much rest as he could get before they set out. Only Orak and John stayed up to keep watch, and although they spent the time sitting in the living room together, neither wanted to talk about travelling to the island, and couldn't think of anything else to say.

After an awkward half an hour of avoiding the subject of their predicament, they both found books in the adjoining study and read. John could understand almost no written Southern Tontoltec, but stared down at the pages and thought about Shoa.

He had not realised that he cared so much until he had seen her in danger. If anyone else in their group had been in the situation she was; he would have done the same thing, he cared about them all. Seeing Shoa in pain, he had been more terrified than he could ever remember being.

Orak looked up from his book and spoke for the first time in over fifteen minutes. "The volcano on Katatua-Shovrus is still active," he said in a worried tone. He had been learning what he could about their new destination, while John had assumed that Mac already knew everything about it.

John looked at the title of the book he had been trying to read; *Sentient Plants, Every Gardener's Dilemma*. "What are the chances of it erupting when we're there though?" he replied, failing to mask his worry.

"Shoa can help protect us against fire, but not thousands of tonnes of fast flowing lava. If it erupts, people in Caracracia will feel the effects. This town and the city south of here will choke on thick boiling ash clouds. We'll be dead no matter where we are when it erupts."

"Oh . . . Okay, that's comforting."

"It's not erupted in over seventy years though, so don't worry too much."

"Why do you think the dreams me and Mac have had about the island are so far apart? In one dream the volcano is erupting; the next it isn't."

"Maybe they are memories from several generations? Have you dreamt it again more recently?"

"Yes, a few days ago, but it wasn't as bad. The mountain was there, but the harpies weren't. It was just cold."

Orak showed him the book, pointing to a paragraph he could read. When the Titan realised that John didn't understand it, he read it out loud in English.

"Katatua-Shovrus was home to the largest known harpy colony. Most who ventured there were killed and only a few survived to warn others. The most famous written account was by an unnamed Telepath who visited the island several months before the most recent eruption. He was attacked by these swarming creatures, and nearly died, but this did not put him off the idea of visiting again. On his second visit to the island, the volcano began to erupt, and he escaped Katatua-Shovrus only to die later from excess smoke inhalation. He reported that the harpies would not survive such a powerful geological event, but few people have returned to the island to ascertain whether the harpies died out during this historic disaster . . ."

John stared at him, trying to make sense of this. "You think the Telepath you're talking about is the one giving us the dreams?"

"No, he's dead, it says so here. I think Kedos has his memories of Katatua-Shovrus, and is sending you them. The latest dreams are Kedos' own memories. He's telling us that the island is safe, that the volcano wiped out the harpies."

"So . . . Why didn't he just tell us this?"

Orak shook his head, "I don't know. Maybe he couldn't. Maybe he could only send it during sleep or in a semi-sleep state. It could be that the only way Mac's unconscious mind could receive his message was in the form of memories?"

"So he is telling us to go there?"

"Almost definitely."

John smiled. Finally everyone in the group wanted to go to the island, and a lot of the doubt he felt about it was gone. "What do you think we'll find there?"

Orak just shrugged. He had thought about it a lot, but he had been more concerned about actually getting there. They had the money to hire a boat, but there was no guarantee that there would even be any at the docks.

Orak shut the book he was reading as it became too dark to continue without lamp light. He and John went upstairs to wake the others. The horse drawn caravan was waiting outside for them.

By morning they were far away from the town, heading south west towards the coastline.

Chapter 48

Maria thought that the quarters that she and Jekka were sharing seemed very basic, until she saw where the rest of the crew and the soldiers were sleeping. There were dozens of bunk beds stacked so close together in the bowels of the ship that people had to clamber over other beds to get to their own. Compared to this, their room looked like a royal suite.

Even the prisoner, Maxwell Stanton, had more space in his cage than many of the free men had in the dormitories. Although food was rationed, Jekka and Maria were given meals twice as large as everyone else, despite asking the chef for equal measures. Maria had given half of hers and Jekka's food to Maxwell, but didn't stay to watch the starving man devour it.

They hit the open sea a day after leaving port, just as Maria thought she was getting her sea legs. She spent much of the following day on the open deck, leaning over the side until the waves settled.

Staring up at the bright red sails, she noticed the huge symbol emblazoned in gold, reminding her of an oriental decoration. The ship was magnificently decorated, and built of high quality polished wood, and she wondered how long it would stay in such good condition.

On the third day, the sea was so calm and the sun so bright, that many of the crew played ball games out on the deck. Maria taught them a modified version of cricket, which lasted until someone batted the ball into the sea. They played a similar game with the spare ball, but it wasn't long before it was knocked overboard and landed on the vessel sailing beside them.

"Someone is going to have to get that," Jekka laughed, "Any volunteers?"

"I'll do it." Maria said suddenly.

"I was joking. We'll just ask someone to throw it back."

"No, I want to go . . . The weapons are on . . . ." she stopped when a soldier walked past. Switching to English, she continued. "This is my chance to get rid of them."

Jekka shook his head, "The men guarding them report directly to Kyra, not me. They won't deviate from their mission, and they won't let anyone near them. You'll need a better plan."

"Sneak in from outside and cut a hole in the hull?"

"You're not putting a hole in one of my ships," he said, "We need to bring them up on deck. I'll call a meeting on that ship, so they have to leave it nearly unattended. They'll still have one guard down there. You'll have to think of a way to deal with him."

"When are you going to call a meeting?"

"Maybe in a week's time. I'll make up something about poor discipline in the ranks, and they will all think I'm referring to someone else and not question it."

As the clouds began to form, the soldiers returned to the cabin. Jekka stayed out on deck even when the rain began, staring out at the calm blue ocean. He had never seen such a vast expanse in his life.

Maria headed for shelter, and watched Jekka from under a canvas canopy. A few minutes later she went back inside.

On her way to the galley, she heard a consistent clanging sound from the back of the ship. Seeing the chef on her way, she asked him whether the prisoner had been fed, but he walked on by without answering.

She found Maxwell in his cell, banging a metal coffee mug against the bars. "Stop that!" she snapped, and he did.

"The room service here is terrible. I've been trying to get someone's attention for an hour."

"What do you want?" she asked bluntly.

"Would a hug be too much to ask for?" he asked, holding out his arms.

Maria's mouth twinged, half smiling, but hid her amusement after that. She heard his stomach rumbling from where she stood and left to get him some food.

She returned a few minutes later with a plate of cold fish and dry bread. "This is what everyone else has to eat, so don't think this is a punishment."

"You're too good to me," he replied with a smile.

Outwardly he showed confidence and indifference to his situation, but Maria could see that his eyes were red from crying.

"Well someone's got to keep you alive; you might still be useful."

"You love me really."

Maria turned away so he couldn't see her quietly laughing. She had to admit he was clinging on well to his forthright charm.

She turned back to take his already empty plate, but when she reached through the bars, he grabbed hold of her hand. His expression had changed to that of desperation.

"I could break your wrist," she said calmly.

"You said I would be free when I told you what you wanted."

"Once we get there."

Maxwell let her go and slumped back into the cage. "They lied to me," he grumbled, "They never told us about the risks. We thought we would be fighting savages, men with sharpened sticks. We didn't stand a chance against the general. If we could hit her, I doubt even a bullet would slow her down."

"Well she isn't human, not as we'd call it anyway."

"And now they've left me here! I have a radio, and nobody tried to make contact!"

"You have a radio? Are you sure it even works?"

"I've still got a pager strapped to the inside of my trouser leg. I know when someone's trying to contact me. I know it works because I made a call when I arrived, but nobody has tried to call back. I guess I'm just another disposable asset!"

"What did you expect from an organisation which starts wars for profit?"

"They deserted me!" he hissed bitterly, "They won't get away with this! I'll help you, if it helps me get back at them! I'll help you!"

Although Maria was sure that they needed all the help they could get, she had to refuse this time. This man couldn't be trusted. "I'll think about it," she lied.

Maria left to take the plate back to the galley. She did wonder whether having an inside man could be a valuable asset, but had no way of knowing whether he was still loyal to his company or not.

After much deliberation, she decided that he should only be released early as a last resort.

Chapter 49

The journey towards the coastline was quicker than anyone had anticipated. After leaving just before midnight, they were looking out at the sea before seven.

Looking down from the mountain road, they could see Jopaka-Rafree in the distance. In the opposite direction they could see the harbour, but not a single sail.

"If we can't get a boat, we'll have to go there," Orak said, pointing to the silhouetted towers several miles away.

The cliff side road grew narrower the closer to the coast they got, until they came across a section which had crumbled away. John peered down over the edge and saw nothing but darkness. The road had fallen into a large cave system, and the gap was even too big for Orak to jump across. Setting the horses free, they deserted the caravan and scrambled down the side of the cliff.

As they got closer to the docklands, it became clear that they weren't going to find any usable vessels. The nearest thing they could see was an upturned hull, floating in the shallow water underneath the pier.

Remnants of the once proud ships were scattered everywhere, now nothing more than driftwood. Orak dragged the hull of the longboat onto the sand, and saw that it was full of holes.

"We won't get far in that," Gloria commented.

"Should we go to Jopaka-Rafree then?" Shoa asked, "We're more likely to find boats there."

"But it doubles our journey. The less time we spend in the water the better," Mac replied.

Orak flipped the damaged boat over and began gathering driftwood.

"Err . . . What are you doing?" John asked uneasily.

"We can make this sturdy enough to use," he replied, "Maybe with a few alterations."

"Aren't you going to need some tools and some, like, nails? And that wood doesn't look strong enough . . . Have you built boats before? I'm not a strong swimmer."

"If your concern is that I'll be too heavy and sink it then don't worry. I won't be in it. I am a strong swimmer."

"What?" everyone else said more or less at the same time.

"I've swum further than this before," he replied, "I'll carry a big chunk of driftwood with me for buoyancy, but the water is warm and I've got the energy."

"It's over nine miles!" Mac exclaimed. Even though it wasn't him swimming, he could feel the water pouring into his lungs and the helpless feeling of sinking into the lake. He was dreading the boat trip for fear of it capsizing. He didn't have the strength to swim, and it would surely finish him off.

While Orak sorted through the pieces of wood and drew up plans in the sand, John and Gloria headed towards an abandoned hut on the opposite side of the pier to look for anything to help with the construction. John wondered whether any of the contents of Gloria's garage would have travelled this far, hoping to find Mark's toolbox sitting in the middle of the wharf.

They walked in silence until Gloria decided to break it. "What are you going to do if she is pregnant?" she said suddenly, catching John off guard.

"Who?" he said stupidly, "I . . . I'm not going to desert her if that's what you're thinking. I really like her; I just reacted badly to begin with. I hadn't planned what happened. If she forgives me, I'd like to try and make a go of things with her."

"John, she's seventeen. Do you really think a relationship will work between you? I think she's a nice enough girl, but you've seen how volatile she is. Don't forget either, that she's not what you and I would call normal . . . If you hurt her again, you know how dangerous she can be."

"I won't hurt her again," he replied, "I've learnt my lesson." Gloria shook her head, "I don't think you have. Are you attracted to her because she's the one you want to be with, or because there's nobody else on this world who you think you can be with? Only a handful of people speak English or understand anything about our culture . . . It wasn't long ago when you thought you were in love with Maria."

"Maria's gone!" he snapped back, "There's nothing I can do about that! If I could bring her back I would, but I can't!"

"I'm just asking you to think about what you're doing, please?"

When they got to the shed they saw that the door was padlocked. John yanked at it to try and break it free, but it was still intact and secure. He was about to turn back to fetch Orak until he saw how rotten the timbers at the side of the shed were.

Wobbling the timbers, he felt that the points where they were nailed to the frame were still strong. Taking a few steps back, he ran at the sidewall and kicked through the soft crumbling planks. Gloria helped drag the woodworm ridden timbers out of the way while John climbed through the gap. "It's not very bright in here," he muttered.

"Anything of use?" she asked.

"It's not a workshop; it's a boathouse, so yes."

Dismantling the back wall with the prow of the wooden canoe, John clambered back out. The pair of them started carrying small kayaks down to the beach. He had also found several lengths of rope and a set of oars.

Once they got back to the beach, John drew up a plan in the sand using the end of the oar. It showed the boat Orak had found, with the two kayaks lashed to its sides as stabilisers. The hull of the boat had been patched up badly, and wasn't watertight, but the stabilisers would be placed lower, so the boat would be raised above the level of the water, effectively turning it into a catamaran.

After everybody agreed on the design, Orak tied the vessels together and asked Shoa whether she could help them out with the water if it started to sink. This unsettled Mac further, so he changed the subject.

"It's getting late. Should we leave setting off until the morning?"

"Agreed," Gloria replied, also eyeing the less than professional looking construction.

As everyone returned to the caravan, John stopped Gloria. "I need to talk to you about something."

"Can it wait until the morning?" she yawned.

"Yeah, sure," he smiled faintly.

He had decided that he couldn't leave it much longer to tell her about the reflection in the puddle. There was no doubt that he had seen Mark Jones, but still had no idea why.

That night, the dream seemed more vivid than ever before.

Chapter 50

The warm weather continued for the crew of the TMV Victory and its sister ships in the fleet. A strong consistent breeze carried the ship at a steady pace in the right direction. Despite the ships wide stabilising hull, it was still at the mercy of the thrashing waves.

Most of the soldiers stayed underneath, hiding from the sweltering sun, while the crew baked out in the open. Maria also stood out on the deck, sheltering in the shade of a parasol, watching the watery horizon bobbing up and down. She had been violently sick over the starboard side of the vessel but was gradually starting to feel better.

"This is ice cream weather," she said to Jekka when he came up to see how she was.

"Do you still miss your world?" he replied.

"On days like this I miss travel sickness medicine . . . and sun cream."

"You could make medicine couldn't you? You are a doctor."

"It's not that simple . . . I'll cope, don't worry about me."

"I will always worry about you Maria. That's my job now. Let's go inside. I don't want you to burn."

Maria folded the parasol away and stowed it in a compartment on the port side of the deck. She followed him to the stairwell, but stopped when she noticed someone sitting up in the crow's nest looking through a telescope. This seemed strange, as they were nowhere near charted land.

"What are you looking for?" she called up to him.

"I saw another ship!" he called back, "Just the top of its sail!"

"What colour?" Jekka asked, clambering up the mast ladder.

"Dark green!"

"What?"

"Dark g . . . DRATHMORKS!!"

Jekka slipped down the mast, stumbling at the bottom. The sky which had been clear seconds before was now filled with chaos. He sprinted down the stairs yelling orders, while Maria watched the watchman desperately trying to clamber down to the deck.

Before he had even placed his foot on the third rung of the ladder, a creature tore through the sail and hacked the rope in two. The crewman tried to grab the rope above but fell too quickly, plummeting to his death.

Maria screamed as the body crashed head first into the deck. She saw and heard his neck snap, and leapt out of the way as his legs fell towards her. The winged soldier shot down from the sail and swiped at her. Maria blocked the sword strike with the dead man's telescope, which tore in two, exploding into a cloud of broken glass. The creature's sword fell from its hands and Maria took the opportunity to escape as it ran across the leaning deck after its fallen weapon.

Running to find cover, Maria saw the battle ready soldiers emerge from a hatch behind her. Their shields rose as they moved into a Roman style tortoise formation.

Arrows flew through the air in both directions, and Maria had to duck and dodge to avoid them. From under the protection of the shields, the grounded soldiers fired crossbow bolts up into the sky, most of which fell back down upon the ship. One struck the deck at an angle directly in front of Maria, causing her foot to catch on the shaft.

She hit the deck head first but staggered back onto her feet straight away. Disorientated and in pain, she stumbled down the stairs. More soldiers ran up past her, almost skewering her on their swords. She ran through the corridors, ending up in the store where the prisoner's cage was being held.

"Set him free!" she ordered the man guarding it, then turned to Maxwell. "If you want to help; now is your chance!"

Out on deck, Jekka watched as more and more creatures swooped down onto the deck. They were vastly outnumbered, and the enemy was hacking through his soldier's shields like they weren't even there. Across the water, he saw the other ships being bombarded by similar surreal assaults and felt that the battle had already been lost.

If they had been on land he would have called a retreat, but there was nowhere for them to go, so they had no choice but to fight. Jekka hurled his shield through the air, striking a Drathmork and knocking it off course. As the beast sped towards him, he picked up the sword of a fallen comrade and speared it through the chest. The creature screeched and clawed the air in front of itself, unable to reach its attacker. With his own sword, Jekka stabbed through its neck to silence it. He withdrew both weapons, before kicking the enemy's body into the sea.

Narrowly missing a crossbow bolt, Jekka hacked apart four more creatures in quick succession before the winged warriors realised that he was their biggest threat. The swarm which had been attacking the Testudo formation left the terrified few survivors to focus on the Commodore of the fleet. Very quickly he was surrounded and had no way of escape.

"Where are the weapons?" the leader of the creatures snarled.

Up until this point, Jekka had no idea they could speak, and was stunned. "They're not here," he lied, "They're being shipped to Alkak-Taan."

"Even your people are not that stupid! Nobody can breach the shores of Alkak-Taan! Where are they?"

Jekka held both swords so tightly that his knuckles turned white. He tried to weigh out his options: should he attack the leader or try to escape? Both ways would inevitably lead to his death. "What will you do with them?"

The Drathmork leader roared and stormed towards him. Throwing down his sword, he challenged Jekka to unarmed combat by beating his chest with his left fist and sticking out his thin reptilian tongue.

"If I win . . . ?" Jekka asked, knowing full well that he couldn't.

The creature just hissed, waiting for the centurion to disarm. When he saw that his opponent wasn't prepared to accept, he crouched down to pick up his discarded sword.

Before he could stand back up, a sudden bang sounded, and the Drathmork felt a wound, which had appeared in his chest. Another muted bang signalled another injury to appear upon the beast's temple, and his soldiers watched as their commander fell.

Frightened and confused, the creatures backed away from Jekka, unaware that he was just as baffled as they were. He watched as the creatures fled from the TMV Victory, but saw that the other two ships were still under assault.

Maria ran out from the cover of the stairwell and hugged him.

"What happened?" he asked her.

"Don't be angry," she replied, causing further confusion.

Jekka turned to see the ship's prisoner standing out in the open, holding the weapon which had been confiscated from him and locked away. Maxwell didn't give Jekka a chance to absorb what had just happened, and rushed over to them.

"They're here for the bombs! They can't fly out with them, but they don't want you reaching the island; they're going to try and detonate!" he blurted out.

Maria quickly translated, but before she could finish Maxwell had sprinted to the starboard side of the ship and thrown himself over the side. "What the hell?" she cried.

A few minutes later, when Jekka had arranged his soldiers to cross to the imperilled ship, a deafening blast sent ripples through the water. A hole had appeared below the water line of the vessel containing the warheads, and water began flooding in.

Not long after, a second blast tore a huge section of the hull apart, and the ship began to crumble apart. "The grenades," Maria said quietly.

Very soon the ship was nothing but flotsam; the bodies of the dead and the payload were sinking to the bottom of the sea.

Chapter 51

The blast had frightened off the creatures that were attacking the third ship in the fleet, but very few of its crew or soldiers on board had survived. Jekka sent boats out to rescue those left alive, but most came back empty.

Among the men fortunate enough not to have been killed by the explosions or the enemy's swords, was an unconscious and burn scarred Maxwell Stanton. He had several small wounds from grenade shrapnel, and had been cut across the back of his leg, but was in good shape considering.

In this state he was no threat to anyone, and as Maria expressed that he had earned some degree of forgiveness, he was allowed to recover in the medical suite. He was also not to be returned to his cell unless he was involved in misconduct.

The rest of the day was spent repairing the mangled sails, and deciding what to do about the damaged ship that was slowly drifting further away. As the number of soldiers was drastically reduced in the attack, there was no problem with overcrowding. The remaining crew could only manage one vessel, and after a brief discussion, the decision was made by Jekka to leave the damaged one and carry on with the mission.

Far more time was spent searching the sky, but without a telescope it was difficult to detect approaching ships. Everyone was constantly on full alert, and sleeping shifts had to be organised for the duration of the journey.

Jekka and Maria offered to stay up for the first shift, along with half a dozen other soldiers. "Twenty" Jekka said quietly to himself, "From a hundred to twenty in just a few minutes."

"There was nothing you could have done this time," Maria told him, rubbing his shoulders to relieve his stress.

"I could have told my men to use the prisoner's machine guns to begin with," he replied solemnly.

"With no training on how to use them? I'm not even sure how to load them, or turn the safety off. The only people you can blame for this are the Alkak-Taan council who sent them."

"Why is it that the worst people to deal with are always in power Maria? Is it the position of power that turns them, or are they just that way to begin with?"

"That's a good question; one people have been wondering on my world just as long as on yours. You're a good leader, nothing will ever corrupt you."

"Especially not the command of twenty men."

He watched as the lonely battered ship, which was once a part of his fleet, vanish into the distance. He looked up at the stars and knew they were going the right way.

Maria hadn't noticed before, as she had rarely looked up at the stars on Earth, but they were much closer together here. It made her wonder where Ithria really was in the universe and how far it was from home. It made her feel small and insignificant.

Jekka apparently was thinking along a similar path, as he asked, "Do you think I would like Earth?"

"No," she replied flatly, "Not the part I'm from anyway . . . . There's so much of it I never got to see."

"There's so much of Ithria I have never seen," he replied, "If we had planes and trains like you, I would go to the flats of Kelcawlrin to see the famous whistling trees and pick you one of its fragrant flowers. I would go to the frozen lakes of Isenbruge and catch the biggest snake fish I could find . . . There's so much on this world for us to see, but there isn't enough time in our lives to see it all."

"This machine Maxwell told me about takes you anywhere, here or on Earth. If we capture the island, then the machine is ours to use."

"But you know we can't. You told me how destructive your world can be. We can't let anybody use it, not even us."

Maria sighed, she felt trapped on this ship and Jekka was squashing her dreams of ultimate freedom. He was right though; the machine had caused enough devastation.

"It might take us longer, but we can still go to these places," he told her, "I'm a free man remember?"

Maria hadn't heard him. Her attention had been drawn by a soldier running across the deck towards them. At first she feared that he had seen another attack, but when she saw a faint smile across his face, she knew it couldn't be.

"The prisoner is awake," he panted. "He says he thinks he has a way to get us to the island . . . and past the defences."

*

John did not sleep much that night. Once again he took a stroll through the darkness, but kept close to the others in the caravan at all times. He knew he had to tell Gloria about her husband in the morning, or Mac would. Although he hated the idea of how she would react and feel, this was not what worried him.

Katatua-Shovrus was just a few miles away across the water. He would probably be able to see it if he found a high enough vantage point. The dreams had been a warning for weeks, and then suddenly they became something else. John didn't know what to expect, and this scared him more than the threat of the harpies themselves.

He stayed up to watch the sun rising, and clambered up the highest hill he could find. Looking out across the ocean he saw nothing but water. John knew that he would not see the island until they were up close, when it would be too late to turn back.

When John returned to the caravan, the others were already awake and cooking breakfast on a campfire in the middle of the dirt track road.

"We saved you some bacon," Gloria said, handing him a plate.

Without much encouragement, he accepted the food. He looked around at the others and saw nothing resembling a smile. They had all agreed to go to this mysterious volcanic island, but now it seemed everyone was having second thoughts. To add to their worries, the journey there would not be an easy one. Orak would be swimming an exhausting distance through turbulent waters. The rest would be drifting across on a jerry built vessel, one of whom was still seriously ill.

An argument was started when Mac refused a blood transfusion from the Titan to keep his strength up. He insisted that Orak needed all of his strength for the trip, and shocked everyone when he said that the last time it hadn't had any effect.

"The infection must have mutated," he explained, "You can't help me anymore. I need Earth medicine."

Mac was as pale as an albino, despite the fact that the sun had given everyone else a dark tan. He was helped into the boat, and made as comfortable as possible. They all noticed that the sound of his breathing was louder than the noise from the breaking waves. Gloria checked his heart rate and looked at John with a worried expression.

John also checked his heart rate then spoke to everyone, "We can't go, not with him in this state. If we go to the city . . ."

"No!" Mac croaked, barely audible, "You have to go to Katatua-Shovrus." Slowly, he pulled out a small leather bound notebook from his robes. "My most recent research . . . into the Anuma link . . ."

"Why are you giving us this?" Shoa asked tearfully, trying to hide the fact that she knew what he was saying.

"It tells you how to find the rifts . . . I know you can figure it out . . . if you work together . . ."

"We need you for this. You've got to stay strong for us."

Orak placed a hand on her shoulder, "You can help him if you find a certain plant. The leaves have anti-biotic properties. Its leaves have five points; they're about as wide as my hand. It has a small blue flower at the base of each leaf; you can't miss it. Can you look for this plant? We need maybe a dozen or more of the leaves."

Shoa nodded. "I won't be long. I'll find it, don't worry," she said hurriedly. An unshared optimism was present in her voice.

Mac watched as she ran off into the hills to help him. He turned to Orak and for the first time ever saw tears forming in a Titan's eyes. "Is it really that bad?" he uttered.

"I'm afraid so," John replied, fighting back his own emotions.

Gloria who had seen hundreds of patients and many of her friends and family depart said nothing.

"How long?" Mac sighed calmly, closing his eyes.

"I don't know. Your physiology is different to anyone I've helped treat before . . . only slightly different, but I don't know how much of an effect that will have . . . a day at best."

"So this is why you didn't want Shoa here?"

"You're family to her now," Orak choked, "We all are."

Mac smiled, and tears started to well up in his own eyes. "I've always wanted to be surrounded by my family at the end . . . If I did find a way back to Earth . . ."

Gloria shook her head, "There's nothing anyone would be able to do." She knew for a fact that he wouldn't survive the journey.

She took hold of Mac's hand. It felt cold. "None of this is your fault," she told him quietly. "You did what you had to do. I understand that now."

As John crouched down to speak to Mac, he heard Shoa yelling in the distance. He turned to see her running back down the hill. She had figured out what was happening.

"You bastard!" she sobbed, hitting Orak in the chest and hurting her fist. "You weren't going to let me say goodbye! I'm not a child!"

"I wasn't . . ." he began, but stopped and turned his head down.

Crumpled leaves fell from her hand, as she crouched down and hugged Mac gently. "You can't go!"

"It's my time," he whispered back.

"No it's not! You can get better!"

John helped Shoa back up and held her in his arms while she wept.

Orak sat down on the ground beside the boat so that he was level with Mac and took hold of his hand. "You are the smartest man I know and you've passed your knowledge on to all those willing to learn. You've done great things in the time you were given; regret not a minute of it. You were a friend to all of us."

"You know what to do?" Mac struggled to say, "It only takes a few drops."

Tearfully, Orak nodded and started gathering up the leaves that Shoa had gathered. Gloria brought him a mug of water, and he rung the leaves out into it. The water turned to a deep green, and he shook the mug gently to mix it fully. "Goodbye," he whispered, holding the mug to Mac's lips as he glugged it down.

A smile broke out across Mac's face, and he slowly closed his eyes. Orak kept hold of his hand while Mac drifted off to sleep. Nobody spoke as they waited.

A few minutes later Orak let go and stood up. John felt for a pulse, but found none.

"He's gone."

Chapter 52

Maxwell was brought to the captain's office in chains. Once the guards escorting him were discharged, Maria unshackled him and led him to a chair beside the desk opposite Jekka's.

Once he was seated, she locked the door behind them and sat down at the end of the desk, facing them both. Maxwell noticed that they both had large hunting knives sheathed to their belts.

"I'm getting mixed signals here," he said jokingly, holding up his unrestrained hands while looking at their sharpened blades.

Jekka's stern expression didn't change. His unflinching steely eyes chilled the prisoner to the bone. Maxwell felt that for the first time, his humour would not help him out at all.

"You destroyed one of my ships and killed many members of my military unit!" Jekka said in concise clear English. "Explain yourself!"

Maria's eyes darted between them and felt glad that she wasn't the focus of her partner's anger.

"I had to get rid of the warheads, Maxwell replied, "It was the only way. The Drathmork's could have detonated the active weapon."

"Could you not have done that without sacrificing my people?"

Jekka leant forwards and glared at the prisoner. Sweat began to form on Maxwell's brow, and he had to fight the stammer in his voice when he answered. "It was the only way I could have done it in time."

"He saved us," Maria cut in. "That bomb would have killed everyone, and made it so nobody could safely sail along the waters of this coast for decades."

"I find that hard to believe, but I know you wouldn't lie to me," Jekka said more calmly in Tontoltec so the prisoner would not understand. "I need to know whether he has our safety in mind and not just his own. Do you think what he did was the only way to save us?"

"I do."

Jekka turned back to Maxwell and switched back to speaking in English. "So you think you can do more to help us?"

"Yes," Maxwell replied, "I think I can get us to the island."

"What do you mean by us?"

"Do you have the four assault rifles and four sets of breathing apparatus that my team and I had when we arrived on this world? There was also a small black device that has a rubber antenna."

Jekka looked at Maria for the answer, and she nodded a reply.

"There was," he said curiously.

"Can you bring it to me?"

"Why? What does it do?" Jekka asked.

"I just want to try something. There's no guarantee it will work, but it could really help you."

Jekka stood up and simply said "No." He unlocked the door and held it open for Maxwell. Over the threshold, two armed guards waited for the prisoner.

Maxwell looked hopelessly at Maria. He watched her stand up and then take hold of the door and slowly close it behind him. "I believe he can help Jekka. Please, can we just listen to his plan?"

"Okay," he replied reluctantly. Opening the door again he instructed the guards to bring the equipment. "I'm listening Maxwell."

A few minutes later, the three of them ascended the stairs onto the open deck above. The sun was not as strong as it had been, but it was still bright. In hindsight, Maria wished she had brought a pair of sunglasses with her from Earth. They all stood with their backs to the sun while the equipment was brought to them.

Maxwell picked up the long range radio communicator and noticed that the screen was broken. Things didn't seem hopeful when he held down the on button and the device failed to switch on.

"The batteries are meant to last for months!" he said, banging it against the wooden floor in frustration.

"Is that really going to help?" Maria asked.

Discovering that violence against the piece of technology had no effect, he removed the casing from the back. Using his fingernails, he cleaned a layer of dried mud from the contacts and rubbed them with his shirt, before slotting it back together. Pressing the button down for a second time, he jumped with delight when the screen lit up.

"Unit Six reporting," he said into the devices inbuilt microphone. "Unit Six reporting, over."

He waited for a response, but heard nothing more than a steady crackling. Repeating his call-in again, he added an alphanumeric code and listened for the reply.

"Maybe it's out of range?" Maria suggested.

"Unit Six, this is Ithrian hub one. Repeat pass code. Over," came a barely audible voice from the damaged speaker.

"Alpha, Delta, Niner, Seven, Seven, Two, Papa, Quebec, over," Maxwell responded.

"Stanton? We all thought you were dead? Over."

"No such luck I'm afraid. I encountered some trouble, but I've found the warheads. Requesting transport, over."

"We need visual confirmation before we allow you access. Over."

"My camera was damaged in the fight. I can't show you, but I've got them pretty close to me. I might not have much time. Over."

"Read me the serial numbers on the weapons, over."

Maxwell released the speaker button. "Shit!" he exclaimed.

Strolling across the deck, he frantically tried to think of a way to bluff his way out of this. His colleagues at the command centre were trained not to believe anything across a radio link without confirmation.

"Stanton, are you still there? Over."

"I've lost the devices!" he snapped back angrily. "I had a window to get them and you fucked it up with fucking protocol! Over!"

"I'm going to send more units through to you in about fifteen minutes to assist you. Over"

"Shit!" he yelled again, releasing the speaker button just in time.

"Okay, this has backfired. Could you bring out some armour? We need a fourth person, and we need to put these breathing masks and tanks on. Looks like we're going in, but not quite how I planned."

*

Orak, John, Gloria and Shoa delayed setting across the sea for another day. Most of them barely had the strength to stand, but all helped lift Mac out of the boat and laid him down in the sand. Once he felt able to, Orak carried him off the beach and onto higher grassland.

They all helped find a suitable place, and agreed on a tranquil clearing from which the coast could be seen. It took most of the morning to dig a shallow grave and after lowering Mac's body into the ground; they held a traditional Tontoltec funeral service.

Shoa felt numb. This had happened so suddenly for her, as it had never occurred to her that he would not get better. For the past few months, he had been more than just her university professor; he had been a mentor, a guardian and a friend.

Orak gave a short eulogy, but was unable to hold himself together long enough to finish. He felt as though he had lost a brother and he felt guilty for all the help he tried to give, as he had only prolonged the Telepath's suffering.

"Why didn't he let us know sooner?" Orak said angrily, "We could have helped him!"

"You know Mac," Gloria replied, "He probably didn't want anybody worrying."

"For all his brains, he was too damn stubborn to ask for help!"

John began to scratch Mac's full name into a piece of driftwood with a knife. After double checking the spelling with Orak, he proceeded to etch a message into the wood.

WaMaktaJrei Kroez
Selflessly gave his life to help others
He will never be forgotten

The other three carved similar messages on pieces of waste timber and staked them in each corner of the freshly dug grave.

"What now?" John asked, unfamiliar with the local funeral rituals. It seemed so surreal that they could just legally bury him here, with no need to report his death to any authorities.

"Traditions change all the time these days," Shoa replied, "Before the revolution, the deceased's family would not work for five days after the burial, but we can't do that. We have to set off in the morning."

"This is stupid!" Gloria cut in, "Even if this island holds a way for us to get home, which face it; we've all been hoping for, without Mac we have no idea what we're looking for. I've looked through his notes, and I can't make any sense of them."

"What other choice do we have?" Shoa snapped back before John had the chance to.

"She's right," John added, "If we go to that weirdly named city, then the war will still reach us. Then we'll have to move again in a few weeks. I'm tired of running and I know you are too."

"I'm tired of everything John. I want to go home more than anything," Gloria sighed.

"Home to what?" he said without thinking. He turned quickly and started walking in the opposite direction.

He heard her footsteps following before she yelled, "What the hell do you mean by that?"

"I didn't mean that," he lied, trying to shake her off but failing. He'd well and truly stuck his foot in it now and had no choice but to break the news.

"Didn't mean it?! I don't understand what you could mean!"

John stared into her eyes and saw confusion. She really had no idea. He took Gloria away from Orak and Shoa before beginning to explain.

"I know I should have told you before, but I didn't know how you'd react and I still don't understand it myself."

"John, what the hell are you talking about?"

"In the dreams me and Mac have . . . had been having, we worked it out that they were someone else's memories right?"

"Yes?"

"Well, in one of the dreams I saw that person's reflection when I was . . . When they were running . . ."

"And?" she asked impatiently.

"It was Mark."

Gloria was silenced for a moment, and then slowly said "What? My Mark?"

This was not the reaction he was expecting. She just looked at him blankly, as if he had just declared that grass was orange. He had expected her to come to some kind of monumental realisation, but instead she just raised both eyebrows and continued to look at him like he was insane.

"Mark is a bank manager," she added, "How would he even get to Ithria?"

"I'm sure it was him."

"Well it wasn't."

At that, she turned away and walked back towards the beach.

"Think about it? Why is he never home?" John called after her.

Gloria just ignored him and carried on. This wasn't the response he had been expecting at all. If Mac was still alive he would have asked him to send Gloria the dream, but even if John had telepathic traits, he wouldn't have been able to do it himself.

He suspected that sooner or later he would be proved right. At the very least, he had given her a warning for what could turn out to be the biggest fright of her life.

Chapter 53

Maria had never felt fifteen minutes go by so quickly in her life. The three of them hurriedly changed into the lightweight armour, and after putting on their thin steel helmets, Maxwell taught them how to operate the breathing apparatus and the assault rifles. A fourth member of the team was recruited; the young soldier named KliPradras who had brought the equipment up to the deck.

"Are you ready?" the skilled mercenary asked them.

Everyone nodded uneasily, proving that they weren't.

"The rift will open from the north west," he added, orientating himself so that he was facing the bow of the ship. Maxwell knew that this plan would work if it was orchestrated by his own team of trained men, but all three people fighting beside him had never fired a gun in their lives.

He felt as though he had barely finished speaking over the radio, when the familiar unnatural breeze blew through his ruffled unclean hair. Electric white fractures cracked through the air, as the breeze grew stronger.

As an arc of lighting formed an opening, he shouted for everyone to aim ready. "Now!" he yelled, opening fire on the masked figures as they broke through into the world.

Maria closed her eyes as she pulled down hard on the trigger, but as soon as she heard the spurt of gunfire and felt the gun jolting she released it. The rattling continued for several more seconds, but after it had stopped she still couldn't bring herself to open her eyes. She had no idea whether she had hit anyone, and she never would.

"Move!" she heard Maxwell shout, as a strong hand grabbed her by the collar and dragged her forwards. She felt the electricity pulsing through her as she was pulled into the storm.

When she opened her eyes the world had disappeared around her, replaced by nothing but blinding white light. Maria felt her eyes trying to shut, but pulses of aerosol stimulant from her gas canister forced her to stay awake.

Her eyes blinked, but upon opening them, the white light had gone. She was looking down upon a linoleum floor, and could hear the faint whirring of machinery. Standing up, she felt her head spinning and saw the other four leaning up against a nearby tiled wall. As she tried to gain some bearings, she staggered towards them and collapsed against the wall.

"It shouldn't last long," she heard Maxwell's muffled voice saying.

Jekka looked as though he was about to throw up, but KliPradras was already walking about the room.

"Where are we?" Maria asked. "Are we on Earth?"

"No, but Earth is just a jump away," Maxwell replied. "We're on Katatua-Shovrus, and we haven't got a moment to waste."

*

Orak had made the decision on behalf of the group that they would leave immediately and not wait until the following day. Despite the other three arguing that it would be better to wait, he responded by saying that they had waited long enough. They had no choice but to go with him.

Irrationally fuelled by grief, he led them to the boat and launched it into the water, desperate to find something to help him forget. With one less member, they were able to carry everyone in the makeshift vessel.

A quarter of an hour into the journey across the sea, Orak was starting to change his mind. By now though, nobody was prepared to turn back.

The boat was quiet for most of the journey, as anything said would be heard by all of them. Nobody wanted to tell Orak how frightened they felt about reaching the island, and he didn't want to admit that he had rushed things.

Gloria didn't want to speak to any of them. She couldn't understand why John would make up such things, but she also couldn't understand how it could be real. The only explanation was that John was mistaken, but he seemed so adamant and she didn't want to trigger an argument while they were all in such a confined space.

"What do we do when we get there?" Shoa asked Orak directly. "What if the enemy is there? I mean, only you and I can fight."

"I can fight." John cut in, feeling offended.

"Not without a shotgun you can't."

"You're right," Orak replied. "They can't fight without weapons, which is why I put these together earlier. Reaching down to the bottom of the boat, he pulled out several longbows from under a floorboard. "There's one bow each, but I only carved twelve arrows in total. If we come across any opposition, it could be to our advantage if we look to be armed."

"I know Gloria can hit an apple off someone's head from fifty paces, but you know how bad I am at archery," John replied.

"Well, let's hope you won't have to use it then."

Orak tucked the handcrafted weapons back out of the way and searched the horizon for a sign of the island. Over the level of the water, he saw a rocky peak and knew they were going the right way.

*

Maria, Jekka and KliPradras followed Maxwell through the modern electrically lit corridor. They moved as silently as they could, and listened to voices through the walls. None of them truly knew what to expect, and Maria nearly shouted at Maxwell when he confessed that he had never actually been to this particular facility.

"You could have told us before!" she hissed, prodding him with the barrel of her sub-machine gun.

"I've seen the floor plans," he replied.

Maxwell proceeded to give a series of complex military hand gestures, but quickly realised that none of the others knew what they meant. Instead, he gestured for them to follow him slowly and quietly.

They stopped when the tiled wall changed into a floor to ceiling transparent plastic partition. The four of them stepped back out of view, but Maria watched from the bottom corner.

The room on the other side appeared to be a laboratory. Everything was stark white and immaculately clean. She looked into it from underneath a table, and could only see the bottom halves of the people walking around in long lab coats. In the centre of the room, she could see what looked like a mortuary table, and a tray of blood stained instruments.

"It's where they make them," Maxwell whispered, "The Drathmorks . . . There's a supercomputer a few doors down where they engineered the genetic codes. There should be a hall full of incubation vats on the other side of the island where they breed prototypes . . . Looks like they're still trying to make the perfect soldiers."

"We have to stop them," Maria replied.

"One step at a time. We need to neutralise any and all threats in this place and deactivate the Anuma link navigation machine, so nobody else can be sent through."

"How do we do that?" Jekka asked.

"Switch it off," he replied simply.

The four of them crept on their hands and knees passed the laboratory, until they had cleared the glazed section. For Maria, it suddenly felt as though the past few months had never happened, and that she was still in the hospital where she once worked. Memories came flooding back, and for some reason it made her think of John and Gloria. *Could they still be alive?* She doubted they would have both been as fortunate as she had.

"We need you here," Maxwell said, sensing that her mind was elsewhere.

"Where are we going?" she asked.

"Here."

They had stopped outside what looked like the door of a bank vault. A stiff metal wheel resembling that of a submarines airlock was locked and controlled by a numerical keypad.

With his fingers crossed, Maxwell typed in the code he knew from the parallel facility on Earth. He watched in utter disbelief as the illuminated keypad lit up green, then turned the wheel to open the door.

The door hissed as it slowly opened, revealing the secrets inside. Maria and Jekka had been told what to expect, but nothing prepared them for what they saw. KliPradras blurted out something incomprehensible, but clamped his hand across his mouth to stop himself making any more noise.

The security door opened out into a huge cavernous space. Towering stone columns reached up to the shimmering glass ceiling a hundred feet above, encircling a gigantic tubular concrete shell. Protruding from the centre of the encased machine was an array stack of metallic pipes, reaching skywards towards the domed roof. Cables thicker than a person's waist trailed across the ground from the colossal machine, through the walls towards another chamber.

From the gaps in the casing, a faint blue glow could be seen, as the machine constantly emitted the same mysterious energy present in every cell of every Spellcaster, Titan or Telepath. Maxwell instructed them to keep their distance; as such high levels of Anuma could be hazardous if they came in contact with it.

"Mark Jones built this?" Maria said in amazement. She had only met the man once very briefly, and he had not struck her as someone capable of a feat of this magnitude. "Where is the off switch then?"

"It's not that simple," Maxwell replied. "I need to figure out the pass code to get into the computer, and then shut each component down separately. The machine is run on twelve nuclear batteries, each the size of a transit van. After disconnecting each one, we need to wait for things to cool down. As soon as I shut the first one down, the alarms will be triggered, and every armed guard on the island will want to find out what is going on."

"Why didn't you tell us this before?" Jekka demanded, raising his firearm at the mercenary's head.

"Because you didn't ask. There's a catwalk up there where you can get a good vantage point of the door. There's another door on the opposite side of the room. One of you will want to guard there."

"Wait, how many guards will there be on the island?" Maria asked. "Will they all have guns?"

Maxwell shook his head, "I doubt they'll be carrying firearms. They'll need to get people in from Earth for that. I don't know how many there will be though."

As they discussed formations, KliPradras tipped over a heavy cabinet and began pushing it towards the doorway. Jekka quickly joined in and once the cabinet was blocking the door, he rushed over to the opposite entrance. After blocking both doorways, they wedged whatever flat objects they could find between the cabinets and underneath the handles of the doors.

"That's bought us time. Now get to work!" Jekka ordered.

"I'm not taking orders from you!" Maxwell snapped back, "I'm doing this for my own reasons!"

Jekka was ready to attack the mercenary, but Maria stood in his way and persuaded him to calm down. "Will you listen to me then Maxwell?" she asked.

"I suppose. I've got nothing against you."

Frantically typing everything he could think into the computer, he tried to imagine what the company would use. The occupants of the island believed nobody could gain access to this facility, so there was a good chance the password was something easy so people would remember it.

"Have you tried 'swordfish'?" Maria asked semi-seriously.

Maxwell had tried every word he could think of. There were millions of combinations. It would take him a lifetime to try them all. The longer he took, the higher the chances of them being discovered were.

Maria looked up at the sky through the glass dome. If the enemies took the less orthodox route, she knew they wouldn't stand a chance.

Chapter 54

The makeshift catamaran drifted into a dark rocky cove. As it collided with the cliffs, the vessel shook, and Orak looked down at the still, deep water. Pushing it along the rock wall, he stopped when the boat was beside a flat outcrop.

They all realised why this island had been used to keep whatever secrets it was keeping. Without rope and climbing experience, it looked impossible to get onto. John began scrambling up a mound of loose rock, but stopped when he came face to face with the vertical cliff. Orak managed to haul himself up to a higher section with his arms, through crimping at the rocks, and was glad that he hadn't tired himself out by swimming here.

Offering his hand to the others, he lifted them up onto a wide step one by one. He felt the flat surface of the cliff and discovered that there were no holds he could fit more than one finger in. At a push, he was sure he could reach the top, but the others wouldn't, especially not Gloria.

"There's got to be another way," he muttered.

"I think I may have one," Gloria replied.

Scrambling back down towards the boat, she started untying the kayak sections.

"I don't think dismantling our only way back is going to help," John said uneasily.

Wrapping the unbroken rope around her arm, she hauled the boat sections onto the rock just in case things went wrong. John and Shoa helped her back up the rubble, and Orak hoisted everyone back up the short cliff section.

After tying a rock to the end of the rope, she handed it to Orak and asked, "How's your underarm?"

"Dreadful. Is this your plan?" he replied.

"Can I try something?" Shoa cut in. She took the end of the rope and untied the heavy piece of stone. "I've seen Spellcasters do this before."

"You'll burn out halfway." John said.

John and Gloria looked at each other in confusion, but understood when a sudden gust of wind whipped up the gritty sand from underneath them. Holding their hands over their mouths, they watched as Shoa's body slowly lifted from the ground.

The rope safely tied to her belt, Shoa ascended up the cliff face, but even from the ground it was obvious that she was sweating. After nearly a minute of struggling to maintain control over the air, she dragged herself up onto the top of the basalt cliff.

A few minutes later, she called down to say that the rope was secure. Orak climbed it first, and then once he too was safely atop the cliff, pulled the rope up with John and Gloria hanging on to it.

As Orak had predicted, Shoa was too tired to move, and he had to carry her on his back from there. The moment John had reached the top of the cliff, he knew where they were. It was as though he had stepped back into his dream, but this time there was no doubt in his mind that this was real.

The sun had set and the moons had risen, bathing the jagged dark rocks in twilight. The breeze was just as cold as it had been in his nightmares, but the whistling wind was now the only thing he could hear. He waited for the screeching of the harpies, but nothing came.

His foot crashed down into a puddle, and he looked down to see the reflection, but the ripples just turned everything into chaos. The mountain from his later dreams dominated the skyline ahead. "This is the place alright," he said to the others.

"There's nothing here," Gloria replied, sensing that they had all made the biggest mistake since they had been on this world.

"There's got to be something here. Why else would Kedos show us this place?" asked John.

"It's not a small island," Orak explained, "There's a smaller volcano a few miles further south from this one, and a strip of land joining the two together."

Shoa looked up towards the crater of the volcano ahead of them. There was no smoke erupting from it, and she saw this as a good sign. Either side of the dark mountain, she could see tiny trees dotted around at the base, and realised just how big and how far away it was. Clambering down from Orak's back, she followed the others as they walked towards the mount.

The further everyone walked, the more they started to agree with Gloria about there being nothing there.

"I hope we can get the boat back together again," said John.

"It was your stupid dreams that led us here," Gloria snapped back. There was no denying that she was feeling irritable. She had placed all of her hopes on this place, and was angry that she had done so without any logical reason.

"I think Kedos wanted us to go this way," John suddenly realised, "This is the exact same place from the dream, and so far we've encountered nothing dangerous."

"That's because there's nothing dangerous here, everything has choked to death on these eggy sulphur fumes," said Orak.

Shoa laughed, but as she did inhaled a mouthful of the toxic air and started coughing.

"Mac wouldn't have coped breathing here," Orak said quietly, "Maybe it was best that he passed before we came."

Just as Gloria was about to tell him that they should never have come here in the first place and that Mac was the only way of them getting home, she caught sight of something moving in the distance. Tapping John on the shoulder, she pointed towards the figure standing beside a boulder twice their height.

"I guess not everything has choked to death on the fumes," Shoa whispered.

Shifting towards cover so that the figure in the distance could not see them, they stealthily approached. As they got closer, the cloaked figure became clearer, but faced away from them. Before they reached them, the figure turned and walked behind the boulder, and a disembodied voice nobody recognised spoke to them all.

"I'm sorry for the subterfuge," it said. The voice was that of an elderly man, and sounded far calmer and more soothing than you'd expect from anyone in such unpleasant surroundings. "Come closer so I can speak to you all in person."

Cautiously they approached. Orak drew his knife, and everyone else held arrows to their bows, unsure whether they would actually fly straight.

"You won't need those yet," the voice said again, but this time not inside their heads. From behind the rock the cloaked man stepped out.

"Kedos?" John asked, relaxing the strain on the bowstring.

The old man nodded as he lowered his hood. His face was pale and gaunt, but his eyes were the same vivid purple as Mac's had been. Upon his nearly bald head were a few strands of untidy white hair jutting outwards, and his few remaining teeth were crooked and stained yellow.

He nodded at John's question. "I suppose you must want some answers?" he asked with a wry smile.

Chapter 55

"I can't get in." Maxwell snapped through frustration, "I'll never guess this password."

"Why did you bring us here then?" Maria replied, still staring at the barricaded door in fear.

"Because I thought I knew it." Maxwell typed in yet another guess, which happened to be one guess too many. An error message flashed up on the screen.

System locked

Speakers all around the room that none of them had seen burst into life. The wailing alarm carried through the whole facility, and Maxwell stared in horror at the monitor. He had pushed his luck too far.

KliPradras began panicking and hurriedly talking so only Jekka could understand him. Aiming at the loud speakers, he fired up at them.

The audio equipment blew apart like cheap appliances and sent sparks flying through the air. Jekka joined in and soon every speaker in the chamber was inactive. It was as if they had gone deaf for a moment, but after a few seconds of apparent silence they began to hear the wailing faintly through the walls.

"We can hear ourselves think now," Jekka added, "What happens now? Should we try to get out of here?"

"We should but we can't, the doors are now deadlocked," Maxwell replied.

"You idiot," Maria snapped. She felt like shooting him, but resisted.

"Don't panic, I can sort this," he lied.

Within minutes, there was a loud hammering on the door they had come in from. It stopped suddenly, and before any of them could say anything, the door exploded open with such force that the cabinet blocking it, flew halfway across the room. The door itself broke from its hinges and crashed down onto the floor.

A spine tingling screech from outside drowned out the sirens for a second, and the creature responsible stepped through the door, one set of legs at a time. The Arachno-Sapien as Maxwell had called it, had to duck down to fit through the door, but stood up in the chamber to reveal its full height of over ten feet.

Without hesitation, Maria opened fire, shortly followed by the other three. Nearly every bullet hit, but the beast's outer shell didn't fracture. It sprinted towards them with such speed that nobody but KliPradras was quick enough to act. Leaping in Maria's way, he took the full force of its sword strike. The blade cut through every rib and punctured nearly every organ in his torso.

Maria screamed and fired upwards at the creature's head, but only struck it once, under the chin at an angle. She stared in amazement as the creature barely reacted, its lower jaw hanging slack on one side. It gave her the time to move away from its path of destruction.

"Get down," Maxwell yelled at her, seconds before firing at the creature via where she had been standing.

The arachnid monster stormed towards him, the bullets ricocheting off its tough skin. Ducking, he narrowly avoided its blade, but fired up at its throat at near point blank range.

As the creature fell, its sword nearly crashed down on Maxwell, but struck his assault rifle with such force that the barrel dented and the weapon flew from his hands. The ground quaked when the hybrid soldier struck it, and Jekka rushed to the aid of his fallen soldier. He looked into KliPradras' frozen eyes and knew that he had died almost instantly.

"They sent it so we'd waste our ammo," Maxwell snapped angrily, rubbing his twisted wrist. He crouched down and prised the gun from KliPradras' hands, then checked the cartridge. "Trigger happy bastard used them all."

"Show some respect," Jekka yelled, shoving Maxwell to the ground, "This man was a hero."

"Yeah, well he was a reckless hero, and my gun is broken and so is my wrist, so you two better make them count, because they're sending more soldiers as we speak."

*

Kedos led the group through the desolate rocky plain, to an area where the ground sloped downhill and away from the mountain. He changed direction so often through the maze of stone and walked so quickly for a man of his age that they all struggled to keep up. He had to stop to allow Gloria to catch her breath as she nursed a stitch. It pained John to see her like this so soon after Mac's death, even though he knew she was fine.

"So you've been living out here all this time?" Orak asked, "Hiding out in the open?"

"There are miles and miles of caves under the mountain, it wasn't hard to stay unseen," Kedos replied, "I had to speak to WaMaktaJrei through my dreams and memories, because if I consciously spoke to him, I could have slipped up and Mradraak would have seen where I was. If he intercepted my dreams, he would have thought nothing of it. I'm sorry I couldn't have been clearer, and I'm sorry about WaMaktaJrei's passing. At least you all got here."

"Err, how come you can speak English?" John asked.

"We've been able to see your world far longer than the people of Tontoltec because this is the epicentre of the link. I was a member of the Alkak-Taanan council, another fellow member and I left our positions when the rest agreed on the plan to try to reclaim our lost empire with the help of the Earth company. There are now twelve members of the council including Mradraak."

"What happened to your friend who left the council with you?" Shoa asked.

"They found him and executed him in front of our people to send a message. I was lucky."

Kedos started walking again without warning, and Gloria had to run for a few seconds to catch up.

"Why did you want us to come here?" she asked.

"Because I knew you wanted to go home, and I thought WaMaktaJrei's knowledge of the link might come in useful."

"For what?" Orak cut in.

"For using the machine to take down the council. Do you hear the alarms in the distance? Sounds like somebody has already tried to use it, and this gives us the perfect opportunity to get inside."

"Inside where? What machine?" Gloria asked. In more ways than one, he was moving too fast for her.

"I'll have to show you, look down there."

They had stopped at the edge of a large crater. The rock walls looked charred from blasting, and the flat base was flat and dusty. Built into the side of a quarried cliff face was a huge solid steel door, as big as the doorway to a Roman Catholic cathedral.

Kedos led them past the crater and much to everyone's confusion, towards a smaller dark hole in the ground. The hole looked so small that they could easily have missed it, and was just over half a metre wide. "It's a low pressure air outlet" he explained, "It gets wider further down."

"I'm not going to fit through there," Orak pointed out, "Everyone else probably will, but not me."

"Which is why I brought these. It will sort out the iron grid lower down as well."

Kedos produced several thin plastic sticks from underneath his cloak. Only Gloria realised what they were. "That's going to draw attention to us," she said.

"You'll have a few minutes to get to the chamber before the guards reach you. I've made a map for you to use."

"You're not coming?" Shoa interrupted, "We don't even know what we're doing."

"I'm confident John will figure out the controls. The password is Gloria."

At that, Kedos vanished from their vision. Gloria looked dumbstruck, staring at the spot where he had been standing. "Why am I the password?" she yelled at the empty space.

"The bastard didn't tell us anything," Orak muttered, placing two of the explosives around the outside of the opening, before dropping one down into the hole.

*

Jekka and Maxwell struggled to slot the fallen door back into place. Dragging the piece of furniture back to hold the door, they searched the room for something else to barricade it. Not long after piling chairs onto the cabinet to weigh it down, something on the other side of the door started knocking.

Maria looked up at the glass dome above and knew it was only a matter of time before the enemy decided to attack, after all, they did have flying soldiers. "How many rounds do you have?" she asked Jekka.

"Sixteen," he replied a moment later, "You?"

"Twenty, I don't think I can do this. If they sent people, I can't kill a person."

"Get a grip, you're a soldier," Maxwell cut in.

"Don't think I won't use this on you," Jekka snapped, rounding his gun on the mercenary.

The banging against the door was cut short by a louder bang further away. Maria felt the ground vibrating for a moment, and then listened out for answers. She could hear shouting but nothing else.

As she got closer to the door, a loud electrical crackle deadened the sound of the guards, and then stopped.

Clambering over the cabinet, she placed her ear against the cold steel door to listen. She could hear voices on the other side but couldn't make out any words. The voices sounded calm unlike the panicked guards.

As one of them came closer to the door, she could just about make out what they were saying. "We've still got one stick left. If it doesn't shift this, nothing will."

"Get back," Maria yelled, scrambling off the cabinet and dragging Jekka away from the entrance. They both aimed at the doorway, waiting.

"Don't hesitate," Maxwell shouted from behind the computer terminal.

Chapter 56

On the other side of the door, Orak led Shoa away from the explosives. Gloria proceeded to usher them further back, and John, taking no chances stood further back than all of them. "It's going to be loud again," he reminded them, placing his fingers in his ears.

Orak closed his eyes and shielded everyone else with his body, and when the explosive detonated, he felt the hot air blast against him and dust fill his lungs. Coughing violently, he tried to look through the cloud of smoke. He heard a rattle, and the next second he was struck by a bullet.

"Take cover," John shouted, trying to drag the wounded Titan out of the line of fire.

"I'm ok, it just went in and out," Orak spluttered, collapsing against the side wall. He felt the hot blood between his fingers and looked down at the tiny hole in his gut. He could not see the massive red splatter on the tiles behind him.

Shoa could hear footsteps from behind them and realised they would soon be trapped. Orak was already back on his feet, but clearly still in great pain.

"What are we going to do?" she asked him.

"Stick to the plan," he replied.

"What plan?" she asked.

Without giving an answer, Orak ran back into range of the guns and lifted up the heavy steel door, which had spun back into the hallway after the blast. Using it as a shield, he charged through the smouldering widened doorway and smashed it into one of the gunners, knocking them to the ground.

"Orak!" he heard a woman scream, causing him to stop dead.

He saw her run to the aid of the fallen man, who was still just about conscious. An unarmed man watched in confusion from behind a terminal, as the other three walked into the chamber.

Orak placed the door on the ground. "How do you know my name?" he asked, focusing on his surroundings with his stinging smoke filled eyes.

The woman looked up and gave a puzzled look, "It is you, isn't it?"

"Maria?" he said slowly, recognising her voice.

Upon hearing her name, John rushed forwards, virtually pushing past Shoa. "You're alive," he spluttered, almost tripping over the door and then Jekka to get to her.

He embraced her in a hug, and could feel that she was trembling. He let go as he felt her slowly moving away from him. He could see tears running down her eyes but only the faintest of smiles.

"I'm sorry we couldn't find you," he replied, mirroring her teary gaze, "I'm sorry we left you all alone."

He saw that she was holding the dazed gunman tightly in her arms, and she simply replied, "I was never alone."

Gloria said nothing to interrupt them, but tapped Orak on the shoulder to remind him of the approaching threat. He picked the door back up and slotted it back in place as best as he could.

Gloria grabbed the fallen gun from the injured man and aimed through one of the gaps in the damaged doorway. "How long do you think you can hold it for?" she asked.

"Not long, we need a better plan again."

"The password is Gloria." Shoa yelled to the man at the console.

"What? That's stupid," he replied, typing in the six letters, "It's far too short, and . . . . access granted, whoever you are I love you."

The sirens shut down almost immediately, but Maxwell continued frantically typing. "What are you doing?" Maria shouted, standing up and running towards him, "We haven't got time."

"I'm viewing the location history," he cut her short.

As Jekka stood up, John found himself collapsing to the floor. He had slipped on a puddle of blood and looked up at Orak, who was bleeding more heavily. "Not you as well," he croaked, shaking his head in disbelief.

"I'll be fine," Orak said once again, "I've had worse."

Jekka tore off a section of his shirt and handed it to the wounded stranger Maria seemed to know. He felt compelled to help as he himself had caused the wound. As he helped the fallen man back up, he heard the rattle of gunfire again, and turned to see the old woman firing through the gap.

"They're coming," Gloria screamed as her weapon stopped dead, "Jesus there's hundreds of them."

"Here we go. Masks!" Maxwell yelled.

"What?" asked Maria.

The light from the machine grew brighter and a wind began spiralling around the room. The blue glow turned to white as the light extended beyond the machine. Soon the whole chamber was engulfed in the soft light, and those not wearing breathing masks instantly fell asleep.

*

The jagged rocky wastelands were no longer a part of John's dreams. The cold wind and the screaming of the harpies had gone, replaced by the murmuring of voices echoing around a stone chamber. He was deep inside an ancient building, walking through the torch lit corridors. John felt himself taking a turn to the right when he was faced with a sculpture of a giant frilled reptile.

At the end of the next corridor, he encountered another sculpture, this time of a perched peregrine falcon, and he walked down the left of the two corridors as it divided. The maze of corridors continued until he reached the source of the low rumbling voices. Among a dozen cloaked figures he saw a mirror and caught sight of Kedos reflected in it.

"You remember the way?" he saw Kedos mouthing towards him.

John shrugged, but as he stepped away from the mirror, the Telepath also vanished. Suddenly his lungs filled with a pungent chemical taste, and his eyes flew open. He felt the plastic mask pressed against his mouth and nose, and pushed them away.

Maria was standing over him faintly smiling. "Did you see anything?" she asked.

"You remembered about my dreams?" he asked, as his surroundings slid into focus.

"That was such a long time ago John," she replied, shaking her head, "Shoa told me about them. Did he show you anything?"

John ignored her; he was staring into the blackness ahead, confused as to how there was so much steady light around them. He saw it emanating from Shoa, as if she had descended from heaven. A second later he saw the source in her hand, a 100 watt light bulb powered by her own electrical output.

"Maria found it in the woods," she explained.

John clambered to his feet and after a moment of trying to regain his balance, rested a hand on her shoulder and led her through the tunnel. "Come on, I know where we're going," he said.

Chapter 57

Shoa quickly started to feel the heat from the bulb, and despite being able to hold fire in her hands, it started to burn. Dropping it as a reflex to the pain, she heard it smash on the ground. Everyone stopped dead, unable to see.

A smaller, more focused beam of light appeared from beneath the barrel of Gloria's assault rifle. A moment later, a second beam shone from Jekka's weapon. They both stood either side of John, several paces behind, and carefully treaded around the broken glass.

"Hold it higher," John instructed Jekka, "I don't need to see my feet."

They moved through the tunnel at a snail's pace due to their limited visibility.

"They didn't give you night vision then?" Maria asked Maxwell, feeling the walls with her fingertips.

"They wouldn't fit with the masks on, so we left them," he replied, embarrassed by the poor management of his former team.

John's mind was frantic, and he suspected this was the case with everyone else as well. They were inside the Alkak-Taanan council building, where decisions on the war were made. They all had an opportunity to dramatically change things thrust upon them without warning. This would probably be the only chance anybody had to stop the conflict, but it would be far from easy. In their party of six, only two were trained killers, and victory would require stopping a group of powerful and ruthless beings twice their number.

The only thing that eased his mind slightly, was that they appeared to be undetected. Maxwell had informed them that the machine would not work again for another hour or so, however, the enemy had Earth communication technology and could still theoretically send a message across. Their long range radios probably weren't quite long ranging enough, and everyone held on to this belief to keep them going.

They had passed every stone animal John had envisioned, and just like in his dream, it ended with them standing in the doorway of a large chamber. Unlike the dream however, the room was empty, and as dark as the rest of the building.

"Do you think they know we're here?" Shoa whispered, lighting one of the wall mounted torches.

In the centre of the room, stood a long, heavy, polished oak table, surrounded by ornate cushioned chairs. In the firelight, they could just about see the detailed painting on the ceiling high above, but couldn't make out what it depicted.

"No," Orak replied, shaking his head, "I just don't think they spend their whole time here . . . I know that nobody but the councillors are allowed in this section of the building, anybody else is a security risk, so we won't encounter any guards or servants."

"Just superhuman politicians," John replied, wishing he had some kind of weapon, "We're going to need a better plan."

"Agreed . . . . This is really starting to hurt."

"And if any of these guys are like you, a handful of bullets won't do much."

Shoa was about to light a second torch when she saw the door on the opposite side of the chamber swing open. She saw the wide startled eyes of a young man, and hurled the fire from her hand, the moment sparks appeared from his fingertips.

The flaming projectile dissipated in mid-air, as a bolt of lightning shot towards her. The lightning arched away and made scorch marks along the table. Gloria and Jekka rounded their guns on the Spellcaster and fired, as he dived behind a fixed wooden bench. The bullets tore through the timber, sending splinters raining down on the councillor.

Scrambling across the floor, he sent a blast of wind towards them. Gloria was knocked off her feet, but Jekka was only pushed back far enough to collide with Orak, who didn't even wobble. The chairs in the centre of the chamber had flown across the room, and it had tipped the large table over. In the confusion, he had escaped.

"Let me get the little runt!" Orak snarled, sprinting through the door and down the corridor after the fleeing man.

"By yourself, you can't . . . ?" John started to say, but saw the Titan vanishing into the blackness before he could finish.

"This wasn't what you meant by a better plan I'm guessing," Maxwell laughed.

Nobody else shared his sense of humour, and Shoa just glared at him. Several minutes later, Orak returned, carrying the unconscious Spellcaster over his shoulder. His clothes were smouldering, and after dropping the man to the floor, he threw down his jacket and stamped down the flames as soon as they ignited.

"One down," he panted.

Dragging the councillor across the floor, Orak pulled the table back up and laid him down on it. Both guns were aimed at his head, while Maxwell's plastic gas inhalator mask was pressed down over his mouth and nose.

Although he knew that this man was one of the many responsible for hundreds of deaths, John couldn't bear to look. He could see that Gloria too was trembling, and that Shoa was nearly in tears. The only one who seemed completely detached was Maxwell, and John didn't fully understand why he was there helping them.

"Where are the others?" Orak roared as soon as the trapped Spellcaster regained consciousness.

"Abria Agada Zubrekaraj!" he blurted.

"I know you speak English!" Orak snarled, "I know you've been working with people from Earth!"

"They aren't here! I look after the building when the others have left! I'm only training to be a councillor. My father is the one you're after!"

Orak slammed his fist into the head of the table, causing two of its legs to snap, throwing the young Spellcaster to the floor. The guns followed his head, but he made no attempt to escape, as his legs were badly bruised. "What good are you then?"

"Please don't kill me!" he whimpered, shutting his eyes so tightly his face crinkled up like a prune. Sweat poured from his hands, and he felt himself sliding across the smooth floor.

Orak struggled to keep the tough image when he realised that this man wasn't who he first believed. Realising the Titan was having a crisis of conscience, Maxwell quickly stepped in.

"We won't hurt you if you help us," he said, "If you try to escape, we kill you. If you lie, we kill you. Understand?"

He nodded, looking up and blinking at the light from Jekka's firearm. "My father and my uncle are on the Council," he stammered, "They gave me the job . . . I don't know anyone else on the Council . . . No, I do. My older brother joined it a few days ago too . . . You're not going to hurt them are you?"

"No," Jekka cut in, "Not if they want to see you again. I think we can come up with a better plan now."

"We can't!" Maria blurted out, but he cut her down with a cold serious stare.

"She's right," John added, "I don't like any of this. This guy has done nothing wrong. We should bargain for our freedom, how else will we get out of here alive? Gloria, tell him we can't hold him hostage."

Much to his surprise, Gloria didn't back him up. "We have to John. This is bigger than just the seven of us in this room. This is about stopping a war. We have to think this through, but the best option so far is this one."

"Look what you're doing!" he snapped, pointing at the gun in her hands, "This isn't you! You're a nurse not a soldier! This place is changing you!"

"Nobody likes this John," Shoa interrupted, "Nobody wants to do any of this, but we're here now. Kedos wouldn't have shown us to the island if he didn't think we could do something to stop these people."

Maxwell glanced at his watch. They had forty-five minutes before the machine would be active again. Forty-five minutes before all hell broke loose. He tapped the watch as a gesture that time was ticking.

"Look, we can't do this without you John," Orak said, "Kedos chose to give the directions to you. He wants you to be a part of this. As none of us really know what we're doing, you have the upper hand in this situation."

"So . . . I'm in charge?" he replied, wearing a perplexed look.

"What?" Maxwell and Jekka said almost simultaneously, while Maria looked at him in disbelief.

Orak shrugged his shoulders, "I guess so. What we do next is up to you."

Chapter 58

"Forty minutes!" Maxwell shouted, subtly reminding everyone of their impending fate.

John still struggled to find the words to express himself. "I've never been in charge of anything this big before," he laughed uneasily. Looking down upon the frightened captive man, he couldn't see a way that anybody else's plan would work.

"Whatever happens, I still love you," Jekka said, taking hold of Maria.

John turned away. He couldn't deal with this too. "Is there any way to get out of this place?"

"You tell us leader," Maxwell replied snidely.

"There's a secret passageway . . . I can show you it," the prisoner quietly suggested.

"Good enough for me," John decided. Orak grabbed the Spellcaster by the collar and dragged him back onto his feet.

Maxwell felt a pang of guilt. It wasn't that long ago when he had been the one being treated like this. In just a few hours, he had changed from a prisoner being relocated, to a key member of this bizarrely constructed team. Ignoring any feelings which contradicted his goal, he followed the group down yet another dark corridor.

"If you're leading us into a trap, I'll snap your neck!" Orak snarled, and felt the prisoner's body tremble under his hand.

"It leads to the laboratories. It's the only way out without using the front gates, which are heavily guarded. Once I get you to safety will you let me go?"

Nobody replied. The young Spellcaster led them to a patch of wall which looked just like any other, except for the fact that it had mould growing around it. "It's not been used in years. They use the main doors to the labs," he explained, pushing it to no effect, "It's pretty stiff."

"What kind of labs are they?" John asked.

"I don't know. I've never been in them."

"Stand back!" Orak cut in. Taking a run up, he sent his foot crashing through the ancient wall, which crumbled to pieces upon impact. Hauling the rubble out of the way, he gritted his teeth at the pain in his gut. The wound was hurting a lot more now, but he wasn't going to let on. "Okay, where do we go from here?"

"Straight on, I guess. Like I said, I've never been down here before."

The hallway beyond the broken wall seemed even darker than the rest of the building. The air smelt musty and was thick with dust, which flew through the air caught in the torch beams like a snowstorm. They walked single file down the centre of the corridor to avoid the huge draping spider webs, but didn't see them until they were already clinging to their clothes and skin.

"I don't like this place!" Shoa hissed.

She stopped when a wall became visible just in front of her. The torch beams scanned the room in every direction, but found no way out, except back where they came from.

"Turn off the light," Orak instructed.

Reluctantly, Gloria and Jekka switched off their torches, but as they did, a faint thin line of light appeared on the wall.

Orak tapped either side of the wall, and then took several steps back. "Will there be anyone inside?"

The prisoner shook his head, but realising that nobody could see him, he said, "No."

Just like before the wall, came crashing down and a blinding light came pouring into the crumbling stone chamber.

Orak kicked the rubble out of the way, and stepped into the brightly lit chamber. This new room couldn't have been more different from the rest of the council building. The surfaces were smooth and clinical, and were bathed in a soft white light. Jekka couldn't help himself from touching everything he saw. The polystyrene ceiling tiles and the plastic coated walls and floor were like nothing he'd seen before. He touched a glass partition and was amazed at how clear it was.

Maxwell was sure a silent alarm would have been tripped, but said nothing. Instead he headed for the nearest computer terminal, "Don't suppose you know the password for these too?" he asked Shoa. Glancing at his watch he saw that they had thirty minutes left. "How far is the exit?"

"I don't know," the captive Spellcaster replied, "I've never been here before."

"So how do you know it's a safer way out?"

"Because I know where the service lines reach the surface, and it's never guarded because nothing can get in there."

"But we can get out there?"

"Yes," he lied, "There's an emergency exit. My dad told me."

"So which way do you think it is?"

"Through here."

The Spellcaster led them through yet another maze of corridors; past banks of high-tech looking supercomputers and doorways, labelled with every warning sign imaginable. The oddly well thought out set of directions took them to a hallway lined with large glass columns, filled with thick clear liquid. In many of the columns were preserved or alive specimens. A sedated Drathmork's eyes slowly followed them down the hall, as its slack jaw lolled up and down.

In another tank, a creature which had clearly not formed right bobbed up and down. Skin had formed halfway across its mouth, but on the exposed half of its un-opening jaw, its teeth were crooked and cutting through its raw gum. Upon its back, was a single shrivelled wing and its irises were completely white. Nobody could bring themselves to look at it, but when they did, they struggled to look away.

"Why are they kept alive?" Shoa asked, clearly sounding distraught.

"So they can figure out what they did wrong" Maxwell answered, before leaning towards Maria and asking "Am I the only one who thinks we're being led into a trap?"

Maria shook her head. She was sure that none of them trusted their guide, but with absolutely no knowledge of where they were, they didn't have any choice but to follow.

They passed another large tank, but this time with wide pipes and wires protruding from the opaque glass. Everyone but the captive Spellcaster tried to peer inside. They were so distracted that nobody noticed their prisoner moving further ahead, and hitting a button mounted to the wall.

A thick clear plastic wall slid across the corridor, separating him from everyone else.

"The exit is just this way," he laughed, sprinting off in the stated direction.

"You little Krithsprore!" Orak roared, slamming his hammer like fists into the barrier, causing nothing more than surface cracks.

They all turned when something beside the incubation tank started bleeping. A light at the top began flashing, and the thick clear fluid inside was slowly drained from around the specimen.

Gloria shot at the glass, which she quickly realised was bullet proof. Nobody knew what to expect, but as the glass container began to separate, whatever was inside wasn't patient enough to wait.

The toughened container was blasted open, sending tiny pieces of clear shrapnel across the room. They all shielded their eyes as the thousands of shards hit them like sand from a grit blaster. The two gunners opened fire, but after just a few seconds they had depleted both weapons. The creature masked by smoke and icy cold vapour, leapt from its plinth and thudded to the ground, unharmed.

Chapter 59

Mradraak passed the static guards and ran through the arched doorway of the council building. At the same time, a towering robed Titan sprinted through, almost knocking over one of the human sentries. The two councillors were followed by a rabble of snarling Drathmorks. Several minutes later, another party of cloaked officials glided into the building.

The Council had been scheduled to meet half an hour later, but after hearing the alarms, they decided to follow their security forces into the facility in order to confront their intruders personally.

"It's probably just Nakabada messing around again," the Titan grumbled, "We all warned him not to use that tunnel. This Earth security technology we're spending all our money on is a waste of time!"

"If he wasn't related to half the Council I would have voted him out, you know I would," Mradraak replied. "But we have bigger issues than him."

"You're still going on about Kedos?"

"He's a threat, you might not see it but I do. Any security breach is a threat."

"You think he's trying to break in?"

"No; he's smarter than that. I should know; he taught me everything I know. He thinks he's better than the rest of us, but his arrogance cost him everything: his influence, his wealth, his land . . . If he's behind this, he's not putting his own life on the line; he's got people under his control everywhere."

The Titan shook his head and laughed, "You're sounding crazy; we're untouchable now, and there's nothing Kedos can do about it."

The final members of the council arrived, congregating in the cavernous entrance hall. Each man was escorted by a small party of personal guards, who joined the hybrid soldiers as they ventured further into the building.

As the councillors began to discuss what could have triggered the alarm, Nakabada came running past the Drathmorks towards them. He nearly dropped to the floor when he stopped running, and braced himself against the wall to stay standing.

All eyes fell upon him, as he struggled to get his words out. "They broke in . . . They tried to get me to help them . . . They let it out!"

"Slow down!" the boy's father yelled, grabbing hold of his son and shaking him to his senses. "What did they let out?"

Mradraak pushed past the gathering crowd, "What did they let out!" he snapped, grabbing the young Spellcaster by the collar and pushing him to the wall, "Tell us!"

"Prototype sixteen!" he croaked, "The scientists failed to terminate it, and the intruders opened his cell!"

*

The vapour sank and spread across the room, before condensing on the cold tile floor. Prototype sixteen stood inanimately, staring at the equally stunned people standing before it. After a moment of silence, the creature heard one of its viewers speak.

"Can it see us?" Shoa whispered nervously.

"How would I know?" Maxwell replied, "I don't get involved in this tampering with nature shit!"

Orak stepped forwards, before ushering the others to move back. At first he thought the creature was entirely encased in a tough black shell, but as he saw the light move over the surface of its exoskeleton, he realised it was metallic.

The dark solid steel plates covered every inch of the bipedal being, with no more than a millimetre gap between any of the hundreds of panels. It became clear that whatever they were looking at had been grown inside its own armour, which explained why the barrage of bullets had no effect. Orak could see no facial features through its small deep eye slits, and the creature appeared to be swaying slightly.

"Okay, we should go," he said decisively, forgetting that he had appointed John as the leader.

Slowly they all backed out of the room, constantly maintaining eye contact with the baffled experiment. Shoa lingered, unable to break her eyes away from the dumbstruck creature. John tapped her shoulder to get her to follow, but caused her to jump with fright. A bolt of lightning shot from her fingertips at the creature, but before she could realise what she had done, the electricity shot straight back towards her.

Catching her as she fell, John dragged her away through an open doorway. "Shoa! Are you alright?" he spluttered, trying desperately to drag her to her feet.

"I'm okay," she coughed, pushing him away, "It missed me, I just tripped and twisted my ankle a bit."

"It's not following us, but we'd still better get out of here," John replied. "Can you run?"

Before waiting to see if she could even walk, Orak grabbed Shoa and threw her onto his shoulder. "Any suggestions as to which way?" he asked.

As the clinical white laboratory ended, and the hallways became stone again, the screeching of the Drathmorks echoed all around them. "This was a really stupid idea!" Gloria yelled at Maxwell, "Why did you take us here?"

For the first time since any of them had known the mercenary, he was speechless. He had no witty comebacks or snide remarks and he was as frightened and vulnerable as everyone else was.

"We're underground, right? So we should head upwards," John added, swiftly changing direction when he saw the bottom of a staircase.

The stairs led them to a long thin balcony stretching all the way back along the hallway they had been running. With such little light, they had not seen what was above them, but now everything seemed slightly clearer. At the opposite end they could see another better lit staircase, and without even looking the other way, they headed towards it.

Each staircase led them closer to the surface. Each new floor was brighter, and with each new breath the air grew fresher. Orak stopped dead when, after losing count of how many flights they had ascended, he found himself looking down into the main entrance chamber. The stairs descended again, in a wide spiral all the way around the circular pillared hall. Painfully bright light poured in through the large open doors, and he could see in detail the dozens of Drathmork and human corpses which littered the floor far below.

"We should turn back," he said gravely, despite knowing there was only one way they could go.

*

The councillors swiftly left the building when they heard their soldiers screaming in pain. When complete silence fell, they began to run.

Nobody looked back as they sprinted up the sloping path through the vast palace gardens. As the Titan approached the walls, he saw more soldiers approaching to aid them, but before they could enter, the wrought iron gates swung shut; trapping them outside.

Hammering on the heavy duty gates, he ordered the soldiers to break through, before attempting to clamber over. Halfway up, he cut open his hand on the razor sharp wire which was in place to stop intruders. The wire detached as he tried to climb back down, and began to wrap around his body as if it had a mind of its own. Before he'd even reached the ground, the wire had bound him with more strength than even he could muster and sliced his body into three.

A fine bloody mist sprayed across all those unfortunate enough to witness the man's death, and the soldiers began backing away. The other councillors watched as the armoured creature stampeded towards them, bearing the swords of two of its many victims.

Nakabada's uncle threw his cloak aside and began sprinting towards the metal monster; zigzagging to avoid any attacks. Once he was close enough, the Spellcaster sent a powerful blast of wind at the creature, knocking it off its feet.

Throwing itself back onto its feet as if its armour weighed nothing, the creature forced the wind to change direction and treble in strength, lifting the Spellcaster high into the air. Stopping the wind suddenly, prototype sixteen watched his attacker plummet to his death.

"Open the gates!" the dead man's brother cried, as he watched the Telepaths flying over it with ease. The blood soaked wire which had cut apart the Titan flew back up into the air and wrapped around the legs of two airborne dignitaries, before dragging them back to the ground.

"You don't have to do this!" Nakabada pleaded, "I set you free; you can go and nobody else needs to get hurt!"

The creature stopped dead in its tracks and stared at the adolescent. Its head swung around in every direction, surveying the scene as if it had only just arrived. It turned back to the frightened and tearful young Spellcaster knelt down on the ground.

"Nobody else needs to die!" Nakabada repeated.

"Die," the creature uttered through the grill of its helmet, merely repeating the boy's last word.

"Not today!" he screamed back, grabbing a discarded sword from the floor and swiping at his attacker.

The blade missed the steel and cut straight into the flesh of the beast's outstretched hand. As its index and middle fingers fell to the ground, the creature let out a scream which burst Nakabada's eardrums.

Flames rose from the ground around the Spellcaster so quickly that he only saw a flicker of yellow light before the fire itself poured into his lungs and engulfed him. Within seconds he was just a smouldering pile of ash blackened bones.

In a fury of confusion and pain, the creature hacked apart the remaining councillors one by one. Soon all was calm again, and the bound gates flew back open.

Fifty swordsmen retreated from the lone soldier as the rogue experiment followed them into the surrounding city.

*

Mradraak watched the whole thing through wide petrified eyes. Once he was sure the bloodthirsty monster was far enough away, he clambered out of the muddy ditch and back onto his feet, throwing aside the body he had hidden beneath.

Staggering back towards the palace, he stopped when the nausea was too strong for him to cope with. Bending over the carved stone drain he couldn't stop himself from vomiting. He had been powerless to stop the massacre. The beast's mind had forced itself into his and paralysed his whole body. It froze its victims to the spot while they watched it kill everyone around them. His ears were still ringing from the creature's scream, a sound he knew would haunt him forever.

Mradraak collapsed back onto the ground. He couldn't find the strength to move, even when he saw people emerging from inside the palace.

Chapter 60

Despite having no ammunition, Maxwell led the group whilst tightly clutching the firearm as if it was precious to him. He saw the robed man kneeling in the mud with tears streaming down his face, but felt no pity. Aiming the barrel of the gun at his former employer, he waited for an excuse to pull the trigger; even if it was only to intimidate. The Telepath remained passive.

While the mercenary kept both eyes firmly upon their unarmed but still potentially dangerous enemy, everyone else surveyed their surroundings. Bodies of all species were strewn across the neatly cut lawns, several still moving but only minutes from death. The majority had died instantly.

"Do you think it's gone? Shoa asked, staring through the gates at the city beyond.

"I don't want to stick around long enough to find out," John replied through chattering teeth. It suddenly dawned on him how cold it was, and he remembered that they had travelled very far north without stepping foot outside until now. Shoa explained to him that they were only a few hundred miles south of Ithria's Arctic Circle.

Orak swiftly walked towards a Drathmork soldier who was choking on its own blood and without hesitation he plunged its own blade through its neck, ending its misery. "We're right inside the enemies territory; we don't have long until more come!" he bellowed.

"But where can we go?" Maria asked, turning to Maxwell and glaring at him as if to say, 'You know this is your fault.'

"Anywhere but here," the mercenary replied. "The machine will be ready again, and they've had time to gather every hired gun on the island or even their mercs from Earth. We won't stand a chance; not without a hostage."

All eyes turned to Mradraak, who was still kneeling in the dirt. Unlike Nakabada, Mradraak was no innocent bystander. Before anyone had a chance to discuss it, Jekka yanked the Telepath to his feet and began tying his belt around Mradraak's hands. He then took the councillor's belt off and tied a knife into his hand, looping it around the prisoner's neck and tightening it so the blade was inches from his throat.

Gloria and John exchanged anxious glances, feeling once again worried by the company they were keeping. Only after Jekka began to drag Mradraak back to the palace entrance did the Telepath seem to become aware of what was happening.

"Don't hurt me," he said, rather pathetically.

Jekka felt his deep seated anger rising to the surface, and fighting his urge to push the blade, he shoved the diplomat into the stone pillar instead. "Start talking! What was that creature?"

Everyone gathered around, partly to listen, and partly to make sure this man who most of them didn't know, didn't ruin their only leverage by killing the prisoner. Jekka stepped back and watched the Telepath struggling to break free from his restraints, or at least move the razor sharp blade away from his larynx.

Maria took hold of Jekka's hand to try and remind him of his peaceful caring side, but noticed John turning away. She turned her attention to their captive who had stopped struggling, and looked as though he was ready to cooperate.

When he spoke, those who had heard his voice as a daunting phonation in his haunting illusions were surprised at how timid he now sounded. "We engineered the creature, or should I say our allies on Earth engineered them, just as they did with the Drathmorks and the arachnoid warriors. It was the sixteenth attempt, and the most successful, but it still wasn't perfect."

"What? You saw what it did! What more did you bastards want from a soldier?"

"It wasn't meant to be a soldier; it was to be a general. The Drathmork were becoming hard to control, so we asked for a creature that could manipulate their minds in the same way I can manipulate human minds. The Drathmork are less intelligent than humans, so controlling them would be easy once we created a compatible mind. We crossed their already heavily adapted genetic material with that of some of our strongest Telepaths, Titans and Spellcasters to make a battlefield general that could control our flying soldiers without being vulnerable to assassination. We grew it inside its own armour to give it a flawless metal exoskeleton, exposing no soft flesh . . . . It was perfect except for one aspect; it wouldn't accept that its purpose was to do our bidding. Its mind was flawed, and would show vastly different character traits during each encounter, as if several beings were living inside one. It was scheduled for termination, but the first attempt at flooding its lungs with toxic gasses failed. The second attempt would have succeeded had it not been set free."

Mradraak was starting to sweat profusely, and wouldn't take his eyes off the tip of the blade just below his chin. He looked up to find that his captors were no longer staring at him, but at the dark open doorway to the palace. A faint sound of footfalls quickly became a thunderous noise of marching and clattering shields. Maxwell pulled the prisoner forwards and held him out in view of the doorway in hope that this would hold back the approaching army.

Maria held on to Jekka tightly, and John felt Shoa's hand taking hold of his.

"We'll be fine," he lied, "Mradraak will order them to stand down." He felt a sword being placed in his other hand, and looked up to see Orak proceeding to arm everybody else.

"We need to let them know we mean business," the Titan growled, psyching himself up for the inevitable bloodshed. He would strike as soon as he saw the white of his enemy's eyes, and he would strike hard.

Maxwell however, didn't look so confident. "This isn't right; they don't sound like mercenaries . . . . Why would they send primitive swordsmen here?"

Jekka snarled at the soldier of fortune, "Primitive! Stand down Earth man . . . Orak; stand down."

"What's wrong with you?" the Titan replied in his native tongue. "They will decimate us in seconds!"

"No they won't," he replied, placing his sword down on the ground. "They won't harm us."

As the first wave of soldiers breached the palace doors, they began to slow to a halt. The crest of Erinthia was clearly visible upon their shields, and as they saw the faces of their commander and his companion, they laid down their arms.

Chapter 61

Jekka took a moment to understand the situation, despite having worked out that the soldiers were his own before they came into the open. Once he remembered the instructions he had left his second in command the day before he left, he began to understand.

Leaping into action, he barked orders, "I want a dozen of you to stand guard at the gates, the rest of you I want inside, and I need five guards to hold the prisoner . . ."

Scanning the soldiers, he quickly realised that something wasn't quite right. Not only were there more than four times the number of soldiers here than there had been upon his ship, but most of them bore different crests upon their shields.

He turned to the acting commander, but before he had chance to ask the question, the soldier started to explain, "They reached it ahead of us sir. They had already taken the island of Katatua-Shovrus when we arrived just under an hour ago."

"But where are they from?"

"General Kyra sent a message south by dragon, it reached the city on the south coast, and they sent everyone they had. They threatened the technicians into showing us how to use the machine, and that's how we got here . . . What happened here sir?"

While Jekka explained everything that had happened in the last few hours, Maria was acting as a translator between Maxwell and the Commander of the Southern army.

The mercenary was presented with an assault rifle, much like the one previously in his possession. He was told that the soldiers had broken into the armoury at Katatua-Shovrus, and salvaged what they could carry, which turned out to be a lot.

"I'd like a party of volunteers to come with me to hunt down that monster," Maxwell said.

Maria looked at him in shock. "Didn't you see what that thing did? I thought you wanted to get home?"

"Will you just tell him?" he replied impatiently.

Maria translated, taking almost three times as long as the original sentence. She waited for the commander's even longer statement before turning to Maxwell and explaining, "None of his soldiers would be willing to go on a suicide mission like this in the heart of the enemy's country. He did tell me that there are about twenty men being held captive on Katatua-Shovrus, all with projectile weapons training . . . You might know them. What's in this for you Stanton?"

Maxwell gave a lopsided smile, "Don't you trust me?"

"You want Alkak-Taan's gold supplies don't you?"

"Not all of it,"

Neither of them had noticed how close Orak had been standing to them, and jumped when he spoke. "As long as you find that creature first, I don't think anyone here cares what you steal afterwards. I'm coming with you."

"So am I," Maria added.

"No you're not."

"Why? Because I'm a woman?"

"No, it's because you're inexperienced. I don't care if he dies, I care if you do. It's my fault you were stuck here, and now you finally have a chance to go home."

Without saying another word Maria walked away. He was right about one thing, she was inexperienced; it was pointless her risking her life over this. Her part in this war was over, but leaving Ithria was the last thing on her mind.

*

At the same time, John had been having a similar discussion with Shoa, but was more forceful in telling her not to go after the escaped experiment. As expected, she was defiant but eventually Gloria was the one who convinced her not to go.

"If that gung ho American wants to go and get himself killed trying to be a hero, I'm not going to stop him. You've already helped out enough in this war. Maxwell needs to go to prove he's changed, don't forget whose side he started out on."

"But Orak is going too. He can protect me," Shoa argued.

"You'll just put him in danger. Orak used to slay dragons for a living, he'll be better off without you dear,"

"There are things that need doing here," John reminded her. "Alkak-Taan has lost nearly all of its government, and we need to be here as the civilian voice of this discussion; everyone else here is military and we need to help form a balanced committee."

Jekka's men forced Mradraak to show them to somewhere where they could hold this vital meeting, then awaited to hear which of them should be present for the discussion. They were led to a large chamber deep underground, dimly lit by hundreds of wall mounted candles. A long, thin oak table spanned the whole length of the depressed section of floor, overlooked by terraces of benches.

The atmosphere would have been unpleasant in this dark, drab room even without such strong hostile feelings in the air. Mradraak was made to sit in on the meeting, as he was the only one who knew the state and current political structure of the country. Jekka and the general of the Southern Tontoltec Army each chose two of their soldiers to attend with them, along with the three civilians and Maria. Orak voiced his opinions beforehand, so his proposals could be taken into account during his absence.

After nearly an hour of intense argument, very little had been decided. Although Mradraak was officially deemed a war criminal, he would remain a member of the governing council for as long as his knowledge and guidance was needed. The group decided to have a short recess, but most members continued the discussion in a less formal manner.

After the debate restarted, matters were resolved much quicker. It was eventually decided that Alkak-Taan was not able to form its own government quickly enough, but its societal problems would degenerate even further if it was entirely ungoverned. They began compiling a list of names of politicians and accomplished men and women from Tontoltec who may be willing to take on the positions of those who had been killed earlier that day.

Orak had mentioned that the Drathmork breeding facilities needed to be located and deactivated as soon as possible, and Mradraak was made to give detailed directions as to their whereabouts. With the Telepath's help, they were also able to have messages sent to every active commanding unit in Alkak-Taan's military. Using the Earth telecommunications technology they had all been supplied with, they were ordered to stand down within minutes of the orders being given.

With threats and wise words, the war which threatened to tear Ithria apart swiftly came to a conclusion. A quarter of a million humans and over a hundred thousand engineered soldiers were commanded to stop fighting all across the globe. The Drathmorks' fury could not be contained so easily however, and anarchy quickly broke out. Battles in Erinthia were tipped in favour of the defending side when their enemies turned on their own men, and those who didn't retreat perished.

The machine on Katatua-Shovrus would be used extensively over the coming weeks to bring an end to the conflict and help heal the wounded nations, but the device's eventual fate was still in much dispute.

That night, the temple was used to accommodate the many hundreds of people who had come through the manufactured rift. Most eagerly awaited the following day when many matters would be finally resolved, while some dreaded having to make the hardest decision of all, the decision that would forever shape the rest of their lives.

Chapter 62

Maxwell and Orak met up with the rest of their team before nightfall and kitted themselves out with as much equipment as they could move with. The captured mercenaries looked downtrodden and showed no signs of elation when they were reunited with their former colleague. They knew how dangerous the mission they were being pressed into was, but had no other choice.

Orak was taught how to use the weapons correctly, as well as the night vision goggles and radio. They had decided to wait until dark to make their move, knowing that their equipment would give them the upper hand. Dragons had far better night vision than most other animals, but this creature had enough humanoid in it to reduce its senses severely.

The plan of attack was entirely Maxwell's idea, and with every new revelation, the Titan found himself respecting his former enemy more than he had anticipated. It was as though the private sector soldier was returning to a long forgotten moral path after years of greed and selfishness. It was proof that people could change. However, they were all aware that their quarry was not strictly a person, and knew it couldn't change.

Orak knew he had to treat the creature in the same way he treated dragons during his hunting days; as a soulless animal. On the other hand, this soulless animal had a human mind, however disturbed or corrupted that mind was.

"Are you sure this will work?" Orak asked for the umpteenth time, warily eying their pressed help. The soldiers looked capable of taking down most prey, but he strongly doubted their conviction.

"To a degree," Stanton replied. With each new response, his confidence seemed to dwindle, adding further to everyone's unease.

The city around them moved quickly as they pressed on, and the cramped terrace housing had changed to large detached official looking buildings almost without them noticing. The largest of these was their destination.

Orak knew very little of the written language of Alkak-Taan, but he did recognise the focal word upon the sign of the huge pillared edifice.

"Gold!" he exclaimed, as he rounded his gun on their guide.

"It's not what you think!" Maxwell replied, holding his hands up in submission, "Sure I want to get something for my troubles; we all can, but that's not why we're here."

"So why are we here?"

"I'll show you once we're inside."

Quietly growling like an impatient lion, Orak lowered the gun and allowed Maxwell to lead the way.

*

The council building provided very comfortable accommodation for those who needed to stay there, but that night, very few slept for long. For many of the soldiers, the battle at Katatua-Shovrus was still fresh in their minds, and they would wake up from nightmares screaming. Some had witnessed such horrors that they felt they would never sleep easy again.

The civilians had seen very little of such things, but still had much on their minds. John, Gloria, Shoa and Maria had commandeered a small common room and ignited the ready laid fire. Gloria was the first to finally fall asleep, and not long after she had, Shoa decided to go on a midnight stroll.

John and Maria were alone together for the first time since they had shared a kiss in John's kitchen many months ago. It was over a minute and a half before either of them spoke. It was Maria who broke the silence.

"I'm glad to see you're safe," she said.

"And you . . ." he replied, struggling to find the right words to continue, "Jekka seems like a nice guy."

Maria just nodded and gave a faint smile. Another long pause later she asked, "Did I tell you how he saved my life?"

John shook his head, "You haven't really told me anything. You seem happy together though . . . What we had, it was only . . ."

"What we had was something very special," she interrupted, finding herself relieved that she was speaking so openly about it. "It could have been, but we never had a chance for our relationship to start. We would have been great, but it's too late now. I'm in love with Jekka. If he asked me to marry him, I would."

John couldn't find a response, his mouth opened and closed a few times, but nothing but air escaped. He had thought and even dreamt about seeing her again, about what he would say, but this eventuality had never come up.

"You're with Shoa now anyway," Maria continued, "If somebody had told me about you two when I first met her, I don't know what I'd have thought. She didn't give us the best impression."

John laughed, "She's grown up a lot."

Maria nodded in agreement.

"But we're not that close. What I feel when I'm with her is nothing compared to what I felt when I was with you."

She looked away, then to the door to make sure Shoa hadn't been there listening. "I'm sorry, but if I could change things I wouldn't. I'm not going back to Earth. I couldn't take Jekka with me, so I'm staying."

"What about your family? You'll be a missing person back home. I probably won't be, my father won't have noticed I'm gone, and Gloria is the closest person to a mother I've ever had . . . I don't have many friends back there either."

"Earth isn't my home anymore. I was going to ask you to send them a message to say I'm alive when you got back, but it sounds like you don't want to go either."

After yet another long pause, John muttered, "What good am I back there?"

"You were a good nurse; you just let things get on top of you."

"No, I was a below average nurse, but here I'm an excellent physician. I can offer Ithria a lot more than I could offer our world."

"Have you thought this through? You don't even speak any of the languages, at least not well enough."

"I can learn, like you did. I'll go back to Whitefalls with Orak and Shoa, reconstruction will keep us all busy for a few months, and after that, who knows. What will you do here?"

"Jekka is being stationed on the island to guard the machine, until a permanent solution is devised. I'll stay there with him. After that, maybe I'll try my hand at being a field medic, or even set up my own hospital . . . Have you spoken to Gloria?"

John shook his head, "Not yet. I will in the morning, maybe I can get some rest before then."

They lay down on facing sofas and within minutes were both fast asleep.

*

"You think he's inside?" asked Bronson; a rather stocky hired gun currently under Maxwell's command, as he peered up at the austere bank.

"No, what would it want with gold?" came Maxwell's patronising reply. "I need you all to familiarise yourselves with the layout once we're inside."

"How are we going to transport all the treasures?" asked another mercenary by the name of Günter.

"We're not. You can take what you can carry once we've completed the mission, but not before because it'll weigh you down."

Led by Maxwell, and backed by Orak to dissuade the pressed men from fleeing, they ascended the pyramid like stairs that raised the building high off the ground. The structure upon this plinth reminded those from Earth of a Roman temple, except it was many times larger than any they had encountered, or seen on TV.

A day earlier, the building had been surrounded by guards, who had now been relieved of duties. Only a small handful of lightly armed men remained, who after Maxwell displayed an official looking document, gave them permission to enter.

The main double doors were left open behind them, and Orak noticed several of the guards running down the steps away from the secure facility. They had been informed of the plan and were vacating the facility, to minimise the number of casualties in case things got out of hand.

The main corridor was lined with thin arrow slits along its walls and there were circular holes dotted all across the ceiling.

"Günter, you and Willis find the door to the rooms on the other side of these walls," Maxwell instructed, "I want one of you on each side. This is the only way into the building, so it will have to come through this way to get in. You'll have a few seconds to unload as many rounds as you can into it; aim for the gaps in its armour. You've got your grenades if it finds you . . . Good luck."

"Where are we going?" Bronson asked, staring further down the long dark corridor.

"To the vaults."

"The armoury first," Orak corrected him. "I'm going to want a backup if this weapon fails."

After searching several rooms, they came across a heavy iron door, in which the top half was a barred window. Through the vertical bars they could see that the room contained every bladed weapon imaginable, as well as over a dozen crossbows. The door looked as though it weighed more than half a tonne, and was bolted in several places. Fortunately, the keys had been left in every one of its locks for them.

After helping himself to an assortment of weighty arms, Orak handed out several lighter daggers to the three other men.

"How's the wound?" Maxwell asked, noticing that there was still blood on the Titan's clothes. "I hope it won't slow you down too much."

"It still hurts a little, but it's closed up now. It won't slow me down."

Leaving the armoury behind, they made their way to the main chamber. Like the armoury, the door looked impenetrable, but just like before, the keys had been left for them.

Orak swung the solid metal hatch open as if it was a plywood cupboard and stepped inside.

"Jesus Christ!" Bronson exclaimed.

To which Orak's response was, "Who?"

Unlike the dark glim hallways, this huge cavernous chamber was brightly lit by tens of thousands of candles. The decorations of gold painted statues and huge areas of stained glass gave it the appearance of a Roman Catholic Cathedral, except that the characters depicted resembled nothing from either of the testaments; new or old.

In contrast with the classical décor, a bank of computer terminals ran along the back wall, which constantly kept an eye on the building and its occupants, using thousands of unnoticeable sensors.

If the building had been a church, the centre of the room would have been lined with pews, but instead there stood a seven foot tall cuboid of steel bars, containing countless bricks of glimmering gold, all branded with the same imperial crest.

Either side of the chamber, there were more cages that contained wooden crates, barrels and chests of insurmountable treasures. Much to everyone's surprise, Maxwell barely looked at the cages, but headed straight towards the terminals.

They all watched him take out a small USB pen-drive and then insert it into a slot on the side of one of the monitors.

"I don't know how long we'll have, so be ready as soon as I start," he said sternly, his commanding voice echoing around the chamber.

"How do you know the recordings are . . . saying the right thing?" Orak asked, wishing he'd asked this earlier.

"Extensive studies, that's what the wacko scientists told me." He spoke into the radio, "Get ready, over."

"Are you sure it will be loud enough?"

"The alarms here are designed to be heard from all over the city, to warn intruders that there's no escape. Here goes . . ."

Clicking open the file, the air suddenly filled with a screeching so loud and haunting it would have reduced even the hardened soldiers inside the vault to tears, had they not been wearing ear protection. The recorded cries of a whole squadron of Drathmorks would surely draw their quarry to them; it was just a matter of time.

Chapter 63

Maria and John awoke at the same moment and looked into each other's eyes across the room. For a moment, they had forgotten where they were, and why they were there.

Gloria rushed over towards them several seconds later, and in their first few waking moments, it was as though the past few months had been nothing but a dream. The eerie sound of the monsters calling out quickly brought them back to Ithria.

"What's going on?" Maria said groggily, reaching for the knife she had left on the floor earlier. Her dreamt memories of being Doctor Bishop had vanished, and once again she was a soldier under her lover's command.

"It's Stanton's plan, it's over a mile away; don't worry," John assured the two frightened women.

After nearly a minute of deafening noise, the screeching stopped.

Gloria sat down and made herself breathe steadily. "I've been on edge ever since we've been here," she said shakily.

"The creature is long gone, it won't be back."

She glared at him in response, shocked that he didn't understand. "I'm not talking about this temple; I'm talking about Ithria. The past few days have been the worst; knowing we can get home, but just waiting and waiting."

John and Maria glanced at each other for a second, then back to Gloria.

"What? What is it?"

"We were both . . . Well, Maria is definitely . . ." John stammered, "I want to stay."

The last thing he had expected was for her to say nothing. Gloria sat there in silence while John explained everything he had told Maria, about how he felt like he had a purpose here, and how he had grown to care about people in Ithria more than anyone back on Earth. When he had finished, Gloria stood up to leave, but stopped and turned to him.

"I can't go back by myself. I can't go home being the only one to have seen what I've seen, with nothing but my own memories of this place . . ."

"I don't want you to go," John cut in, "But I can't expect you to stay. I know you could never stay, you said it yourself."

"I'm a missing person. How can I go back to my job? How can I go back to Mark after everything I've learnt about him?"

"Do you want to?"

There was no dispute in her mind; the answer was no. She had nothing left on Earth, but she felt in her heart that she was too old to adapt to life on a new world.

"You don't have to choose your old life over this one; there are other answers. Earth is a big place," John continued, "And now you're free to see it all."

"You don't mind if I go?" Gloria asked, almost feeling rejected.

"You've looked out for me my whole life; with my career, my education. You were there when nobody else was . . . but it's time I made it on my own."

"He won't be alone," Shoa cut in, placing her hand upon John's shoulder. Nobody had noticed her return, and she seemed unfazed by the intermittent monstrous screeching.

"If he's got you and Orak to protect him I've got nothing to worry about have I?" Gloria said tearfully.

"It's not like you'll never see him again; the machine will always be there to make a gateway between our worlds."

"No dear, it won't, and we can't use it, not for ourselves. We all know how many problems it's already caused."

"Oh . . . I guess this is a proper goodbye then . . . When are you leaving?"

"This morning I suppose . . . No point delaying."

Whilst everyone waited to hear from Maxwell's team, Gloria went through the meagre possessions she had collected over the past few months, deciding what to take with her to Earth. Many of the clothes she had accumulated would look strange to people back home, but others were far too nice to discard. There was a small leather bag containing souvenirs such as a handcrafted knife, arrow heads and crudely blown glass medicine bottles. Everything she owned fitted neatly into a backpack.

She had arranged for someone on Katatua-Shovrus to open a gateway for her to leave through as soon as Orak returned.

*

Orak glanced at the large digital clock display upon the vault wall, which declared it to be quarter of an hour after Maxwell had first played the recording. The gut-churning noise was played for only thirty seconds at a time, but regularly at two minute intervals, and he was thoroughly sick of it.

"No more Stanton!" he demanded, "This isn't working."

Maxwell muted the recording, "Well, I know it's done half of what it was meant to," he replied. Orak looked at him puzzled, so he explained, "It's not attracted the Drathmorks; thank God."

"Are you saying that was a risk?" he asked, tightening his grip on the salvaged battle axe in his hands.

"Not a strong one . . . Do you have any better ideas?"

"We could spread out, go out and look," Bronson suggested.

The mercenary received nothing but blank stares in response. He glanced at the man to his left, whom he had forgotten the name of, who was also looking at him as if he was stupid.

"Ok, bad idea then," he admitted, avoiding eye contact with all three men. "We may as well stock up on treasures while we're here . . . No point standing around doing nothing."

"First good idea you've had all day," said the unknown mercenary who until this point had not said a word. He spoke with a deep drawling Texan accent.

"Not until you complete the mission," Orak stopped them. Even though their enemy's gold was within their reach, he was not prepared to steel from a country on the brink of financial depression. He knew the effect losing the war would have on Alkak-Taan.

"We've failed the mission, the plan didn't work. There's no reason why we shouldn't . . ."

"SHH!" Maxwell interrupted, holding up one finger, "Gunfire!"

Everyone stopped arguing immediately and listened. Sure enough there was a faint but undeniable rattle of an assault rifle being discharged. The next second they all heard the loud bang of a grenade detonating.

"It's here!" Bronson blurted out, grabbing his gun from the floor.

A second explosion followed by a screeching not dissimilar from Maxwell's recording told them that prototype 16 was still alive, and that Günter and Willis weren't.

Silence followed, and the four armed men took their positions behind whatever obstacles they could find, whilst still in sight of the door. They each checked that they still had their grenades, but found less comfort in the fact that they had them, than they had before.

"If I'm gonna die, I'm going to take this bastard down with me!" Bronson snarled, as he heard heavy metallic footsteps approaching.

As the creature's shadow came into view from around the corner, he hurled the first explosive towards it and ducked back behind the gold cage. The blast was drowned out by the monster's roar of pain.

Close up, it no longer sounded like the creatures it was built to command, but more like the ferocious call of the dragon it was made from.

Enraged, the iron clad beast stormed into the vault, smouldering and trailing blood. On first sight of the creature, Bronson ran from his hiding place towards the back of the vaults, forgetting that there was no other way out. A lightning bolt travelled thirty feet through the air and struck him in the small of the back, scorching his flesh and stopping his heart instantly.

"FIRE!" Maxwell yelled.

Both mercenaries stood up above the crates they had been hiding behind, and unleashed the full power of their automatic weapons. The cartridges were depleted almost before Orak could fire off his first few rounds, and the two men ducked back down.

The crate that the Texan was hiding behind, was suddenly blown to pieces, and he was thrown back onto the cold hard floor, cracking his skull open. Maxwell quickly shifted position just before his hiding place too was turned into dust.

Orak watched the creature through a gap between two large cardboard boxes. He knew that his cover wouldn't stand a chance against prototype sixteen's powers, so he hushed his breathing and shrank down as small as he could. Through the thin space, he could see that the creature's neck and a large area of exposed skin on its left arm, was badly burnt where several armour panels had come off. It appeared that the explosives had done some damage.

From across the room he heard Maxwell's foot striking wood, and the beast turned its head to explore. Without allowing himself time to think Orak, lifted the battle axe, bursting through the boxes, swung for the monsters head.

The axe blade struck metal with an almighty clang. He had missed the neck by inches, and as the heavy weapon bounced across the room, nearly decapitating the Titan; the creature's helmet was torn from its head by the force. Dented and blood stained, the elaborate horned piece of armour came crashing down, chipping the solid stone floor.

Orak saw the hybrid's face for the first time and he was paralysed by the shock of what he saw. He had not expected it to look human, but what he saw barely looked alive. The metal covering had formed the outer layer of its flesh, and without it the creature looked as though it had been skinned.

Set deep inside its large dark sockets, the creature's small yellow eyes stared at Orak, and its jaws full of thin, crooked and misshapen teeth, snapped viciously in his direction.

Prototype sixteen raised its hand ready to smite its attacker, but as it did, Maxwell hurled himself from behind one of the many crates, and fired off a single shot.

The creature's head jerked violently to the side, but the beast remained standing. Blood was pouring from its temple. Both men could see that its eyes were rolling, and as Maxwell lifted the barrel of his gun to fire again, the creature stumbled. The mercenary pulled the trigger, but the weapon just clicked.

"I'm out! Orak! Fire!"

The Titan scrambled across the floor for his assault rifle, but as he did the creature bolted for the exit. Once Orak had regained a weapon, he too realised that its ammunition was depleted.

"There's no exit wound," Maxwell realised, "The bullet is still in the fucker's head. He won't last long."

"You think!" Orak snapped, snatching up the axe and running through the open doorway, "It didn't even fall!"

Once he reached the main gates, he realised that their quarry was long gone. Even in its current state, and with most of its weighty armour still upon itself, the creature was much faster than he was. Orak knew that this wasn't over.

Chapter 64

Orak and Maxwell returned to the temple in the early hours of the morning, feeling lucky to be alive. When the creature had arrived in the vault, they had both prepared for the worst, but as relieved as they were to have survived without further injury, they were beginning to feel the disappointment of failing.

When they explained to everyone, the general response was that they did all they could, and that the creature couldn't live long with such an injury. This was no consolation to either of them though. Maxwell knew of cases where humans had survived such injuries, and prototype sixteen was far more resilient than any human. One solace for him however, was the fact that he had managed to scavenge enough treasures to comfortably retire on the proceeds.

"You didn't get to be the hero you wanted to be," Orak had said.

"I feel I've done my bit," had been his response.

Maxwell didn't see anyone else before heading to the designated rift opening chamber. He thought about saying goodbye to Maria; he had grown to admire her, but he knew she wouldn't reciprocate his feelings. He wanted to tell her that it was because of her that he switched sides, but he felt it was easier for him to just fade away. A gateway was opened at his request, and Maxwell Stanton left Ithria forever.

*

Orak arrived back, just as a meeting between the newly imported politicians of Alkak-Taan was being held. These new members would form a temporary government until the country was ready to elect its own officials. He was allowed to sit in, and was glad of the chance to take the weight off his feet.

"The threat of the Drathmorks still exists," a short grey haired man was saying, "From what Mradraak has told us, almost a quarter of a million have been bred, and most of those are still alive. On top of that, thirty legions of the creatures which have been named Arachno-Sapiens have been created. Most of the populations of both are currently residing in the uninhabited Parga Islands, without purpose or leadership; they aren't our immediate concern."

"What is our main concern?" was the response.

"The creature which will provide them with a purpose . . . Professor JaVrei. Were you successful in your mission?"

Orak slowly shook his head, "I don't think so."

"Then we may have a very big problem."

The Titan didn't stay for the rest of the meeting. He had said all he came to say. Orak climbed into one of the sturdier bunks in the living quarters and fell into a very deep sleep.

*

It was almost midday when he woke up, and he woke tired and groggy. John had tried to shake him awake, but had resorted to emptying a bucket of water over his friend's head. Orak swatted the air around him frantically, nearly knocking John out.

"Whatayawant?" he grumbled.

"Gloria is leaving," John replied solemnly, while Orak towelled himself off and changed into the dry clothes that had been left for him, "Think she wanted to say goodbye."

The two of them went to the common room, where Shoa and Maria were sat at a coffee table. Gloria was there aswell, with a single backpack at her feet. They all stood up when they saw that the others had arrived.

Shoa rushed towards the Titan and hugged him, "I'm glad you're alive." She tried to kiss him on the cheek, but even on tiptoes she could only reach his chin.

"I hear you didn't quite complete your mission," Gloria added, "On the plus side, you showed everyone that the enemy can bleed. I know that when the time comes, you'll do all you can to finish the job."

"Thank you" Orak replied, "Are you sure you want to go back so soon, there's a lot you haven't seen of Ithria . . . ?"

"I'm sure. Besides, there are things I can do to help on my side of the Anuma link. The war was started by my people too, and I have a link with the company that caused it all."

"You're going to destroy the company?" he asked, puzzled.

"I'm going to do what I can."

Orak took her small age-weathered hand in his huge rough paw and shook it, "It's been an honour knowing you. Good luck on whatever ventures you pursue."

Shoa was next to say her goodbyes, she began to shed tears, which caused Gloria to cry too. Neither of them had realised how much they had grown on each other. When they first met, Shoa would never have believed she would befriend this old woman, but here they were, parting as friends.

Maria felt strange when it was her turn to say her goodbyes. She had known Gloria before either Orak or Shoadrina, but because she had not been through everything with her on this long adventure, she was almost a stranger in comparison. What felt stranger, was the fact that one of her few reminders of Earth was leaving. All she had left in this world to remind her of her home was John and even he was going on a separate path to her.

John kept his goodbye as brief as he could. He was saying goodbye to the closest thing to a parent he cared to know, and he didn't want to delay the inevitable, in fear of breaking down. They hugged and waved goodbye, promising to look after themselves and to make the most of their lives. Gloria vanished through an invisible hole in the air, never to be seen by Ithrian eyes again.

Epilogue

Gloria's arrival on Earth was far softer and more controlled than her landing on Ithria had been; the technicians had made sure of that. They had taken her straight to the town she called home, but not to her own house. She had asked to be dropped outside John's residence, as he had given her instructions before she left.

In the kitchen cupboard she found the stacks of notes just as John had left them. Apart from the huge amount of dust that had gathered, and the smell of mould wafting from the fridge, it was as though nothing had changed.

Stuffing them into her backpack, she looked around to see if there was anything else to take. John had told her it was all hers, as he would never be coming back for it. After deciding to leave the rest of the house as it was, she left for her own home.

The house looked like it always had, and the inside hadn't changed much. Just as when she'd left, Mark was away on business. He had probably been home only a handful of times, but she expected he had reported her as a missing person after seeing the 'evidence of theft' in the garage.

Although she barely saw him these days, she felt that he had once loved her. Why else would he have used her name as the password at Katatua-Shovrus? No matter what he felt for her, she would never forgive him for his role in Ithria Ltd and its crimes against alien nations. Her first port of call was their bedroom, where she hurriedly packed only her best clothes and anything that would fit in her handbag. Once that was done, she headed for the study.

Mark had always trusted her; not enough to leave the file drawers unlocked, but enough to keep important documents at home. Breaking the drawer open with the knife she had acquired on Ithria, she took out the documents and began sorting them into piles: those to send to Maxwell Stanton once she found out where he was, and ones to send to the police. She knew Maxwell would act when he found out the identities of those who had left him stranded on another world.

Logging onto the computer, she used the passwords her husband had foolishly left written down to hack into the database of the bank he ran. She knew his bank was cover for the personal and expense accounts of the whole company he co-ran, and through the database she had access to over ninety percent of its liquid assets. Transferring the funds to a new offshore account in her name, she made sure Mark had nothing to fall back on.

The cash would come in useful to make her escape. Heading straight for the airport, she bought a one way ticket on the first international flight she could find. Hoping the destination would be sunny and without looking back, she set off on her new life as a wealthy single pensioner.

Sequels

Coming soon
The Firestone Shard
The Dragon Rider

Lightning Source UK Ltd.
Milton Keynes UK
UKOW041043241012

201105UK00001B/62/P